The
Seeds
of
Change

Books by Lauraine Snelling

Leah's Garden × 1

The Seeds of Change

LAURAINE SNELLING

with Kiersti Giron

BETHANYHOUSE
a division of Baker Publishing Group
Minneapolis, Minnesota

© 2021 by Lauraine Snelling

Published by Bethany House Publishers
11400 Hampshire Avenue South
Bloomington, Minnesota 55438
www.bethanyhouse.com

Bethany House Publishers is a division of
Baker Publishing Group, Grand Rapids, Michigan

Printed in the United States of America

Library of Congress Cataloging-in-Publication Data
ISBN 978-0-7642-3569-6 (trade paper)
ISBN 978-0-7642-3570-2 (cloth)
ISBN 978-0-7642-3571-9 (large print)
ISBN 978-1-4934-2978-3 (ebook)

Scripture quotations are from the King James Version of the Bible.

This is a work of fiction. Names, characters, incidents, and dialogues are products of the author's imagination and are not to be construed as real. Any resemblance to actual events or persons, living or dead, is entirely coincidental.

Cover design by Dan Thornberg, Design Source Creative Services

Author is represented by the Books & Such Literary Agency.

21 22 23 24 25 26 27   7 6 5 4 3 2 1

I dedicate *The Seeds of Change*,
and the rest of the LEAH'S GARDEN series,
with great love and admiration,

to Wendy Lawton,

agent extraordinaire, deep friend, sister in Christ.
She has made my life richer on so many levels.
Another of God's gifts to me.

Forsythia

Because it flowers in late winter or early spring,
forsythia stands for spring sun and anticipation.
After the cold of winter, we are all longing for the sun,
and the bright gold of first-blooming forsythia
cheers us beyond measure.

Forsythia is a shrub, and branches can be easily forced
by cutting them on the diagonal,
placing them in a tall vase or bucket of water,
and checking them daily.

Nothing says spring is almost here
like the bright, cheerful forsythia.

1

LINKSBURG, OHIO
MAY 1865

I truly hate that man."

"Lark, you know Ma said we should never hate anybody." Larkspur's sister Forsythia, third of the Nielsen daughters, spoke out of the side of her mouth, the way they had learned so as not to be heard by anybody else. Especially in church. Forsythia had spent a good part of her young life trying to keep her older sister out of trouble.

Larkspur refocused her attention forward, clenching her fingers in her lap to keep from leaping out of the pew.

Deacon Wiesel raised his Bible, the pages rippling from the force of his shaking. His voice nearly tore the hinges from the doors. "Women, if you are indeed following God's Word . . ."

Larkspur watched the red of his face deepen. Perhaps a heart attack? A stroke?

"You are ordered to submit to your husband's every utterance. God says so, right here." The words thundered, and spittle spattered the pulpit. "If you are not married, your father is in charge. For too many of you, your mouth is your biggest sin."

Little pig eyes slit nearly shut, he stared right at Larkspur as if daring her to speak.

Lark returned stare for stare, knowing she was aggravating the deacon but no longer caring. According to him, women should never raise their eyes—only a downcast posture was proper.

Forsythia laid a gentle hand on Larkspur's shaking knee, and Lark felt an elbow digging into her left side. Her sister Delphinium was only reminding her that were their mother here, she would be mortified by the actions of her eldest daughter. Surely she had taught her daughters better than to let their emotions show like this in church. But then, Ma had never met Deacon Wiesel or watched him drive their dear Pastor Earling to his deathbed. At least, Lark sure found it suspicious that the two men had gone for a buggy ride and only the deacon returned alive, lamenting that their pastor had died in an accident. But how had Wiesel survived a runaway horse and Pastor Earling hadn't? And if their mother could see how the weasel took out his furies on his wife . . .

Lark glanced at Climie Wiesel, cowering in a forward pew. Bruised, bones broken, terrified he would one day abuse their dreamed-of children, Climie made excuses for her husband whenever she and Larkspur talked. But they all knew that Climie had lost that last baby and those before because the deacon beat her so badly. When Wiesel got liquored up, there was no stopping him. They all knew that, but their mother had gone on to heaven before Climie started taking refuge with the Nielsens when her husband went deep in his cups. Sadly, often not soon enough.

Something had to be done. After the accident, Deacon Wiesel had taken over, ignoring all efforts of the other church leaders to find a new pastor. Larkspur tried to shut down her mind by running through multiplication tables. It didn't help. She tried adding columns of three numbers. Nothing helped. She raised her head when she no longer heard the weasel haranguing them with the Bible verses.

But he was staring right at her. "Women, obey your husbands, for that is the word of the Lord."

For Forsythia's sake, Larkspur stared down at her clenched hands. She was shaking so hard the entire pew shuddered. *Thank heaven I am not married, and if all men are like you, I never will be.*

At a faint thud from the front of the church, Larkspur looked up.

Climie had slumped over in the pew where she sat. Fainted from the sheer force of her husband's hypocrisy?

Lark half rose to go to her.

"Young woman," Deacon Wiesel fairly roared, "sit down!"

"Your wife, sir." Lark shook off Forsythia's restraining hand and stood to her full stature, taller than the deacon himself if he hadn't been in the pulpit. "She's fainted."

"She has merely fallen asleep. You should concern yourself with hearing the word of the Lord and leave my family to me."

Mrs. Smutly, the woman on the piano bench who thought Deacon Wiesel ordered the sun to rise in the morning, gave a firm nod and cast a disapproving glance at the slender woman collapsed in the front pew.

Lark once again matched Wiesel glare for glare, then pushed past her two sisters and strode up the outside aisle toward the exit as if she were stomping ants. She ignored the scowls she could feel stabbing her and let the outside door click shut behind her. Shaking her head, Larkspur sucked in a deep breath, pausing at the top step to inhale the clean, quiet air.

"'Onward, Christian soldiers . . .'" The closing hymn floated out through the walls and windows, giving no hint of what had gone on inside.

Or what was going on inside of her.

She had to get away before the congregation was released from the evening service. Deacon Wiesel would make his way up the aisle to stand at the door and greet everyone, and she didn't want to be here when that happened.

Starting down the walk to the street, she heard her siblings exiting behind her.

"You've done it now." Her brother Anders, the eldest of the Nielsen clan, joined her. "I'm going back to the store. You're welcome to join me. Dealing with numbers always calms you down."

Larkspur shook her head. "If someone came in, I might bite their head off."

"Why can't you just ignore him? Or stop going to church?"

"That would really do it. Both Pa and Ma would be shuddering in their graves."

"Wait, Lark," Delphinium, next in age below Larkspur, called from behind them. "Let's walk together."

"I don't think you want to hear or even feel what I am thinking, Del."

"We know what you're thinking, but it doesn't do any good."

"Look, several of us from the board have written to the head church office requesting that they send us a new pastor," Anders said. "Till then, we'll have to ignore him."

"Ignore when his poor abused wife keels over in the front pew?" Lark demanded.

Anders stopped at the wooden porch of Nielsen Mercantile, which had been started by their father. "So what are you going to do, then?"

"I'm going home, that's what I'm doing." Larkspur turned to her sisters. "You can go back there and make nice with everybody, but I'm finished." She stomped ahead of them, the other three trailing behind.

"What are we going to do?" Delphinium whispered. "When she gets like this, she won't back down."

On the corner of the next block, rowdy piano music poured out of the swinging door of a saloon, inviting passersby to come on in. The sisters automatically stepped off the boardwalk to move to the other side of the street.

"Deacon Wiesel already blames Lark for all his problems. He thinks she influenced Climie and turned her against him. Now he's going to come after us, and if he doesn't do that, he'll at least tell everybody else how horrible we are, and there go our reputations right down the drain." That was Lilac, the youngest of the sisters at nineteen.

"Reputation isn't the most important thing here," Forsythia's gentle voice cut in. She caught up to Larkspur and put her hand through her sister's arm. Forsythia said nothing more, just walked quietly with her for a few moments.

A measure of peace seeped into Lark's bones bit by bit, radiating from her sister's spirit. She lowered her stiff shoulders with a sigh. "I just couldn't sit there anymore."

"I know."

"When I saw Climie crumple . . . Isn't there anything else we can do?"

Before Forsythia could respond, someone burst through the saloon doors and charged across the street in the waning light, nearly running into them.

"You gotta help me! I'm in bad trouble." Their baby brother, seventeen-year-old Jonah, grabbed Larkspur's hand and tried to drag her across the street.

"Jonah George Nielsen!" Larkspur jerked her hand free. "What in the world do you think you're doing?"

He fell to his knees, clutching her skirt. "He's a new man in town, and he's got all our money, and Bernie gave him a deed, and he's got that too and . . ." His words tripped over each other, tumbling into a cacophony of sound.

Shaking her head, Lark pulled him back to his feet. "How

many times have you promised me you would stay out of that place?"

"Just this once! All I ask is that you come help me. You know cards. We were just playing for a good time, but I think he's cheating." He sucked in a deep breath. "You could stop him."

Lark sighed. "The stupidest thing I ever did was teach you to play cards."

"He would have learned from someone else." Delphinium had caught up and rolled her eyes. "Come on, Jonah, just come home with us, and—"

"I can't. Jasper lost his horse and saddle, and Bernie bet his land."

"And lost it. Won't you fellows ever learn?" Del asked.

"He's cheating, I know he is."

"Makes no never mind. Had you stayed out of the saloon, you wouldn't be in this mess." Larkspur stared at her youngest brother. Were those tears in his eyes? Was he that afraid? She noticed details no one else did, and that tended to help her win at cards, but she'd promised herself not to help him again.

But since, according to Deacon Wiesel, she was a fallen woman anyway—and worthless, at that—she straightened her spine and sucked in a deep breath. Maybe giving someone their comeuppance would be a relief to her feelings right now.

Turning to her sisters, she said gently, "You go on home, and I'll bring Jonah in a little while."

"Larkspur, surely you're not going to—"

"Just go on home and put on the coffeepot. This won't take long."

"Oh, dear Lord, protect us." Lilac glared at the youngest of the family. "You, Jonah George Nielsen, are nothing but trouble. Have been since the day you were born."

Jonah swallowed and nodded, penitence dripping from his

eyes. "I know, but this is the end. Just get me out of this, Larkspur, and I promise I'll never gamble again."

"We've heard that before," Del said.

Larkspur tucked her arm in Jonah's and gave a tug. "Let's get this over with."

2

As they entered the saloon, Larkspur thought of the two dollars in her reticule. Surely that would be enough to get in the game. She knew she would have to lose some before she could clean the floor with the varmint. That would teach him to come into their little town and destroy some of the boys who should have been men by now.

Cigar smoke cast a silvered haze across the room. The piano player stopped playing when he saw Larkspur but picked up again at the bartender's barked order.

"Well, well, look who's here." Bonnie Belle, the hostess, greeted them. Her look at Larkspur was questioning, but she kept her smile in place. "Welcome."

"Thank you. I just came to see what Jonah has been raving about." Lark patted his arm and batted her eyes.

Demure, simpering, and with her smile sweeter than sugar and her voice the low contralto of a siren, she let Jonah lead her to the card table where a fine-looking gentleman, puffing his cigar, rocked his chair back on two legs.

"Hey, boy, you brought a lady in here. What will your mama say?" the man teased.

Larkspur held her handkerchief up to her nose. "I'm just curious as to what Jonah finds so fascinating here. Do you mind if I sit and watch?"

If only Deacon Wiesel could see her now. That thought lent wings to her charade. At least she might prompt some justice in one place today.

"Ah, sweet lady, house rules say that observers can't sit at the table. Players only. You ever played poker before?" The stranger's dark eyes studied her through the smoke ring he blew.

She nodded. "Jonah has been trying to teach us. It's a good parlor game during the winter."

"Well, you just sit down and make yourself at home." The stranger glanced around the table. "Anyone else want to play awhile longer?"

Larkspur nodded for Jonah to pull out her chair. She smiled at the other players.

The visiting gentleman had the manners to stand and remove the cigar from his mouth. "Jonah, would you introduce me to this lovely lady?"

"I, um . . ." Jonah gave a jerky nod. "Miss Nielsen, I'd like you to meet Mr. Ringwald."

"My friends call me Slate," the stranger added.

"A pleasure to meet you, Mr. Ringwald." Larkspur tipped her head and cast him a gracious smile. Considering the situation, she wasn't sure she wanted him to know her name, but manners were manners.

"So." Ringwald sat back down and rubbed his hands together. "Who else still wants to play?"

Jonah's best friend, Bernie, closed his eyes as if in prayer. He had been in and out of the Nielsen house ever since the boys started school. "Not at all," he murmured. After all, she'd taught him the game too. He glanced up at the dealer as if asking permission, since he'd just lost his last dime.

An old guy who'd given up sometime earlier tossed a couple of dollars in front of Bernie. "You can pay me back."

Larkspur studied the gambler from under her eyelashes as she fumbled in her reticule, seeming to search for her money. A black cutaway coat of fine wool, pleated white shirt with cuff links at the wrist, a ring that held a rather obtrusive shimmery stone. Not a working man by any means, at least not at what she would call *working*.

"Ah, there." She carefully smoothed out the two dollars she laid on the table, then looked up with a timid smile.

"That'll get you started," Ringwald said before looking around. "Anyone else?"

"Come on, Art, you still got some cash in those deep pockets of yours." Bonnie Belle patted the top of Mr. Holt's bald head. "Just play a hand or two, give these young sprouts a chance to learn from a master."

Mr. Holt wagged his head. "Ah, why not?" And pulled his chair back up to the table.

Larkspur smiled sweetly at this friend of her late father's who was still a good friend to their remaining family. "Good to see you, Mr. Holt."

"I'm rather surprised to see you here," he said in a low voice, glancing at Jonah and then back to her.

"And I you." She tipped her head to the side. "I just wanted to see what Jonah finds so intriguing here."

"I'm only here tryin' to keep an eye on him." Mr. Holt shook his head, keeping his tone low. "Not that I've been much good."

"If no one else wants to join us, let's begin." Ringwald shuffled the cards, then ran them again through cupped, manicured hands. Once more, and he set the deck in front of Jonah, who cut the cards and nodded. While Ringwald dealt four cards to each player, Bonnie Belle exchanged the money laid on the table for chips.

"Two card poker. Everybody take a look and make your choices." The gambler leaned back in his chair and lifted the edges of his cards, examining his hand, then discarding two.

Larkspur watched Ringwald carefully. Far as she could see, he'd not cheated on that hand. Probably figured he didn't need to. She'd be an easy mark. "Sir, may I ask a question?"

He removed his cigar from the corner of his mouth. "Why, of course, Miss Nielsen. Ask away."

"That means I can only keep two cards, correct? And I can't draw any?"

"That's right, young lady." His smile showed off a gold tooth.

They went around the table discarding until it came to her. She fingered one card, then another as if trying to decide. She chewed her bottom lip, then discarded two, including one of her best.

"Bets."

The other older fellow folded and laid his cards on the table.

Lark could feel all eyes on her. Fumbling, she pushed one chip into the growing pile.

"I'll raise you one." Ringwald slid two more chips into the center of the table.

Jonah did the same. Holt followed suit. Bernie dropped his cards on the table, shaking his head. So it was Lark's turn again. She moved her chips around, twitched her nose, and pushed in two more chips. Ringwald upped it to three this time. Jonah folded. Mr. Holt pushed his chips in, keeping an eye on Larkspur. When she gave him a rather pathetic questioning look, he slightly nodded.

"I'll take pity on the lady," Ringwald said. "Only one more this time."

Holt stayed in, Lark dithered, finally shook her head, and laid down her cards. Shame to waste what could have been an excellent hand had she kept that original king.

Holt called on the next round, and everyone laid their cards face up on the table. Even so, Lark had the winning hand, but since she'd folded, she got a tsk-tsk from Mr. Ringwald. Holt won.

"What a pity, miss."

"Silly me." She didn't dare look at Jonah full on, but when she shot him a glance, he shook his head as if disgusted with her.

Good. Let's play the part. She managed to look totally confused. On the next hand, she folded without betting. It would have been a good hand to truly gamble on, but she needed to convince them she hadn't dared play on it.

Ringwald laid down a worthless hand and gave her a look of pity. Had she pushed further, she might have taken him. Was he cheating? He hadn't used it to his advantage yet if so.

"Maybe I'm not cut out for this," she said on the next round. "It's so different from playing at home in the parlor. I thought I knew how to play." *Don't overdo it,* she cautioned herself.

"Don't be too hard on yourself, miss. It takes time and practice. Plus a little something that, well . . . some have and some don't." Ringwald cut her another smile.

Was he flirting with her? Could she use that to her advantage? A frisson of danger tickled Lark's spine. *Careful . . .*

Another round, and time to discard. She kept her best cards and ordered herself to keep a straight face. Perhaps a tiny frown. Appearing to study her own cards, she watched Mr. Ringwald.

While the other men kept their focus on their hands, he kept an eye on the other players. His gaze followed when they picked up their cards, when they discarded. But why?

His dark eyes caught hers. Lark flashed a coy smile and ducked her gaze back to her hand. She ran her thumb over the edge of her cards, both spades. A good hand. But was that a slight dent in the corner of the ace? Her scalp prickled. It was. A dent as if from a fingernail. She'd heard of gamblers marking cards that way. And this was Ringwald's deck, wasn't it?

Her mind spinning, she focused back on the table. The pile of chips in the center grew. Holt, Ringwald, and Lark were still in. Holt called and laid out his cards. The gambler did the same. Lark flinched and laid hers down. A queen and a ten.

"Does this mean I won?" She injected a note of astonishment into her voice. Holt pushed the pile of chips toward her. "Oh, good, now I can keep playing." She stacked them carefully to the side and sent Ringwald a delighted smile.

He nodded, though his eyes studied her.

Careful, he'll be on to you. Or know you're on to him.

She lost the next hand and better than half her stash. "Maybe I better quit. I hate to slow you all down."

"Ah, miss, that's just part of the game," Ringwald said. "Perhaps your luck will turn."

She heaved a sigh and nodded. "I s'pose." She glanced at Jonah, who shrugged, sticking to his part.

"All right." She sucked in a deep breath. "I sure hope my big brother doesn't come in here and drag me out."

The words rang partly true. She'd lost all track of time during the game, but night had fallen outside the saloon windows. Bonnie Belle lit the lamps inside. Holt coughed and pulled out a handkerchief to blow his nose.

"Anyone for changing the game?" Ringwald shuffled the cards while he looked around the table.

"To what?" she asked.

"Oh, let's say five-card draw?"

"But you don't have to draw five each time, right?"

"That's right, miss. We just have five cards in our hand instead of two."

She won the first hand and beamed at the gambler. "Thank you. I like this game better."

"Glad to be of service, my lady." Ringwald dealt the next hand.

She watched the pile of chips in the center of the table grow, monitoring her hand but watching Ringwald more, her certainty increasing that he had marked the cards. She caught several more in her hand with fingernail scores, so tiny others probably wouldn't notice.

The fourth time around the table, Bernie laid his cards down. Jonah only had two chips left, so he shook his head. "Good luck, sis."

Holt met the raise and stared at Ringwald. Lark pretended to count her chips, then did the same.

The three of them laid their cards down. Ringwald won with a straight.

Bernie slapped the table and muttered something Lark pretended not to hear.

"What luck." Mr. Holt's voice rang faintly ironic.

On the next round, Lark watched Ringwald so closely that she didn't pay much attention to her own hand and discarded one she shouldn't have. But the gambler seemed to be able to tell when other players were bluffing, and she even thought she saw a tiny ink mark on the back of a couple of the cards. If she was right, no wonder he could tell what other players would do.

"I raise ya two." Holt threw in his chips and laid his cards face down.

Both Lark and Slate complied.

Holt fanned out his cards. Two pairs.

"Tough luck, Holt." Ringwald blew another smoke ring and laid his cards out. A straight flush.

He shouldn't have gotten that, not after winning the last round with a straight. The odds were too high. Lark spread her cards, three of a kind. A decent hand, but not good enough. Not against a cheat.

"Well, perhaps we should call it a night." His grin flashing with its gold tooth, Ringwald raked in his winnings. "Bonnie Belle, change these chips to cash for me, please?"

"Excuse me, sir, but I don't think I'm ready to quit." Lark straightened her shoulders and met the gambler's surprised gaze. "I'm just beginning to understand the finer points of this game. And isn't it only polite to let the rest of us try to recoup?"

Ringwald chuckled without humor. "Bit late for a proper lady like yourself to be out, isn't it?"

She turned to Jonah with pleading eyes, inwardly urging him to go along with her charade. "You don't think Anders will come after me just yet, do you?"

Jonah hesitated. "Guess not."

Ringwald grunted. "Fine." He grabbed for the cards. "Let's get to it, then."

This time she needed to let Ringwald know she knew he was cheating. Not too obviously, though, or he'd be humiliated and thrown out of the saloon—and that wouldn't end well for any of them. She could feel tremors beginning in the pit of her stomach.

She turned to Bonnie Belle. "Could I please have something to drink?"

"Of course. What can I get you? Perhaps a sarsaparilla?"

Lark glanced at her brother, who nodded.

"Don't you worry, miss, it can't hurt ya none," Bonnie assured her. "Coming right up."

"Thank you." Lark glanced at Ringwald in time to catch a slight smirk just before he downed the glass by his hand. It seemed to her he'd had a number of drinks, since Bonnie Belle kept his glass full. Might that work in her favor?

"Can we get back to our game?"

Lark picked up the sarcasm that sugared the gambler's words. He wasn't flirting now. "Oh, of course. I'm sorry to cause a problem." She fluttered her hands some as she settled herself back in the chair and sent him an apologetic glance. "Please, go ahead." She wished she dared ask him to put out his cigar in the ashtray by his hand.

Ringwald dealt the cards, his movements faster now, as if he couldn't wait to get the game over with.

The round went quickly this time, and Ringwald kept his bets low. No doubt wanting to protect his winnings. Soon they all spread their cards on the table. Holt won.

"Well, that's more like it." With a relieved grin, Holt gathered the modest pile of chips.

Ringwald would want to quit before losing any more. If she was going to make her move, it had to be now.

Lark bumped her glass of sarsaparilla with her elbow. The bubbly brown liquid sloshed over the table, ruining many of the still-scattered cards.

Ringwald swore, shoving his chair back out of the way of the spill. "What in tarnation?"

"Oh, I'm so sorry." Lark pressed her hand to her mouth. "How clumsy of me. We'll have to get new cards." She lifted her gaze to Ringwald's, narrowing her eyes below her fluttered lashes.

He stared at her. Red crept up his neck, though it might only be noticed by someone watching him carefully.

Good, he got her point. Or *was* that a good thing?

"Not to worry, Miss Nielsen." His voice calmer, the gambler flicked a drop from his sleeve with exaggerated coolness and reached in his coat pocket. "I have another deck."

"Oh, I couldn't ask you to risk your cards around a butter-fingers like me again." Lark fluttered her hands as the hostess cleaned up the mess. "Bonnie Belle, doesn't the saloon have a deck we could use?"

The hostess hesitated, then nodded. "I'll get it, miss."

Mr. Holt and Bernie exchanged glances. Jonah jiggled his foot. Mr. Ringwald withdrew his hand from his pocket, the red of his face turning deeper.

Everyone knew now. Lark avoided Jonah's gaze, her heart beating fast while she kept the innocent look firm on her face.

Had she made a mistake? But the gambler needed to be stopped somehow.

"Here you are, Slate." Bonnie Belle laid a fresh deck in front of the gambler.

"Fine." Ringwald snatched up the deck. "Let's speed this up a mite. Haven't got all night." He shuffled, some cards slipping through his fingers in his haste, then dealt, the cards flying toward the players so hard that a couple landed on the floor.

Jonah bent to pick them up and used the chance to whisper to Lark. "You've made him mad."

She knew that. But maybe he would slip up.

Ringwald started the betting so high that Lark swallowed.

"Your turn, Miss Nielsen."

The knives in the gambler's voice tightened Lark's chest. She counted out the required number of chips and glanced at Jonah. Both he and Bernie shook their heads. She figured neither one had enough left to meet the bet. She slid her chips into the center and waited for Mr. Holt. Surely it wouldn't be just her and this scoundrel.

Ringwald took a long draw on his cigar, puffing an eye-stinging cloud of smoke in her face. "Raise you five."

Lark and Holt both complied.

"Think you can go five more?" Ringwald stared at Lark, his gaze daring her. A muscle in his jaw jumped.

She half shrugged and slid the required amount to the center. Her stomach clenched, but she made sure her face didn't show it. She had a good hand, but everything rested on Ringwald being too thrown off by losing his deck to be careful. Her mind kept muttering, *Please, God. Please, God.* Never in her life had she prayed for such a thing as this.

"I raise ya two." Holt threw in his chips and laid his cards face down.

Both Lark and Slate complied. The gambler threw his chips in the center of the table and took another swig from his glass. His dark eyes watched her—unreadable—but his fingers twitched on the table.

Mr. Holt laid out his hand. Three of a kind.

Ringwald slapped his down. A high card, but that was it.

Lark laid out hers. A flush.

"Well, I'll be." Holt chuckled. "That's it for me."

"Another round." It was not a question. Ringwald gathered the cards while Lark did the same with the chips she'd just won.

She made sure she didn't look at Jonah or Bernie. She'd never seen this much money at one time in her life. She straightened her back, wanting nothing more than to go home and crawl into bed. Reaching into her reticule, she withdrew her fan, spread it, and fanned herself gently as if she'd not a care in the world.

This time Ringwald's hands visibly shook as he dealt the cards for the final round. A vein pulsed in his neck.

Lord, what have I done?

"How many?" Venom laced the words.

Lark studied the cards in her hand. Three of a kind already. How could he have dealt her a hand like this? "One, please." She laid one card down and slid the new one into her hand. Another six, giving her a pair. *Thank you, Lord God.* She nodded.

When her turn came again, Lark laid out her cards—a full house—as did Ringwald—two pairs.

Jonah knocked his chair over leaping to his feet, Bernie right along with him.

"Congratulations, Miss Nielsen. I've never seen anything quite like this." Holt stayed in his chair, watching the gambler, whose ears seemed about to emit steam.

"Thank you, Mr. Ringwald. Especially for your encouragement when I was about to stop." Larkspur waited, sensing his gaze on her, while Bonnie Belle exchanged the chips for cash.

The phrase "only by the grace of God" swam through the clamor in Lark's mind.

"Never seen a lady play like that." Ringwald bit out the words around the cigar in his mouth. "Might think you knew what you were doing all along."

"Now, how could I do that?" Lark stood from the table and lifted her chin to meet his gaze. "But since I won, I'll thank you to release the title to the land I hear this young gentleman bet." She gestured to Bernie. "I'll pay whatever recompense is needed from these winnings. And the horse and saddle you lifted off some other young player too."

The gambler lunged to his feet, his chair crashing over.

"Why, you little—" Muttering something vile under his breath, Ringwald snatched the deed from inside his coat and threw it on the table. "Fine. You can have your land back." He glared at the cowering Bernie. "And that other numskull can have his horse and saddle, for all I care."

"Please allow me to reimburse you, Mr. Ringwald." Larkspur held her voice steady.

"I won't take money from a woman. Even a shameless hussy like you." The gambler stepped near, so close she could smell his breath and see the glint of his gold tooth. "But don't think I'll forget you, Miss Nielsen. You'd do best to steer clear of me, or you'll have more than your sniveling brother and his friends to worry about."

3

I think you'd best back up, Mr. Ringwald, if you know
what's good for you." Mr. Holt stepped between Lark
and the gambler.

Bonnie Bell slipped up behind Lark and handed her an envelope of cash. "Be careful, miss," she whispered.

"I'll walk you home," Holt said, taking Lark's arm with a
firm grip. The look he sent Jonah and Bernie made sure they
did not argue.

She tucked the envelope in her reticule along with her fan
and followed Mr. Holt's lead, nearly running to keep up with
his stride. They'd just stepped down onto the boardwalk, the
saloon doors swinging behind them, when she heard something
smash inside.

If Holt had not had her hand clenched to his side, she might
have turned to see what had happened, but he steered her firmly
toward home.

"Go get your brother," Holt ordered Jonah. "Tell him to get
to your house right away."

Bernie went with Jonah as they ran back to the mercantile,
where Anders lived in the quarters above the store.

Her three sisters met Lark and Mr. Holt at the door. "What happened? It's after midnight. Are you all right?" Their questions peppered them like buckshot.

Lark sucked in a deep breath and huffed it out. "I won."

Her three sisters sat around the kitchen table. "Are you all right?" Delphinium whispered again.

"She's in a state of shock. Ladies, your sister is in mighty deep water." Mr. Holt's voice softened. "Show them, Lark."

Sinking down on one of the chairs, she pulled the envelope out of her reticule and laid it on the table. They all stared at the thick tan envelope as if it were about to ignite.

"How much is in there?" Lilac looked to Mr. Holt.

"Somewhere over five hundred dollars."

"Are you sure?" Forsythia shook her head. "It can't be."

"Count it." Lark sucked in another deep breath and propped her elbows on the table, making it easier to rub her eyes. "Lilac, will you get me a wet cloth, please? The cigar smoke in that place was . . ." She shook her head. "Lord, help us."

"What are you going to do with all that money?"

"Pay back your loss, Mr. Holt." She looked at the man leaning against the dry sink. "How much do I owe you?"

"You don't owe me a cent. I went into that game with my eyes open, and you won fair and square. That's yours."

"But—"

"No. I won't listen to any argument. Right now we have to figure out a way to keep you safe."

"Infuriating the deacon and gambling all in one night." Forsythia squeezed Larkspur's shoulder. "You've outdone yourself."

"Good thing Ma and Pa aren't here to see this." Lilac handed her sister the dripping cloth.

Lark buried her face in the cool wet towel.

She lifted her head when they heard boots on the front porch.

Holt started forward but stopped when Anders burst through the doorway. Lark swallowed again, not realizing she'd been holding her breath.

"What in the world have you done now?" Anders asked.

Jonah came in right behind him. "She bailed me and Bernie out of deep trouble. Jasper too."

Anders shook his head. "Larkspur Grace Nielsen, do you have any idea what kind of trouble you're in?"

She stared at him, feeling stronger by the second. "All I did was win at cards."

"A woman playing poker in a saloon in this town is bad enough." Anders clamped his jaw. "But you made that man look like a fool. I ran into a fella on my way who was there and was coming to warn us too. Apparently Ringwald's threatening to get even."

"What if Jonah had won? Wouldn't it be the same?"

"No. He'd entice the boys back with the hope of winning more tomorrow."

"So then . . ."

Anders slammed his hand on the table. "You're a young woman who pulled the fleece over that man's eyes. You made a fool of him. I'm sure you went in there playing the hesitant sweet young woman who didn't know the game."

"Not to mention flirting with him," Mr. Holt muttered.

Anders cut a glance at her. "You didn't."

"Not really. That is, I didn't mean to." Lark flushed despite herself. "And I told him we played poker as a family on winter nights, as a parlor game."

Anders stared at her, arms crossed over his chest.

"He was cheating." Lark glared right back at her brother. "Cheating people right out of their livelihood—horse, saddle, land. He couldn't be allowed to get away with that."

"She has a point there," Mr. Holt put in. "She showed that swindler up, and that's a fact."

Anders huffed out a disgusted breath. "It makes no difference anyway. The deed is done. The only way I see it, we need to get you out of town for a while. You could go visit Tante Grete for a month or so."

"Are you serious?" Lark pressed the towel to her face again. Surely what she had done was not that bad.

"I have a small house out by the lake, you could stay there to begin with." Holt nodded as he spoke. "You would be safe there."

"So I just disappear?"

"What about the rest of us?" Del asked. "All the gossip . . . and the diatribe from Deacon Wiesel will never end. He'll bar us from the church because we're her sisters."

Lark stood and opened the damper before lifting the lids on the stove to set a fire in the few remaining coals. "If we're going to stay up talking, I need some coffee. How will you explain my disappearance to the good folks of Linksburg?" She tossed in some shavings and blew on the coals till smoke curled, then laid in kindling and a couple of larger pieces of wood. "And besides, I've not done anything against the law. If a man won that kind of money, people would congratulate him. And if we had a real pastor again, I would not be the brunt of the weasel's fury. But if no one ever stands up to him, nothing will change."

"Be that as it may, the reality is you are in a mess, and that means the rest of us are too," Anders said.

Lark shut the stove door and sat back down. Maybe they needed a different solution—completely different.

"Remember when we talked about going west?" She watched shock freeze the faces around her. "Well, we did. There are no men around here of good husband material, and we've got to do something with our lives now that the war is over. Anders can stay and run the store. Besides, if we all left, Josephine and Anders could get married and move into the house here."

"I don't want to go west." Jonah shook his head. "No and no."

"They could use a man along, if they're actually going to do this, for safety and help." Anders frowned. "I've got the store and Josephine, but what's holding you here? If it weren't for you, we wouldn't be in this fix in the first place."

"They don't need me," Jonah insisted. "Lark is as good as a man. She's as tall as many and a better shot than most."

"So what are you going to do, then?" Lark threw up her hands. "You're the one who keeps wanting adventure. And getting into trouble instead."

Jonah squirmed in the chair. "I—I'll work with Anders at the store."

Anders studied his younger brother. "Why the change? I've been trying to get you there for ages."

"And I had to about break your arm to get your help when I was running the store." Lark narrowed her gaze at him. Was that a flush creeping over her little brother's ears? "There's a girl, isn't there?"

"No!" Jonah scrubbed his hand over his hair, his ears turning scarlet. "I mean, I helped Lila Johnson find baking soda when I was in there the other day. She said she didn't know what she would have done without me. So I can be good at helping people find stuff."

"At least when they are pretty daughters of livery stable owners." Lark rolled her eyes. "If you're going to stay, you'd best be serious about it."

"I am." He did sound serious.

"There can be no gambling. None! No going to the saloon for anything." Anders's eyes sparked fire. "And if I catch you at it, you are out on your own. Out of the store, out of the house, out!"

Silence pulsated in the room. Only the growing fire snapped and spit.

Lark huffed out a breath. "Now that that's settled, back to our original problem. The more I think about it, the more it makes sense, and not just because of this situation. I think the female portion of this family should head west."

A collective breath sucked the air from the silent room.

Lark looked around at her family, only her heavy eyebrows twitching. Were they as observant as she was, that would tell them she was anything but certain. "Think about it. We have some money saved, and with this windfall, we could probably buy land rather than homesteading, which might be difficult as women." Her breath came fast, belying her confident tone. Could they really do this?

Anders stared at her, tapping a forefinger against his chin. "If you want to go, Jonah had an interesting idea earlier. Do you think you can turn into Clark again?"

"Become a man again?" Larkspur raised her eyebrows. When a letter from Anders during the war had told them he was injured and in a prison camp, Lark had turned herself into Clark. Taking a horse and wagon, she had driven behind Confederate lines and brought him back. Anders had been certain it was just in time for him to be buried next to their parents in the church graveyard, but with the good nursing of his sisters and nourishing food, his strength returned. While he still limped and always would, and he had lost part of one hand, he took over the family store from Lark once he had healed. "Yes. I think I can."

"You mean travel on the train, right?" Forsythia asked.

"No, it doesn't go far enough yet," Lark said. "But we could take that covered wagon Anders got all outfitted for that man who changed his mind when his wife died." She looked at her brother. "Should we get oxen or mules?"

"I'd say oxen, slower but more dependable. And besides I know a man who has four up to sell."

"The same man?"

Anders nodded.

"I don't want to go west in a wagon. It'll take forever." Forsythia shuddered. "Don't look at me like that. I'm entitled to an opinion." She hugged her arms over her chest. "Besides, where would we go? All the way to Oregon?"

"I think it's too late in the spring to go that far. We'd have to overwinter somewhere or settle somewhere on the way." Del set the cookie jar in the middle of the table. "The coffee should be hot pretty soon."

Lark stared at her. "How do you know all that?"

"I've been reading accounts from folks who survived the journey. Some of the letters could break your heart."

Anders stood and crossed to the parlor, where his father's desk and bookshelves took up one corner. He returned with a pad of paper, a pen, and an inkwell. Pulling his chair up to the table and sitting down, he continued. "Ma always said start with a list, so that's what we're doing." He looked at his sisters. "What?"

"You look and sound so like Pa." Lilac blinked and sniffled.

Anders started writing. "Kansas is closer, and so is Nebraska."

"I've read good things about the land in Nebraska." Delphinium leaned forward. "And it might be far enough not to worry about the gambler tracking you down."

"May I make a suggestion?" Mr. Holt took another chair. At their nods, he continued. "We have to get Lark out of town by morning. I heard what Ringwald said, and he meant business." He looked at her. "You can pack a few things into saddlebags and take Lilac's mare to the lake. Pack food, too, although there are staples in the pantry. One of my friends up there makes sure the house is always ready. We used to go up there when we could. Nora loved the lake. Meanwhile, we'll figure things out. If you all decide to do this, we'll get the wagon ready and packed, and the girls can stop there and pick you up the next day."

Lark shook her head. "Impossible."

Anders studied their friend. "No, no, pay attention. I think he's got a point. Protecting Lark is the first thing, and you need to leave before dawn."

"I'll go along and make sure she gets there, then turn around and ride back. We could take the buggy. . . ." Holt thought a moment. "But riding is faster and would draw less attention."

"Why do I feel like I'm being railroaded here?" Lark asked.

"Because you have to listen to someone else for a change." Del patted her sister's shoulder as she made the rounds refilling coffee cups. "We're all agreed, right?"

Lark looked around the table and saw slow nods from everyone there. "But how will you know what to pack of mine? This is moving, not just going for a visit."

"Don't worry, none of us gets to take much." Forsythia looked at Anders, who nodded. "I'll make sure the trunk contains the Bible and a few other books." She heaved a deep sigh. "I'm sure there is no room for my piano, but we can tuck the fiddle into the wagon, and the mouth organ won't take up any room at all." She gave Jonah a pointed look. "If you join us someday, you can bring the guitar."

"Take it now." Jonah shrugged. "Maybe the rest of us will come someday." He looked to Anders, who was shaking his head.

The grandfather clock in the parlor chimed three times.

"I'll go home, get saddled up, and be back within half an hour," Mr. Holt said. "Jonah, would you please take care of my animals this morning?"

Jonah nodded.

"Lilac, go saddle up Starbright. And not with the sidesaddle.

Remember, Lark will be Clark." Anders raised his eyebrows. "You still have that slouch hat?"

Lark nodded. She'd kept the hat she had worn as Clark. That trip had taken her a month, but they had returned. This time they likely would not.

While they'd been talking, her mind had been running around, calculating how many miles they could travel in a day, how many weeks traveling time they had till frost, how far their money would go. But she needed to focus on the present. What could fit in her saddlebags for tonight? She'd need the rifle scabbard and ammunition. Good thing their father had made sure all his children could shoot straight. Forsythia even had a knack for knife throwing.

Lark rose. "I'll be ready." Her mouth said the words, but her mind screamed, *I don't want to leave home*. Were they really doing this? "Forsythia, make sure you pack Ma's flower seeds and whatever vegetable seeds we have left. Just think, perhaps we could find land to build Ma's dream of a seed company. Remember, she thought Lilac and Forsythia should design the seed packets and catalogs? That seemed an impossible dream, but perhaps it's not anymore." She sighed. "Who knows, there has to be a reason for all of this."

"You're right. It bears thinking about." Delphinium handed a heavy cloth bag of supplies to Lark. "We'll bring the rest."

Lark nodded. "And now I become Clark again. Who ever thought this would happen?"

Anders was buckling the saddlebags in place on Starbright when Holt rode back into the yard.

Lark hung a bag of food over the saddle horn, checked the girth one more time, and swung into the saddle. Fighting tears, she nodded down to her three sisters. "See you soon."

"Go with God." Anders squeezed her hand one more time. "I'll come someday on the train to visit. Write often."

Jonah shook his head slowly. "All because of me."

"There will always be a place for you, no matter where we are," Lark said.

She nudged her mount forward, Holt by her side. She knew if she looked back, she'd never leave. God only knew what lay ahead, and He was sure closemouthed. That thought didn't stop her tears.

4

"I sure hope this was the best thing to do." Forsythia watched Lark's form disappear into the darkness atop Starbright.

"Let's go get some sleep. Morning is almost here." Delphinium took Forsythia's arm, and together the three sisters climbed the stairs to their bedroom, Jonah right behind them.

Without bothering to change into their nightdresses, they lay down and flipped light blankets over themselves to ward off the wee hours' chill.

Lilac's and Delphinium's breathing soon evened, but Forsythia lay staring at the darkened ceiling.

Going west—was this really happening? How had everything changed so fast? All because of a couple of evil men. Not that things hadn't changed before. Losing their parents. Losing the man she loved in a war that took so much. Now she was to lose her home too.

But what did she have to stay for? Maybe a new beginning could be a good thing. Yet tears burned her throat in the darkness. *Lord, you know. Please lead us.*

"What in the world?" Forsythia blinked awake some time later, fighting to come out of a deep sleep.

"Someone is pounding on the door," Delphinium whispered. "Where's Jonah?"

"You know he can sleep through anything." Forsythia swung her feet to the floor and tiptoed over to the window that overlooked the front porch.

"I know you're in there," yelled a raucous voice. "You better get down here before I break down the door."

"I'll answer the door." Forsythia threw her dressing gown around her. "Del, you can run the fastest, so you go get Anders. Wake up Jonah too."

"It's Deacon Wiesel."

"I know. Run."

Del reappeared a few seconds later. "Jonah's not in his room."

Forsythia nodded and waved for her sister to hurry before stepping back to the window. "My land, can't a body get any rest around here?" she called down to the deacon.

"Get Miss Larkspur down here!" he hollered back.

Lord, save us. Thank you for getting Lark out of here. Mr. Holt was so wise. "We're coming." Should she get the shotgun off the wall? Or her knife? Lark had the rifle. *Please give me wisdom.*

The deacon banged on the door again. "Get that Lark out here."

At least he had the decency to stay on the porch, but he'd obviously been drinking. Where was Jonah?

"I'm coming, I'm coming." Forsythia detoured into the kitchen and lifted the old muzzle-loader off the wall. While it wasn't loaded, it would make a good scare tactic and a possible club. Holding it in the crook of her arm, she stopped at the door. Lilac came up behind her. She glanced over her shoulder to see her youngest sister with the rolling pin in one hand and the big knife in the other.

Wiesel continued banging on the door. Surely the neighbors had heard him and someone would go get the sheriff.

Forsythia shot up one more prayer and opened the door a crack. "Why, Deacon Wiesel, isn't this a bit early for house calls? I'm sorry, but we don't even have the stove lit yet to make coffee." She surprised herself with such a genteel voice. Knowing him, he'd probably been taking his frustrations out on his wife before he came here.

"Where is that Lark?" His breath nearly knocked her over. Drink and chaw. What a combination.

"You mean Miss Larkspur?" She put the emphasis on the *Miss.*

"Don't you go correcting me, missy. If you don't let me in, I'm going to break down this door and—"

"And what?" Jonah paused under the arbor over the gate in the picket fence, then slammed the gate shut behind him.

"Don't you smart-mouth me, you young good-for-nothing. Get your sister out here."

"Well, I don't rightly know which of my sisters you might be referring to." He looked at Forsythia in the doorway. "You know who he means?"

"He was yelling for Larkspur."

"Oh, that sister."

"His banging woke us up. How should I know where she is?" Stepping out from behind Jonah, Del yawned for good effect and patted her mouth. "Pardon me. What time is it anyway?"

All played their parts well. *Please, Lord, get Anders here before anyone gets hurt.*

"Jonah, do you know where Lark is?" Lilac asked, leaning around her older sister.

"Oh, of course I do," Jonah said, easy as you please. "Why, she left early this morning when Uncle Leroy came to get her. Aunt Bessie slipped and fell, and she wanted Lark to come help her. It's a shame her own children are too far away to come quickly. I'm surprised she didn't wake you."

"Why, me too. Did she say when she'd be back?" Forsythia asked. Was that the kitchen door she heard?

"What's going on here?" Anders stepped up beside Forsythia. "Deacon Wiesel, I hear you've been raising a ruckus. I hope you didn't wake all the neighbors up too."

"Your sister . . ."

Anders's eyebrows almost disappeared under his hat brim. "Yes? Which one might you be referring to?"

"Why, Lark, a'course."

Able to breathe easier now that Anders had arrived, Forsythia studied the man before her. *Please, Lord, let him know nothing about the gambling.*

"Why—why, she stood right up in church last evening, got up and left before I even finished the sermon. Caused a ruckus, she did," Wiesel complained.

"As the eldest in the family, since our parents passed on to their reward, I will be sure and pass on your message," Anders said. "Was there anything else?"

"She's been corrupting my wife with her misuse of Holy Scripture, turning her against me."

"Seems to me she helped bandage up your wife a couple of times after she fell or met some other misfortune." Anders stared the deacon down. "Could you tell me why your wife didn't go see Dr. Hunsaker?"

Wiesel glared over his shoulder at Jonah, who had moved closer behind him. "I-I guess that ain't none of your business."

"Perhaps you should go apologize to our neighbors for waking them up with all your ranting and hollering." Jonah took another step closer.

Anders stepped out on the porch. Even though he was still a little thin and weak from his imprisonment, he towered over the ball-shaped man with the mean mouth and snake eyes.

"She's hidin' in that house, I know she is. You let me in, and

I'll find her." The deacon raised one fist, then thought better of it and took a step backward, bumping into Jonah.

"I think you owe my sisters an apology." Jonah spoke softly, then made a show of sniffing the air. "Smells like you've been hitting the bottle." He raised his voice. "Anders, seems to me a letter to the head church office might be in order. As president of the board, mightn't you want to let them know how our deacon is behavin'? I thought he was supposed to be an example for us younger folks."

Forsythia rolled her lips together to swallow her response. This had gone from a frightening confrontation to something they would laugh about later. Interesting the difference because two men had arrived. Not that she would usually refer to her younger brother as a man. At least her heart was no longer jumping right out of her chest.

"I'm sure when Larkspur returns, she'll be glad to discuss all this with you." Anders leaned against the porch post as if he hadn't a care in the world. "And perhaps by then we'll have a new pastor in our church so the burden isn't so heavy on you."

Forsythia caught the gleam in her brother's eye. She knew he and a group of the men of the church had written letters to the head office and were talking about sending a delegation to get Deacon Wiesel relieved of his position.

That old phrase "if looks could kill" sure fit here. Wiesel spun around and elbowed Jonah aside on his way to the gate. In his drunken rage, he stomped clumsily off the path and through one of the prettiest corners of Ma's garden, which was known throughout the town and beyond.

Lilac gasped and started forward, but Forsythia held her back. No point engaging with the man further this morning.

"You ain't heard the end of this," Wiesel flung over his shoulder as the gate slammed behind him.

The three young women joined Anders, who sat down on the steps.

"Thank you for coming so quickly," Forsythia said.

"Never went to bed. Made lists of what can go in that wagon and gathered some of it up. I hate having to do this in such a rush, but I wouldn't put it past him to go on a drunken rampage and hurt someone other than his poor wife."

"Good thing Mr. Holt thought ahead enough to get Lark out of here."

"Now to get the rest of you out of here too. He's worse'n an angry boar hog." Anders shook his head. "He wasn't like this before Pastor Earling passed on."

"Power gone to his head?" Del asked. "That's what Lark said one time."

"He ruined Ma's primroses." Lilac's voice quivered.

"I know. He's violent every which way, it seems. We'll just have to ask Josephine to plant more." Forsythia stood. The sky was lightening toward dawn. "I'll get breakfast on the table."

"Stay for breakfast?" Del asked Anders as they all filed into the house.

"Thanks. I thought Jonah and I could get the trunks down from the attic. I still can't believe this exodus is actually going to happen." Anders sighed, looking troubled. "You should have a man along."

"We'll have Lark, and she's stronger than many men and more than capable."

"But, Sythia, she's still a woman."

"She was able to bring you home in spite of the battles going on and the ruffians who tried to steal her horse and you nearly dead." The words came forth sturdily, but Forsythia's chest still ached at the thought of leaving home.

"I know, and I will be forever grateful, but . . ."

"With her strong features and dark eyebrows, she can look

the part more than the rest of us too." Forsythia filled the coffee-pot.

Lilac turned from setting the stove lids back in place now that she had the fire going. "When are you and Josephine planning to get married?" She placed the cream pitcher on the table, then stared at it. "We won't have milk or cream."

"People can live without milk and cream and eggs and all kinds of food." Forsythia gave the mush a stir. "I've not made biscuits over a campfire before, but I guess we'll learn how."

By the time breakfast was on the table, the three trunks waited in the parlor, and Del had emptied and wiped them clean. To sweeten the musty odor, she brought lavender sachets from the wooden box their mother had used to store her dried herbs and garden seeds.

Anders said grace, and Lilac set the bowls of mush around the table. "We better be thankful for all the good things we are leaving behind." She blinked and swallowed, but the tears burst through her attempted dam and rolled down her cheeks. "I don't want to leave home."

"We all agreed," Forsythia said softly, blinking hard.

"Why did Lark have to go in that saloon? She's always charging into things." Lilac glared at Jonah and headed out the back door.

Del stood to go after her, but Anders shook his head. "Let her be. Better to work it out here than on the trail."

The silence was broken only by an oriole singing in the ash tree that shaded the south side of the house and the scrape of spoons on the bowls.

"More coffee, anyone?" Forsythia pushed cheer into her words. She couldn't deny Lilac's point, but they were family. And family stuck together.

Anders raised his cup. "I figure we'll park the wagon behind the store and have everything ready to load tonight under cover of darkness. I'll make a diagram of where everything needs to go. I'm hoping you can leave before dawn tomorrow. It's a good thing I've done this before, and the wagon was mostly loaded already when Sam's wife died and he decided not to go."

"How were you able to refund his money?"

"He hadn't paid it all. Was planning on the last payment on departure, but now we have the barrels of flour and slabs of bacon, sacks of beans and coffee that you need. The oxen are freshly shod too. I've been studying maps, and it looks like you could take the National Road across Ohio and join the Oregon Trail in Independence. It goes through Nebraska, so you could easily stop off there if that is where you decide to settle. One of my officers in the army hailed from out there and moved back after he was wounded and discharged. He's an attorney. I'll write to him and see what I can find out to pass on to you."

Forsythia nodded. At least that gave them something of a plan. "Give me the list so we can start packing."

Lilac came back into the house, her face more at peace. "Ma always said to use bay leaves to prevent weevils. We should put bay leaves in all the foodstuffs."

"Good idea." Forsythia sent her a smile.

They heard Mr. Holt talking to his horse before he mounted the steps and entered at Anders's invitation.

"Sit down and have some breakfast while you tell us what happened." At Anders's invitation, Del rose to fetch the coffee-pot and kettle of mush while Lilac brought dishes from the cupboard.

Holt brown-sugared his mush and poured cream both on the cereal and into his coffee. "We made it without anyone notic-ing us, at least as far as I could tell, and Lark let the horse out to pasture before we ate. I left her getting ready for bed and made my way home. 'Bout fell asleep on my horse, so it's a good thing he knows the way." He paused to eat a few bites and wash it down with coffee. "I tried to give her all the information I could about taking care of the oxen and the wagon, since I've had some experience with 'em on my farm. She's got a good head on her shoulders, but . . ." He heaved a sigh. "I hate to see you four undertake such a strenuous ordeal all by yourselves."

"You didn't tell her that, did you?" Jonah asked, his face wrinkled.

Holt shook his head. "Nope, I know better'n that. Best way to get folks all fired up is to give them unasked-for advice." He looked at Anders. "You got any maps to send along?"

"I do, some 'specially for folks heading west. We were just talking about that. Lark did a good job running the store while I was gone. I imagine she was the one who ordered the maps. I know I hadn't before I joined up with the Ohio brigade. I guess that's why my sisters figure they can do this—they helped so many others."

"True, but they didn't make the trip. I'd feel a lot better if they could join someone else from around here."

"We can join up with a wagon train in Independence, assuming we can get there in time," Del said. "It's mid-May already, and the trains start leaving in April, I think."

"Can I get you anything else, Mr. Holt?" Forsythia asked.

"More of that coffee, if'n you don't mind." He held up his cup. "Then I need to get some sleep so I can show you all the way to pick up Miss Lark." He looked around the table. "You're still planning on leaving before dawn tomorrow?"

Forsythia's head spun. So much to do.

Anders nodded. "Just praying we can keep their departure from Deacon Wiesel."

"It's a shame we can't figure out a way to get him out of commission for a while." Holt drained his coffee and set the cup on the table, staring at it for a long moment. "Just such a rush."

"Like Pa always said, 'Just do the best you can.'" Anders stood.

"Jonah, you come with me. You can pack boxes in the back while I take care of the store. Or I'll pack the boxes, and you mind the store."

"I don't know." Holt's head moved slowly from side to side while he studied the embroidery on the doily in the center of the table. "All this hurrying could cost you your lives on the trail because you don't have something that didn't get packed in the rush." He looked at Anders. "Think about that, all right?"

That afternoon, Forsythia took a break from packing and stepped out to soak in Ma's garden one more time. The primroses struggled up bravely in the sunshine despite the deacon's careless stomping. She gently fingered the irises budding along the fence. They would miss the graceful lavender blooms this year.

She found Del bent in her favorite corner by the lilac bush, digging up several of their mother's rosebushes.

"I want to take these four with us." Del wrapped burlap around the root balls. "I don't know if I can keep them alive on the way, but I want to try. Those apple seedlings too. It's too early to collect seeds from all her flowers and vegetables, so we'll just have to take what we've already saved." Tears caught in her voice. "Do you think Josephine would send us more later?"

"I'm sure she will." Forsythia hugged her sister's shoulders. "We should plant that garden in Ma's honor wherever we settle. You know, like we were talking about earlier. Not just for ourselves, but a place where others can come and buy her seeds and starts, benefit from all the wisdom she taught us. A real horticultural business. What do you think?"

"We could call it Leah's Garden, after Ma," Lilac said from behind them.

"Leah's Garden." Del sniffed and reached for Forsythia's hand to pull herself up. "I like it."

Del wrapped both her sisters in her arms. Forsythia blinked into her older sister's shoulder, wishing Lark were there too. *Lord, we're stepping into the unknown. So much ahead, and so much we're leaving behind.*

5

The oxen moved out when Delphinium, walking to their left, hupped and flicked the whip before dawn the next morning.

Lilac sat beside Forsythia on the wagon seat, sobbing on her shoulder. Tears dripped off Forsythia's and Del's chins too.

Mr. Holt and Jonah rode alongside on their horses, shadowy in the darkness. The men would lead them to where Lark was waiting.

Forsythia patted her little sister's knee. "We'll get through this. I know God is with us. He'll never leave us, and as far as I can tell, we are doing His will." She sure hoped so.

"I-I'm not afraid." Lilac sniffed and pulled a bit of soft cloth from her apron pocket. "I just don't want to leave home." She wiped her nose and tears. "I think Lark is happy we're starting on a new adventure. That's what she called this—an adventure."

An adventure to Lark maybe, but, Lord, I can see so many things that could go wrong. Forsythia's thoughts piled on top of each other and weighted her down like boulders. She knew she was supposed to trust in God to lead and guide them, but . . . *Lord, you seem so far away. Please don't turn your back on us.*

The four-up team of oxen plodded along. How could they cover twenty miles a day with beasts that didn't even trot, let alone walk faster than this? She could hear her father saying, *"Sure and steady wins the race."* There had been so many bits of wisdom stored in his silver-crowned head. She should have brought some of his journals just so she could hear his voice, at least through the written word. He had encouraged all of them to write journals, saying they were a mark of a thinking being. Hers had been sporadic, to say the least. Anders was the most consistent. Where would they even find journals out west?

At least her tears were drying. Maybe that was a good part of traveling with oxen—it gave one time to think. The moon cast shadows of the trees that lined the road. The whoosh of the wings of an owl on the hunt made her look up and watch as it flapped in and out of the moonlight. Up ahead it swooped down. A scream rent the air. The owl gained altitude again, a rabbit hanging limp in its talons.

The way of life. She knew there were plenty of rabbits and that the owl needed to eat and feed its family. God set it up this way.

Lilac flinched beside her. "Poor bunny."

"You can go back and sleep on that pallet, if you like."

"I know. I thought about it." She tucked her hand under Forsythia's arm and leaned on her shoulder. "Maybe later."

Del raised her voice. "Jonah, you make sure you keep that garden weeded. Shame to have wasted all those seeds if you don't."

He pulled his horse back to ride beside her. "Who's going to eat all that, since you won't be there to put food by for the winter?"

"I guess you and Anders better put up the screens for drying. I'm sure some of our friends will appreciate all that produce and put some by for you too."

"I think Anders and Josephine ought to get married soon and move into the big house, and I'll sleep above the store."

And get into trouble without anyone looking out for you. The thought brought Forsythia's eyebrows up. "Remember, you promised—no more gambling. Nor drinking either." She raised her voice. "Or Mr. Holt will attend to you, right?"

Mr. Holt reined his horse back. "Why will I attend to this young man here?"

"If anyone catches him in the saloon or drinking or carousing in general." She shook her head. "No, never mind. We can't ask that of you. He knows wrong from right, and he keeps saying he's an adult, so he needs to behave like one."

Holt shook his head. "Drinking and gambling are supposedly the realm of men. Some boys just start earlier and pay the price sooner. Between Anders and me, we'll keep him too busy to have time during the day. Can't speak for the night."

"I know. None of us can. It's all his choice." Forsythia finished with an internal, *Please, Lord.*

"How much farther, Mr. Holt?" Lilac raised her head to ask.

"Oh, we're about halfway there. Then we'll all sleep for a while, let the beasts graze, and then get you back on the road in the daylight."

"I see." Lilac nudged her sister. "I think I'll take you up on the pallet offer, unless you want to sleep."

"No, you go ahead."

Sometime later, when they reached the little house by the lake, Holt and Jonah unhitched the oxen and let them loose in the fenced pasture to graze. "We'll let them drink at the trough after they cool down," Mr. Holt explained.

Lark met her sisters at the door. "Bring a pallet in, and you three can sleep in the bed."

"We could sleep outside. It's such a beautiful morning." Del hugged her older sister. The sky in the east turned pearly gray, etched with pink clouds.

"We're going to be sleeping outside plenty. Enjoy a bed while you can."

A while later, Forsythia woke to the sounds of someone starting a fire in the round-bellied stove. She lay and watched Lark, now dressed in her new persona as Clark, blowing on the tiny flame started by a flint. Her sister's beautiful dark hair was shorn shorter than many men's, and her faded, rolled-sleeve shirt and pants hitched up with a belt above worn boots completed the picture. Her boots would be doing a lot of walking in the days and weeks ahead.

Forsythia sat up and stretched. "Is there an outhouse here?"

"Good morning to you too." Lark smiled at her. "Out behind the house." She pointed to a door on the back wall.

Forsythia left her shoes by the bed and headed outside. The dew on the grass soothed her feet and soaked the hem of her dress. Something else to be thankful for. They would not see outhouses along the trail.

"We'd better appreciate a hot breakfast," Lark said, dishing up the bacon and scrambled eggs while Lilac poured coffee into metal cups. "Thank you for this cozy house, Mr. Holt. I can see why your wife loved to come here. Trees for shade, water to wade in. Such riches."

"We thought often about moving here, but you can't leave a farm for any length of time. You all get on the road, and I'll clean up here and shut the house down again."

"Oxen are hitched up and ready to roll," Jonah said, coming through the door. He joined them at the table. "I'm sure going to miss all of your cooking. Did you talk to Anders about moving the wedding date sooner?" He looked at Forsythia.

"I did, and he said they are seriously considering it. I wish they could have had the wedding before we left, but that couldn't happen."

Anders and Josephine had grown up together but only recently decided that their friendship was a good basis for marriage, perhaps because of Anders's near brush with death. If Josephine had had her way, they'd have been married the day Lark brought him home over six months ago. Anders had refused until he knew he could manage the store again and make a life for his future family.

With everyone ready and the wagon loaded, Lark stepped up beside the oxen and lifted her whip, pointing it down the road. "Lord, as you blessed the Israelites with the crossing of the Red Sea, so we ask that you bless us as we head west into our new life. We thank you in advance. Amen."

She flicked the whip, and the oxen began to move.

Jonah rode near Lark, who walked beside the off ox. He kept his voice low. "I know you're glad to be leaving and see this as an adventure, but please be careful. I mean, I know you are always careful, but . . ."

Lark gave him a look from under the brim of her slouch hat.

"I know, I know. Who am I to talk? But I never thought . . ."

"Ja."

"You sound like Pa, but . . . but I . . . Sorry sounds like such a mealy word."

"And what would Pa tell you?" She walked with her gaze straight ahead.

"To think of others before myself." He paused and snorted. "Actually, he'd tell me to think before I do anything. I can hear him saying, 'You got to think and ask God for guidance.' I'm sure Jesus didn't want me in the saloon."

"Nor me either. I fell in the same trap you did, and look what it has cost us." She shook her head, regret lacing her chest. "Lord, protect us."

"I better get on back. Write soon so we know how you're faring."

"Now you sound like Anders."

"Guess that's not such a bad thing." Jonah pulled his horse back toward Mr. Holt. "You ready to head back?"

"Anytime you are."

They said their good-byes, and the girls watched them go. Tears dripped down Lilac's cheeks as she perched atop Starbright. "What if we never see them again?"

"Then we'll live with that." Lark, ever practical, motioned Lilac to bring the horse alongside her. "Keep your eyes out for something we can have for supper. Rabbit, squirrel, quail, doves. Get out the shotgun and make sure it's loaded with small shot. We'll set snares every night, as there are rabbits all around here. Remember that time I brought in a deer and Pa was nearly flummoxed? He wasn't sure he wanted his daughters to be so proficient with firearms. But if I hadn't been, I never could have brought Anders back."

"Did you have to use your gun?"

"I did. Ran off a pair of ruffians who thought my horse and wagon should belong to them. I shot one in the leg and the other in his shooting hand. He was right upset about that, but they both hightailed it away. It took my heart a while to settle back down where it belonged. Other times I stopped at a house or farm and was welcomed right into the family. I never could have made it without the loving and caring people along the way. I was able to buy a bag of oats in one town, but so many were barely hanging on themselves. They'd gotten real handy at hiding the supplies they had to keep the raiders and soldiers from stealing them blind."

"Forsythia gave up. She said we'd never see either you or Anders this side of heaven."

"It took a lot longer than I figured it would, but when I left home, I had no idea what I was getting into. All I knew was that God told me to go and He would get me there and back. Perhaps some evening around a campfire on this trip, I'll tell you more about what I saw and experienced. One thing for sure, I knew the hand of God was around me."

"Do you feel that now?"

"Not so much, but then, we aren't in any danger yet. But I do feel certain this is His will for us."

"I'm glad somebody does," Lilac muttered into her chest.

Lark patted her younger sister's knee. "It's going to be hard, but it'll come out good. You'll see. Think of this as an adventure. You know, you could write lots of stories from this trip."

"I thought of that. Did I tell you I brought Pa's last two journals along?"

Lark rolled her lips together to keep from laughing. Leave it to Lilac. "Good for you. Found a hiding place for them, did you?"

"In the trunk with all our clothes and some of the bedding. I brought two of Ma's paintings too."

"And paints and brushes? Canvases?"

"They don't take up much room. Not like the piano." Lilac patted the mare's neck. "I know how heartbroken Forsythia was to leave the piano, and I cried right along with her."

"But Del has the guitar?"

"She hung it in a sling from the roof hoops. Anders helped her, muttering all the time. And we have the fiddle."

Lark thought of the harmonica she kept in her satchel. Pa had taught her and Del, while Mrs. Saunders had been Forsythia's piano teacher for years. They'd been born into their love of music and art of all kinds. And their mother's garden was known even beyond their town as a place of peace and beauty.

"And we're leaving it all behind." As usual, Lilac seemed able to read Lark's mind.

"Not all of it. We have seeds, the rosebush starts, and diagrams of the garden. Sythia told me about Del's idea—when we find our new home, we'll name it Leah's Garden, in honor of her. Someday when the railroad comes near to wherever we are, we'll have Anders and Jonah send us more starts and bulbs, irises and lilies."

"More fruit trees too."

"And nuts."

"What are you two talking about up there?" Forsythia called from the wagon seat. "Does someone else want to ride up here and keep watch? I'll walk and guide the oxen for a while."

"I will," Del answered.

When the wagon stopped, Forsythia clambered down. "Can we get a drink?" She stretched, bending over to pull some tension from her back. "I hope we can stop by a creek or river or something tonight."

"The water keg is full." Lark headed for the barrel strapped to the side of the wagon and dipped into it so they all could drink.

"Anders mapped out towns and such for us," Forsythia said. "We might be able to purchase some fresh fruits and vegetables that way."

Lark hung the water dipper back on the hook by the barrel. She then showed Forsythia the basics of guiding the oxen with a few simple commands of the whip. It was amazing how different driving oxen was from driving horses.

When they stopped for dinner, Del handed around ham sandwiches and cookies they had packed from home. Though the bread was nearly as dry as crackers, they ate it anyway, knowing these were probably their last sandwiches for months.

When they started off again, Lilac mounted Starbright, Del took over driving, and Lark and Forsythia walked beside the oxen. They drove through one small town, with people waving at them and two young boys walking with them for a time.

"How far you going?" asked one.

"California," Lark answered, just in case that gambler lived up to his threats to come find her to get his money back. In all the throes of getting going, she'd nearly forgotten why they left.

"Pa says that's a long, long way away."

"Yep."

"On the other side of the world," added the other one.

"'Bout so."

"Good luck, mister." The two waved and dropped back.

Lilac rode up beside Lark. "Did you change your mind? I thought we were going to Independence, Missouri, then on to Nebraska."

"That we are, but if someone tries to find us, I don't want to leave a trail."

"Oh, like the gambler."

"We don't know if that man will live up to his threats, but we aren't taking chances. I want to get far away from Linksburg as quickly as possible."

Late in the afternoon, Lark rode ahead and found a creek for them to camp by, riding off the road a short way to find a good camping place shielded from view.

"There's a perfect place others have used," she told her sisters. "It even has a fire ring."

"Good thing." Forsythia pushed her sunbonnet back off her head to feel the breeze now that the sun was going down. "I'm beat."

And to think this was only day one. Lark studied her sisters. *We'll take some hardening up, that's for sure.*

6

hat a lovely spot.

Lark and Del unhitched the oxen and, after lowering the wagon tongue to the ground, led them forward to lift the yokes from their necks. The animals shook their heads and then their whole bodies.

"Can we wade in that creek?" Lilac closed her eyes and spun in a circle. "After watering the animals, of course."

"You all go ahead. I'll water and hobble the animals." Lark waved them off. "Just don't take long. We need to find wood." *Just for tonight*, she told herself. *This life is new to all of them.* She'd had the search for Anders to help prepare her for this. "Come on, Sadie, let's get a drink."

Sadie, Sam . . . they needed to think of names for the other two oxen. *Soda and Sarge?* Lark chuckled. She led the animals to the creek and let them drink their fill. When they raised their heads, water dripping from their jaws, she herded them back up by the wagon and set about hobbling them, then did the same for Starbright. Something about the peace of the falling dusk and the song of the creek made her pause and draw in a deep breath. Inhaling the animal smells along with that of the trees and grass, she tucked the sights and smells away in her heart.

She started a fire with flint and stone from the tin and some dried leaves and kindling she found, then grabbed the metal coffeepot and headed up-creek where the water would be pure. Dipping the coffeepot into the burbling water, she shook her head at seeing her younger sisters still knee-deep in the creek's flow.

"We need firewood," she called. Trying to make her voice stern didn't quite work. She envied them, but someone had to be in charge and make sure supper happened. After all, she'd walked farther than any of the others.

Lilac soon came hurrying into their campsite with an arm-load of firewood.

Lark nodded her thanks. "We need to remember to put some wood in the wagon in case we hit a rainstorm."

"Which will happen sooner than we planned." Lilac pointed to the west, where black thunderheads were chasing away the sun.

Lark blew out her disgust. They were prepared for rain with slickers hanging from one of the hoops, but she would prefer to be near a barn or someplace to shelter. Lightning forked the burgeoning blackness. She dumped out part of the coffee water so it would boil more quickly, then threw in a couple of handfuls of ground coffee. The others hustled back with more wood.

"Break it up and stack it in and under the wagon," Lark instructed. "What did you plan for supper, Del?"

"I was planning to make biscuits and fry the beans with bits of bacon."

"Better get the beans in the frying pan, quick. We can eat in the wagon."

Thunder rumbled in the distance. The animals continued to graze, ignoring the drops that spattered as the wind kicked up. Forsythia handed out the slickers, shivering all the while.

The mare threw up her head, wind catching her mane. Lark snapped a rope to her halter. "Just to be safe, girl." Patting Starbright's neck and watching the sheet of rain draw nearer, she blew out a breath. *Please, Lord, protect us from this storm.* She drew the mare into the shelter of the trees, but the oxen kept right on grazing.

The others had retreated to the wagon, carrying the steaming coffeepot and sizzling frying pan. Lark leaned against Starbright's warm shoulder, and the mare went back to grazing the sparse grass around their feet. The storm hit like an upturned bucket of water. Thunder roared closer and closer as lightning stabbed the sky.

When the thunder crashed right over them, Starbright jerked her head up against the lead. Lark murmured to gentle her down, all the while locking her hand in the rope right under the mare's jaw.

"Look at that, heading on east." She puffed out a sigh of relief. The torrent soaked everything around them but didn't hover over them. Within a couple of minutes, the rain went from drenching to dancing and then to dripping. "Okay, girl, go join the oxen." She unsnapped the lead rope and stopped to look at the fire pit. There would be no trying to restart the fire.

"Come and eat, Lark," Del called. "The coffee is still hot too."

"You don't have to ask me twice." She joined the others crammed in the rear of the wagon.

"Fried beans are really good when you're as hungry as I was." Lilac handed her big sister one of the metal plates Anders had supplied.

"Where are we going to sleep?" Forsythia asked after a jaw-popping yawn.

"Two can sleep in here, and I'll spread the oilcloth on the ground under the wagon for the third," Lark said. "We'll be taking turns keeping watch, three each night. Who wants to go first? I'll take the third until daylight."

"I can go first. Will we start a fire to fix breakfast?" Forsythia asked.

"I think not. Everything will still be wet. We'll eat what we have."

When Del woke Lark for the third watch, the moon was flying so bright that even the grass etched shadows.

Lark stretched and pointed to the bedroll. "I kept it warm for you. Isn't this glorious? Kind of like a benediction after the storm."

"Thanks to the moon, I could keep track of our grazers. They kept wandering despite the hobbles. But they just laid down a few minutes ago. Guess they finally got full." She tucked her boots under the foot of the bedroll and slid in between the blankets.

Lark rubbed her hip where there must have been a rock hiding in the grass. Sleeping on the ground was going to take some getting used to. She poured herself a cup of cold coffee, and her mind leapt to the road ahead, all the unknowns. Had they brought enough supplies? Would the money she'd won stretch far enough to set up a whole new life? Had they even left early enough in the season to join a wagon train? During the storm, she had questioned the wisdom of leaving home like this.

"Lord, you know I've prayed about this, and I so hope I was listening for your answers. We could still turn around and go home if you think that's best. I don't want to be out of your will. Thank you for never leaving us alone."

With the moonlight so bright, the stars were dim. Her father had loved the stars, taught her the major constellations and how to navigate by them, little dreaming she would ever need that knowledge.

When dawn cracked the eastern skyline, she roused the

others, no closer to being sure of God's will. Everything had happened so fast—and all because of her actions. As light colored the sky so they could see more clearly, she rounded up the animals while her sisters dressed. Del helped her yoke the oxen.

The sun just glimmered on the horizon when they bowed their heads for Forsythia to pray for God's blessing on each of them, the animals, and the long day ahead.

"And thank you, Lord, that you moved the rain on quickly so we needn't be concerned about muddy roads. Please bless our travels today, and thank you for your protection and guidance hour by hour, day by day. We rejoice and praise your holy name."

They all said the closing "amen," and Lark checked on Forsythia up on the wagon seat, Del on the horse, and Lilac walking with her.

"All ready?" She hupped the oxen, flicking the slender whip at the same time.

"This sure was a nice place to camp," Lilac said, looking back. "In spite of the rain. Do you think we'll find another wagon to travel with soon?"

"I hope so. There's safety in numbers."

"True. But probably not as much peace. As I fell asleep, I felt such a sense of peace, as if God was surrounding us with angels."

"Thank you, I was concerned that . . ." Lark shook her head, a sudden lump in her throat. "Let's just say God used you to answer my prayers this morning."

"Where's Sythia?"

Forsythia heard Lilac's question from her pallet inside the wagon. It was dawn on their fourth day, and Forsythia felt wretched.

"I don't know. I saw her head to the creek a bit ago. Del?"

"Did you check the wagon?" Del suggested, and Forsythia groaned.

Lilac found her wrapped in a quilt and huddled in the rear corner. "What's wrong, Sythia?"

"Just leave me alone, okay? I'll be better by tomorrow." *Please go away.* Forsythia always longed for her mother's comfort when her cycle arrived with miserable cramps and a head-ache. It didn't happen every month but often enough to make her dread it.

"I'll bring you a hot rock." Lilac disappeared.

Oh, I wish I were back home. Even though Ma had gone on to heaven, so she could no longer bring tea and a comforting hand, Forsythia could still have made a cup of ginger tea to help relax the cramping. Sometimes her mother would read to her from her well-worn Bible, and then they would talk about the blessings God was sending down. Ma called times like this the curse of Eve, something she had also suffered.

"But be encouraged. After I had my first baby, I no longer had the monthly curse, at least not the cramping. So you can look forward to that."

Forsythia jerked back to reality when Lilac returned and handed her a hot rock wrapped in a small blanket. "Thank you."

"I can't find the herbs, though I know we packed them, or I'd make Ma's tea for you."

"You're so like our ma." Forsythia nestled the warmth against her lower belly. *I want to go home.* Tears leaked over her cheeks. *I didn't want to come on this trip.* All because Lark couldn't keep from saving Jonah's hide one more time.

"You want some breakfast?" Lilac asked.

"No, thanks." Forsythia bit back a groan. She could hear the others clattering about outside but tried to ignore them.

"Lilac, let her come and get her own breakfast," Lark called.

Lilac turned toward the opening at the back of the wagon. "But you know Forsythia struggles—"

"No, she just gives in. Ma always babied her. It's time she grew up and . . ."

Forsythia curled into a tighter ball, hurt pinching her throat on top of the cramping.

Lilac propped her hands on her hips. "Just because you don't—"

Lark snorted in disgust. "Let's just get on the road. Forsythia will be all right by tomorrow."

"She was supposed to drive today," Del snapped back.

"You can drive, Lilac can ride, and I'll walk."

"I planned on knitting. We're going to need warmer winter things where we're going." Del often knitted as she strode along and still managed to keep from stumbling.

"One more day won't make a big difference." Lark's voice came out gruff, as if she really were a man. "Just calm down and—"

"Me calm down? Have you listened to yourself? Why don't you just go hunting?" Del must have slammed the coffee jug back into the lidded cooking box outside the wagon by the sound.

"Just stop it. I'll drive today." That was Lilac.

"Fine," Lark snapped. Forsythia heard the creak of the saddle and then the sound of Starbright's hooves loping down the road.

Forsythia groaned and cuddled closer to the hot rock. This was their first big fight. It would probably not be their last.

She dozed for a while. When she awoke, the rock was only warm and so of little use. *Why am I the only one who suffers so?* Perhaps walking would help.

She asked Lilac to stop the oxen for a moment and clambered out, then walked beside Del, breathing in the morning air. The sunshine warmed her muscles, easing the cramping.

The sun was past the zenith when they reached a creek. Still no Lark.

"Let's rest and lunch here—nooning, I think they call it," Del said.

They unhitched the oxen, then Lilac unyoked one ox from each pair and re-yoked them facing the other direction, a trick learned from Mr. Holt. That way the animals could graze in a circle around each other but not wander too far.

Forsythia dug in the food box and handed a biscuit to each of her sisters. "What if something happens to Lark? How will we know?"

"We just go forward until we find a good place to camp and trust that she's all right."

Del spoke so reasonably that Forsythia felt almost foolish in raising the concern. But what if . . . ? Her mind flitted around, seeing her sister with a broken leg or arm, unable to get on the horse. *What if she never shows up again? What do we do?* No matter how disgusted Forsythia was with Lark's saving their little brother yet again, or the hurt of her words this morning, the thought of life with no Larkspur was nearly as bad as when Ma died.

She kept pace with the plodding oxen as they continued down the road. *Lord, your Word says you are our strength and our shield. You know every breath we take and every step we make. You are our rock and our redeemer.* Her mind slipped into song.

"'Rock of Ages, cleft for me, let me hide myself in thee . . .'"

The sun had started its downhill slide when she saw a horse and rider coming toward them. "Lark. Thank you, Lord God, you kept her and us safe."

Their sister stopped a ways ahead and waited for them. What did she have hanging from the saddle?

As they drew nearer, Lark reined the horse around and rode

beside Forsythia. "Sorry I took so long, but I shot a deer, and I knew it would rot before we could eat it all. There's a hamlet with a store nearby, so I kept a rear quarter and traded the rest for some supplies. Tonight we'll have venison steaks along with bread and cheese and rice. Even eggs for breakfast. We'll dry as much of the venison as we can. I'm thinking we might stay an extra day to finish that. There's a good place to camp a mile or two ahead."

"We were worried about you, that you'd gotten hurt or something." Lilac glared at her.

"Sorry, but had I brought the whole carcass here . . ." She blew out a sigh. "It was a difficult decision, but I figured it was for the best."

When they arrived at the spot she had found, they set up camp as usual but made a longer fire. Lark used the tailgate as a table and sliced four slabs of meat to fry for supper.

"How will we dry the meat?" Forsythia asked.

"I saw a picture that showed Indians weaving thin slices of meat on sticks and setting them to hold over the coals. We'll need lots of coals. We'll cut willow sticks and sharpen the points. One end for the meat, and one to stab into the ground."

Lark and Lilac took knives to cut from a thicket up the creek a ways. When they returned, the steaks were sizzling in the frying pan, and Del had sliced most of the rest as thinly as possible. "We can boil most of the rest, so we should have several good meals besides the smoked and dried pieces."

Lark squeezed Forsythia's shoulder as she passed. "Feeling better?"

Forsythia nodded and felt the worry band around her chest loosen. They were back to working as the team they had been raised to be. *Thank you, Lord.*

Forsythia had the middle watch that night, as it was Del's turn to sleep through. She sang to herself to keep awake, checked the fire and the meat, and walked out to where the oxen lay, chewing their cuds. Starbright nuzzled her, hoping for the sugar treat she used to get.

"Sorry, girl. No more sugar lumps. No more cookies. We had it pretty easy at home, though we didn't realize it."

The mare nickered softly as Forsythia moved away. She sat on the hunk of applewood they'd brought along, a piece of home. Poking the fire with a stick sent sparks rising, like lightning bugs dancing in the dark. With no moon yet, the dark was so dense that she felt closed in until she looked up at the stars God had strewn across the sky. "Lord, all this you created, and yet you love me and ask me to spend time with you. How can I be so blessed? And thank you, the misery is gone."

She got up to put more wood on the fire. *May my praises rise to you as the sparks fly upward.* She heard the flap of wings and hoot of an owl. Some critters rustled in the brush. How easy it would be to let fear take over. She used to be afraid of the dark, but her father would take his girls outside at night to learn about the stars and the birds and animals that hunted and moved around during the wee hours.

"What do you think, Pa, of your daughters heading west like this? Ma never wanted to leave her home. She wanted us all to marry good men and bring her grandchildren to love and enjoy. I can see her loving our children, like she did those at church when we no longer needed to be held and rocked and sang to." She poked the fire again. "Lord God, I want to be like my mother." And her father. She was so thankful Lilac had brought some journals after all. One of these days she'd read through them.

The next day, when it was her turn to ride in the wagon, Forsythia lifted the guitar off the hook on one of the hoops and tuned it, then picked out a tune. Lively or poignant, the music lifted their hearts along with their voices. As usual, they slipped into harmonizing as naturally as breathing. They sang songs that made them giggle and others that drew tears. "Arkansas Traveler," "Beautiful Dreamer," "In the Sweet By and By," and "Fairest Lord Jesus."

> "Beautiful Savior! Lord of all the nations!
> Son of God and Son of Man!
> Glory and honor, praise, adoration,
> Now and forever more be thine."

When Forsythia strummed the final chord, she wasn't the only one wiping her eyes.

"Thank you, Sythia, that was lovely. Perhaps one of these evenings we can bring out the fiddle and mouth organ." Del clasped her hands in her lap as she sat astride Starbright.

"Makes me even more homesick." Lilac blinked and wiped her eyes. She flopped her sunbonnet over her shoulders to let the teasing breeze play with her hair. "You think Pa and Ma are up in heaven, looking down on us?"

"And wondering why we ever left home."

"I think Pa would have wanted to head west. He was so sick of all the division that was happening with the war, he wanted to go someplace where that wasn't a problem. As if that were possible."

Del stopped the horse and dismounted. "Come on, Lilac, you ride Starbright awhile. That always makes you feel better."

They waved at a family in a wagon going the same direction, but much faster, who pulled out around them. The two boys in the back waved and whistled.

"Where ya goin'?" one hollered.

"West," Lark answered.

"To California to find gold?"

The younger boy chimed in. "That's where I'd go. Maybe when we get older."

"The gold will all be mined out by the time we get that big." The older boy punched his brother's arm. The younger punched him back, and they almost tumbled out of the wagon as they scrapped.

"They remind me of Jonah, but he didn't have a brother that close to his age," Forsythia said.

"So he teased me." Lilac shook her head. "And I played with him the most." Their mother had often reprimanded her youngest daughter for her unladylike behavior. "I remember wishing I could wear pants like Jonah did. I didn't think it fair then, and I still don't." She rode up next to Lark. "Are pants easier than skirts?"

"Easier? Indeed. But wool pants scratch the insides of your legs. Mighty uncomfortable." Lark took off her hat and wiped the sweat from her forehead, then put it back on. "I like this hat better'n sunbonnets too."

"If I had my way, I'd wear a wide-brimmed hat like yours but made of straw. Let the air in better." Lilac untied her sunbonnet and hooked it over the saddle horn. "Any idea how close we are to Columbus? We can pick up the National Road there, and that'll take us to Independence."

"I'll ask at the next town. I've been thinkin'. I hate to go through towns all together, just in case Deacon Wiesel or Ringwald come looking for us. So I figure you can head north and circle around the town, and that way we won't have a horse along either. Sythia, you huddle down in the wagon under a blanket. Then we'll just be a man and his wife heading west. I'll stop and chat if necessary. All agree?"

Lilac stared at her eldest sister. "You amaze me. I'd have never thought about things like that at all."

When they approached the village where Lark had traded the venison, they put her plan into action. Within a short while, they relaxed on the other side of the town. No one had noticed them or paid attention. Forsythia folded up the blanket and climbed out of the back of the wagon.

"That was getting plenty hot." She pushed her sunbonnet off her head and let it hang down her back. "Ah, that breeze is a gift. You think the gambler would really ride west after us?" Just the thought of someone trailing them made her shudder.

"I have no idea. He seemed mighty prosperous, and the only one of us who might know is back home. And if ever I hear he's been back to the saloon, I swear . . ."

Assuming they ever saw their brothers again in this life.

7

The days fell into a pattern as they plodded south and west. Their plan to join up with a western-bound wagon train at times seemed beyond reach. How late they had started pressed on Lark's shoulders. Late May already, and wagon trains started heading west in late April, from what she understood. Was it foolhardy to think they could reach Independence before all the wagon trains had left?

One night when they had finished eating and were sitting around the fire, Del stopped digging a stick into the dirt and looked around at her sisters. "What if we asked around if there are any places for sale in some appealing spot on the way to Independence? I mean, we've not bought land or committed to living in Nebraska."

"What if Ringwald is tracking us? We're only a couple hundred miles from home." Lark shook her head. "We'll ask at the post office in Columbus if there is a letter from Anders. He and I decided he'd send it to the Jimson family. That way if the gambler comes lookin', there'll be no trace of us."

Forsythia looked up from her mending. "You're really worried about him, aren't you?"

"He didn't like losing, and that was a lot of money."

"Some folks will die to get even. I say we keep going." Lilac stood. "Let's play some music." She returned from the wagon with the guitar and the mouth organ.

Forsythia took the guitar and tightened the strings. "Give me a C."

Lark blew the proper note. When they were tuned together, Forsythia strummed a few chords, and her fingers set to picking. Their mother's favorite hymn wrapped around them. By the end of "Abide with Me," they were all wiping their eyes.

"It makes me miss her all the more." Lark sniffed. "How about something livelier?"

Forsythia set her foot tapping, and "Turkey in the Straw" circled the wagon.

"Now, that was mighty fine." A male voice came from the trees along the creek.

Oh, Lord, protect us. Lark played the mouth organ with one hand and picked up the rifle at her side with the other. "You're welcome to join us." She made sure to keep her voice low like a man's.

Forsythia started picking again, her fingers wandering over "Jesus, Lover of My Soul."

"My mama used to sing that ever' night."

"The coffee's still hot."

"I hate to bother you. . . ."

"No bother." Lark stared into the dark. Like an apparition, a form separated from a tree and shuffled into the firelight. "I'd appreciate it if you leave your gun behind."

"Not loaded. No shells."

She raised hers. "Just lay it down, then."

He slowly did as she said and stood again. "Your music woke me up. Thought I'd died and gone to heaven."

"You live around here?"

"No, I'm on my way home."

"From the war?"

He nodded.

Lilac shifted beside Lark and whispered, "Can I pour him some coffee?"

Lark nodded. "How long since you've eaten?"

"I got a squirrel yesterday. Last of my ammunition."

Del stood and moved to the wagon. "Our biscuits are like rocks, but they're filling."

"I didn't come for food. Just wanted to tell you thanks for the music." He took the cup Lilac handed him. "Thank you, ma'am."

"Sit a spell," Lark said. *Lord, please keep me from making a mistake here. Set up a hedge of protection around us.*

He crossed his legs and lowered himself to the ground on the other side of the fire, dipping the biscuit in his coffee. "Thank you."

He has manners and that softness of speech, neither north nor south. Who is he under all that grime, both body and clothes near worn out? Lark studied him from under her hat brim. Scruffy beard, army uniform so old you couldn't even tell which side it was from.

"Where's home?" she finally asked.

"We had a fine farm in West Virginia, but there's nothin' left of it. A neighbor said one side or the other burned it to the ground. I think my folks died of broken hearts at all the carnage. My younger sister married a man from Illinois, and no one had heard from her since. My two brothers both died in the battles, one in blue and one in gray. I have no idea where my older sister is. A mining company had taken over the land by the time I got back. I was the firstborn and spent the last months of the war in a prison camp. Thought I would never live through that. But when they opened the gates, I staggered out and headed for home."

"To find nothing there." How horrible that would be. Lark knew about prison camps, having rescued her older brother from one. But this was not the time to bring that up.

"So where you bound for now?" Lilac asked.

The man didn't answer. Forsythia kept picking out hymns on the guitar, a shawl of beauty and comfort that seemed to wrap around them all. The fire sent up sparks when Lilac jabbed a stick in the coals that lay glowing in shades of vermilion, gold, and white hot.

"Sir, where did you learn to play the harmonica like that?" The stranger wrapped his hands around his coffee cup. "Nothin' can sound as lonesome as a hobo harp."

"From our pa. Our folks taught us that music expanded the mind and soothed the soul."

"What else do you play?"

"Oh, piano, fiddle, harmonica . . . whatever we put our mind to. Or have at hand." Lark felt a yawn coming on. "Mornin' comes before dawn, so we better be turning in. Let's close with Ma's favorite."

Forsythia played a few chords and moved into the beginning. They all sang, full harmony holding up an ocean of sadness, though Lark kept her contralto soft to keep from giving anything away. When a baritone blended in, Lark switched to her harmonica, and they finished after a couple of verses, sliding into humming.

As usual, Lark closed with a blessing. "And now may the Lord bless us and keep us. May He lift up His countenance upon us, and give us His peace." *And protection*, she added in her mind.

"Thank you for giving a wanderer a cup of coffee, biscuit, and this mighty fine taste of home." The stranger rose and tossed the dregs from his cup into the fire. He tipped his hat to all of them and faded into the darkness.

The sisters stood, and each fell to her evening chores. Tonight

Forsythia was on duty first, Del on the middle watch, and Lilac the final.

"Do you think he'll still be here in the morning?" Lilac asked.

"We don't even know his name," Lark said.

"Nor he ours. But he did call you *sir*, so you played your role well." Del moved the coals around so none were touching. The coffeepot sat off to the side, ready to be filled again first thing.

Lark checked on the hobbled oxen and horse before she turned in. The oxen were lying down, chewing their cuds, and Starbright nuzzled her chest. She palmed a bit of biscuit she'd stored in her pocket. "You keep watch now, you hear? Let me know if some stranger comes in the night."

"All is well?" Forsythia asked when Lark returned to the wagon.

"So far. You keep that rifle in hand and wake me if you hear anything unusual."

"I will. You get some rest."

Lark fell asleep praying for the man with no name, for both protection from him and for him. Mostly she woke to any unusual noises, so when Lilac woke her just before dawn, she stretched and felt like she'd had a good night's rest for a change.

"All is well," Lilac said.

"Glad to hear that." Lark pulled on her boots and clapped her hat back on her head. Her hair was getting longer again after a few weeks on the trail, but then, that soldier had his tied back with a strip of leather.

They were on the road again about an hour later, just as the last star faded overhead.

"No sign of our visitor?" Lark was walking beside the wagon.

"None. I'm not sure if I'm grateful or sorry." Del let her sunbonnet fall down her back so she could feel the morning breezes. She'd given up keeping her face and arms anything but tan. "He seemed so sad." She leaned forward and patted Starbright's neck.

"He appreciated good music, so I guess we blessed him too. I know playing like that sure relaxes me." *But I wish we had learned his name.* Look at all he'd endured. Made it out of a prison camp only to find the home he'd dreamed of was no more. Why didn't he stay there to rebuild?

"Lark," Lilac asked from the wagon seat, "do you ever dream of what lies ahead of us, the place that we'll find in Nebraska?"

"Maybe some, but mostly I think about the next hours, miles, where we'll find a good place for the night. Having enough food, keeping us safe." Details, numbers, and plans ran through her mind so fast she had to limit her concentration. "So far, we've done well."

"I know. I thank our Father every night and whenever I think of Him during the day for the way He is protecting us and providing what we need."

"I've started a supply list for when we find a store again." Del tipped her head back, the better to feel the breeze. "I find myself thinking of home rather than what's ahead. I watered the roses and apple tree starts this morning."

"We should send someone ahead to scout for us," Lark said.

Lilac, always eager to be on horseback, traded places with Del and rode on ahead.

As the sun inched farther along its daily arc, both the animals and the humans darkened and dripped with sweat. Del tied a rolled cloth around her head to keep sweat from dripping into her eyes.

When Starbright trotted back, Lilac announced, "There's a creek a mile or so ahead with some big trees. It'd make a great stopping place for dinner and watering the animals. A mile or so beyond that is a town, and after that is Columbus. We can turn off and bypass Columbus and pick up the route west again, or we can drive right on through. I remember Anders talking about the Columbus Arsenal. Said he'd heard it's a mighty busy place. The railroad's already there, probably because of the military."

"Thanks, you did well." Lark nodded. "We'll go on through and check at the post office to see if there's a letter from Anders. We'll stop where you said, but not for long. I'd like to put Columbus behind us before we stop for the night."

The road grew busier the closer they came to Columbus. Farms with fields of hay and grain lined the roads, of which there were several running north and south. Buggies and riders on horses passed them going both ways as they plodded along. The dust hung in the humid air, coating everything so that the sweat running down their skin left streaks. The clouds that blocked the sun held their moisture, killing any breeze.

While most folks waved, one rider slowed to ride beside them. "Where ya headin'?"

"Oregon Trail." Lark, now riding Starbright, answered for them.

"Got a ways to go, that's for sure. You lookin' for work? There's plenty goin' on here, what with the building of the arsenal this side of town. Government orders, ya know."

"Why now, when the war is over?"

"Troops still head out, and there's people movin' west like you folk. They're buying rifles but not paying much."

"Thanks for the information." Lark nodded a farewell and urged her mare forward. Getting out of Ohio was paramount. Especially since the railroad made travel this far easy and thus even more dangerous.

What if they'd been so careful for nothing? The thought tensed her shoulders. *Keep your eyes on Independence.* "I think I'll go on ahead and find the post office," she told Forsythia.

Nudging Starbright into a trot, she pulled away from the others. Perhaps she should have sent Forsythia ahead, but her sister didn't like riding in public without a sidesaddle.

Lark found the post office without difficulty, and after wrapping Starbright's reins around the porch railing, she paused to read the wanted posters on the wall. Folks asking after boys who had gone off to war and so far not returned. Most probably never would. Thinking of the young man who'd sat with them the night before, Lark shot a thank-you heavenward that she had been able to bring Anders home.

"After you, ma'am." She nodded to the older woman who came up behind her as she stepped toward the post office door, tipping her hat at the same time.

"Thank you, young man." The woman fluttered her fan, and the tiny breeze that passed over her shoulder made Lark wish for the one she used to have at home. It was a shame they hadn't put a couple in the wagon. They wouldn't have taken up much room.

When it came her turn, she nodded at the woman behind the counter. "You have any mail for the Jimsons?"

"I'll look and see. Might take a minute or two."

Lark waited, listening to the conversation of the two ladies behind her. "Blue uniforms—that's all we see around here anymore. This is far worse than during the war."

"It's not safe to travel these roads at all."

Lark picked up the letter slid across the wooden counter to her. Anders had kept his word. "Thank you, ma'am. Lord bless you."

She almost paused in shock that she had said that. All because she was so thrilled to see her brother's handwriting.

She stepped to the side. "Excuse me, please." She tipped her hat to the two gossipers. "Thank you for the warning." She strode out of the post office, their tittering following her through the door.

When she caught up with the wagon, Lark waved the letter. "We'll read it when we stop for the night, so keep your eyes peeled for a possible spot. I'll scout ahead."

Dusk had fallen, drawing the moisture from the soil to create wispy bits of fog, when they finally turned off the westbound road to set up camp along the banks of the Scioto River. The animals set to grazing as soon as they were hobbled, only pausing when led down a gentle slope to the river. Starbright drank, then raised her head, ears pointing at something across the water.

"What do you see, girl?" Lark stared too.

"Something is bothering her," Lilac said softly. The horse dropped her head and drank again. Lilac guided the oxen from standing knee-deep in the water back up the bank so they could graze where the grass was thick. "Did you see anything?" she asked Lark when she brought the horse to join the cattle.

"No." But Lark's scalp still prickled.

8

A scream shattered the night chorus.

Forsythia rolled to her feet before the scream ended abruptly. Lark was up before her, gun poised. Lark ratcheted a shell into the chamber and then eased around the back of the wagon without making a sound. Forsythia stood back in the shadows, knife in hand.

They both froze and held their breath in order to hear where the sounds were coming from. Scuffling and a grunt told them where to go. Starbright snorted, then screamed.

Lark motioned Forsythia to go around one way while she went the other, stopping behind a tree. Another grunt and an expletive.

Forsythia rounded the front of the wagon to see Del in the moonlight, one man trying to hold on to her as she slammed an elbow into his stomach and kicked him in the shins. A second ruffian was struggling to bring the mare under control, but Starbright reared and jerked him off his feet.

Lark stepped out from her cover, gun cocked and aimed. "Let her go."

A string of cuss words answered her.

"I said let her go."

"You drop that gun, or I'll kill her. It won't take much—just a slice from ear to ear or a quick snap. Less blood that way." Moonlight glinted off the blade of a knife. "Just give us that there horse and a steer to butcher, and we'll be on our way."

Lark nodded and started to lower the gun.

"That's right." The man chuckled. "Now give my friend a hand with the mare there. Meanwhile I'll bring this little filly under control." He grabbed Del tighter around the neck and started to drag her toward the brush.

God, help me. Forsythia let her knife fly.

The man dragging Del grunted and stumbled forward, pulling her to the ground with him.

The other robber let go of Starbright and faded back into the woods.

"Get off me, you worthless piece of . . ." Del struggled, trying to push the man away.

Forsythia rushed forward. Lark helped pull the body off Del so she could stand up.

"What happened?" Del wiped tears off her face. "I thought for sure he was going to kill me."

Lilac arrived. "Forsythia threw her knife."

Lark felt for a pulse at the side of the man's neck. "She sure did. Bull's-eye."

"I-I didn't mean to kill him." Shaking, Forsythia fell to her knees.

Lark jerked the knife out of the man's back.

Good Lord, deliver us.

Lark wiped the knife blade on the man's filthy and now bloody shirt. "You saved your sister's life. I didn't dare shoot for fear of hitting Del." She gathered the sisters into her arms.

"I went over to see what was bothering Starbright, and that piece of trash grabbed me. I at least screamed before he got his hand over my mouth. He nearly suffocated me." Del dug in her pocket for a handkerchief and blew her nose, tears streaming down her cheeks. "Forsythia, you saved my life."

Forsythia leaned against Lark, Lilac rubbing her back. "I-I killed a man, a human being."

"You nailed him right between the shoulder blades."

"All I could think—he was killing my sister."

"They thought they could sneak in, steal our horse, and be gone before anyone noticed. After all, a woman was the only guard." Lilac hugged Forsythia. "They sure underestimated us."

"What are we going to do with the body?" Del shuddered again.

"We're going to take his knife, see if he has a pistol or any money. Then we'll drag him into the woods and let the animals take care of the rest." Lark set her jaw.

"You don't think we should bury him?" Lilac asked, her eyes wide.

"No. This might not be the Christian way, but that other man might return and bring friends, so we can't take the time. We'll do what I said, then yoke the oxen, eat something, and be on our way. I think we should start praying for another wagon to travel with. We won this time, but there's safety in numbers."

"But I killed him. Pa would be horrified." Forsythia couldn't stop her hands from trembling. Hands that had just taken a human life.

"He's the one who taught you to throw a knife," Lark said.

"I know, but the Bible says 'thou shalt not kill.'"

"True, but the Israelites went to war, and God backed them up. In fact, He fought their battles for them. I believe He was right here protecting us."

"You really believe that?" Forsythia breathed a bit easier. Maybe there was hope for her after all.

They all stared down at the body. Confederate pants, blue

Union shirt, hat of no account, and boots that might have been stolen, since a bit of shine remained. Lark dropped to her knees by the body and handed Forsythia the knife. Flinching a bit, Lark dug into the man's pockets, pulling out several coins. The pistol stuck in his pants she handed to Del, then unbuckled his belt that held ammunition and gave her that too. A sheath with another knife was strapped to one calf and hidden in his boot. Patting his chest, she found a small leather bag on a rawhide loop. Inside hid a gold piece, probably stolen. The back pockets yielded a filthy rag. The knife in one boot made her check the other. Lark shook her head at several bills folded over each other. Confederate money, worthless now.

"Isn't this stealing?" Lilac asked.

"Could be called that on one hand, but we can use it better than some coyote. If his buddy comes back, you can be sure I don't want him to have this. It's all stolen anyway, I suspect."

"I have a thought," Del said. "Since he can no longer use his boots, what if we pulled them off and left them someplace others might find them? We could leave the gold piece in there too."

"Good idea. Come on, let's drag him out of here and pull off his boots where we leave the body. Boots were priceless during the war, and these still have a lot of use in them."

Huffing and puffing, they dragged the body to a willow thicket by the river.

"Let's at least say a prayer over him." Forsythia shuddered again. "It's thanks to me he didn't have time to repent and ask God's mercy for himself."

Lark removed her hat and said a brief prayer. Then they left the body there, Lilac carrying the boots back to the wagon.

By the time dawn drew a faint line of yellow across the horizon, they were on the road again. As the sun shot higher in the sky, dark clouds formed in the west. A wind kicked up, lashing the trees along the road.

"Go on ahead and see if there might be somewhere for us to get out of the storm," Lark told Forsythia. "But hurry back. This storm looks to be right fierce."

Forsythia nodded and nudged Starbright with her heels. Fat drops were kicking up puffs of dust on the road by the time she rode back. "There's a big grove of pine trees up ahead. That should offer us some protection."

Lilac handed out slickers from the back of the wagon just in time for the downpour to hit, drenching them all.

Forsythia arranged her slicker to cover the saddle, too, and huddled into it. That pine grove couldn't come soon enough. The temperature was dropping as the wind whipped the trees on both sides of the road. At least they had dry firewood if they needed to camp in the grove.

After they'd huddled under the pine trees for nearly an hour, the lightning and thunder passed over them, and since it looked like the rain might keep up, they pulled back onto the road and trudged westward through puddles and running creeks, mud and rainwater slowing them down even more.

The rain had slackened to mist by midafternoon when they paused at a creek that was striving to become a river. It didn't look terribly deep, but it was wide enough to cause consternation.

"How deep?" Del asked from the driver's seat.

"Sythia, ride through it and see. We know the wagon will float, since we sealed all the seams before we left home. But if waiting overnight might make it safer, we can do that." Lark looked toward the west, where the sun had managed to poke a few holes in the cloud cover, stabbing light streams to brighten the land.

Forsythia guided Starbright into the creek. Cool water nearly reached the horse's belly until she slipped in a hole in the middle and struggled to get her footing again, the current trying to push them downstream. Forsythia kept the reins tight to help keep her mount's head up. Starbright shook when they reached the other side, making her rider laugh. It was good to laugh again after last night.

"Thank you, God," muttered Del. "Stay out of that hole in the middle, and we should be okay."

Using her walking stick as a probe, Lark kept up-creek and beckoned to Del to move the oxen into the water. By the time they reached the other side, the wagon had almost floated but settled back as the teams dug in to pull it out.

Forsythia drew a deep breath. After the horror of last night, this crossing seemed almost easy.

"Well, if that's the worst we ever cross, we can consider ourselves lucky. We better grease those axles tonight. It's a good thing we brought both grease and tar along, thanks to Anders's thinking ahead." Lark wiped the sweat off her forehead with the back of her arm.

"I wish I'd read more of those books about traveling west." Del stepped down from the wagon. "Someone else can ride. I'd rather walk a ways."

Lilac flicked the whip on the ground, putting the oxen into action.

Forsythia let Lark take the horse and climbed into the wagon. *Thank you, Lord, a chance to rest awhile.* If only she could stop remembering the thud of that man hitting the ground.

A couple of nights later, screams jerked Lark out of a deep sleep. *Not again.* On her feet and rifle in hand before she had time to think, she heard Del murmuring at the back of the wagon. "What is it?" Other than her sisters being awake, nothing seemed amiss.

"Sythia had a horrible nightmare." Del held her sister in her arms, murmuring soothing words and stroking her back.

Lark puffed out a breath she didn't know she'd been holding, her heart hammering back into place. "I'll go check on the animals."

The indigo skies were lightening in the east, and the sun would be up in another hour. Far too short a time to go back to sleep. Starbright nickered softly as Lark approached, and nuzzled her chest.

As trees emerged from the dark, so the trail to the water could be seen, and Lark removed the hobbles from the mare and led her down to the little river to drink. A cardinal stuttered, then heralded the dawn with its special song. Lark looked upriver to see two deer drinking on the opposite shore. Starbright lifted her head, water dripping from her muzzle, ears pointed at the pair.

The shattered peace tiptoed back in. Hopefully, they could find land like this with a creek and big trees. What would the terrain be like in Nebraska? She led Starbright back to camp, where her sisters had started breakfast.

"Everyone, make sure you have a loaded gun with you whenever you leave the camp from now on. We don't want a repeat of the other night." Lark managed to keep her shudder to herself. She'd known there might be thieves about—Anders had warned her repeatedly—but what could they have done differently? That was the big question.

You could have stayed home, her inner voice said. *If you hadn't gotten in such a snit at church and then gone into that saloon . . .*

If Del had died, it would have been my fault. And now my little sister has to live with knowing she killed that man. Lord, why do I feel like you are so far away?

She looked across the fire to see Forsythia staring into the mush she was stirring. Of them all, Forsythia was the deep thinker and the one least likely to share her thoughts. She and Pa had many long discussions about the meaning of Scriptures and books they'd read, about the why's behind how the world spun and men treated each other. Pa had called her tenderhearted.

Lark looked up at the song of a meadowlark soaring toward the brightening sky. Soon the sun would be up, chasing away the memories that came with the night. She shuddered. How could she forget that man's voice? It was grating, but still she could tell he was enjoying himself. When she thought about the other man who had escaped, she hoped one of the horse's hooves had connected with him.

Lord, let that awfulness be the worst thing that happens on this journey.

9

Walking, riding, driving—how to get away from that horrible night?

"What's going on, Sythia?" Lark asked, falling back from walking with the lead ox.

"I'll be fine."

"Not what I asked you."

Forsythia stared down into the concern on her sister's face. She felt the tears start again, tears that seemed to live right under the surface, the slightest nudge causing them to overflow.

"The nightmare?" Lark asked.

Forsythia nodded and shook her head, then shrugged, almost all at the same time. *All I want to do is go home.* That thought jerked her flat like she'd hit the end of a rope running.

"Hey, Lilac, leave the letter writing and lead the oxen, will you?" Lark called toward the back of the wagon.

"Sure. Something wrong?" Lilac tucked the paper and pencil back in the bag and made her way to the front to find Forsythia raining tears. She climbed over the bench seat and down to the ground, taking the whip from Lark. "Sythia, it's going to be good again. God promised."

Forsythia fought to smile through her tears. Lark waited for her at the back of the wagon with open arms. They sat on one of the long wooden boxes that held kettles and other cooking needs. Leaning into the comfort of sisterly arms, Forsythia failed to stop the sobs.

"If screaming will help, do so. Pound on the box. You can even pound on my knee." Lark jiggled her leg.

"If it would, I might." The words stuttered between the sobs.

"I did, and it does."

Forsythia turned her head to stare at Lark, shock drying up the tear well. "When?"

"One night when I was trying to find Anders, a puffed-up officer told me to give it up and go home. Quit wasting my time. If Anders was indeed in a prison camp, he'd never come out again except in a wagonload of cadavers going to a mass burial."

"Oh my . . . you never told us any of that."

"I figured it was bad enough for me to know without inflicting it on all of you."

"I'm so grateful you didn't follow that advice. To think we came that close to losing Anders forever." Forsythia felt like she could have wrung out her handkerchief. Instead, she flapped it a couple of times and mopped her eyes. "Thank you."

"Now, let's talk about what is happening with you." Lark clasped her hands together, elbows resting on her knees.

"I keep seeing my knife stuck in that horrible man's back. It all happened so fast, I didn't even think about it. I just threw it."

"Pa trained you well."

"He didn't train me to kill a man."

"Perhaps not, but he did mean for you to defend yourself, or in this case, your sister. They say the first time is the hardest."

Forsythia choked on the words. "I won't do it again."

"That's why soldiers are trained by repetition so that shooting or stabbing or whatever they need to do is a reflex action, and they do it without thought. They also know that their job is to save their comrades as well as themselves. You were saving your sister's life and possibly all of our lives. That man was enjoying what he was doing."

"Will the nightmares and the horror ever go away?"

"That's a God job, I think. Only He can see inside of your head. So we'll pray, all of us together tonight, for Him to wash all this from your mind and soul. Remember, whiter than snow—that's His cleansing power."

"You ever thought of being a preacher?"

"God made me the wrong sex, according to certain people we used to know."

Forsythia didn't even try to stop the giggle she felt start in her toes and scrub its way out. "Lord, thank you. I am learning anew to trust you, this time with my mind and my heart. I trust your healing." She sucked in a lung-filling breath and held it, almost feeling the release of . . . of she knew not what. "So now, when I feel like screaming, I go ahead and do so, only screaming, 'Lord, help!' or 'I trust you, Lord!'" Another giggle escaped. *Thank you, Lord.* "But what if the emotions overcome me again?" She clenched Lark's arm, feeling her whole body tense.

"Remember when we were little and if we were hurt or frightened, how Ma would sit down in her rocker, gather us into her lap, rock oh-so-gently, and sing to us?"

Forsythia tipped her head back, trying to dam the flow before it began. "Oh yes, I remember." Her whisper allowed sweet tears to trickle down her smiling cheeks. "I remember." A pang of mother-sickness rather than homesickness stabbed her heart. She watched the dust puffing out behind them, smelling and tasting the dryness of it. "Thank you, Larkspur. I feel like I could sleep for a week."

"You can lie on the pallet and sleep as long as you need to."

Lark turned and took Forsythia's hands in hers. "When—if—they come again, we will all pray together. We will beat this thing."

Forsythia felt her head nodding.

Lark clambered back onto the wagon seat.

"All is well?" Lilac called from her position beside the oxen.

"All will be well," Lark responded. "Remember Ma quoting some woman of long ago? 'All shall be well, and all manner of things shall be well.'"

"Possibly. That's a good thing to remember. How about we stop when we reach some shade? Move around and take care of the animals?" Lilac suggested.

"Good idea." Lark turned and smiled back at Forsythia, something of Ma's love in her eyes. "All shall be well."

"We'll find a good place to camp with enough grazing and then stay there an extra day to give the animals a rest," Lark told them a couple of days later. "Sythia, you want to ride ahead and find us a place to stop for the night?"

"Be happy to."

Once mounted, Forsythia nudged Starbright into a lope and sat back to enjoy the rocking motion. She slowed to a jog through a small town made up of a mercantile, livery, church, a few houses, a school, and a saloon. Why did there always have to be a saloon?

She waved at two boys sitting on the steps of the mercantile, sucking on peppermint sticks. "Are we in Indiana yet?"

The two boys looked at each other and giggled. "Uh-huh."

"You know anyone who might like to sell us some eggs, maybe milk too?"

"Uh-huh, my ma has lots of chickens."

"Where might we find your ma?"

"At our house." He pointed over his shoulder. "You want I should take you there?"

Forsythia rolled her lips together to keep a straight face. "Now, that would be a mighty neighborly thing to do."

Both boys jumped up and trotted up the road with her, then turned onto a wide path. When they neared a house, they ran ahead, yelling, "Ma, Ma, we got comp'ny."

Forsythia trotted up the lane, an orchard on one side and a pasture with several cows on the other. Chickens scratched around a house that hadn't met a paintbrush in a long time. A black-and-tan hound crawled out from under the porch and, after a prolonged stretch, trotted out to greet the horse and rider, tail wagging.

A woman wearing a faded apron and a bright smile pushed open the screen door and stepped out, a rifle leaning against the wall. A little girl peeked out from behind her. "Welcome, stranger. The boys said you're looking for eggs and perhaps a chicken?"

"We are indeed. My sisters—and brother—and the wagon are some ways behind me."

The woman patted her daughter's head. "Where you headed?"

"Nebraska by way of Independence, Missouri, where we plan to join a wagon train."

"Well, we've got eggs. 'Sides milk and soft cheese, and I can slaughter a chicken, if you've a mind. Oh, and butter. The store you passed buys from us too."

Forsythia's mouth watered.

"I can butcher that chicken while you go back and bring your wagon here. Late as it is, you might could overnight here, fill your water barrel from our well. It's safe here."

"I sure appreciate your offer. I know we'll want the food you mentioned, and I'll pass on your invitation. It'll probably be an hour or so before we get back."

"That'll be fine."

"Thanks."

Forsythia turned Starbright around and nudged her into a slow lope back to meet the wagon. *Thank you, Lord Jesus.* She found herself humming the words, adding more until the words and notes had become a song, one that made her want to shout and sing it out. And get it written down.

When she saw the wagon ahead, she leaned forward enough to urge Starbright into a gallop. The wind on her face tried to tear her hair out of her bun, and her sunbonnet beat a tune on her back.

"My land, girl, what's goin' on with you?" Del called as Starbright slid to a stop, grinning nearly as much as her rider.

Forsythia beamed at her sisters. "I have the best news."

"What, we are in Nebraska?" Lilac grinned back at her.

"Not hardly, but I met a family who sells eggs, and they invited us for supper and to spend the night there. They have two boys who were sitting on the mercantile steps in town, and they waved and I stopped and I followed them. . . ." Her words tripped over each other before running together.

Lark raised a hand from the wagon seat. "Whoa. I think I missed half of what you said, so start again, and perhaps slow down a bit."

"Sorry." Forsythia wanted to hug them all.

"Forsythia Peace Nielsen, I've never seen you so excited." Del stroked the horse's sweaty neck. "She was in such a hurry to share her news, she made you race back to us. Sorry, girl."

"I know." Forsythia leaned forward and smoothed Starbright's mane to one side. "Just think, girl, you might get to spend the night out in a pasture. No hobbles."

She told her tale again, more coherently this time, and in less than an hour, their wagon rolled up at the end of the family's lane. The two boys were waiting for them and caught a ride up to the farmhouse.

"Does your family do things like this often?" Forsythia asked them.

"Not much. Not many wagons no more."

"What is your last name?"

"Herron, ma'am. You can stop here. Pa will show you where to park your wagon." The boy leaped from the wagon seat to the ground while his brother slid off the horse, their dog running from the house, barking a welcome.

Someday, Lord, let us welcome strangers like this. The smile Mrs. Herron wore to greet them underlined Forsythia's thoughts.

With the oxen and Starbright set free in the pasture, they followed their host back to the house, where Mrs. Herron had cookies and lemonade set on a table under a tree.

"I think I must have died and gone to heaven." Lilac bit into a cookie. She answered the beckoning of the eldest Herron daughter, and they sat side by side on one of the various logs that made up a circle.

"It looks like you have company often," Forsythia said.

Mr. Herron nodded. "We have church out here when the weather permits. In the barn or the house otherwise."

"You're a minister?"

"Of sorts. I figured the Bible talks about meeting in homes, so we could do that too. Someday we might try to build a church building, but for now . . ." He waved his arm to encompass the place. "Meeting at night allows folks to get their work done and then come worship. It's a shame you can't stay for our meeting tomorrow night."

Please, Lark, please, Forsythia caught herself pleading. *Let us stay.*

Why was she hesitating?

'Cause I don't know what's best to do, that's why. To enjoy the

evening and head out at first light? Or accept the invitation and ignore her fear? Fear. *Why in the world am I afraid of this blessing?* When she thought of it that way, Lark felt like kicking herself. She could feel her sisters' eyes on her. "Thank you, Mr. and Mrs. Herron, for your gracious invitation. I wish I could think of some way to repay you."

"Repay?" Joseph Herron burst out laughing. "Ah, Clark, we're only sharing what God has so richly blessed us with." He clapped his hands on his knees and stood. "Everyone, let's get our chores done."

Lark almost offered to help in the kitchen but clamped her mouth shut just in time. That would be a dead giveaway. "I haven't milked cows for a while. Could I help you so I don't forget how? After all, we're hoping to have livestock again when we find our land."

"Up in Nebraska, you said?"

"Yes, sir."

"Well, we wouldn't want his hands to get soft, would we, boys?" Mr. Herron asked his sons, grinning.

Taking her place with her forehead planted firmly in a cow's flank, Lark let her mind wander. The cow's swishing tail brought her back to a three-legged stool in a barn in Indiana. "Easy, old girl," she murmured, glancing at the cow's head to see she was finished with her grain. "I'm hurrying as fast as I can. You have a lot of milk to be pulled out." *Someday I hope we will have cows like this, pigs and chickens, a new home with new friends in a town that only you know about, Lord God.*

She swung the milk bucket off to the side when she finished and stood to stretch. "You have a milk can to pour this into?" she asked Mr. Herron.

"Up by the grain bin. You sure you want to milk another?"

"Yes, sir, I do." Milking cows was a great place for letting one's mind roam. Unless you had a kicker who liked to plant her foot in the bucket.

As Lark poured the steaming milk through the straining cloth spread over the mouth of the can, she inhaled. *Perhaps you should tell this man who you really are,* whispered that voice inside her head. *And perhaps I shouldn't,* her other side answered back.

Her shoulders inched upward toward her earlobes, where they seemed to reside permanently these last weeks. Could it have anything to do with needing to be constantly on guard? She hadn't realized the pressure till arriving at this taste of heaven. Tears pricked unexpectedly. That wouldn't do.

"You all right?" Mr. Herron asked as he paused beside Lark.

"Will be." Lark cleared her throat and flexed her fingers. "It's been a while since I milked."

They ate supper at a big oval table that managed to seat them all, four sisters, five children, and their parents. Afterward, while the girls put the kitchen to rights, Mr. Herron and the boys hauled wood out to the fire pit.

"Mr. Herron," Lark asked, "do you mind if we get out our instruments? We have a guitar, fiddle, and harmonica. We just need to tune them up. I thought perhaps we could all sing a bit."

"Well, bless my soul, what a gift that would be. And a mouth organ, no less. Now, that surely don't take up much room in the wagon."

"No, it doesn't, but the others don't either, as we hang the cases from the ribs of the wagon." She looked over at hearing giggles and saw Lilac with her paper and pencils out, probably drawing one of her comical animals for the children.

Lark dug her harmonica out of her shirt pocket and settled on a log.

One of the little girls scooted up next to her and grinned up. "My name's Essy. It's special to have you here to play." Her lisp made her big smile and friendly eagerness even sweeter. "Someday, when I get big, I want to play one of those."

"You could play it right now." Lark showed her how to blow into it and make different notes. "You hold it like this." She heard the others tuning up and blew a C, making the little girl grin even more. "Sometimes you have to blow gently and other times harder." Lark placed the harmonica in Essy's small hands. "Blow on this side."

Several notes came out. Essy handed it back. "Can we do that again tomorrow?"

"We certainly can." *I guess that means we're staying over another day.* She glanced up to see her sisters nodding and beaming.

She played the opening bars of "She'll Be Coming 'Round the Mountain," and the others joined in singing and clapping. Other songs followed, and soon the Herrons were calling out their favorites.

"Isn't that some pretty? Never thought I'd get to hear your music-makin' again." The male voice brought the musicians to a halt as they turned to gape at the speaker.

"Isaac, glad to see you, son." Mr. Herron stood to greet the young man, and one of the boys leaped up and ran to grab his hand.

Lark stared at him, shaking her head. She'd thought never to see the drifter again, and here he walked up right in the middle of singing, like before. At least now they knew his name was Isaac.

"You know these folks?" Herron asked.

"I met them one night on the trail. Heard music and singing as if from a heavenly choir. I thought to stay away, but I couldn't, and here you all are days westward."

"How come you're here?" Lilac asked.

"I was hungry and stopped at the store to ask if anyone

needed some work done in exchange for a meal, and they sent me out here. The Herrons made me feel like family and told me about a neighbor who needed some help, so here I still am."

"We want him to stay, but he only agreed to a little while. Sit yourself down, son," Herron urged.

"Will you play some more?" Essy's whisper could have carried back to the store.

"What would you like me to play?" Lark asked.

"'Mary Had a Little Lamb.'"

One of the boys groaned, but his mother gave him a look.

Lark chuckled inside as she played. The memory of her mother giving Jonah that same look made her blink back tears. *Someday, Lord, I want a daughter like this.*

"Let's have one more and then call it quits. Morning comes mighty early here," Mr. Herron said.

The sisters swung into "Blest Be the Tie That Binds," and everyone stood to sing.

As the notes drifted off like the smoke from the fire, Mr. Herron took the hands on either side of him, and the others followed suit. "Dear Lord, thank you for the gifts you have given us, like this time together. And may you, our good Lord, bless and keep us. May your face shine upon us and fill us with your peace."

They all drifted off to their beds, and Lark decided not to set any watches. They'd all get a full night's sleep.

The next day was one of rest for themselves and the animals, and the Nielsen sisters looked forward to the worship service that evening. It was nothing like the service at their church at home. Dusk sneaked in while they were singing, which led into Mr. Herron reading Scripture, followed by observations rather than a sermon. He asked for comments, and some of the attendees added their thoughts. Then they prayed for the needs and praises people brought up. Someone started singing and the others joined in, followed by a time of silence—to let the Spirit speak, Herron said. Awe and reverence floated around like the fragrance of sweet peas in spring.

"Let's sing the doxology and say our benediction together."

Never had that song sunk into Lark's heart like this. Praise God from whom all blessings flow indeed. It was so sweet to worship with other believers with no officious hypocrite twisting God's words.

"I wish you could stay longer," Mrs. Herron said, hugging each of them. "I'll have breakfast ready for you in the morning so you can be on your way."

"I sure enjoyed your music again. To think—two nights in a row." Isaac gave them a nod. "The Lord bless and keep thee."

"And you also. If you ever get to Nebraska, I hope you can find us, Mister . . . ?" Del quirked a brow.

"McTavish. And, Miss Nielsen, I will make every effort. You're heading down to Independence, right? I pray God's protection on you all the way." Isaac McTavish touched his hat with the gentle courtesy that sat as easily on his shoulders as the tattered jacket.

"And we you."

Saying good-bye in the morning, with extra eggs, a cooked chicken, and a loaf of bread added to their load, made leaving even harder. Lark raised her hand in a final salute and left the temptation to remain behind. They couldn't, not with the danger that could be following. This was such a welcome reprieve, but there were sure to be hard times ahead.

Lord, please find us a wagon train to join up with, and let us not be too late in the season. One with folks like these would really be appreciated.

10

"How I hated to leave there," Forsythia said.

"I know. Me too." Del heaved a sigh.

Forsythia situated the folded blanket behind her back as she leaned against the cooking box, then dug her journal and pencil out of her bag. Fumbling in the bottom of the bag, she dug out the pocketknife she kept there and sharpened the pencil so she could begin to write, catching up on the last few days.

Lord, the only gift we could give the Herrons in return was our music. And to rejoice in being bathed in their unending flow of love. How could they share what they had so freely? Only by the grace of God. That's what Mrs. Herron said. I felt at home there from the first moment we stopped the wagon. How can love permeate even the grass and the trees? I can understand through flowers, but there . . . a pasture for our animals, grass to cushion our beds, good food and laughter. And then to think that Isaac McTavish appeared too. He said that night at our camp that he hoped to see us again, but we didn't even know his name. And now, O Lord, we pray for a wagon to join us. Thank you for all the blessings you poured out upon us. Amen.

She dashed away a tear ready to splash down on her journal pages. At least the pencil did not smudge from tears like ink did. She tucked the pencil and journal in the bag and stared out the back of the wagon at the road ribboning behind them as they headed onward.

That afternoon she rode Starbright on ahead, looking for a place to stop for the night. Streams were fewer now, but she spotted a ribbon of blue dotted by trees along its shoreline. A river—an honest-to-goodness river. She touched her heels to the mare's sides to reach the shoreline, where indeed there were places other folks had camped. Cattails and water grasses lined the shore here, but around the bend there looked to be an open spot.

Staring out from the shade of her sunbonnet, she nudged Starbright into the water. "You can't have much, but we'll be back soon, and then you can drink your fill."

When she tugged on the reins, the horse raised her head and turned to go back to the wagon. *Perhaps we can all swim there tonight and catch fish for supper.* She set Starbright into a rocking-chair lope so she could tell the others.

That night, with fish sizzling in the pan thanks to Lilac, the stars a canopy of twinkles thanks to the Lord God, and the smoke driving away the mosquitos, Forsythia brought out the guitar, picking rather than strumming. With each note separate, they seemed to rise with the smoke and float above the treetops. The monster oak whose branches provided shelter for them rustled in the breeze that danced around.

They finished their supper, drinking the last of the milk the Herrons had sent with them before it soured, leaving only enough for pancakes in the morning. After scrubbing their tin plates and the frying pan with sand in the river, Lilac took the first watch.

Forsythia roused from a deep sleep when Lilac shook her shoulder.

"I think I hear something," her sister whispered. "Am I going crazy? Can you hear that?"

"What?" Forsythia sat up. "Someone crying?" She strained her ears. "Nah, can't be. Must be a bird calling."

"No." Lilac raised a hand. "Someone out there is crying."

"Any idea which way it is coming from?" Lark slid from her bedroll.

"Let's split up." Forsythia stood as Del sat up, rubbing her eyes. "Lark, you go that way. Del, you stay here, and Lilac, you and I will go this way."

"Maybe there's a house somewhere around here." Del shook her head. "We sure could use a moon right now."

"Take the guns," Lark said. "Shoot once to let us know where you find them and twice if you need help."

Forsythia made sure she had her knife in its scabbard, and Lilac picked up the handgun they'd taken from the thief. Lark and the Winchester headed north along the shore, and Forsythia and Lilac went south.

They slogged through a marshy spot and paused to listen. The cry came again, closer this time. Beating off mosquitos, they forged ahead, the brush trying to scrape their clothes and skin away.

"Ouch!" Forsythia stopped to unsnag her skirt before it was ripped off.

They could indeed hear a child wailing. They broke out of the brush to see a wagon with a hooped canvas top just like theirs. As they drew nearer, they could see coals from a dying fire and an outline of someone in the wagon.

"Hello? We've come to help you," Forsythia called.

"Oh, thank God." A man's voice.

"Pa, don't leave." A child.

Forsythia and Lilac sprinted the final distance.

"I'm going to shoot to tell the others where we are, so don't be afraid of our gun." Lilac pointed the pistol in the air and pulled the trigger. The shot sounded like an explosion.

The man beckoned from the back of the wagon. "My wife is ill, and the baby might be coming and—and—" He broke down sobbing. "Thank God you're here, that someone is here. God sent us angels. Here in the wilderness, someone heard and came."

Forsythia and Lilac paused at the tailgate of the wagon. A woman lay on a pallet, one arm around her small sobbing child.

Dear Lord, how we need your help now. What do we do? Forsythia nodded to Lilac and mouthed, *Pray*. "Sir, could you and your little boy move out of there to make room for me to see to your wife?"

"Oh yes, of course." He jumped down and reached for his child. "Come on, Robbie, let these kind ladies help your ma."

"Go." His ma pushed the boy with a weak hand.

Once the man and his son were on the ground, Forsythia climbed into the wagon and knelt beside the woman. "We heard crying, so we came. How long have you been sick?" The reek of vomit and intestinal sickness permeated the wagon.

"Thank God for your good ears. It started a couple of—" She paused to suck in more air and blew it out before inhaling again.

"Are you in labor?"

She shook her head. "I-I don't think so. Too early. Oh, your hand feels so cool."

"You have a fever."

"I know. Been coughing some. So weak."

"When did you eat last?"

She shrugged. "No idea, lost track of time. Thomas tried to feed me, but it-it didn't stay down."

"Drinking?"

"Thirsty."

"Lilac, bring us a cup of water."

When she had the cup in hand, Forsythia slid her other arm under the woman's head and held her so she could sip. The woman coughed immediately.

Forsythia sat back on her heels. *Lark, Del, please come quickly.* But she was the one who had studied and grown the herbs after their mother died. "What is your name, ma'am?"

"A-Alice." The whisper came fainter as the woman drifted off to sleep.

Thomas, Alice, and Robbie. Forsythia nodded as she climbed out of the wagon. And a baby on the way.

When Lark arrived, the three sisters talked together too low for Mr. Thomas to hear. "We've got to get her cleaned up and taking spoonfuls of herb tea and ideally beef or chicken broth. Either way, we need hot water. I say, first we ask him to get the fire built up and pray they have a big pot."

"We could bring our wagon here to use our pot too," Forsythia suggested.

"If this is dysentery, it's contagious. I'm surprised the mister isn't showing symptoms, or the boy." Lark chewed on her bottom lip. "I'm trying to remember what I know from bringing Anders back. Dysentery is what killed so many soldiers in the prisons. It spreads terribly fast."

"So perhaps this isn't that."

"I guess we'll see." Lark walked over to the man at the fire. "Mr. Thomas, first thing, we need hot water for tea and a lot more water to get your wife cleaned up. Is that all the wood you have?" She pointed to the few pieces lying off to the side.

He nodded. "I'll get more."

"We need your largest pot too." Forsythia twisted her hair back out of the way and rolled up her sleeves.

He nodded and stood, but his son clamped both arms around his leg.

Lilac squatted beside the little one. "Hey, Robbie, I'm going to hold you while your pa goes to get more wood. We need it to help your ma." She scooped him up, arms and legs flailing.

"Pa!"

Del could probably hear his shriek back at the wagon, but Lilac held him, speaking softly until he settled down.

Forsythia nodded to her. "Just like gentling a horse, isn't it?" Lilac had always had a way with animals and babies of any kind. "You take care of him, and I'll take the pot down to the river for water." She looked over to see the fire catching on the wood Thomas had added. He set a small pan of water from a bucket under the wagon on a rock on the fire's edge, then headed back into the woods.

"Pa?"

The child's whimper tore at Forsythia's heart. "Thank you, Lilac. Poor little one. Must be three or four, you think?"

"About that." Lilac set him on her hip so she could use her other hand to pat his back, swaying all the while. "Pa went for wood, Robbie. He'll be back."

"Wood?"

She used her apron to wipe his face and dry his eyes. "Uh-huh. He went for wood."

Forsythia hauled the iron pot down to the river and filled it, then hauled the heavy pot back to the fire, where Thomas and Lilac were breaking up several branches to add to the flames.

"I'll get more." Thomas left again, but this time his son only sniffed and laid his head on Lilac's shoulder. Lark dragged a huge branch into camp, dumped it, and went back out.

"I need my herbs, and I just thought of the chicken we have left. We could set it to boil." Forsythia studied Lilac. "Why don't you let me take Robbie and you run back to our wagon? You're much faster than I am. Get the things we need and ride Starbright back?"

Lilac nodded. "Robbie, my sister will hold you, and I'll be back as fast as I can so we can help your mama."

He sniffed again and nodded, letting Forsythia take him without a whimper.

"I think he's exhausted. I'll have his pa put him down to sleep as soon as he gets back."

"Good." Lilac patted the child's back. "Good boy."

Forsythia swayed as Lilac had, murmuring, then singing softly as she felt Robbie relax against her. Despite the circumstances, her heart warmed at holding the little boy. Would she ever have children of her own?

Mr. Thomas returned with more wood. At Forsythia's suggestion, he reached into the wagon for a pallet, spread it under the wagon, and tucked his son under the light blanket.

"Mr. Thomas—"

"My name is Thomas Durham." He tipped his head slightly. "Did I hear you say your sister will bring another pot?"

"Yes."

"I'll—" He stopped. "Alice." He strode back to the wagon at his wife's call. Forsythia followed.

"Thirsty. R-Robbie?" Alice said.

"Robbie is sleeping on his pallet under the wagon. Ladies from another wagon are here to take care of you."

Forsythia went to the fire and used her apron as a hot pad to pick up the pan of warm water. "Mr. Durham, could you please get me a spoon?"

He dug in a box and handed her one.

Climbing back up in the wagon, Forsythia tested the water and held the spoon to the woman's lips. "A spoonful at a time. Hold it in your mouth if you can, then swallow." *Lilac, hurry.* Mrs. Durham was so weak, and the baby mounding her belly . . . *Lord, help her keep this down. Please, Father, help us.* "More?"

Another spoonful. *Lord, please.* She sat down on the edge of the wagon bed and heard horse's hooves. *Thank you.*

Mr. Durham had started another fire, so he took the big pot

from Lilac's hands and strode off toward the river. "Thank you," he called back.

Lilac tied the horse to a wagon wheel and lifted the sack she'd attached to the saddle. "I have herbs here. I'm not sure what you need, so I brought several. Del is cooking the chicken so we'll have broth."

"She kept two spoonfuls of warm water down."

Mrs. Durham retched, and the water drooled out her mouth.

"Guess not." Forsythia took the pan back to the fire, where she sprinkled several herbs on the water and set it back on the rock to heat. She dipped a finger in the large pot of water and shook her head. "Not hot enough yet."

Lark returned, dragging more branches. "It sure will be easier to find wood in the daylight, which looks to be on its way."

"What if we bring our wagon closer?" Forsythia suggested again. "It'll make caring for her easier."

Lark nodded. "We'll have to take turns sleeping. I think Mr. Durham is very near the end of his rope."

"I wonder how long they've been here," Lilac said.

Forsythia shrugged.

Mr. Durham returned with another pot of water and set it on the new fire. "I'll go find rocks as soon as it's light enough."

"Mr. Durham, we're going to give your wife a bath. Do you know if she has a clean nightdress or something to wear?"

He shook his head and shrugged at the same time. "Clothes and bedding are in the trunk."

"When did this start?" Forsythia asked.

"Yesterday morning. She mentioned the night before when we camped that she didn't feel well but said we should keep going, so we did." He shook his head. "She got so sick so fast, so we stopped here by the river about midafternoon."

"I see. Did you and Robbie eat last night?"

He nodded. "Leftover beans and biscuits."

Lark joined the conversation. "Mr. Durham, we're going to bring our wagon over closer as soon as we can. In the meantime, have you checked on your oxen?"

Durham shook his head. "I took 'em to drink and hobbled 'em. Heard one bellow not too long ago."

"You feed the fires, and I'll go see about them." Lark stepped into the shadows.

Forsythia stirred the simmering herbs and set the kettle back from the flames to let it steep. The fragrance that rose told her it was ready. "I could use a cup."

Mr. Durham brought one from the box in the wagon.

"Do you by any chance have any honey or molasses?"

He nodded and brought that.

Forsythia dipped tea out of the kettle, added a drop of honey, and stirred. *Please, Lord, help her keep this down.* With the sky lightening, she could see their patient more clearly. Holding the cup and spoon in one hand, she softly called Mrs. Durham's name. "I brought you some herb tea to help soothe your stomach."

A slight nod told her that Alice heard, and she opened her mouth as soon as the spoon touched her lips. She swallowed and coughed, spewing droplets all around. Her forehead wrinkled.

"Lilac, I need your help," Forsythia called.

"I'm right here." Lilac slid her arm under the patient's shoulders and propped her up. This time the liquid slid down Mrs. Durham's throat.

"Easy." *Please, Lord, please.*

They waited awhile, then did it again. And waited.

Lilac gently laid Mrs. Durham back on her pallet. "Can we . . . ?" She nodded to the mess.

Forsythia nodded. "Alice, we're going to wash you up and get you a clean bed too. My name is Forsythia, and my sister Lilac is going to search in your trunk for clean linens and something for you to wear."

At the woman's barest nod, the two proceeded.

Lark returned and joined Mr. Durham in breaking branches and chopping larger pieces for the fire. "I'll fix some breakfast."

After bathing Alice and changing her sheets, Forsythia and Lilac bundled the soiled bedding and garments into the large laundry pot Del had brought. They paused long enough to eat, then kept on boiling the wash, stirring with a straight green willow stick Lark cut. She had stripped off the bark to make the work easier. Hauling the soapy wash to the river, both Forsythia and Del took off their boots, hitched up their skirts, and waded into the water. By the time they'd rinsed all the laundry, both were nearly as wet as the wash.

"It's a shame we can't go swimming." Forsythia handed Del one end of the sheet, and together they twisted the water out.

"In our clothes?" Del motioned back toward camp.

"Why not?" Forsythia almost dunked herself and then remembered the man working around the wagon. "No, you're right."

After wringing everything out, they draped the linens over bushes and branches to dry. When they got back to camp, Mr. Durham had scrubbed his wagon and collapsed under a tree, finally getting the rest he sorely needed.

As the morning sun climbed, Del and Forsythia took turns spooning tea into their patient and rejoiced when Alice kept it all down. Bathed and in a clean nightdress, Alice finally slept after taking some of Del's broth.

Weary to the bone, Forsythia sank onto a fallen log and watched Lilac entertaining Robbie. He shouted with glee when Lilac let him perch on Starbright's back while she walked the horse around. A very different scene than when they'd arrived. *Thank you, Lord. Thank you.*

Late in the morning, Forsythia and Lark headed back to their wagon for a rest, while Del and Lilac took a shift. They met another wagon heading down toward the river.

"You camped down there?" the husband asked Lark after stopping their oxen.

"Back up a ways." Lark tipped her hat up. "But there are good spots by the river. We're just helping some folks camped there who fell sick."

"Poor souls." The wife smiled at them from the wagon seat. "You're good to help your neighbors."

"Huh. We'll steer clear of any sickness." The husband glanced at his wife and the three children's faces peeking from behind her. Another boy in his early teens rode horseback alongside the wagon. "Can't let anything hold us up from joining a wagon train this late in the season."

"Where are you folks from?" Lark asked.

"Ohio. Headed to the Oregon Trail. You?"

"Same."

Forsythia smiled up at the wife. She seemed kind, more so than her sour-faced husband. "Perhaps we'll see you on the trail."

"If we all make it soon enough." The husband hupped the oxen and nodded at Lark, ignoring Forsythia. "Thank you kindly."

Forsythia studied Lark's face as the wagon lumbered on. Brow tightened, her sister strode on ahead without a word. Forsythia followed, a tightening in her middle. Yes, they needed to press on. Time was running out. But how could they leave the Durhams behind?

11

"W"e need to get moving again," Lark said.

"I know, but what about Mrs. Durham? Do you think she's strong enough?" Forsythia asked. They were gathered around their campfire after helping Mr. Durham put his son and wife to bed before himself.

"Guess we'll see in the morning. He's getting restless to leave too." Lark poked a stick into the fire, causing sparks to spiral up with the smoke. "I keep remembering something about wagon trains not starting out after a certain date. I know we're getting late in the season, but what that man said concerns me." Calculations circled through her mind—how many miles a day they could make, how many miles still to Independence.

"Leaving them behind doesn't seem right either." Forsythia slapped at a mosquito on her arm. "Pesky things."

"We could take turns riding with them to take care of her." Del pushed herself to her feet. "But since she can drink from a cup now, probably the best way we can help is to keep Robbie with us."

Lark nodded. "I'll go talk with him in the morning. We won't get as early a start as we'd like, but even ten miles is better than none." Tension tightened her shoulders again.

"I set the snares, so perhaps we'll have fresh meat for tomorrow." Lilac climbed under her blanket.

Restless even in her sleep, Lark woke before the others and went to check on the animals. *As of tonight, we go back to taking turns at watch again.* She stroked Starbright's favorite spot between her eyes and leaned into the horse. Was Jonah staying out of the saloon? And any other way he could get in trouble? When were Anders and Josephine getting married? Would they find letters from home in the Independence post office? Were those two evil men still looking for them? She tipped her head back and stared at the disappearing stars as light bloomed in the east. *Lord, I sure wish the Durhams would choose to stop when we come to a town with a boardinghouse and stay long enough for Alice to regain her strength.* The question, of course, was how long that might take. Another thought chased after that one. The Herrons were only one day back. They'd take the Durhams in for sure, or help them at least. Perhaps Mr. Durham could work for them. Thought piled on thought, but any reminder of the Herron family created a warm circle around her heart.

She heard Del starting the fire for breakfast and the others greeting her. They had invited Robbie and his pa to have breakfast with them. Forsythia planned to go tend to Alice. *Better get going,* Lark told herself. She gave the mare one last pat and returned to the fire.

"I'm going to water the animals, unless you need something else," she announced.

"Good morning to you too." Del set the pot of water on to heat as well as the coffee. She turned to smile at her older sister.

Lark nodded. "Point taken."

"Good morning," Forsythia said around a yawn. "I checked on our patient during the night, and she seemed to be sleeping peacefully. I thought I'd make some gruel with that chicken broth and feed her that. See if she can keep it down. I'll make up more of the herbal tea too."

"We're having mush for breakfast. Lilac is out checking the snares. It makes me dream of fried rabbit for supper, and I'm setting beans to soak. Should have done that yesterday." Del tried to cover a yawn. She nodded toward the other wagon.

Lark turned and nodded to Mr. Durham, who was approaching. "Good morning."

"I've come to tell you my wife and I want to travel with you today."

Lark nodded. Good. "Breakfast will be ready soon. I'm going to water our teams, then yoke them up. You need some help?"

"That'd be appreciated. Do yours first, then mine?"

Lilac strode into camp holding two rabbit carcasses and set to dressing them. "We'll eat good tonight."

Both spans were yoked up when Del announced breakfast. The rabbits were dressed and wrapped in a cloth, Mrs. Durham was taken care of, and Forsythia had brought Robbie, bouncing and chattering along, back to the wagon with her.

Del dished up the mush and drizzled a dab of molasses on each bowl before handing them around. "Sythia, you want to say grace?"

"Lord, thank you for always being with us. Please bless this food to our bodies and the hands that made it. Amen."

When they finished eating, Lilac and Robbie scrubbed the bowls in the river. They returned with Robbie even bouncier than before.

"We saw a duck and her babies! Ma needs to see the babies. She likes any kind of babies."

Lilac squatted down beside him and said softly, "Baby ducks are called ducklings."

"Ducks and ducklings."

"That's right."

"Show Ma?"

"You'll have to tell her about them." Lilac stood and ruffled his hair.

When they were ready to travel, Lark paused as she stepped up to the bench seat. "You goin' to ride Starbright?" she asked her youngest sister.

Lilac grinned back at her. "Of course. Come on, Robbie, you can ride with me."

She mounted, and Del lifted the boy up to sit in front of her and patted his knee. Lark hupped the oxen and headed south on the trail worn into a road. Mr. Durham waited for the dust to settle and then followed them.

Lark exhaled. *It's good to be moving again.*

"Is she awake?" Lilac asked softly, riding Starbright near the tailgate of the Durhams' wagon. "Robbie wants to say hello."

Forsythia nodded. "Come on, Alice, I'll help you sit up." She braced her weak patient with her knees. "I've got you."

"Hey, Ma, Lilac and me are riding Starbright," Robbie crowed.

"I see that." She blew him a kiss.

"We saw a mama duck and her . . ." He grinned up at Lilac. "And her *ducklings* swimming behind her."

His mother nodded and blew out a weary breath. "I'll . . . see you . . . later."

Forsythia smiled at the little boy and gently settled her patient back on the pallet. She picked up the guitar she'd brought with her that morning. "I think we need some music here. Do you like to sing, Robbie?"

"Uh-huh. Ma sings lots."

"Oh good." While she spoke, Forsythia plucked at the guitar strings. "How about 'Come, Thou Fount of Every Blessing'?"

Miles down the road, when they paused for much-needed refreshment for animals and people alike, Lilac clutched Robbie's hand while he slid down to the ground and then dismounted herself. With no trees around, only the wagons offered shade. The oxen stamped and swished their tails against the flies, and the humans drank water from the barrels on the sides of the wagons, stretching and moving around.

Lark and Mr. Durham filled water buckets and gave each animal a short drink, then checked hooves and under the yokes to make sure no sores were developing.

"Why don't I take your place with Alice and you ride?" Lilac suggested to Forsythia.

Forsythia nodded. "Thank you. She's sleeping much of the time. When she wakes, I help her drink right away."

"I'll do the same." Lilac dropped her voice. "Is she worse?"

Shaking her head, Forsythia pondered. "She's keeping everything down, so she's not worse, just terribly weak. But she's more aware when she's awake now. She says she's thirsty."

"I'll get my bag."

Forsythia shaded her eyes with her hand and looked back the direction they'd come. "Someone's coming. It looks like a buggy."

The driver pulled his team to a halt. "Good day, folks. Headin' west?"

Lark nodded and smiled at the well-dressed woman seated behind the man with the reins. "Good day, ma'am."

"Where are you heading?" she asked, her stylish hat nearly hiding her eyes.

"Independence, Missouri, hopefully in time to meet up with a wagon train heading to Oregon."

She nodded. "I see. You should be there in two or three more days. If you need more water or supplies, we have a mercantile about two miles ahead that has helped outfit many wagons. We have a place with trees where you can camp, too, and a well for water."

"Why, thank you, ma'am. Do you by any chance have a doctor in your town?"

She shook her head. "I'm sorry, but we're still looking for one to open a practice in our town. Doctors are scarcer than turtle teeth out here."

"Ma'am." The driver turned slightly.

"Yes, almost ready." She looked back at Lark, shaking her head and setting the red flower on her hat bobbing. The feather matched the color of her ensemble, as did her gloves. "I hope you decide to stay over, even a day or two."

Lark nodded, and the driver flicked the reins to set the buggy off at a trot.

"Will we stop?" Forsythia asked. Her heart leapt at the thought of civilization again, but Lark's brow furrowed.

"How about you think on what we need and pass the word back. How is Mrs. Durham doing?"

Forsythia took Starbright's reins from Lilac. "Not vomiting, but she's so weak. Robbie's napping by his ma."

If only the sleep would give Alice some strength to recover and carry the baby to term. *Please, Lord.*

Lark walked with the lead ox, watching to see if any of them were limping. Anders had reminded her several times how to care for their mode of transportation.

She added grain to the list growing in her mind. It would be good to stock up before they reached Independence, as prices might be higher there.

It wasn't long before they reached the outskirts of the town, which boasted a shady, fenced pasture and a well, just as the woman had promised.

"You'll enjoy that, won't you?" Lark gave Sadie a scratch behind her stubby horns. She halted the oxen next to the fence, where a gangly young man leaned against the gate.

"A lady in a buggy a ways back told us we could spend the night here."

"Sure." The boy straightened and took a piece of grass out of his mouth. "Cost you a dollar per wagon."

"A dollar?" Lark stared. "Just to camp?"

"Take it or leave it." He shrugged and put the grass back in his mouth.

Lark glanced back at Forsythia. Atop Starbright, her sister tipped her head toward the Durhams' wagon. They didn't have much choice, not with Alice's condition. And they needed supplies. But Lark nearly choked as she placed the dollar in the boy's hand, then another for the Durhams. She doubted they had that kind of money to spare. At least she had her gambling winnings, strange as that still felt.

"Make yourselves comfortable." He swung the gate open for the wagons to pass through.

They stopped the wagons under some spreading oaks near the well, unhitched the oxen, and lifted their yokes. Sam and Soda immediately started grazing, while Sadie and Sarge took time to rub the day's weariness from their heads and necks against the tree trunks first.

"A whole dollar?" Lilac crossed her arms. "That's pure robbery."

"I know." Lark lifted her hat and let the breeze blow through her hair. "We'll stay just one night, especially since they don't have a doctor here. Want to come with me to the mercantile?"

"Sure." Lilac retied her sunbonnet strings. "Man and wife again?"

Her sister's teasing wink made Lark smile. Thank God for her sisters.

The mercantile was well stocked, at least. They refilled their stores of beans, flour, bacon, and even fresh eggs to pack in the cornmeal. The store sold wood for those staying in the camp overnight. Lark eyed the tagged bundles with a raised brow. Would they at least let them gather kindling for free?

The bell on the store door jangled.

"Ah, you found us." The lady they'd met on the road swept up beside Lark, red flower still bobbing in her hat. "I trust you are finding all you need?"

Lark met her gaze. "You didn't mention the charge for camping here."

"Are you not satisfied with the site?"

"It's fine, but—"

"Nothing comes free, you know. Water, safety, rest—we provide all these for weary travelers. You can always go elsewhere." The woman smiled, but a hint of steel laced her voice.

Savvy businesswoman, Lark would give her that. This close to Independence, weary travelers must be aplenty.

Lilac stepped up, eyes alight.

"Look, Lar—Clark." She held out two tablets and fresh pencils. "Can we? For Sythia and me?"

Lark checked the price. Not as high as she'd feared, considering. "All right." Her sisters deserved a treat for all they'd put up with on her account and for serving as God's angels to the Durhams. Not that they'd been raised to do any differently.

The total for their purchases still made Lark swallow, but at least they'd be stocked for a while. No doubt prices might still be higher in Independence. She tried not to let her mind start running numbers again.

"So that lady owns this place?" Lark counted out coins after the woman had swept out of the store.

The mustached man behind the counter chuckled. "And half the town. Even the saloon."

No wonder. A regular monopoly.

"We should have gotten something for Robbie." Lilac glanced at the jars of candy on the counter.

"Your son?" The store clerk cut a length of brown paper to wrap their bacon.

"A little boy in a wagon traveling with us," Lark said, lest Lilac forget and say something to give them away. "His ma's been sick."

"Here. Take him a peppermint stick." The clerk lifted a glass lid and handed the candy to Lilac.

Something in Lark's chest eased. So generosity did exist in this town.

"Thank you kindly." Arms laden, they stepped out into the sunshine.

As their wagons rumbled out of the pasture the next morning at first light, Lark rode up next to Forsythia. "Someday wherever we end up, we're going to start a boardinghouse or hotel. A place that will treat folks right."

12

I'd like to have stayed there another day, but I can't afford it," Mr. Durham said.

"You're sure your wife is strong enough to go on?" Lark asked from Starbright's back.

"She says she is." Durham looked to Forsythia, who shrugged. "Thanks to Miss Forsythia."

"We might have layover time in Independence. Depending on when the wagon trains leave."

Lark knew her concern was showing. If it weren't for Forsythia making sure his wife was as comfortable as possible . . . She still wished the Durhams had turned back and stopped at the Herrons', but they were insistent that they continue. She'd heard rumors that wagon masters could refuse a wagon if there was sickness. If Sythia could get Alice strong enough to sit up on the wagon seat . . . *Lord, you know this situation. What do we do?*

Traffic increased the closer they drew to Independence. Late in the afternoon, they stopped at a general store for information. Inside, the man behind the counter gave them instructions as to where the wagon trains formed up.

"The wagon master, name of Ephraim Hayes, told me they're

waiting on a couple more wagons. You might be the answer for him."

Lark and Mr. Durham exchanged glances. "Thank you."

Back at the wagons, Lark told the others the news and led the way, swinging out around the town proper and stopping near a circle of wagons. She and Durham stepped down and went searching for the wagon master, asking those they encountered. They finally located him by his wagon, busy greasing the axles.

"Mr. Hayes, we heard you were lookin' for more wagons," Lark said.

The wagon master stuck his paddle in the bucket of grease, wiped his hands on his pants, and nodded. "Who are you? Where you from, and where you goin'?"

"Name is Clark Nielsen. My wagon is from Linksburg, Ohio. Myself, my three sisters, two span of oxen, and a mare." Lark looked at Mr. Durham.

"Thomas Durham. My wife and I and small son have one span of oxen and a smaller wagon."

"Adequate supplies?"

"Used the lists sent out. How many are in your train?" Lark studied the man who might be responsible for their safety.

"Twelve so far. The two of you make fourteen. You related?"

"No, met up a few days back."

"What kinda arms you carryin'?"

Lark answered his questions carefully. One repeating rifle, one muzzle-loader, and a pistol. Good thing she'd bought more ammunition at that last store.

"And how many can shoot and hit their target?"

"All of us. My youngest sister is best at reloading, but she can shoot, too, and she's a good hunter."

Hayes cocked an eyebrow. Obviously he didn't think much of female shooters.

"Our father made sure all of his children could handle fire-arms. He started us young."

Hayes turned to Thomas. "Durham, is it?"

Mr. Durham nodded. "One rifle, one shooter."

"I see. And where might you all be headin'?"

"My sisters and I are thinking on southern Nebraska. We don't really want to cross the Rocky Mountains. It depends on what kind of land we can find. We're thinking to homestead or buy."

"And you, Durham?"

"We were planning on Oregon, but the more I hear about the Rockies, the less I want to attempt that, so we might stop in Nebraska too." Durham looked to Lark, who shrugged.

He's afraid his wife won't make it that far. Lark kept her thoughts to herself. She had a feeling the real strength in that little family lay with the missus. And right now, that was slim.

"Let's go look at your wagons," Hayes said.

As they walked toward the waiting wagons, Lark asked, "How many trains have you taken west?"

"Three, this will be four. As the railroad expands west, wagon trains will be a thing of the past. I got me a good plot of land in a beautiful valley in Oregon. My wife and two children are there, along with my brother and his family. This train'll be my last."

Lark led him to their wagons, introduced him to her sisters, and invited him to look around.

"I see you got a guitar back there. Musicians?" Hayes asked.

Lark nodded. "We've done some entertaining back home."

"On the road too?"

She nodded. "A good pick-me-up."

"We can always use some music in the evenings." He looked up at Lilac on the horse with Robbie in front of her. "You the hunter?"

Lilac shrugged and adjusted Robbie. "Me and Clark."

Hayes turned to Durham. "That your boy?"

"Yes, sir."

At the Durham wagon, Hayes tipped his hat to Mrs. Durham, who sat up on a couple of boxes padded with folded quilts. She was knitting, and Forsythia was stitching on a framed piece.

Durham introduced his wife, and Forsythia smiled at Lark's introduction.

Hayes studied her for a moment. "And you can shoot?"

"Would you like to set up a test? I can also throw a knife. My father wanted his daughters to be able to defend themselves if ever need be, considering we were fighting a war. He wanted us to be self-sufficient." Forsythia's voice was steady, with no hint of her struggle from her last knife-throwing incident.

"Unusual man." Hayes shifted his jaw.

"He was. He and our mother also made sure we got a good education. Any one of us could teach school, if need be."

"Or farm or run a store." Lark leveled a look at Hayes. "Or fight."

"I see." He tipped his hat again. "Good day, ladies. I'm sure we'll get to know each other on the trail." He turned to Lark and Durham. "I'll need you gentlemen to join a meeting before supper to sign the contract and go over our bylaws. I also heard tell two more wagons are nearing town. I'll give them one more day, and then we move out at the crack of dawn on Monday. So if you're needin' more supplies, now's the time. I'll tell you the lineup on Sunday. I suggest you move your wagons north and east to get closer to grazing land. Give your animals a rest. There's water there too. Make sure your water barrels and canteens are full."

The families watched him stride off.

Lark blew out a breath. Apparently they had been weighed and found acceptable—though she doubted that would be the case if Hayes knew her gender.

She grinned at her sisters and shook Durham's hand. "Guess we're bound for the promised land." *Thank you, Lord.*

From atop Starbright, Robbie gave a whoop. Lilac smiled and hugged him.

Since they'd stocked up in the previous town, only Lark headed into Independence to check for mail. Hopefully there'd be another letter from Anders before they hit the trail, and she had a packet to send him from them. Forsythia, Del, and Lilac stayed behind to set up camp and help the Durhams.

She stepped into the post office, blinking in the dimness after the bright sun outside.

"Any mail for the Jimson family?" She tapped her fingers on the wooden counter, waiting. It would be good to hear from Anders.

"Here you go." The clerk handed her four letters.

Four. What riches. She'd have thought two at the most. Lark paid for the postage on her letters to Anders, then hurried outside and leaned against the hitching post to examine the envelopes.

Two from Anders—or rather, Anders and Josephine Nielsen, the return address said. Lark smiled. So they had gotten married. One from the Herrons, bless them. And one unmarked envelope. Mr. Holt? Another friend? She'd find out when they opened the letters together tonight.

Her heart lifting, Lark swung up on Starbright again. Joining a wagon train just in time, and four letters from home. She sang softly as they trotted back to camp. "'O for a thousand tongues to sing my great Redeemer's praise . . .'"

She found their wagon and the Durhams' just to the east of the circle of prairie schooners, the oxen grazing with others in the grassy field. Del and Forsythia stooped over a newly kindled fire, starting supper.

Robbie came running to meet her. "Guess what, guess what. There's an Indian, a real one."

"Is that so?" Lark chuckled and dismounted.

"A Pawnee guide the wagon master has." Mr. Durham followed his son, shaking his head. "I don't know how I feel about having him along."

"No doubt he knows the territory better than even the wagon master." Lark shaded her eyes to look across the circle of wagons where Robbie pointed. She could barely make out a slender young man talking with Hayes.

"Still. I'd rather not have a heathen skulking nearby, not around my wife and young'un."

Her spine stiffened. "We're all God's children, are we not, Mr. Durham?"

He gave a noncommittal grunt.

As the sun slanted lower in the sky, Lark and Durham gathered with the other men around Hayes in the center of the circled wagons. Smoke from cooking fires and the aroma of mingled suppers spiced the air.

"You're all here because you want to be." Hayes raised his voice to be heard above the surrounding clatter of pots, chatter of women, and scamper of children. "You're bound for Oregon or California, or points that direction. And you know there's safety in numbers. I'm Ephraim Hayes, and I'm your captain. Just as if we were on a ship, what I say goes. No arguments." He clapped a hand on the shoulder of the young Indian man beside him. "This here is Kuruk, our Pawnee trail guide. He knows these parts like the back of his hand. His name means *bear* in his language, so I call him Little Bear. You can too."

Murmurs, curious glances. Little Bear leaned against a wagon behind Hayes, his expression neutral.

"This document lays out the rules and regulations for this wagon train all the way to our destinations." Hayes held up a written paper. "I'm going to read through the articles aloud. Any objections or questions, speak your piece now or hold your tongue later. Understood?" He leveled a glance around the circle.

Nods, shifting of feet.

Hayes began to read, laying out regulations for decision-making, for adding or withdrawing members, against drinking and gambling—Lark's cheeks heated at that—and regarding river crossings and private property rights. Some men started to lose interest, but the rules seemed fair.

"You may now sign if you agree to be bound by this contract." Hayes laid the document on a rock along with a pen, and the men filed in to scrawl their names.

"You may have noticed we have an article against Sabbath-breaking." Hayes raised his voice above the swelling murmurs, and silence fell again. "Whatever your personal convictions, the wagon train will not travel on Sundays. Tomorrow morning the Rev. William Green will hold a church service for the camp. Monday morning we move out."

Lark stepped closer, waiting her turn to sign the contract. She passed near Little Bear and gave a friendly nod.

He nodded back, still reserved, but his eyes smiled a bit.

"You been on many of these wagon trains?" Lark ventured.

He looked no older than Anders, dressed in a woven hunting shirt and leather breeches. Under his shaved head and scalp lock, his face was young, unthreatening. He made her miss her brothers.

Little Bear shrugged. "A couple of times. I know the trail, though."

"Where do you live?" She hoped she wasn't pressing too far.

"My family is on the reservation north of here." He dipped his head politely and stepped away.

Lark watched him slip behind the wagons, her heart tugging

strangely. What must it be like to serve as guide for foreigners invading his people's land? The thought cast a different light over her excitement for setting out. And yet he chose to go along with them.

"You going to sign, young fella?"

"Sorry." Lark stepped up and added her signature to the document, making it as manly as she could.

Well. That was that.

She went back to the wagon.

"There's really going to be a church service tomorrow?" Forsythia dished up beans and hot corn bread for supper.

"So Hayes said. Sounds like it'll be a weekly occurrence."

"Maybe they'd let us bring some of the music," Del said.

"Not a bad thought."

"Come on, eat quickly so we can read the mail." Lilac reached for her plate.

After supper and washing up, Lark pulled the letters from her satchel, running her fingers over each envelope. Her sisters gathered close.

She opened the letter from Anders dated the earliest and began to read.

My dear family,

We have much news here, but first I want to thank you for the missives you have sent. Lilac, do you mind if we share your drawings with others? You depict life in a wagon so well that we could turn these all into a picture book. And Forsythia, Mrs. Smutly played the chords of the song you sent, and now we are singing it regularly. Josephine enjoys the piano so much, as do we all. Mr. Holt is a frequent supper guest. He says his ranch is so lonely, especially since another of his ranch hands is itching to head west. He said he wouldn't be surprised if one morning he wakes up with one less employee.

Josephine and I missed you dreadfully at the wedding, which really wasn't much of a wedding, but we did have our new pastor officiating at the service. Jonah was my best man, and her sister stood up for her. Her mother and aunt made a special dinner, and that was about it. Our biggest question is why we waited so long. Yes, I know the many reasons, and they are all valid, but we so missed all of you here to celebrate with us.

Since Reverend Spalding and his family arrived only three weeks ago, he has been cleaning house. Deacon Wiesel was relieved of his position, and Climie barely lived through it and lost another baby that never saw the light of day. Wiesel has now left town, but Reverend Spalding refused to let Climie go with her husband, no matter how Wiesel ranted and raved. She is healing well but will be disfigured for life. She has moved in with Josephine's parents to assist them in their later years. Now Grandma Larkin is able to enjoy her family more, and Grandpa is getting good care.

Needless to say, we are so grateful for Rev. Spalding and his lovely wife. They have two children still living at home. Their eldest son is in college and planning to follow in his father's footsteps.

I hate to leave you with this news, but Wiesel left town still blaming our family for all his troubles—Lark, especially, which is not a surprise. As far as we know, he has no idea where you might have gone, other than west.

I must close. Lark, I wish you were here to take care of the store books. You are far better at that than I am. Josephine loves our house, and I must say I do not miss living above the store. Jonah seems to be shaping up, and we keep praying for God to work His miracles there. Jonah helps out at Holt's ranch at times too.

Farewell and thank you for the wonderful letters. With love and prayers from all of us here.

> *Your brother and sister-in-law,*
> *Anders and Josephine Nielsen*

"So much good news." Forsythia clasped her hands around her knees and scooted closer to the campfire. "You said there is another, more recent?"

"Yes." Lark opened the envelope. Reading the words made her miss Anders something fierce, and even Jonah, troublemaker that he was. Though it sounded like that might be changing. She prayed so.

My dear family,

I hope this letter catches you before you leave with the wagon train. I have been marking your progress on a calendar, so we have some idea of where you might be. Thank you for the letters you have sent, which we read over and over.

Much has happened here, and some of it is not good. Jonah sneaked his way back to the saloon, so though it nearly killed us, he no longer works at the store or lives above it, and until he can learn to live up to his promises, he is not welcome here either. I now know the horrible sadness of the father in the story of the prodigal son. I pray our prodigal brother will come to his senses and return to those who love him no matter what.

I am not that father, though, because I cannot allow him here if he doesn't mend his ways. He has to decide and adhere to his decision to live without booze and gambling.

Arthur Holt has hired him to work on his ranch full-time, but the same rule applies: If you return to the

saloon, you will be on your own. He says Jonah is working hard and hopefully too tired at night to have any desire to go to town.

The mercantile is doing well, even better now that
Josephine has taken over the bookkeeping and Climie is
our newest employee. You can see her blossoming, as my
Josephine says.

I have heard of some land available in southern Nebraska. A man wants to sell his homestead property near
a town called Salton. I do not know the rules for purchasing a homesteaded property, but I am in contact with an
attorney in Salton, under whom I served in the war. This
is rather convoluted, I know, but we shall see.

Love from your brother,
Anders Nielsen

Lark's heart sank, despite the news about possible land. *Jonah,
Jonah, truly you are like your stubborn biblical namesake. Lord,
what is it going to take to knock some sense into his head?*

Her sisters sat subdued around the fire.

"He'll come back someday, Lark." Lilac reached out to squeeze
her arm.

"I sure hope so." Lark opened the letter from Mrs. Herron
next. Its warmth and homey bits of family news lifted all their
hearts. What a precious connection that had been.

"Who is the last letter from?" Del asked.

"No clue." Lark slit it open and read.

To Clark "Jimson,"
I decided I needed to inform you that your little
brother got a bit in his cups and bragged about your new
last name and where you're bound for. I felt honored that

he shared that bit of information with me, as I feel it is time to move on, perhaps to points west, once the railroad comes through.

I wanted to remind you that I have not forgotten the way you made a fool of me and left me nearly penniless. I do mean to repay you, however long it may take for our paths to cross again.

Slate Ringwald

Lark's fingers stiffened on the paper, the words settling cold in her belly. What in land sakes had Jonah done now?

13

"Forward, ho!"

The call echoed down the wagons pulling into line in their assigned positions.

Forsythia and Del looked at each other on the wagon seat and nodded. Forsythia murmured their farewell prayer. "We're on our way. Dear Lord, guide and protect us. Give Mr. Hayes wisdom beyond his usual in his responsibility for all these people and all the things that can happen on this journey. And, Lord, if you will, bring full healing to Alice and her baby."

Del added the "amen" and reached over to hug her sister. "It's going to be long, but I do believe this is God's plan for us, that He has the perfect place all picked out."

Forsythia nodded and pressed back the worry lingering from the letters two nights ago. Surely Ringwald's missive had just been a threat. He wouldn't take the time and effort to track them all the way to Nebraska. Nor would he know exactly where they aimed to go—provided Jonah hadn't also revealed that bit of information. Tension tightened Forsythia's shoulders again. *Oh, little brother, when will you learn wisdom or at least common sense?*

Lord, you are a shield about us. You are our glory and the One who lifts our heads . . . I trust you. I choose to trust you. Peace eased out the tension again. *Thank you.*

She looked at Lark, who strode along beside the lead ox. The weight she'd seen there Saturday night seemed gone for the moment. All their burdens had lightened some with the church service yesterday morning, especially when their family had been invited to lead the singing with their instruments. Now, head high, shoulders back, Lark looked the epitome of a man embarking on the next stage of an exciting adventure.

Lilac rode beside her, Robbie in front. As usual, he was talking to Lilac, to the horse, and shouting at times to his mother, who at least was starting the day sitting in the back of their wagon, which was in front of the Nielsens'. She waved back to her son. The extra day's rest had strengthened her considerably.

Del nodded toward the Durhams' wagon. "That's thanks to your patient doctoring, you know."

At the word *doctoring*, Forsythia thought about the man driving the end wagon, two behind theirs. Dr. Adam Brownsville. The final addition to the train, and the one Mr. Hayes had been waiting for. She'd noticed his eyes first. While he looked tired, his rich brown eyes held a confidence and warmth that inspired trust immediately. What a gift for a doctor. The rumor was that he was late because he had to bury his wife two days before they reached Independence. Which explained the grief also in his eyes. The poor man. What a heartbreaking start to what they must have hoped would be a new adventure together.

The sun climbed as the oxen plodded on. After their nooning rest, the heat rose, as did the dust, blowing into their faces in choking clouds from the wagons ahead.

"I didn't miss this part when we were on our own." Del held her handkerchief over her mouth.

Forsythia coughed and nodded. "I'm going to walk awhile. And check on Alice." She climbed down.

Heading forward to the Durhams' wagon, she waved at Lilac and Robbie on Starbright. They certainly had become an inseparable pair.

She paused beside Thomas Durham, who walked beside his oxen. "How is Alice?"

He shook his head. "Not so good."

Alarm gripped her. She climbed into the back of the wagon where Alice lay, eyes closed, one hand resting on her mound of belly. "Alice?" Forsythia stroked her hair. "How are you doing?"

Alice's eyes fluttered open, and she gave a faint smile. "Fine. A little weak."

Forsythia breathed a bit easier. Perhaps Mr. Durham was overly worried. But when she felt Alice's pulse, the thready rhythm concerned her. "Have you eaten?"

"A little gruel."

"We need to get some more nourishment into you." Forsythia couldn't cook anything, not until the wagons stopped for the night. If only they had milk. Perhaps one of the other families who had brought a milk cow might spare some. "I'll be back."

Hurrying, she found her way to Lark, who was leading Starbright and visiting with the husband of the family behind them. Del had taken over droving the oxen, while Lilac sat with Robbie on their wagon seat.

"Clark," Forsythia interrupted when she could, "I'm sorry, but Mrs. Durham has weakened. Do you know of any families with a milk cow?"

"Saw one three wagons ahead," the man Lark had been talking with said. "They might be glad to share."

"Thank you."

Half an hour later, Forsythia climbed back into the Durhams' wagon with a cup of fresh milk, one of their own eggs stirred into it with a little sugar. "Alice, see if you can drink this. It'll give you strength."

"Strength . . . I need." Alice smiled and tried to lift her head. "Especially when this little one comes along."

"We're going to have you strong and well before then." Forsythia propped her up, but Alice sagged on the pillows. *Dear Lord, please.* On a second try, they got her settled, and Alice drank half the concoction before turning her head away.

"No more." She was asleep by the time Forsythia climbed down from the wagon.

"How is she?" Mr. Durham hung back from his oxen.

"I got some nourishment into her." Forsythia rolled her lips together. "But you're right—she's weaker."

He said nothing, but the misery in his eyes cut to her heart.

Lord, show us what to do. The dysentery seems better, and no one else has gotten sick. So what is wrong?

As night fell, the company circled the wagons and set the animals free to graze within. Ephraim Hayes gathered the heads of households for another meeting, though anyone else was free to join this time. After making sure Alice drank the remainder of the milk, Forsythia went with Lark while Del and Lilac started supper.

"We made a good start today, folks. Covered near twenty miles. We gotta do that every day, at least, if we're going to make it over those Rockies before winter."

Murmurs and nods of agreement.

"I want to introduce a new member of our train who, due to unfortunate circumstances, was unable to be present at our first meeting. I know we're all glad to have a doctor around. Dr. Adam Brownsville is traveling with his nephew, Jesse. Please make these gentlemen welcome."

Forsythia craned her neck to catch another glimpse of the kind-eyed doctor and the young man with him. Jesse had a gentle face and spoke with a stutter. He looked with adoring trust at his uncle.

Mr. Hayes dismissed the meeting, and the group broke up to visit and drift back to their cookfires.

Forsythia touched Lark's sleeve. "I'm going to talk to Dr. Brownsville, ask him about Alice."

"Good idea."

She had to wait for several men to finish talking with the doctor and his nephew, but at last Dr. Brownsville turned to her.

"Forgive me, miss. Did you wish to speak with me?"

"Yes." Forsythia held out her hand to meet his warm, quick grip. "First, let me say how terribly sorry I was to hear about your wife." Empathy gripped her chest again with the words. She knew the pain of losing your beloved.

"Thank you." Lines of grief bracketed his eyes, yet he smiled beneath his neatly trimmed brown beard. "And you are?"

"Oh, I beg your pardon." Forsythia's scalp heated. "Miss Forsythia Nielsen. I'm traveling with my sisters—and brother Clark." She nodded across the clearing at Lark. The lie caught on her tongue, but she pushed the discomfort away. This way was best under the circumstances, they'd all agreed.

"And you wished to ask me . . . ?"

"Yes." Why was she scattered all of a sudden? "The family in the wagon in front of ours—the wife is ill. We've been nursing her as best we can since we found them a week ago, but she's growing weaker. At first it was dysentery, we thought, but now I'm not sure. And she's pregnant, over seven months along, as best we can figure."

"I see." The doctor frowned. "Might I come take a look at her? Would she and her husband be willing?"

"I'm sure they would." Relief flooded her. What a gift to have a doctor in this train. "Would you like to follow me now?"

"Certainly. Just let me explain to Jesse."

A moment later, Dr. Brownsville returned, bag in hand. He smiled at Forsythia. "Ready?"

"He seems a nice young man, your nephew." She led the way, skirting darkened wagons and firelight. Oxen lay resting, chewing their cud after the labors of the day.

"He is. He lost his parents years ago and has been passed from one part of the family to another, finally landing with me. I hope this journey will be a good, fresh start for him. He's all the family I have now."

Forsythia fell silent, honoring his grief. Only a few days, so fresh. How many more would be buried from this wagon train before they reached their destinations? She pushed away the morbid thought.

"Here we are."

Thomas stooped near the Durhams' fire, clumsily tidying up from supper. Robbie sat on the ground near him, whining sleepily. Poor little boy, it was past time he was in bed. Alice, of course, was too weak to do anything about it, and Thomas seemed unable.

Forsythia cleared her throat. "Mr. Durham, you remember Dr. Brownsville from the meeting? He's here to take a look at Alice, if you're willing."

"Much obliged." Durham straightened and came to shake the doctor's hand. "We don't know what's wrong with her. I hope you can help."

"I'll see what I can do." Dr. Brownsville squatted to Robbie's level. "And who do we have here?"

The little boy leaned against his father's leg, a finger in his mouth. "Robbie." He sniffled and wiped his sleeve across his nose.

"Would you like me to finish tidying up, Mr. Durham, while the doctor sees to Alice?" Forsythia offered. "That way you can get Robbie to bed."

Thomas nodded as if the thought hadn't occurred to him. "Sure." He lifted his son and led the doctor to the wagon.

Forsythia busied herself with the Durhams' dishes, scouring burned beans from the pot as best she could in the tepid dishwater. Dishes done, she wrung out the cloth and hung it to dry from a hook on the side of the wagon. She shook her head. This family needed help.

She turned to see the doctor climbing down from the wagon, lantern light from within framing his bearded silhouette against the canvas cover. He alighted with a soft thud on the dirt.

Forsythia approached him, drying damp hands on her apron. "What do you think?"

"Hard to say." The doctor blew out a breath and rubbed his beard. "As you said, no dysentery now, but she is weak and running a slight fever."

"That's not good. What about the baby?"

"I can hear a heartbeat, fairly strong. We won't know more until she gives birth—hopefully not for some weeks. She isn't strong enough now."

"Do you see any signs of labor?"

"She says she's been having some tightenings, but that's also normal at this stage." He shook his head. "All we can do is try to get her strength up with rest and nourishing food. And pray."

"Yes." So he was a praying man. Not a surprise, from what she'd seen of him so far. "I asked the folks ahead with the cow for some milk and whipped it with egg for her today. They said we could have more in the morning."

"Good. Crumbling a biscuit and soaking it in the milk might help too."

Forsythia nodded. "We'll try that. Thank you so much, Doctor. I'm very grateful for your input, and I know the Durhams are too."

"Sorry not to be of more help. I'll check in on her as I can, and please keep me informed, Miss Nielsen." He gave her hand a squeeze, then released it. "They are blessed to have friends like you and your family."

Forsythia watched him disappear into the darkness, headed for his wagon. *Bless that man, dear Lord, for his kindness. Heal his heart. And please, Father, bring strength and healing to Alice and her little one.*

Durham appeared at her side, lantern in hand. "Robbie's asleep. Alice too. Doc tell you anything else?"

"She's running a slight fever." Forsythia rubbed her arms against the evening chill. "We need to focus on getting her strength up before the baby comes."

"She has to get better." His voice hollow, Durham extinguished the lantern and hung it from the wagon side. "I don't think I can live without her."

14

They could do with some fresh meat.

Lark watched a hawk soaring overhead. It circled lower, then dove for its prey. A rabbit, most likely. This grassy region must be full of them, and the woods by the Kansas River not far away would hold more prey. Someone should organize a hunting party. Wasn't that the job of the wagon master? When she thought about it, that made sense.

Lilac pulled Starbright up beside Lark and dismounted. "Want to ride awhile?"

"Where's your other half?"

"Robbie? He found a friend two wagons up."

"A week into the journey, and you're already deserted." Lark gave her sister a teasing grin.

Lilac smiled back. "I'm glad for him. You should go see. They're having so much fun."

"I will. I want to speak to the wagon master about a hunting party. Interested?"

"Sure. Great country for rabbits." Lilac handed over Starbright's reins.

"That's what I thought." Lark swung up onto the mare. Trying to skirt the worst of the dust clouds alongside the rows of plodding oxen, she trotted past wagons until she found Mr. Hayes near the front of the train.

"Morning, sir." Lark tipped her hat, making sure to keep her voice low. She had to be especially careful about her disguise now that they were surrounded by so many people. "Have you thought about organizing a hunting party?"

"Already sent a couple out earlier this week." The wagon master eyed her. "I figured you needed to stick around for your sisters."

"I told you all of us could hunt." Lark fought a surge of irritation. And she'd thought dressing as a man would avoid these prejudices. "Would you mind if I gathered another?"

"If you like." He gestured with a nod. "Take Little Bear with you. He's a good hand at snares."

"So is my little sister." At Hayes's raised brow, Lark lifted her chin. "Best hunter in our family, sir."

"If you say so. Make sure everyone has returned before dark."

Blowing out a breath, Lark rode back to her wagon, stopping to invite a couple of men she recognized along the way. After finding her first interested hunter, she reached the wagon where Robbie had made a friend.

Sure enough, Robbie perched in the crammed back of the wagon, enthralled in a game of wild horses with a pigtailed, freckle-faced little girl of about four. With a carved wooden animal apiece, the children whinnied and snorted their horses into a corral of wooden crates and barrels.

"Having fun, Robbie?" She smiled at him. It was nice how little being male or female mattered at that age. Not so for grown-up folk.

He raised his horse high with a whinny. "Mr. Jesse made us these horses! He said he'd make a cow next."

Mr. Jesse? She'd solve that mystery later. "Is your father around, young miss?"

The little girl nodded hard, flapping her pigtails. "He's driving our oxen."

The father proved eager to join the hunting party.

Lark stopped to mention the idea to Thomas Durham, but as she'd suspected, he didn't want to leave Alice. She promised to share the game and headed back to tell Lilac. That made four for their party so far, including her and her sister, five with Little Bear. Maybe she should ask the doctor. She didn't see him when she stopped at his wagon, but his nephew walked alongside their two span of oxen.

"Morning. Dr. Brownsville around?" she asked.

"No, sir—I-I mean, he's t-tending somebody. Little boy got his toe run over by a w-wagon wheel."

"Oh dear."

"H-he'll be all right, my uncle says." The young man smiled with a warmth that would make anyone forget his stutter.

"That's good news. Sorry, tell me your name again?"

"Jesse, sir."

"And I'm Clark." She shook his hand. "You wouldn't be making wooden animals for those children a few wagons up, would you?"

In response, Jesse reached into his pocket and pulled out a half-carved cow. Already she could see the skill of the carving.

"You have quite a gift."

"M-makes the children happy."

"So it does." What a tender heart in this often hard world. "I don't suppose you'd want to join a hunting party, Jesse?"

"I'm supposed to d-drive the oxen. But my uncle might. I'll t-tell him when he gets back."

"Do that if he's back within an hour. Otherwise he can come another time." They parted with friendly nods.

All told, they gathered seven people for the excursion: Lilac, Lark, Little Bear, Dr. Brownsville, Martin Wheeler—the father of Robbie's little friend, Sarah—and two other men. Some of them looked askance at Lilac joining the group, but soon she and Little Bear were comparing snares and swapping tricks of the trade.

Letting Little Bear and her sister set the snares, Lark took Starbright and rode ahead of the wagon train into the woods along the Kansas. They'd be crossing this river tomorrow, according to Mr. Hayes—their first big river crossing.

The cooler air amid the trees caressed her face, and Lark lifted her hat to let the breeze through her cropped hair. *Lord, you've brought us this far. Take us safely across the river. And if you'd bring us some good meat today, that would be mighty fine.*

A squirrel darted across a branch, and Lark raised her rifle and fired. The small animal dropped like a rock. *Thank you, Lord.* A good squirrel stew might bring some strength into Alice Durham's bones.

When the party gathered back at the wagons that evening, they counted nearly a dozen rabbits—mostly thanks to Lilac and Little Bear—plus a number of squirrels and pheasants. No deer, but perhaps another time.

They divided the game, and Lark took a skinned squirrel and rabbit to the Durhams' wagon. She found Forsythia there talking with Thomas.

"Brought you some meat."

"I appreciate it." Mr. Durham took the carcasses, then stared down at them. "Now if only I knew how to cook 'em. Alice always did that."

"Why don't we cook the rabbit for you, Mr. Durham?" Forsythia suggested. "We'll make a big stew of it along with ours, then bring you some."

Lark said nothing until they were out of earshot by their wagon. "Sythia, we can't do everything for them. One of these days that man is going to have to step up."

"I know. But Alice is even weaker today. She's got to regain some strength. If us making extra stew helps toward that . . . well, then, so be it."

Lark wouldn't argue with that.

Thunder and rain woke them in the night, and they moved their bedrolls under and inside the wagon for cover. By morning the trail had turned into a muddy, soupy mess. Hayes ordered the wagons to spread out more to avoid sinking too far into the mud.

Once they moved out, Lark hadn't taken twenty paces before she was grateful for her men's boots, already caked nearly to the knee.

"Well, this dress will never be the same." Del, walking beside her with a shawl over her head, made a face. She'd been trying to hold her skirt out of the mud, but the bottom twelve inches was already slick with muck. "Think Mr. Hayes will postpone the river crossing?"

"He says no. The rain could go on for days and raise the river higher, so we'll go ahead." At least the rain was falling lighter now. Lark glanced at the Durhams' wagon ahead. She hoped Alice wasn't still running a fever. It could be dangerous for her to get chilled.

The wagons gathered at the edge of the Kansas River and loaded one by one onto the ferries. Despite the rain and rising water, by day's end they all made it safely across, though one family's mules spooked midriver and nearly dragged their wagon off the ferry before the husband got them under control. Then Lilac surprised everyone by bringing in a deer from the surrounding woodland, just as the rain cleared and the wagons circled.

Overhead, the moon lit the edges of parting clouds, stars pricking in a clean-washed black sky. Relieved chatter rose through the camp, along with cooking odors and woodsmoke.

"Thanks be to God." Forsythia shivered and held her hands out to their sparking campfire. "I've never been so wet in my life."

"Get yourself warm." Lark draped a woolen blanket around her sister's shoulders, worry blooming. Sythia always came down with things easily. "And no checking on the Durhams tonight. Sleep—and that's an order."

"Sythia."

Forsythia woke from a deep sleep to Lilac shaking her shoulder.

"I'm sorry, Sythia, but Mr. Durham says Alice is in labor."

Oh no. Forsythia sat up from her warm cocoon of blankets and pressed her fingers to her eyes. *Please, Lord, no—it's too soon. Let this be another false alarm.*

"He says to hurry. Shall I come too?" Lilac asked.

"Yes, please. You've got experience birthing animals."

Please, God, please. She gathered whatever supplies she could think of. "Del, could you go for the doctor?"

"Lark already did." Del slipped a shawl around Forsythia's shoulders and squeezed her arm. "Want me to come too?"

"Maybe—I don't know. Yes, we'll need someone for Robbie, at least."

The sisters made their way through the darkness toward the Durhams' wagon. The moon had set, and only the stars were bright above, cold and clear. With the camp sleeping, all was silent but for the occasional whimper of a child or distant yip of a coyote.

And a moan from the Durhams' lamplit wagon. Forsythia's chest tightened.

"We're here, Alice." She climbed up, Del and Lilac staying below for the moment.

Alice lay panting on the makeshift bed with Thomas kneeling beside her, her forehead and throat shiny with sweat. Robbie huddled sniffling in the far corner, obviously just awakened.

Forsythia's heart sank. This didn't look like a false alarm.

"When did it start?" She climbed in to join them.

"Maybe an hour ago—I don't know. She didn't wake me at first." Thomas smoothed his wife's hair with a shaking hand.

"Thought it was . . . just the tightenings again. Didn't want to think . . ." Alice cried out, gripping Thomas's arm with a strength Forsythia hadn't known she had.

They needed to get the little boy out of here. "Robbie, sweetheart, will you come to me? Del is going to take you to our wagon to sleep while we help your mama."

Without hesitation, he crawled over the rumpled bedding to Forsythia's arms.

Alice touched his nightshirt sleeve as he passed. "Robbie . . ."

Forsythia scooped him up and turned him around. "Say good night to Mama, Robbie. You'll see her soon." *Please, Lord, let it be so.*

Robbie waved and blew a teary kiss. Forsythia passed him down to Del's waiting arms.

"Lilac, can you come up here? And, Mr. Durham, perhaps you could get down for a while. There's just too little room." And his own panic was too obvious, though she wouldn't say that.

"I'll be right outside." Thomas pressed a kiss to his wife's clammy forehead, then climbed down to make room for Lilac.

Together the sisters examined Alice as she lay spent from the last contraction. Her pulse was fast, her temperature still elevated. And when Lilac checked below her nightdress, she shook her head at Forsythia.

"She's definitely progressing. Second baby and coming early . . . I don't think we have much time."

"Hello?" Dr. Brownsville's voice came from behind the wagon.

"Thank heaven." Forsythia crawled to look out the canvas flap. "Thank you so much for coming, Doctor."

"How is she?" He climbed into the wagon with them, his kind eyes and black bag lending a certain steadiness to Forsythia's heart despite their cramped quarters.

"Seems like the baby's coming—and fast. Is there anything we can do?"

The doctor examined Alice and shook his head much as Lilac had done. "Just do our best to help her through this. And pray. Let me go see if Mr. Durham has any hot water."

Of course. She should have thought of that first thing.

Waiting for the doctor, Forsythia and Lilac took turns cooling Alice's forehead with a damp cloth and letting her squeeze their hands through the pains. They were coming harder and faster now, barely letting Alice catch her breath in between.

"Hold on, sweet girl. You're doing so well." Forsythia stroked Alice's damp hand, so weak now even when she gripped as hard as she could.

"Please." Alice's voice came as merely a breath, but at the pleading in her eyes, Forsythia leaned close to hear. "If I don't . . . make it through, take care of my boy, my . . . Robbie."

"You will make it through, dear one." Forsythia pressed Alice's fingers, willing strength into them.

"But if . . . I don't."

Hot tears pricked. "Then yes. Of course."

Alice smiled, her eyes closing as she rested back on the pillow for a moment. Then she grimaced, curling forward with a guttural groan.

"Doctor?" Lilac called out. "I think she's trying to push."

Dr. Brownsville appeared, shoving back the wagon flap. Gray light filtered in as dawn approached. He assessed the situation with a glance.

"Miss—Forsythia, was it? Sit behind her, please. We need to prop her up a bit. Miss Lilac, would you help hold her legs?"

They shifted into position. Alice groaned long and shrill.

"We're right here with you, Mrs. Durham." The doctor's voice came reassuring and steady. "We're going to help you deliver your baby, all right?"

A faint nod.

Please, Lord. Please help her. Forsythia pressed her cheek against Alice's sweaty hair.

A moment, and then Alice arched forward with a scream, pushing hard. Fluid gushed.

"That's good, Mrs. Durham. Very good. Let me just check to see if I can feel your baby."

Forsythia stroked Alice's arm, murmuring prayers and hymns, whatever might be comforting.

"Your baby is on its way, Mrs. Durham." The doctor sat back on his heels. "And quickly too. But he or she is coming feet first. I'm going to need to help you deliver, all right?"

Alice sobbed a nod, her head lolling weakly on Forsythia's shoulder.

"On this next contraction, I need you to push with all your strength and then some, you hear me? You can do this, Mrs. Durham. We're all right here with you."

He'd barely finished speaking when Alice's body tensed again. She arched away from Forsythia, clawing her knees as she pushed from strength beyond herself.

"Good, that's good. We've almost got a baby here. Once more."

A keening cry from Alice, and a baby girl slid into the doctor's hands, tiny and still.

In a quick motion, Dr. Brownsville cut the cord and wiped the infant's mouth and nose. He flipped her over and slapped her bottom. Nothing.

"Doctor." Forsythia's voice caught. "She's bleeding." In the dawning light filtering through the canvas, dark red spread through the bedding beneath Alice's legs.

"Try to get her breathing." The doctor pushed the tiny form into Lilac's hands. "Mrs. Durham—Alice—I need you to stay with me. We need to get your afterbirth delivered." He kneaded her flaccid abdomen firmly. "Help me, Miss Nielsen."

"Alice, sweetheart, see if you can push once more," Forsythia urged into the mother's ear. Alice sagged against Forsythia's shoulder, unable even to lift her head.

"Come on, little one." Lilac worked over the baby, pressing the tiny chest and patting the little bluish cheeks. "Breathe. Please breathe."

Dr. Brownsville caught the afterbirth in a gush of blood. "Forsythia! Help me. Her womb needs to contract to stop the hemorrhaging."

Forsythia scooted from beneath Alice's limp form to help massage her belly, almost pounding. *Please, God. Please, God.* The prayer moved in rhythm with their hands.

"My . . . baby?" Alice's eyelids fluttered.

Forsythia glanced at Lilac. Eyes filled with tears, her little sister shook her head.

"Stay with us, sweetheart." Forsythia squeezed Alice's hand. "Your family needs you."

"Robbie . . . Thomas."

The doctor's mouth set in a grim line as he tried to stanch the bleeding with linen. "Get her husband."

Tear-blinded, Forsythia scrambled down from the wagon and almost crashed into Thomas Durham.

"What's happening? The baby?"

"She's asking for you." Forsythia dashed the tears from her eyes as he clambered up. *Oh, Lord.* She peered back inside the wagon.

Mr. Durham knelt by his wife, clasping her hand. "Alice, no. Don't leave me."

"Love . . . you." Alice blinked long and slow, then glanced at Forsythia, standing at the back of the wagon. "Take care of . . . my Robbie."

She nodded hard. "I will."

A sigh and a smile, and Alice closed her eyes.

Lilac, holding the tiny, still bundle, choked on a sob.

The doctor checked Alice's pulse, then sat back, shoulders sagging in defeat. "She's gone."

15

It rained again the morning they buried Alice and her baby, a soft mist that dampened the sheet wrapped around the mother and infant and mingled with the tears on the mourners' cheeks.

Rev. Green, who held church services for the wagon train, spoke comfort from Scripture. The twenty-third psalm and the part in Revelation about God wiping all tears from all eyes. But nothing covered the broken sound of Thomas Durham's sobs.

Robbie clung to Lilac, his face pressed into her shoulder against the rain. He'd hardly let the sisters out of his sight since losing his ma. Forsythia held Del's arm close to hers. Would Thomas even be able to care for his son?

When the reverend nodded to them, Forsythia, Del, and Lark stepped up with guitar, fiddle, and harmonica. Softly Forsythia picked out the melody.

"Jesus, lover of my soul,
Let me to thy bosom fly,
While the nearer waters roll,
While the tempest still is high:
Hide me, O my Savior, hide,

Till the storm of life is past;
Safe into the haven guide;
O receive my soul at last."

She closed her eyes as she played, words rising from memory and her heart. *"Safe into the haven guide . . ."* Alice was there now. But oh, the grief left behind.

Several men shoveled damp earth over the body, and the crowd dispersed.

Forsythia stopped by Dr. Brownsville and Jesse. "Thank you, Doctor, for all you did for Alice and her child."

"It seems I'm not much good at saving lives of late." Lines of grief etched his face, though he smiled sadly. "Thank you also, Miss Nielsen. You did all you could for her." His arm around Jesse's shoulders, he headed back toward his wagon.

Forsythia watched him go through the rain, her heart aching for him.

She woke two nights later from another dream of her knife in the back of the man she'd killed, that image mingled with nightmares of Alice's blood spreading, of the tiny babe buried with her mother without ever drawing breath. She sat up shivering and rested her head on her knees.

Lord, it seems like there's death everywhere I go. But no, this thought is not from you. I reject it in the name of Jesus. I know you have not forgotten us. But this is so hard.

She lifted her head at a barely heard sound. Had something woken her besides the dreams? There, again—a child's whimper. Mournful, abandoned.

"Ma . . . Ma."

Robbie. Her heart twisted. Forsythia got up and walked toward the Durhams' wagon. Should she interfere? Thomas would have to learn to cope sometime. Perhaps comforting his son would be a step in that direction.

"Ma. Maaa!" Robbie's voice rose in panic.

Forsythia stopped on the edge of their campsite and called softly. "Mr. Durham? Do you need anything? It's Forsythia Nielsen."

"I want my ma. Where's my ma?"

"Robbie?" Forsythia peered through the darkness and crossed to the bedrolls beside the dying campfire.

Robbie sat up in a mass of tangled blankets. Mr. Durham's bedroll, she could see now, was empty.

"Where's your pa, little one?" She gathered Robbie in her arms.

"I want my ma." Hiccupping, he clung to her neck.

"I know, sweet boy." She pressed a kiss to his tousled hair. Thomas must have gone to relieve himself. "I'll sit with you till your pa gets back, okay?"

Forsythia sat down and stirred the glimmering coals, then wrapped a blanket around both of them. Humming a hymn, she rocked Robbie till he fell asleep and her arms ached with his weight.

But Mr. Durham did not return.

Lugging the sleeping child, Forsythia walked back to their wagon. Lark was sitting up.

"Everything all right?"

"I'm not sure. Robbie was crying, and I can't find his father. It's been at least an hour."

"That's not good." Lark stood. "Want to lay him down here?"

Forsythia tried, but Robbie woke when she released him, screaming.

"Ma, no, Ma. Want my ma, my ma!"

Fighting tears herself, Forsythia tried to comfort him, but Robbie arched and thrashed. Del and Lilac were up now, and Lilac took the little boy, but even her attempts at comforting were to no avail.

"Can't you keep the kid quiet?" A grumbling call came from a nearby wagon. "Some folks are trying to sleep."

Forsythia set her teeth. The child had just lost his mother. Couldn't whoever Mr. Grump was understand that? She took Robbie back from Lilac's arms.

Lark pushed to her feet. "I'll go explain. We'll need a search party come dawn if Durham's not back."

Holding Robbie close, Forsythia walked a bit beyond the circle of wagons into the cool of darkness. The breeze caressed their hot faces, and Robbie's wailing quieted to sobs. He laid his damp cheek on her shoulder, little arms tight around her neck.

"You see the stars, Robbie?" she whispered into his hair. "So many stars, way up in the sky, see? The Bible tells us that God knows each of their names. And He knows each of our names too. He knows yours. And He loves you. He's going to take care of you and your pa."

"And Ma?" Robbie drew a stuttering breath.

"Yes." Forsythia held him close. "He's taking very good care of your ma too." She swayed to and fro under the stars, humming snatches of hymns and lullabies until Robbie's breathing evened and the limp weight in her arms told her he was finally asleep.

She returned to their campsite and lay down with Robbie under her blanket till the sky lightened toward dawn.

Lark came back with Little Bear following. "Little Bear will help us track Durham. We've got a few other men to help search also." She checked and loaded the rifle. "Hayes has agreed the wagons won't start out till we find him."

"Go with God." Forsythia sat up, blinking back exhaustion, and checked to be sure slumbering Robbie was warm enough. *Please, Lord, don't let this be another day of tragedy.*

"I can't abide a man who would just run off and leave his young'un."

Lark gripped her rifle and bit her tongue, keeping back a

retort. Otis Bane, the man from the wagon behind theirs who had complained about Robbie's crying, certainly was free with his opinions. Too bad he'd joined the search party.

"We about ready to head out?" Otis spit a stream of tobacco juice into the grass where they'd gathered by the Durhams' wagon. "I don't want to hold up the wagon train any more'n it has been already."

"We're just waiting for the doctor." Lark kept her voice steady. "If Mr. Durham is injured, it will be wise to have him along."

"Have to say, that family's had their share of bad luck. Should've stayed behind in the first place, wife ailing and all."

Lark clenched her jaw. *Hurry up, Dr. Brownsville, or you may have another injury to treat.*

"Come now, that's a bit harsh," Martin Wheeler said. "They were just seeking a new start, like the rest of us."

Lark shifted her attention to Little Bear, who was examining the ground by the Durhams' cold campfire. "Find anything?"

"He crouched here awhile, then headed that way." Little Bear tipped his head to the east and stood.

"Think you can find him?"

"We will see." Little Bear nodded. "Here comes the doctor."

With Dr. Brownsville added to their number, they set out, a couple of men on horseback, the rest on foot. Birds rose from the dewy grass around them, twittering morning songs. Scattered tufts of cloud were gilded and pinked in the east above them. Such a beautiful morning, if it weren't for the weight of worry. *Father God, be with us. Guide us to Thomas.*

Little Bear led the way, tracking quickly over soft bare ground, then more slowly when they entered the tall grass. Lark marveled at all he could tell by a bent grass stem, a faint impression in the dirt.

Little Bear circled back to speak to them. "He's tired. Heading toward the creek."

"Maybe he's resting down by the water." Martin seemed to have taken the role of encourager, bless him.

"Maybe."

"And leave his son like that?" Otis shook his head. "Terrible careless."

Little Bear slowed, the trail harder to find as the grass thickened.

Otis grew impatient. "We should spread out, use our numbers." He reined his horse. "Can't tell if this Indian fella even knows what he's doing."

And he did? Lark kept her tongue in restraint with effort.

"I'm heading up the creek. Anyone with me?" Otis asked.

"I'll go with you." Dr. Brownsville gave Lark a look that said he'd keep an eye on Otis.

She nodded, grateful. She'd just as soon not have Otis along. He'd certainly be of no help whenever they found Thomas.

"There's the trail." Little Bear bent over a matted patch of grass. "He stumbled here. Not far now."

Moving quickly, she and Martin followed the young Pawnee man into the trees skirting the creek. The bubbling of water reached their ears.

Little Bear paused on the creek bank, examining the damp earth, then headed south, following the stream. His moccasins swift and silent, he climbed onto a couple of boulders, then paused at the top, gazing at something on the other side. He turned and motioned to Lark. "Here."

Lark followed, leaping over stones in her path. She scrambled up beside Little Bear, then froze.

Thomas Durham lay facedown in the creek.

"Oh no. Lord, no."

Lark and Little Bear clambered down into the water and hauled Thomas up onto the bank. With Martin's help, they flipped him over. Blood and creek water soaked Thomas's head and shirt. One look at his face, and Lark knew he was gone.

"Is he dead?" Otis crashed through the bushes, leading his horse. The doctor followed.

"I'm afraid so." Lark swallowed. How much heartache could this family endure? Or rather, how much could Robbie? He was the only one left.

Dr. Brownsville came forward and checked Thomas for a pulse, looked in his eyes. He shook his head. "He's been dead several hours."

"What, killed hisself?" Otis spit into the creek.

"Hit his head." Little Bear touched the gash on Thomas's head, then motioned to a nearby rock smeared with blood. "Stumbled, then fell in the water."

Had he been drinking, found liquor somehow? Or was he just crazy and exhausted with grief? He'd talked about not being able to go on without his wife, but Lark hadn't known . . . She pushed back the guilt trying to clamp her chest. This wasn't their fault. They'd done all they could.

"We'd better get him back to camp." Martin closed Thomas's eyes and stood. "He deserves a decent burial."

"Hope we can make it quick." Otis swung onto his horse. "The sun's climbing, and the wagon train's been delayed enough already with this nonsense."

Lark shot to her feet and leveled a glare at him. "A man has died, Mr. Bane. Have a little respect."

"Respect, eh? Guess you never heard of respect for your elders, young fella." But he fell silent after that.

"Put him on my horse." Dr. Brownsville rose and helped Martin and Lark haul Thomas's waterlogged body over his saddle. Then they started a sober procession back to camp.

Little Bear touched Lark's arm. "I'll go ahead and tell Mr. Hayes."

"Thanks. For everything." Lark thought of something else. "Warn my sisters, too, would you? I don't want his little boy to see."

Little Bear nodded, understanding in his eyes, then darted ahead.

Mr. Hayes met them at the outskirts of camp, shaking his head. "Such a shame. I've set some men to digging another grave."

"Thanks." Lark swallowed, her throat aching. "I'll go see about his son."

Del met her before she even reached the wagon. Wordless, her sister held out her arms, and Lark walked into them. They held each other tight.

"How are we going to tell Robbie?" Del stepped back and wiped her eyes.

"I really don't know."

In the end it was Forsythia who told him, holding Robbie on her lap in the shade of the wagon while the others stood nearby. The midmorning sun already burned hot.

"Sweetheart, you know how we couldn't find your pa this morning?"

"Uh-huh." Robbie turned his wooden sheep in his hands. Jesse had been busy.

"Well . . ." Forsythia looked up at Lark, tears in her eyes.

Lark shook her head. She didn't know how to do this either. *Lord, give her the words.*

"Well, your pa was missing your ma an awful lot. So he went to heaven to be with her."

"Pa's gone too?" Robbie twisted to look up into Forsythia's face.

"I'm afraid so, little one."

"I wanna go see Ma." Robbie's lip trembled.

"I know." Forsythia held him close. "But your ma asked us to take care of you until someday when we all get to go to heaven and be together. So we're going to do that, all right?"

Robbie sniffled, staring up into her eyes. Then he dropped his gaze back to his sheep. "Okay."

Well. Lark drew a long breath. Maybe the child was too full of grief to endure any more. Or his father had wandered away too much lately. Or this was simply God's mercy in the moment.

The sun had passed well beyond noon by the time the burial was ready. Once again, Reverend Green spoke over the grave.

"Thomas Durham follows his wife and child far sooner than we would like. In these times, we are reminded that 'our light affliction, which is but for a moment, worketh for us a far more exceeding and eternal weight of glory; while we look not at the things which are seen, but at the things which are not seen: for the things which are seen are temporal; but the things which are not seen are eternal.' As we move forward into the unknown on this journey, may we fix our eyes on what lasts for eternity."

Standing beside Forsythia and Robbie, Lark breathed in deeply through her nose, keeping back the unmanly tears. So much loss already. What had she brought her family into?

The reverend said a final prayer, and shovelfuls of dirt hit the wrapped body in the ground.

"Now can we get movin', Mr. Hayes? We've already wasted the better part of a day."

She didn't need to look to know who was speaking.

"I'm afraid it's a bit late for that." Ephraim Hayes squinted up at the sun. "Not enough hours of daylight left to reach another good campsite with water. We'll wait until tomorrow."

More grumbling voices joined Otis this time.

"We're already late in the season, you said it yourself," said a man Lark didn't know.

"Next time a fool gets hisself killed, let him stay where he lies. Not worth punishing the rest of us for it." Otis raised his voice.

"Quiet," Mr. Hayes roared. "You'd do well to remember who's in charge here. Everybody back to your wagons and behave yourselves. We move out at first light. If anyone else feels reason to complain, be grateful it's not you lying in the ground."

The families dispersed, still murmuring among themselves. The sisters headed back to their camp, Robbie in tow.

Martin's wife, Thelma, crossed over from their wagon carrying a covered dish and a spider skillet. Her little girl tagged at her heels. "I thought you folks could use a hot meal." She lifted the towel on the dish. "I brought you some fried squirrel and fresh corn bread."

"How kind you are." Forsythia reached for the food. "You didn't have to do that."

"Well, you folks have been taking care of that poor family like they were kin." Thelma rested her hand on her child's head. "'Bout time someone took care of you."

The kindness in her voice brought a lump to Lark's throat. "Thank you, ma'am. We surely appreciate it."

The scent of crisply fried meat and fluffy corn bread brought on a hunger she didn't know she had. Together they sat, gave thanks, and ate in grateful silence. Even Robbie perked up enough to eat a big piece of corn bread and half of Lilac's squirrel before falling soundly asleep in Forsythia's arms. Exhausted, poor little man.

Lark set aside her plate and leaned her head against the wagon, suddenly too tired to hold it up. *Lord . . .* She was asleep before she finished the prayer.

"Lark?" Lilac's hand on Lark's shoulder startled her awake a while later.

She raised her head, blinking.

"Sorry." Her little sister sat down beside her. "I was thinking maybe some music would lift everyone's spirits. All right if Del and I invite folks to our fire tonight? I'll ask Mr. Hayes."

"Sure." Lark rubbed her stiff neck. Leave it to Lilac.

The sisters had started preparing supper when Mr. Hayes walked up. "Do you folks have a few minutes we can talk?"

"Of course, but can we talk and fix supper at the same time?"

Del's smile could welcome any stranger, let alone a person she had already met.

Lark turned from splitting wood from a dead tree they had downed and cut with the crosscut saw. Anders had insisted they needed one and hung it over hooks on the outside of the wagon. That saw had become mighty popular. "How can we help you?"

"It's about the Durham wagon." Hayes tipped back his flat-brimmed hat. "I know you were traveling together, but with both the mister and missus gone . . ."

Forsythia spoke up. "Before she died, Alice asked if we would care for Robbie. I guess she knew her husband's weakness. I told her we would."

Hayes nodded. "I see. So, then, you should have the wagon and supplies to help care for the boy." He looked to Lark, who nodded.

"I—we figured that when we get to where we're going, we'll try to contact members of their families."

"I planned to search through a box Alice mentioned in the hope there are some names and addresses there," Forsythia added. "I know their family Bible is in that box. She asked me to read from it often. That's a place to start."

Hayes slapped his knees and nodded as he stood. "Good, glad to hear that. You might get some questions or complaints from others, but as far as I'm concerned, the matter is closed."

"Thank you."

After supper, a small group gathered around their campfire. With the familiar feel of the mouth organ in her hands, Lark harmonized to her sisters' playing. They started with Robbie's favorite, "Oh! Susanna."

Voices joined in from the circle, some tapping their feet. Lilac smiled across her fiddle, and Lark nodded at her sister. They played a few more folk tunes, and then Forsythia picked a quieter melody and started to sing.

"Come, thou Fount of every blessing,
Tune my heart to sing thy grace;
Streams of mercy, never ceasing,
Call for songs of loudest praise."

More voices joined from surrounding wagons. Folks came to stand close, mothers holding small sleepy children, fathers' impatient faces softened by the music.

Lark closed her eyes, something unwinding in her middle as she played.

"Here I raise my Ebenezer;
Hither by thy help I've come;
And I hope, by thy good pleasure,
Safely to arrive at home."

Hither by thy help we've come indeed, dear Lord. Guide us through the rest of the way. And please, let today's grave be the last for a good long while.

16

It sure was pleasant sitting around a fire, surrounded by friendly faces.

Adam Brownsville took the cup of coffee Forsythia held out to him with a nod of thanks. *Miss Nielsen*, he should say, even in his head. Yet she had quickly become Forsythia to him. How had that happened? He stroked his beard, once a dark rich brown like his hair but now shot with silver, a habit he had when pondering. His right leg, wounded in the war, ached something fierce at times, and he hated to spend his meager collection of medications on himself. Perhaps the Nielsens had an herbal remedy in their stores.

Clark, the older brother, had invited him and Jesse to join them for supper tonight after a long day on the road. Mr. Hayes had pushed the train harder to try to make up for the lost time, and a weary haze hung over the darkened campground.

Here, though, in the Nielsen circle, he felt the first lifting of his spirits since he'd laid his Elizabeth in the ground. Could that only have been a few weeks past? It felt like a lifetime ago. Yet sometimes he still woke in the darkness, reaching for her beside him, and the pall of grief took his breath once more.

"How did you learn to carve like that, Jesse?" Lilac, the youngest Nielsen sister, drew little Robbie onto her lap. Together they examined his nephew's latest creation—a rooster or duck, from what he could see.

"One of m-my other uncles." Jesse ducked his head and fiddled with his pocketknife. "I l-lived with him before Uncle Adam, till he p-passed on."

"Well, you are certainly gifted." Clark picked up the cow and studied the detail. "You might sell these for good money someday."

"You th-think?" A shy grin crept over Jesse's face.

Adam's chest warmed. The poor boy had known a rough life. This journey would be a good new start for him, please God. Even if not the fresh start he had hoped for himself and Elizabeth.

"That was a mighty fine supper, ladies." Adam held out his empty bowl as another of the sisters—Delphinium—collected the dishes. "Best venison stew I've had in a long time."

"Where did you grow up, Doctor?" Forsythia sat down and clasped her hands around her knees. Her golden hair caught glimmers of the firelight.

"Illinois." He sipped his coffee, savoring the hot brew. "Lived there all my life till now, except for medical school, and had a practice of my own. Then I was conscripted into the Union army, but thank God I was wounded and sent home. The war ended not long after that."

"What started you west?" Clark asked.

"My wife, Elizabeth." He hesitated, warming his hands around the tin cup. "Her lungs had been weak since childhood, and she was getting worse. We thought the air out west might help—that it was a chance for her. But she took a cold not long after we left home, and it turned to pneumonia. We made it to a boardinghouse in Independence, and I tried to treat her there. But her lungs . . . I suppose they were just too damaged."

Silence fell around the campfire.

"Sorry." Adam cleared his throat and attempted a smile. "Didn't mean to bring everyone's spirits down."

"No." Forsythia's voice came tenderly with compassion. "Thank you for sharing with us."

"We're so sorry for your loss." Lilac hugged Robbie. "It seems like there's been too much of that lately."

She was so right, and somehow they had managed to be caught in the middle of it all.

"You folks certainly have a gift for music." He tried to lighten the mood. "That gathering last night was something. Have you always played together?"

"As long as we can remember." Clark stirred the fire. "Our ma always said music was good for the soul."

"That it is."

"So where are you headed? Oregon?" Lilac cuddled Robbie as he sleepily shifted in her lap.

"California was our plan. Better climate for my wife. Now . . . I don't know. Still heading there, I suppose. I've left everything of my old life behind, and doctors are in demand wherever one goes, fortunately—or unfortunately."

"We'll be leaving you in Nebraska, then." That was Delphinium. "Our oldest brother has told us of some homestead land for sale there."

"I've heard there's good farming in that country." Nebraska— there was an idea. Maybe he and Jesse didn't have to go all the way to California after all.

Two wagons sure were a lot more difficult to manage than one.

Striding along beside their oxen, Lark wiped her forehead with her sleeve and sighed at Del's holler for help from the wagon ahead. The Durhams' span was giving her trouble again.

Lark called for Lilac to take over beside Sam and Sadie and jogged up to help. The oxen tossed their heads and bellowed beneath the yokes.

"Settle down, now." Lark smacked the near ox on the rump. "Behave yourselves."

"I guess they miss Thomas." Del cracked the whip and shouted sternly. "Hup!" The oxen lurched forward but still shook their horned heads in protest.

"We should check their yokes tonight, make sure nothing is rubbing their necks." Lark swatted at a fly. "Who knows how well Thomas was keeping things up at the end."

"Good idea."

Forsythia peeked out the front of the Durhams' wagon. "Settled them down?"

"I think so. What are you up to?"

"Robbie's napping on his ma's quilt. I'm looking through the box where she had their Bible, seeing if there are any papers that will tell us about their family."

"Find anything?"

"Just a letter with the address of a great-aunt so far. I doubt she would take Robbie, but we can write to her and ask if she knows of anyone else with a claim."

With the oxen settled down for now, Lark headed back to their wagon and untied Starbright from walking behind.

"Want a little exercise, girl?" She swung up onto the mare's back, scanning the prairie surrounding them. It would be time for another hunting party soon.

"Still hassling with that dead man's oxen?" Otis Bane called, flicking his own whip. His voice grated on her nerves. Too bad he had to have the wagon right behind theirs.

"They're just getting used to new handlers."

"You'd better not slow us up none. It's bad enough Hayes won't let us travel on Sundays. I've been talking with some of the other men, and we agree it's a fool shame to waste one day out of every week."

Lark tipped her hat to the man's sour-faced wife, Louise, on the wagon seat and nudged Starbright with her heels. She trotted out of earshot of the man's complaints, riding alongside the wagon train. *Lord, I know you want us to love all people, but some of them sure do try the soul. No wonder his wife looks like she's perpetually sucking on a lemon.*

They ate supper that night with Martin, Thelma, and their daughter, who were quickly becoming good friends. After eating, Robbie and Sarah made a barn for their animals under the wagon.

"It's so nice for her to have a friend." Thelma collected the dishes.

"For Robbie too." Lark sipped her coffee.

A bellow of pain cut across the camp.

Lark dropped her cup and stood. What in the world?

"Help—please, someone help!" A woman's cry this time, and not far—the Banes' wagon behind them?

Lark and Del rushed over.

"His leg." Louise bent over her husband. Otis lay groaning on the ground, clutching his thigh. "He was chopping wood, and the axe missed."

Even with only firelight, Lark could see blood streaming onto the ground. She yanked off her belt. "Del, give me your kerchief." They had to slow the bleeding, or Otis would bleed to death right here. "Louise, go for the doctor."

Fretting, his wife hurried off.

Lark wrapped Del's kerchief around the wound and cinched her belt tight above it.

Otis swore. "Tryin' to cut my leg off?"

"Trying to save it."

The doctor arrived, and Lark stepped back as Martin ran up too.

"Quick thinking with the tourniquet," Dr. Brownsville said after a brief examination. "Let's move him over by the fire, and I need light, several lanterns at least. The wound will need stitching once we stanch the bleeding. Mrs. Bane, do you have flour?"

The small woman nodded and hurried to her stores.

"And Clark—" the doctor hesitated— "might your sister Forsythia be willing to assist me? She was very skilled with Mrs. Durham."

Lark nodded. "I'm sure she will."

Together she, the doctor, and Martin hauled Otis onto a blanket by the fire, him fussing and cussing all the way. Then Lark fetched Forsythia while Martin collected lanterns.

"Good." The doctor nodded, satisfied when they had assembled four lanterns around the leg. "Now, Miss Nielsen, if you will help me clean the wound, please. I'm going to loosen the belt."

Blood spurted as soon as he removed the tourniquet, but he and Forsythia worked well together, quickly cleaning the wound and stanching it with flour despite Otis's groans and protests.

"Now, Mr. Bane, we're going to stitch up your leg. Clark, would you help Forsythia hold him steady?"

"Tarnation. Can't a man get a lick of whiskey first?" Otis growled.

The doctor sighed. "There's some medicinal brandy in my bag, Miss Nielsen."

Despite the swig of liquor Forsythia brought, Otis hollered plenty through the stitching. Practically lying on the man's ankles to hold him down, Lark shook her head. Some men could be such babies. She guessed that was why God gave childbearing to the womenfolk.

"Quite a character, isn't he?" Martin said as they parted ways once Otis was snoring in his wagon.

"That's one way to put it. 'Night." Lark nodded, and she and Forsythia headed for their bedrolls.

"Never a dull moment, is there?" Forsythia yawned and slid her arm through Lark's. "Maybe tonight we'll actually get a decent night's sleep."

If only.

The next day, after checking the oxen carefully for any tender spots, Lark took a turn driving the Durhams' team. They seemed calmer, adjusting to the new routine, new masters. *Thank you, Lord.* She drew a long breath, trying not to inhale too much dust.

"Indians!" The cry passed along the wagon train. "Behind us."

Lark twisted her head to look. Sure enough, a small group of figures on horseback had just crested a grassy knoll behind them. Her scalp prickled, but more from fear or intrigue, she wasn't certain.

"What do we do?" Forsythia called from driving their own oxen.

"Wait for Mr. Hayes, I guess." Lark looked back again. Already the riders were closer.

A few moments later, Mr. Hayes came riding up. "Circle the wagons."

Her heart pounding, Lark brought the oxen around as Forsythia did the same with her spans. Quicker than she would have thought, the wagons formed a passable circle. She guessed their practice those early nights was paying off.

The Indian riders had come within a hundred yards now. A dozen men, some shirtless, some wearing woven hunting shirts like Little Bear's. Most had shaved heads with a slicked-back scalp lock and a few feathers.

With her sisters and Robbie tucked safely into their wagon, Lark gathered with the other men, rifle in hand.

"Get a look at them," John Manning said. "Would make good target practice." He cocked his firearm and sighted through it.

"Enough. There'll be no shooting today, please God and if I can help it." Hayes leveled a glare at Manning, who lowered his rifle. "They look to be Pawnee. Little Bear is going to talk to them. Most likely they just want food or to trade."

"Trade for what? Our women?" Grumbling and murmurs spread among the men till another glare from the wagon master made them subside.

Hayes nodded at Little Bear, who approached the group of riders. He communicated with them in a mixture of spoken and sign language, from what Lark could tell. The riders consulted with each other, then handed something to Little Bear. He strode back to the circle of wagons.

"They want food. And guns."

"Guns? They think we'll arm them just so they can shoot us and take our scalps?" The murmuring rose louder this time.

"And what food? We need all the provisions we got just to make it to Oregon."

Little Bear held up his hand. "In return, they offer these." He held out an elaborate belt of intricate red-and-blue beadwork.

"What are we supposed to do with that?" That was Manning again.

"Can't eat fancy beadwork."

Hayes raised both hands for silence. "We've got to give them something, folks. We want to keep this friendly."

"They also like that mare." Little Bear inclined his head at Starbright.

"No." Lark's throat squeezed. *Please, Lord.* "She's the only horse we've got. Won't they take anything else?"

Little Bear met her gaze, then nodded. "I will speak to them."

"All right, what provisions can we spare?" Hayes surveyed the group. "Anyone got an extra sack of flour? Side of bacon? Milk cow?"

Some men averted their eyes. Others reluctantly headed to their wagons.

Lark hurried to her family. Between their wagon and the Durhams', surely there was something they could spare. Del helped her dig through their stores. They found a bag of beans in the Durhams' wagon, and a sack of cornmeal and one of salt from theirs.

She hauled the goods over and added them to the growing pile outside the circle of wagons. Not every family had contributed, but hopefully it would do.

Little Bear approached the group again. The men's voices rose louder this time, and by their gestures, they weren't happy.

Lark's stomach tensed. She tightened her grip on her rifle. *Please, Lord, let this not end in bloodshed. On either side.*

Their Pawnee guide came back. "They still want a horse. Or a cow."

The men shook their heads, shifted their feet. "Let 'em fight for it."

"Quiet, you fools." Hayes's patience was drawing thin. "Nielsen, if you won't spare the horse, what about an ox?"

"We need them, sir, to pull our wagon. Unless . . ." Could just one ox pull the Durhams' wagon with no one riding in it? Perhaps some of the belongings could be emptied out and left behind to lighten the load further. "What if we gave them one from the Durhams' wagon?"

The wagon master nodded. "Do it."

Lark ran to the wagons as Little Bear went back to make the proposal. She explained the situation to her sisters, and Forsythia and Lilac helped her unyoke the ox while Del held a confused Robbie.

Little Bear appeared beside her. "They will take that."

Lark nodded, fighting resentment. They could manage, but any loss of animals was a huge one. She didn't like the other men's attitudes toward the Indians, but it did seem an unfair exchange for a few pieces of beadwork. But for everyone's safety . . .

Little Bear helped her lead the ox over to the band of Pawnee. Two men dismounted to receive the bellowing animal being dragged away from the others. They patted the animal over, smiled, and nodded. The other Indians collected the gathered provisions and handed their beaded items to Hayes.

One young man handed an intricately decorated purse directly to Lark, with a gesture she didn't understand. She glanced at Little Bear.

"For you, he says."

Shock coursed through her at the feminine gift. Did he . . . ? She looked up at the smiling young Indian.

"For your woman," Little Bear continued.

Oh. Her scalp heating, Lark nodded her thanks.

The band rode away, horses laden with goods, the ox trailing behind.

Lark watched them go with a mingling of relief and heaviness in her chest.

"Thank you." Little Bear walked alongside her as they returned to the wagons.

"Didn't seem I had much of a choice." Lark glanced back at the riders disappearing over the prairie. "Those were your people?"

"Different band. They are South Band. I am Skiri. But we're all what you call Pawnee."

"So that was why you needed sign language to understand them?"

He tipped his head. "Some. Our languages are similar, but not quite the same. But they need food. That is the same."

Lark frowned. "Your people are short on food?" For the first time, she thought about how thin the bare chests and shoulders of some of the men had been.

"We used to eat buffalo. Now many are moving west because of the settlers. My family is on a reservation in Nebraska. The government is supposed to give us food, but it doesn't always come. We need to go west to find the buffalo but cannot leave the reservation."

"Oh." She'd never heard Little Bear talk so much. "Is that why you work as a trail guide? To help your family?"

He inclined his head in acknowledgement, then hurried off at a call from Hayes.

Lark slung her rifle over her shoulder and headed back to her own family. They might have lost the ox, but she'd learned a bit. And maybe made a friend.

Heading to a nearby stream to draw water after they made camp that night, Lark passed a small knot of men gathered around Otis Bane, who sat on his wagon seat with his injured leg on a pillow. Though he'd missed all the excitement today, he seemed full of opinions, as usual.

"I say Hayes doesn't know what's best for this wagon train," Otis was saying. "You can't just give Indians whatever they ask for. What if they ask for our women and children next?"

"And we've already lost far too much time." Manning leaned in. "Tomorrow's Sunday, so you know what that means."

"That's what I'm saying. A whole 'nother day we could be on the trail." Otis raised his voice as Lark passed. "And a good ox, eh, young fella?"

Lugging her buckets, she ignored him. She hated the sense of unrest that hung over the camp. What would Hayes do about it? What *could* he do?

The next morning, families gathered in the sunshine for the worship service. Sitting beside her sisters near the front, Lark breathed in the sweet scent of dew on grass. A meadowlark warbled nearby, singing its song of praise even as the Nielsen sisters tuned their instruments.

"Let's begin with 'Fairest Lord Jesus.'" Forsythia strummed a chord.

At first only their family's voices raised in song, but little by little, more joined in, swelling the sound into a chorus.

> "Beautiful Savior! Lord of all the nations!
> Son of God and Son of Man!
> Glory and honor, praise, adoration,
> Now and forever more be thine."

The darkness and heaviness over the wagon train lifted away under the beam of sunshine and praise.

Thank you, Lord. Lark closed her eyes. *Maybe we're going to make it after all. If Mr. Hayes can shut down the complainers.*

17

Somewhere they had crossed into Nebraska. Forsythia hupped the oxen, taking her turn at droving. Her sunbonnet flapped against her face in the hot prairie wind. They were making progress toward the land that would be their new home.

Anders had sent the same letter to Topeka that he had to Independence, wanting to make sure they received it. He'd included the address of the attorney he wanted them to meet in Salton, with instructions for Lark to see him when they arrived. But there was no further word of that awful gambler, Ringwald, nor of Deacon Wiesel. *Thank you, Lord.*

"Guess what." Lilac came riding up on Starbright, her hair windblown, and slid off the horse. Her eyes sparkled with excitement. "Little Bear just sighted a small herd of buffalo ahead."

"Really?" Forsythia craned her neck to try to see around the wagon train, but the billowing clouds of dust blocked her vision. "What will we do?"

"Mr. Hayes says we'll stop till it passes. Some of the men are trying to get him to let them shoot a couple, but he says no, we're not prepared for a proper hunt." Lilac pushed back her sunbonnet. "I just want to catch a glimpse of them up close if I can."

"That would be something, all right." As the wagons ahead of her rolled to a stop, Forsythia flicked her whip to halt the oxen. "Whoa."

"What's going on?" Del called from driving the Durhams' ox behind them. They'd decided to switch positions so the Nielsen wagon drove ahead of the other.

"Buffalo." Lilac led Starbright back to explain to Del.

Lark strode up. "Want to go see the herd?"

"I know Lilac wants to." As a distant rumble reached their ears, Forsythia's stomach fluttered with excitement despite herself. "But I should stay with the oxen."

"You girls go ahead. I'll stay with the animals." Lark smiled, her dark eyes full of big-sister generosity. "Never know if you'll encounter a sight like this again."

Del didn't care, so Forsythia and Lilac hurried to the front of the wagon train, hand in hand, lifting their skirts as they ran. The ground shook now with the thunder of the approaching herd.

They pushed their way into the crowd of travelers at the front of the train, everyone jostling for a view.

"Look." Lilac pressed Forsythia's fingers. "Aren't they something?"

Above the din of their hooves, the huge dark heads and shoulders of the beasts rose amid clouds of dust like moving mountains in mist. They tossed their wooly heads and snorted, but thankfully kept their thundering path across the trail, not toward the wagons.

Forsythia squeezed back and nodded. *Lord, thy creation never ceases to amaze.*

A small herd, Lilac had said, yet it seemed to go on and on— the choking dust, the pounding hooves, the majestic animals— Forsythia even glimpsed a calf or two.

As the last of the buffalo passed, a man suddenly rode out on horseback toward the stragglers near the end. Raising his rifle, he aimed and shot. One buffalo stumbled, then wheeled dazedly. Catching sight of the rider, it paused, then shook its massive head and charged toward him.

Mr. Hayes gave a shout. The horse under the rider—Forsythia could see it was John Manning—danced frantically in place, the man fighting to get it to turn, to get away. The wagon master swung up on his own mount and rode toward the wounded animal, shouting, but he was too far—another instant and the buffalo would reach Manning.

Then the wooly beast roared and toppled to the side. Another quiver and it lay still, two arrows sticking from behind its shoulder.

From atop his horse on the other side, Little Bear lowered his bow.

Forsythia gasped out a breath she didn't know she'd held. *Thank you, Lord.* Lilac clung to her arm. They'd no great love for John Manning, but nor did they want to see him and his poor horse gored to death before their eyes.

Manning was now getting the talking-to of his life from the wagon master. Meanwhile, Little Bear dismounted and led his horse to the fallen buffalo. He knelt quietly for a moment, then began to skin the carcass.

Mr. Hayes returned to the wagon train. "And that, ladies and gentlemen, is why I said no shooting." He glared at the assembled crowd. "Thinking you can shoot into a herd of these creatures without proper know-how is as dangerous as poking a rattler. But since this foolishness didn't end in tragedy, thanks to our guide, let me have a few volunteers to help skin and gut the animal. We'll divide the meat among the wagons and have steak tonight."

A few tentative cheers.

Still a bit shaken, Forsythia and Lilac made their way back to their wagons.

Lark met them, but when they poured out the story, she just nodded and held up a hand, her brow furrowed.

"While we were stopped, Jesse spotted some buzzards circling off to the side of the trail. I'm going to see if anything needs tending to." Lark swung up on Starbright.

Sobered, Forsythia nodded and watched her sister ride off. Her brother, to anyone else watching. Lark filled the role faithfully, and it seemed no one suspected any differently. So far.

A few minutes later, Lark came loping back and slid off Starbright almost before she stopped.

"About a mile away there's a wagon broken down. Father dead, mother close to it. Two little children—you'd better go get the doctor. It's a good thing the train is still stopped."

Forsythia ran, lifting her skirts to her ankles.

"Dr. Brownsville?"

He looked up from checking his oxen's hooves. "What's wrong?"

"Clark found a family that needs help. Their wagon broke down off the trail—it's those buzzards Jesse saw."

He set his pick aside and reached inside the wagon for his bag. "I'm coming."

Forsythia was out of breath by the time they reached the broken-down wagon, the doctor striding ahead. She could smell the stench of death and sickness even before she saw the poor man's body lying under the wagon, flies buzzing like smaller versions of the buzzards overhead. No oxen or horses—they must have been cut loose or run off.

A small child's whimper came from inside the covered wagon.

"Go ahead." Doctor Brownsville inclined his head. "I don't want to frighten the woman."

"Hello?" Forsythia lifted the canvas flap aside. "We've come to help you." She climbed up.

Sunlight streamed over a thin mother lying amid barrels and bundles. A newborn baby squalled at her breast, wrapped in a soiled blanket. A little girl, perhaps two years old, stared at Forsythia with big blue eyes swimming in tears.

"Thank . . . heaven." The mother gave an exhausted sob. "Answered . . . prayers."

Forsythia pushed aside more filthy bedding to reach the woman and her children. This woman had not only given birth but been ill, by the look and smell—perhaps dysentery like Alice? Or worse, given her husband's passing. *Oh, Lord, what are we dealing with here?*

"A doctor is here to tend you. May he come in?"

"Of course." The woman waved her hand weakly.

Forsythia scrambled down to make room for the doctor. "Careful, it's a mess."

He climbed into the wagon. "Dr. Brownsville, ma'am."

"Lena . . . Olsen. Thank God you have come."

Olsen? Forsythia perked up her ears. The name sounded Norwegian. She'd wondered from the woman's accent, faint though it was.

"Miss Nielsen?"

She peeked into the wagon.

"Would you take her, please?" The doctor handed the toddler out to her.

"Here, little one." She smoothed the little girl's tangled blond hair. Her skinny little legs clung to Forsythia's waist. When had the child last eaten?

"How long since your husband passed, Mrs. Olsen?" The doctor listened to her chest and felt her forehead, looked into her sunken eyes.

"Two, three days . . . not sure. He died the night before . . .

this one was born." Her voice trembled, and she lifted a shaky hand to her newborn's head.

"Were his symptoms the same as yours? Diarrhea, vomiting?"

A faint nod.

"We need to get some liquids into you. You're very dehydrated." The doctor lifted the baby, who wailed afresh. "Has he nursed?"

"Some . . . don't have much milk."

"We'll take care of your children. Don't worry." The doctor climbed out of the wagon, the infant in his arms.

"What do you think?" Forsythia jiggled the little girl.

"She's extremely weak. Heart rate rapid, dehydrated. We'll do what we can, but she may not make it."

"What do you think it is?"

"The symptoms could be many things—bad food or water, dysentery. Or cholera, but I don't want to think that yet. She's weak from childbirth too."

Forsythia swallowed. The cholera epidemics of recent decades were still fresh in everyone's minds. "Why don't I take the little girl back to camp and fetch some water?"

"Good."

At a sudden thrashing from within the wagon, they both turned.

"Oh no." The doctor thrust the baby into Forsythia's free arm and hauled himself back into the wagon.

"What is it?" Juggling both children, Forsythia strained to see.

"She's convulsing. Must be the dehydration." The doctor tried to hold the woman down. "Mrs. Olsen, we're here, I've got you. God help her."

A few more moments of thrashing, then the woman lay still.

"Is she . . . ?"

"Still breathing, but barely." Dr. Brownsville blew out a sigh. "I don't know what else to—"

"My babies?" Lena Olsen opened her eyes.

"Bring them." The doctor beckoned.

Forsythia passed the little girl up to him, then climbed up herself with the baby boy.

"Sofie. And little . . . Mikael." The mother tried to lift her head but couldn't. Instead, she met Forsythia's eyes with a fierceness that went to her heart. "Take care of them . . . for me."

Dear Lord, was this really happening again? Forsythia nodded, unable to force words past the lump in her throat.

Lena closed her eyes and breathed her last. The doctor bowed his head.

"Mama!" Sofie reached for her mother and started to cry.

Numb, Forsythia cradled little Mikael, who had mercifully fallen asleep. *Father, what do we do now?*

In a daze, she and the doctor got the children back to camp, sending Lark, Jesse, and Martin back to bury the bodies as quickly as possible. With the buffalo herd passed and the meat distributed, folks were eager to get moving again. Meanwhile, Del and Lilac helped Forsythia bathe the children and get some food into their bellies.

The doctor examined them, making a game of his stethoscope with little Sofie and looking over tiny Mikael, who still had his umbilical stump.

"Are they all right?" Forsythia pulled an old nightshirt of Robbie's over Sofie's small blond head.

"Seem to be, other than hungry and dehydrated." The doctor handed the newborn over to Del. "I don't see any signs of infection or illness."

Forsythia breathed a sigh of relief. The doctor passed a hand over his face and beard, a habit she'd noticed when he was weary. He'd certainly had cause to be weary of late.

Lark returned. "We decided to burn the wagon, just to be safe, since we don't know what they had. We'll start up again now, Hayes says. Try to make a few more miles before dark. Folks are impatient."

Dr. Brownsville stood. "I hate to ask it of you on top of Robbie, but do you think you can take the children? At least for now?"

What choice do we have? They have to be taken care of. Forsythia looked to Lark. Her older sister hesitated, gave her a hopeless look, then nodded. "We'll have to find some milk for the little one somehow."

Martin walked back from their wagon. "Hayes is calling a meeting of all the men tonight to try to iron out some of the ill feeling lately. Maybe you can find another family willing to take the children." He held out a pail. "Our cow is going dry, as she's with calf, but here's a little milk to get him started." He nodded at the baby.

"Bless you." Forsythia took the pail. What a gift these friends were.

"We can ask about other milk cows tonight too. I know there's one three wagons ahead with the family who shared milk when Alice Durham was ill, but I don't know how much they can spare." Lark wiped her forehead with her sleeve. "We'd better get the little ones in the wagon. I'm going to start up." She nodded at the wagons ahead beginning to roll.

Dr. Brownsville turned to head back to his wagon, but Forsythia stopped him. "It's been one thing after another lately. Are you all right?"

He smiled, though it didn't reach his eyes. "We go where needed, don't we?"

"You are a godsend to this train, that is certain."

He pressed her hand ever so briefly. "As are you."

Adam Brownsville could smell the tension in the air that evening as soon as he arrived at the meeting.

The men had gathered near Hayes's wagon, the area lit by lanterns hung along its side. A small folding table sat near the wheel, and Little Bear leaned off to the side. Many of the men murmured among themselves, Otis Bane's strident tones easy to pick out above the rest. John Manning's too.

Clark Nielsen approached, and Adam made room beside himself. Though at times something about the young man bothered Adam, Clark and his family were the closest thing to friends Adam had so far in this group. And it wasn't like he could put his finger on anything specific.

"I've never had such a cantankerous train," Hayes muttered near the doctor's shoulder, making his way through the crowd.

Adam stepped aside, offering a look of empathy.

Hayes strode to the front and slapped a piece of paper down on the table. "Meeting come to order." He planted his feet and stared around the group, the men's voices gradually quieting. "It has come to my attention that certain of you have some disagreement with the way I've been handling things. If you've got anything to say, the time is now."

Silence reigned for a moment, but then Otis hobbled forward, nudged on by Manning and a few other men.

"Well, sir, I do have something to say. And I'm not the only one who thinks it."

"And that is?"

Otis looked at his followers for support. "We think you've been making some mighty bad decisions of late. Panderin' to the Indians. Takin' time off from being on the trail for, well, unnecessary reasons. Keepin' us from organizin' a proper buffalo hunt when the opportunity presented itself. Even wastin' a whole day every week when we could be makin' tracks for that promised land."

The wagon master shifted his jaw. "Is that all?"

Otis looked over his shoulder again, then back. "Ain't it enough?"

"Good. Thank you for stating your opinion."

A bit nonplussed, Otis hobbled back to his spot.

"I have listened to your grievances, and now I ask you to listen to me." Hayes raised the paper in the air. "This here document was signed by all of you some weeks ago when we started out on the trail. You all agreed, freely and of your own accord, to be bound by these rules and guidelines all the way to Oregon or however far you stay with the train. I am now going to read these articles aloud once more, as it seems some of us have mighty short memories."

The men stood silent as Hayes read the entire document, then looked around the group once more.

"Let me repeat a few things. I am the wagon master. What I say goes. You may not always agree, but I didn't take on this position without being over this trail a heap of times. I may not always know what's best, but I know a sight more than you do. We stop when I stop, and we go when I go. And about Sundays, you all signed your names to this document that you'd honor the Sabbath and our God, whether you believe in Him or not." He flattened the paper. "Your teams need that day of rest even more than you do. Your oxen can't pull your wagons if they're worked half to death. And we're not going to make it to Oregon unless we can start pulling together as a team. This is the last gripin' and bellyachin' that I want to hear till we reach Willamette Valley. Any questions?"

Silence. Hanging heads.

"Good." Hayes straightened with a sigh. "Dismissed."

Adam raised his hand. "Mr. Hayes, if I could?"

"Yes, Doctor?"

"As you may know, we found two orphaned children on the trail today. Clark Nielsen and his sisters have graciously taken them in for now, but they have already taken on the Durhams' son and wagon after the parents passed. I was wondering if any other family might be willing to open their hearts to these little ones."

"How old are the children?" someone asked.

"A newborn boy and a girl about two."

Several shaking heads. Other men looked away.

The doctor bit the inside of his cheek. No one? "Could anyone wet-nurse the infant?"

Nothing.

"Guess that's your answer," Hayes said. "Sorry, Doc."

"One more thing, then." Adam cleared his throat. "Would anyone have an extra milk cow to spare? Or at least be willing to share some milk? The baby needs it urgently."

Clark shot him a grateful look.

A middle-aged man raised his hand. "We might."

"All right, then." Hayes nodded. "Get some sleep, folks. We move out at first light."

Adam followed Clark to speak to the gentleman with the cow.

"Josiah Hobson." He shook the young man's hand, then the doctor's. He looked at Clark. "We've got two milk cows along. We've got seven kids, so we need 'em. But I guess we could spare one for a while. Want to take her over to your wagon?"

"Can we pay you for her?" Clark asked.

"We'll figure that out later." Hobson patted the young man's shoulder. "Just come get her for the little'un."

"Thanks." Clark followed the man with a grateful nod to the doctor.

Thank you, Father. Adam headed back to his wagon and Jesse, grief and gratitude warring in his weary mind. *At least there is some kindness left in this world.*

But all these orphaned little ones. What would become of them?

And what was it about Clark that dug at him?

18

Forsythia couldn't get the baby to take the milk.

Cradling a screaming Mikael on the wagon seat, she set the milk-soaked rag aside and shifted the newborn to her shoulder. "Shh, little one." She patted his back. Her shoulders and neck ached with tension. *Lord, why won't he drink?*

Lark looked up from driving the oxen. "Still nothing?"

"Nearly." Forsythia fought the urge to cry.

Lark cracked the whip a bit harder than usual. "This is why taking on other people's children doesn't work. What do we know about raising babies? None of us is a mother."

"Well, we couldn't leave them there," Forsythia snapped. "Can I help it if dying mothers keep giving me their children and no one else in the train wants to be bothered?" Her throat ached. She was so tired.

Sighing, Lark turned the oxen over to Lilac and reached up for the infant. "Give him to me awhile."

"We've got to get more milk down him." Forsythia held on to Mikael. "He's only had a few teaspoons since yesterday. If he doesn't drink soon . . ." Tears of worry and exhaustion cut off her words. Between the baby's wails and poor little Sofie sobbing for her mama, she'd hardly slept last night. Her sisters were up, too, of course, but she felt a responsibility—after all, Lena Olsen had asked *her* to care for her children. Just as Alice had. *Lord, why me? I want children of my own, but I surely wouldn't have chosen this.*

"Get some sleep, Sythia." Gently but firmly, Lark took the baby and rubbed his back. His wails calmed a bit. "You're no good to him worn out like this." She met Forsythia's gaze, apology in her eyes. "Sorry for being short."

Too weary to argue, Forsythia lay down in the stuffy warmth of the canvas interior and let the wagon's jolting rock her to sleep.

She woke when they stopped for nooning and climbed out to find Lilac taking a turn with Mikael. She was trying a spoon this time to offer the fresh milk they'd drawn from Buttercup, the Hobsons' cow, that morning.

"Come on, little one. Drink." But as soon as the milk trickled down his throat, Mikael sputtered and coughed, twisting his tiny face away.

"It's like he doesn't understand what it is." Gently, Lilac poked the tin spoon between the baby's pursed lips again. "If he knew, surely he would take it."

"Or he just wants his . . . m-a-m-a," Del spelled, holding Sofie on her lap. At least the waiflike little girl was eating, taking bites of cold biscuit and bacon from Del's fingers as if she'd been starved. Which was not too far from the truth.

Several women from other wagons gathered around, offering advice and encouragement.

"Maybe try when he's sleepy," Thelma Wheeler said, reaching to smooth the baby's downy head. "Instinct might take over?"

"It doesn't always." Louise Bane shook her head, mouth pinched. "We tried to nurse my sister's young'un after she died bearin' him. He followed her within a week."

Forsythia's middle twisted at the tears that sprang into Lilac's eyes. She squeezed her little sister's shoulder. "Well, we're not going to let that happen."

Lark and Lilac joined one of the now-daily hunting parties for the afternoon, so Jesse took over driving the Durhams' oxen while Del drove theirs. As the late afternoon sun slanted over the prairie, Forsythia walked beside the wagon, Mikael sleeping on her shoulder. At least he wasn't crying, but his quietness since noon worried her. The baby seemed weaker, not moving as much, and she'd only gotten him to take a few more drops. Would he follow the dire path Mrs. Bane had predicted? *Please, Lord, no.*

"Miss Nielsen?"

Forsythia squinted against the sun. A young woman she'd only seen across camp approached, her hand shielding her eyes. Her red hair caught the setting sun.

"I'm Maggie O'Malley. I hear you're havin' trouble gettin' milk down the wee one." She nodded to Mikael. "I was wonderin'— would you let me try?"

Forsythia stared at her stupidly, too tired to compute.

A faint flush colored Maggie's fair cheeks. "I've a five-month-old baby of my own, you see. Might I take him into your wagon?"

Understanding dawned, and Forsythia nodded. "Oh, of course. Oh, thank you."

"I thought of it when me husband first told me of the foundlings you'd taken in. But I didn't think I'd have enough milk for both babes, not all the time, and I heard you'd gotten the cow. But today—well, I thought maybe I could at least help him over this rough spot." Maggie climbed into the wagon as she spoke, then unbuttoned her bodice with one hand, holding out the other for Mikael.

Forsythia laid the baby in her arms. Mikael squirmed and whimpered.

"Here, little one." Maggie held him close. "There now, you know what to do."

Forsythia sat silent, hardly daring to breathe. *Please, Lord.*

"Come now. Just take it, my love."

Mikael fussed again. And then—a faint clicking sound. Then he was suckling—and swallowing.

"Oh, thank God," Forsythia whispered, tears spilling over. "Thank you, Maggie."

Maggie cradled the newborn close, crooning snatches of an Irish lullaby. Mikael nursed on one side, and then she switched him to the other.

"Maybe," the young mother said softly, "if you brought the rag or spoon you've been tryin' now . . ."

"Of course." Forsythia scrambled out of the still-moving wagon. She grabbed the jar of milk they'd drawn at nooning and soaked the corner of a clean rag in it. Still praying, she climbed back up in the wagon.

"He's sleepy but still nursing." Gently, Maggie unlatched Mikael, who wailed a protest.

Into the open little mouth, Forsythia slipped the milky rag. Mikael opened his eyes in astonishment at first, then closed his mouth and sucked the rag.

"Oh, thank you, Father." Forsythia dipped the rag again and again, Mikael sucking for another good fifteen minutes. Then he fell asleep, his head pillowed on Maggie's calico sleeve.

"He just needed to remember how." Maggie brushed the baby's downy smudge of hair with a gentle finger. "Didn't you, darlin'?"

"We can't thank you enough." Forsythia sat back, weak with gratitude. "Truly."

"Just let me know if he needs a little boost now and then, aye?" Maggie handed the baby back and rebuttoned her bodice. "But I think you might be over the worst of it."

The wagons circled at sunset, and Lark and Lilac returned with a brace of prairie chickens and a fat jackrabbit.

"We saw buffalo again, but too far away." Lilac's eyes sparkled with excitement. "Little Bear says he'll try to organize a real hunt soon, though. How is the baby?"

"So much better." Forsythia laid a sleeping Mikael in Lilac's eager arms. "Thanks to Maggie O'Malley."

"Maggie who?"

Forsythia explained while Del cooked the prairie chickens, frying one and stewing another for a rich broth. They invited the doctor and Jesse to eat with them.

"We're beholden to you folks for all the meals you've been giving us." Dr. Brownsville scraped a spoon around his bowl and then wiped his beard. "Not that I'm complaining."

"Goodness, Doctor, it's this train that's beholden to you." Del held up the ladle. "More stew, anyone?"

"Me." Robbie held out his tin plate.

"What do you say?" Del cocked her head.

Robbie scrunched up his face. "Please." Sofie sat beside him on the ground, gnawing a drumstick held tight in her tiny hands. Robbie glanced at her. "And Sofie and me need more biscuits."

"Sofie and I." But Forsythia smiled and handed each child a fresh one.

The two children had regarded each other dubiously at first, but now they seemed to be making friends. She'd seen Robbie sharing his carved animals with Sofie earlier, now numbering a horse, a cow, a sheep, a rooster, and a goat, thanks to Jesse's skillful hands.

The baby whimpered, and Forsythia went to fetch him from the makeshift bed they had fashioned in the back of the wagon. Lilac warmed milk from the evening milking, and Forsythia sat to feed him, using a spoon this time. He coughed at first but then slurped eagerly, his tiny pink tongue lapping like a kitten's.

"That's a blessed sight to see." Dr. Brownsville knelt beside them and laid a gentle hand on Mikael's stomach. "His color and hydration are better."

Forsythia dipped another spoonful. "At the rate he's going, we're going to wish we had a bottle or at least something larger than a spoon."

"You might try a small tin cup."

"I c-could make a cup."

They both turned to Jesse, who looked up shyly from his spot by the fire.

"There's a thought." The doctor patted the baby and stood. "What do you have in mind?"

"I could carve one with a little sp-spout. Easier for him to d-drink from than a big cup."

"That it would be." Forsythia smiled at the young man. "Bless you, Jesse."

They said their good-nights after washing up. Robbie and Sofie had fallen asleep where they sat, so Lilac and Del picked them up and tucked them into bed still in their clothes. Lark doused the fire and scattered the coals.

"'Night, Sythia."

"'Night." She lay down beside the baby in the wagon, heart full of gratitude. *Thank you, Father, for your faithfulness today. Thank you that Mikael is taking milk. Thank you for . . .*

She was asleep before she finished the prayer.

Saturday brought an early start and a whiny, clinging Sofie. Del took over with Mikael while Lark and Lilac drove the wagons, and Robbie went to play in Sarah's wagon.

At Lark's suggestion, Forsythia took Sofie up on Starbright with her for a while. She quieted down, gazing at everything around them with big eyes, her tiny fists clenched in the mare's mane.

"You like this, sweet one?" Forsythia smoothed the little girl's wispy fair hair, woven into two tiny braids by Del that morning. Sofie nodded and twisted her head to see a meadowlark spiraling into the sky. "That's a birdie."

"Buh-dee."

"That's right." Forsythia smiled, though the headache that had been niggling at her since she woke up was pounding harder under the sun's beating rays.

By the time she and Sofie slid down for the nooning stop, her stomach was roiling. From the motion atop the horse? Or something else?

Something else, she decided, heaving in the prairie grass behind the wagon a few moments later.

"Sythia, you all right?" Lark poked her head around the wagon.

"I hope so." She straightened and wiped her mouth, then reached for the corner of the wagon bed, dizzy. "I—maybe not." She bent over to retch again.

Del appeared. "Is she sick?"

"Looking that way."

Forsythia leaned against the wagon side. Del felt her forehead. "You feel feverish. We better get you in the wagon."

"Let's put her in the Durhams'. Keep her separate from everyone else."

Lark helped Forsythia climb up into the wagon, fixing a bed amid the sparser barrels and boxes. She lay down and tried to sleep, only to be woken by retching again.

By midafternoon, the runs had started. Forsythia tried to make it down out of the wagon to go in the prairie grasses each time, and again and again she failed. Her clothing and the bedding were quickly soiled with stench.

"I'm so sorry," she whispered to Del, coming to give her a fresh sheet yet again.

"None of that, Sythia." Her sister bundled the reeking sheet and smoothed out the fresh one. "Good thing Ma always taught us to keep plenty of clean linen, right?"

Lark came to check on her next.

"You all shouldn't keep coming in," Forsythia protested. "I might be contagious."

"You know the rest of us have sturdier constitutions than you." Lark smoothed the damp hair back from Forsythia's brow. "And you were the one who was closest to Mrs. Olsen, other than the doctor."

"The children?" She'd hardly seen Mikael all day.

"They're fine. Robbie and Sofie are playing in our wagon, and Robbie is being quite the big brother. Del and Lilac have the baby well in hand. Don't you worry about us. Just get yourself feeling better." She held a cup to Forsythia's dry lips. "See if you can sip some of this broth."

She managed several swallows, then gagged and shook her head, falling back on the pillow.

"The doctor is coming to look in on you. He would have been here sooner, but a child stepped on a hornet up the train a ways. Started to swell up."

"Oh no." Forsythia covered her eyes. "I hate for him to see me like this."

"And you care about that why?"

Forsythia moved her hands to see Lark regarding her with a meaningful quirk of brow. "I . . ." Her brain was too muddled to puzzle out an answer.

By the time Dr. Brownsville arrived, after two more bouts of vomiting, Forsythia honestly no longer cared.

He didn't like this.

Adam sat back after examining his newest patient. Forsythia

lay amid the freshly changed bedding, eyes closed, her breathing and heart rate rapid from stress and fever.

"Do you think it's dysentery?" Clark asked from just outside the wagon.

"Good chance." Adam closed up his bag. "She probably caught it from the Olsens. I'm glad you're keeping her apart. It can be terribly contagious."

"I know." Clark chewed his lip. "I got my brother out of a Confederate prison camp."

"Then you do know. What have you given her?"

"Broth, but she's started to refuse it. Warm water. Del is making some slippery-elm tea, which soothes the digestive tract."

"Good. Keep pushing the liquids, even if she tries to refuse. Dehydration is our greatest worry right now." He climbed out of the wagon. "I'll be back to check on her again."

"Doctor." Clark followed him. "Do you think it could be cholera?"

That dreaded word halted Adam's steps. Not that he hadn't thought it already.

"I don't know. The fever isn't typical for it, but it's hard to say for sure. Children are very susceptible to cholera, and they haven't gotten it, so that's a good sign."

Clark nodded, but Adam could see the worry in his face. He laid a brief hand on the young man's shoulder. "I'll do all I can for her, you know that."

"I know. I hate for her to be jostled in the wagon so much."

"Let me speak to Hayes. Perhaps he might be willing to give us an extra day of rest."

But when Adam spoke to the wagon master, Hayes shook his head. "Tomorrow's already Sunday, so you have that. But I can't hold back the train any longer. You've seen how antsy folks are. We've been delayed enough as it is."

"Even if it means putting one of our own members' health at risk?"

"I can't put one above the needs of the whole group." Hayes eyed him. "You're sure it's nothing that puts the rest of the wagons in danger?"

"We're taking every precaution." Adam could tell that answer didn't satisfy, but what more could he say?

The wagon master shook his head. "Keep me apprised."

Adam checked on Forsythia before bed and again the next morning before the Sabbath church service.

Clark, Del, Lilac, and the children joined the others for worship, yet the group seemed sparse and forlorn without Forsythia's steady presence.

Adam forced his gaze forward to the reverend rather than wandering back to the Durhams' wagon. Even when she said little, Forsythia seemed to radiate peace and a quiet strength that he found himself desperately missing. He closed his eyes but couldn't keep focused on the sermon. *Lord, please heal this precious young woman. And do whatever is needed with the place she seems to have taken up in my heart. After all, Elizabeth has been gone barely over a month. Surely this is not healthy.* Much less proper.

The Nielsens closed in song, as usual, yet without Forsythia's guitar and lovely soprano.

After the service, Adam stopped by the Nielsen wagon again. Del and Lilac were washing laundry in two kettles of hot water.

"I'm trusting Mr. Hayes will see this as necessary Sabbath breaking." Del wiped her forehead with her sleeve. "We don't have much choice, not without an endless supply of linens."

"I expect he will." Adam glanced at the wagon behind. "How is she?"

Lilac shook her head. "I gave her more slippery-elm tea, but she vomited it back up. Clark is trying some broth."

Adam met Clark coming down out of the wagon. "Any success?"

He grimaced and jumped to the ground. "Not much. She took about half of this." He held out a tin cup.

"Shall I see her?" Adam glanced up at the wagon.

"She's fallen asleep, I think. Maybe in a little while."

Adam shouldn't feel so disappointed.

After making camp that night, his evening examination sent tendrils of alarm up the doctor's spine. Forsythia was worse. Still expelling watery diarrhea, she could hardly lift her head from the pillow. Adam felt her dry, hot cheeks and looked into her eyes. She blinked back blankly.

How he missed her gentle smile.

"We'll take turns sitting with you tonight, Miss Nielsen. You won't be alone. Let me see what your sisters might have for you to drink."

He climbed out and nearly ran into Lilac, who held Sofie on her hip. "She's been crying for Sythia. Can I hold her up just to see?"

"I'm afraid not." Adam steered her back toward their campfire. "Where is your brother?"

"Chopping wood." A tremor in her voice, Lilac led the way.

Clark straightened from the pile of kindling and what scraps of log they had scrounged from along the creek bank. "How is she?"

"She's very dehydrated, I'm afraid. And weak. We've got to get more fluids into her."

"What about some peppermint tea?" Del asked. "Mama always said it soothed the stomach."

"Worth a try."

The wagon master approached out of the shadows and nodded to the group. "She well enough to travel?"

"I'm afraid not." Adam blew out a breath. "She needs at least another day of rest." Probably more, but if God was merciful, a day could make a difference.

Hayes shook his head. "'Fraid we'll have to go on without you, then."

"What?" Clark dropped a chunk of wood.

"Can't hold the train back any longer, not if we're going to make it over the Rockies before snowfall. Nor risk cholera to the other wagons, or whatever she might have." Hayes met Clark's gaze, a trace of regret in his eyes. "I'm sorry, young Nielsen. But it's what we've got to do."

Clark gripped the ax handle and glanced at his sisters, at a rare loss for words. Del had come near, too, cradling the baby, with Robbie tagging at her heels. They stood silent, dumbfounded.

Adam met Hayes's eyes. "If they are forced to leave the train, then I will leave too."

"Mighty rash of you, Doctor." The wagon master's nostrils flared. "And mighty unfair to the rest of the folks in the wagon train. You're the only doctor we've got. Better think it over."

"I have." Perhaps only for several seconds, but it had been enough. "As a doctor, I go where I am needed. And where I am needed right now is here."

"Suit yourself." Hayes spat the words, angrier than Adam had seen him yet. "And on your own head be it." He turned on his heel and strode away.

"You didn't have to do that, Doctor," Clark said at last.

"I think I did." The enormity of the decision hadn't quite sunk in yet, but of that much he was sure. Though he probably should inform Jesse. "I'll check on your sister again in the night." Nodding good night, he stepped away toward his own wagon.

"What are we going to do?" he heard Lilac whisper as he walked away.

A question too big to ponder just yet. Tonight, care for For-sythia. And in the morning, ask God what step was next.

At dawn, they woke to see the long line of wagons ahead of them start off and roll away in a cloud of dust and creaking of harnesses.

"Well, Lord, here we are. Now what?" Adam asked.

19

Lark sure had not seen this coming.

While Del and Lilac started the fire and breakfast the next morning, Lark surveyed the empty grassland around them. Three wagons alone on the prairie with four sisters—one terribly ill—three orphaned children, and a bellowing milk cow. Oh, and a doctor and his nephew. Keeping up her disguise while being thrown together with these men added yet another worry knot to her stomach.

Lark grabbed the milk pail and greeted Dr. Brownsville as he approached their campsite. "You didn't have to do this, you know. Stay here."

"Just as you didn't have to take in these children?" His smile seemed forced. "How is she?"

"We're heating some of the broth from the prairie chicken and will see if she can keep it down." Dr. Brownsville showed concern for all his patients. But was there something different in his care for Forsythia? She wasn't sure. "Feel free to check on Sythia. I've got to milk Buttercup. She's been carrying on since dawn."

Josiah Hobson had graciously agreed to let them buy the

cow for a reasonable price. At least they had milk for the baby and the children.

"Easy, girl." Lark squatted beside the cow and patted her smooth, tawny side. She grasped the teats, and warm milk hissed into the pail. Right, left, right, left. The familiar rhythm eased the tension from her back and shoulders. Lark leaned her forehead into the cow's comforting warmth. *Lord, all this didn't come as a surprise to you. But it sure did to us. Guide us, please. And heal Sythia.* Leaning back to squint at the morning-gilded sky, she put all her heart into that last bit.

Birds rose and dipped in a cloud of wings over the waving grasses as she stood, milk frothing in the pail. She patted Buttercup's side and moved her picket to a fresh grazing area. "Thanks for the good milk."

Mikael was squalling for his breakfast. Del jiggled and shushed him on her shoulder.

"Doctor checking on Sythia?" Lark set down the pail.

"Mm-hmm. Hush, little one."

Lilac dipped up a cupful of the fresh milk and carried it to Del. "Here."

"Thanks." Del poured the milk into the spouted cup Jesse had carved, which looked rather like a small wooden creamer. "This special little cup does help. But I need to figure out a way to tend Mikael and still be able to drive the oxen and do other chores, especially with Sythia ill."

"Maybe we can make you a sling out of some of Ma's fabric. Loop it around your shoulder and chest to keep him close but your hands free."

"That's a good idea."

Lark poured the rest of the milk into the freshly scoured milk can. "I think we'll only travel until we find a good campsite today, someplace with more shade, and then rest. We all need it, Forsythia most of all. Then maybe I can find a farm or something nearby where we can find out how to get to Salton. Could be we're closer than we think."

The doctor appeared from the Durhams' wagon. "Got that broth ready?"

"Here it is." Lilac ladled steaming liquid into a bowl.

"I'll take it to her." Lark took the bowl and added a spoon. "How does she seem to you, Doctor?"

He hesitated. "She's awfully weak. And dehydrated. Even if she doesn't want liquids, we'll need to try to force them today. It might help to wrap her in wet clothes too."

"Really?" Lark raised a brow. She hadn't heard that one before.

"The skin can absorb more than you might think."

Lark climbed into the wagon, balancing the bowl. "Hey, you."

Forsythia's eyelids fluttered. She tried to smile. "Hey."

"I brought you some broth." Lark laid her hand against her sister's hot, dry cheek. "Sip." She tipped the spoon against her lips.

Forsythia sipped, gagged, and turned her head away. "I can't."

"You've got to, Sythia." Lark forced away the panic that pushed up her throat. *I will trust and not be afraid.* "I know you don't want it, but it's important. Just another sip."

Forsythia managed two more spoonfuls, shuddering with the effort.

"Good girl." Lark sat back. "We'll try some water next or more tea."

Forsythia seemed to have already fallen back asleep, her face so pale it pinched Lark's heart. She climbed back down and headed to the campfire where her sisters and the doctor waited.

"She took some, but not as much as I'd like." She showed the bowl.

"We'll need to try some sort of liquid every hour," the doctor said. "She's still losing it with the diarrhea, though it's not as violent now."

Lilac looked up from fashioning a length of linen into a sling. "I'll soak a nightdress in the creek to put on her as soon as I try this on Del."

Del came near, burping little Mikael on her shoulder. "You think this will work?"

"I don't see why not. I know immigrant women wear their babies this way, and Indian women, too, I think." Lilac stood and wrapped the cloth over Del's shoulder and under her arm, holding the baby firmly in place, then tied the ends on her shoulder. "How does that feel?"

"Good." Del adjusted Mikael and tried moving about. "I don't even have to hold him in place, he's so secure. Thanks." The baby blinked from his snug new position against her chest, then yawned and settled to sleep.

Together Lark and Lilac wrapped Forsythia in the wet night-dress and added a damp sheet, forcing water down her before and after.

Weary from the ordeal, Lark hupped the oxen on their way, the doctor taking over the Durhams' ox while Jesse drove their wagon. *Lord, I never would have asked Jesse and the doctor to stay with us, but I am grateful.*

The morning sun at their backs, they headed northwest, what she hoped was the general direction of Salton. Once they found a good campsite, she'd see about actually getting there.

The sun had climbed high and started its descent before Lark spotted a clutch of trees ahead. Water. And shade.

They pulled into the grove of cottonwoods flanking a bubbling creek. Lark stopped the oxen and drew a long breath. The shade cooled her eyes from the unrelenting prairie sun, and the trees' heart-shaped leaves rustled and danced overhead.

Lilac came back from checking the creek. "The water is clear and sweet. Thick cover for deer too. Can I go hunting?"

"Sounds fine to me." Lark glanced back at the doctor, who set the brakes on the Durhams' wagon and then approached.

"Looks like a good spot." Dr. Brownsville pushed his hat back and wiped his forehead. "Thinking to stay here a few days?"

"I think so. Forsythia needs the rest—we all do, really." Weariness suddenly crashed over Lark like a summer storm. *Thank you, Lord, for this place.*

They unyoked the oxen and hobbled them to graze along with Starbright and Buttercup.

Lark checked on Forsythia again. Still weak but stable. The wet clothes seemed to be keeping her fever at bay also. She managed to get her sister to swallow a little more water and broth.

Dr. Brownsville lifted the canvas flap and peeked into the wagon. "Let me sit with her awhile. You're exhausted."

"If you're sure." Lark climbed down and surveyed their camp. Livestock peacefully grazing, Del watching the napping children on a blanket. Lilac had taken her rifle and Jesse and set off to see what game they could find.

Maybe Lark could actually lie down herself. She stretched out on the soft grass near the wagon. *"He maketh me to lie down in green pastures: he leadeth me beside the still waters. He restoreth my soul. . . ."*

She woke sometime later to Robbie and Sofie's happy chatter. Yawning, Lark sat up to find the children playing with their wooden animals on the blanket, Del watching them while feeding Mikael nearby.

"Glad you slept. You needed it." Del smiled.

"Guess so." Lark stood and stretched. "Shall I check on Sythia?"

"The doctor's still with her. He doesn't seem to want to let her out of his sight."

She had noticed. She didn't know whether to be worried or hopeful. Dr. Brownsville seemed like a good man—an excellent one, in fact. Her heart would rejoice for Sythia to find marriage and family after losing her love in the war. But he'd lost his wife so recently . . . wasn't it too soon?

Lord, one more thing to trust you with.

"Look, Sofie. The horsies can eat the grass." Robbie galloped his carved steed off the blanket and onto the surrounding meadow.

Sofie's wide-eyed gaze never left Robbie. She lifted the figure in her own tiny hand. "Cow?"

"Sure, cows can eat grass too. Come on."

Sofie crawled over and joined her cow with Robbie's horse.

"Munch, munch." Robbie exaggerated his sound effects, making a face. "Munch-munch-munch."

A delighted giggle squeaked out of Sofie.

"She adores him." Del smiled at the children. "Take the baby for me? I could use a break. And a visit to the necessary—or rather, the bushes."

Lark cradled Mikael's tiny form, warm and fragile. The baby bobbed his head against her chest. "Looking for more milk, little one? Or trying to see the view?" She lifted him to better see their surroundings. Mikael opened his deep blue eyes wide, gazing at the shifting sunlight and shadow in the dancing leaves overhead. Lark pressed a kiss to his downy head, savoring the sweet baby scent.

"Your sister's sleeping." The doctor's voice surprised her from behind.

Lark turned, her neck prickling. Would he wonder at her bestowing such a womanly kiss on the baby?

He gave her a slightly odd look but continued. "Her hydration seems better, and the diarrhea seems less—hard to tell. But we need to start getting more nourishment in her. She's terribly weak."

Robbie ran up and tugged at her trouser leg. "Mr. Clark, I need somethin' from my wagon."

She shook her head. "Sorry, Robbie. We can't let you or Sofie in there right now. Miss Sythia is sick."

"But it's my wagon." His mouth turned down. "I want to show Sofie the top Pa gave me."

"Sorry, little fellow." The doctor squatted at Robbie's level. "You'll have to wait a few days."

"But it's from my pa." Without warning, Robbie's lip trembled, and tears threatened. "I want my pa."

"I know you do, son." The doctor tried to pull Robbie into his arms, but the little boy resisted.

"I want my ma!" The tears spilled over with a vengeance.

Sofie, still sitting on the blanket, watched with wide eyes, then let out a sympathetic wail.

A hard lump in her own throat, Lark shifted the baby and bent to try to comfort Robbie, but he kicked out, arms flailing, then threw himself on the ground with a howl. Del returned and scooped up the sobbing Sofie.

"What happened?"

"Not sure—both of them went off all of a sudden. I guess grief hits in waves, even for children."

"Of course it does." Del pressed a kiss to Sofie's hair, rubbing the little girl's back.

Robbie still lay kicking and sobbing on the ground, but his cries gradually lessened. Lark bent to rub his shoulder.

"I know, Robbie. I know it hurts to lose your pa and ma." She fought tears herself. They all knew loss in this group. Maybe that was one reason God had chosen them to shelter these little ones. Even if sometimes she felt they didn't know what they were doing.

At a shout from the trees, Lark looked up and nudged Robbie. "Look, Lilac and Jesse are back. What do you think they brought?"

Sniffling, Robbie sat up, then a smile broke through his tears. "Deer?"

"Looks like it."

He swiped his fist across his eyes, then jumped up and took off running. "Lilac!"

"Hey there, Robbie boy." She slid off her horse and scooped him up. "Look what we got." She nodded to the deer slung across Jesse's saddle.

Jesse's gentle face split in a grin. "She g-got it with one shot."

Even Sofie's tears mellowed at the distraction. By the time the sun set behind the trees in a blaze of rose and gold, Lilac, Jesse, and Lark had skinned and quartered the deer. Del cooked some into broth and stew for supper, and they thinly sliced the rest to dry for jerky, winding the meat onto sticks and propping it over the coals.

"It's a good thing we'll be here a few days. The meat will take time to dry." Lilac wiped her hands. Robbie stuck close to her, not letting her out of his sight.

That night they sat around the fire, bellies full and grateful, the scent of woodsmoke and drying venison wafting over them. Jesse played animals with the children.

Del rejoined the circle. "I got Sythia to take some venison broth. Maybe tomorrow we can try a bit of stew, see if she can keep it down."

"Try boiling some rice in the broth to start," the doctor said. "Easier on her stomach."

"Good idea. Too bad we don't have a farm-raised chicken. That would be more tender than wild game."

Conversation soon faded into weariness, and the doctor and Jesse headed over to bunk down under their wagon. The sisters spread their bedrolls, and Lilac snuggled Robbie and Sofie under her blankets like two little bear cubs with their mother, her presence seeming to comfort them through the nights.

"I'll take the first watch." Lark poked the fire. Now that they lacked the protection of the whole wagon train, they'd have to take shifts again. "The doctor said he'd take the second."

"Wake me for the third, if the baby doesn't first." Yawning, Del lay down beside Mikael with a tired chuckle. "But he probably will."

Lark leaned her head back and gazed at the sparkling span of stars scattered across the black sky. Much to be thankful for, but much still uncertain. Sythia was still so weak. And tomorrow Lark would need to see if she could find a farm, maybe even a store. They needed some supplies. And where exactly was Salton, anyway? Without a known point of reference or a number of miles to calculate, her mind grappled for solid ground.

The next day after breakfast, she saddled Starbright and headed out, praying for direction. Surely if she stayed along the creek, civilization would crop up somewhere.

Riding along the trace, the grass high as Starbright's belly, her mind took off on adventures of its own, going back to the night their lives fell apart. She could still see the gambler dealing the cards and then staring at her, veins pulsing, as she gathered up the pile of winnings. His threats stayed indelibly etched on her mind. *Lord, I have no idea how he would find us so far from home, but* . . . she had no doubt he could. If that money meant so much to him. And not just the money, but his pride—far more dangerous.

She stared out across the grasses rippling in the wind that seemed always to be blowing. It wasn't the money at all, she knew. It was the horror that a woman had beaten him. Had called him out for cheating, even if not with words. Had she been a man, he might have forgiven her, but she was a woman. And to top it off, she had won fair and square. Surely the news had not gone farther than the limits of Linksburg. After all, who would spread the gossip?

An image of Deacon Wiesel plastered itself across her mind.

Good thing those two didn't know each other. Get the deacon drunk, and he would blab anything.

Lark heaved a sigh. "Only you can protect us, Lord."

Starbright flicked her ears back and forth.

Lark leaned forward and patted her neck. "All we have to do today is find a store and the directions to Salton. That's all."

A short while later she saw smoke rising in tendrils over the prairie and followed it to a tar-papered cabin and a spreading farm.

Thank you, Lord. She reined the mare and called out to a beanstalk of a man hoeing in the cornfield. "Morning, sir. Any general stores around these parts?"

The man pushed back his battered straw hat. "There's a little mercantile up that road a piece. Hardly enough to call a town, just the store and a saloon, mostly. But you can get yourself some basic foodstuffs, if that's what you're needin'. Where ya headed?"

"We were on the Oregon Trail, but we're on our own now. How far is it to Salton?"

The man whistled. "Good thirty, forty miles north of here."

So a three-day journey. Well, at least that gave her some idea. She'd ask more specifics at the store. "Much obliged."

"Anytime. We were strangers on the trail once too." The farmer grinned, showing a friendly gap in his teeth. "Anything else I can do for ya?"

Lark spotted some plump chickens scratching between the chicken coop and the house. "Now that you mention it . . . would you be willing to sell a chicken?"

Half an hour later, Lark rode into the "town" with a fat young rooster tied to her saddle. She swung down and tied Starbright to the hitching post. Inside, the supplies were simple but well stocked. She bought more beans, cornmeal, and salt to replace what they'd given the Pawnee, and a few treats to tempt Forsythia's appetite—cheese and some dried apples to stew. Also soap to scrub down the Durhams' wagon once Sythia grew well enough to leave it. With all the extra laundry, they were running low.

She and Starbright trotted back into the camp before sunset laden with goods. "Look what I got." Lark slid off the horse and held out the chicken. Then she stopped short.

Forsythia reclined on a makeshift pallet by the campfire, wearing a clean, dry nightdress and propped up on pillows against a box. Though her face was still pale, she smiled when she saw Lark and held out her hand.

"Sythia." Still clutching the chicken, Lark handed off Starbright to Lilac and fell to her knees beside her sister. "You're better?" Tears of relief choked her throat.

"Dr. Brownsville says so." Forsythia smiled at the quiet, bearded man who sat by her side. "And I feel it, thanks to all of your good care."

She said *all*, but her eyes seemed only for the doctor, who gazed back at her with a look that made Lark swallow.

Lord, thank you so much that Sythia is better. But what are we going to do about this?

20

They'd made it.

Lark stopped the oxen and heard Del and the doctor do the same behind her with the other wagons. Before them, the late afternoon sun slanted its rays over the growing town of Salton, nestled on a grassy plain along the Salt Creek.

"Is this it?" Lilac hurried up, pushing back her sunbonnet to see better. The children trailed at her heels.

"That's Salton. And Salt Creek." Lark nodded to the creek flowing to the east of them. "The salt flats must be that way. Let's make camp here. I'll head into town in the morning."

And find that attorney Anders had written them about. *Lord, are we close to getting our land?* The thought lent wings as she unyoked the oxen and hobbled them to graze.

Del approached, Mikael snug in his sling against her, and shaded her eyes against the setting sun. "Interesting landscape. So different from most waterways. There's fewer trees."

"The salt in the water, probably." Lark bent to examine the plant growth along the creek bank. "Look at these. They're kind of like asters." She caressed the purple blooms with her fingertips.

Dr. Brownsville approached, Forsythia leaning on his arm. Though still weak, her smile made Lark's heart sing. The extra week of rest had helped, and though it had taken three days to get to Salton, traveling slowly, Sythia didn't look any the worse for wear.

"What a beautiful sunset." Forsythia sighed. "It's so nice to see something outside the canvas cover again."

The doctor moved his hand to cover hers on his arm, a tender gesture that quickened Lark's heart.

"Let's start supper." Del gave Lark and Lilac a significant look and nodded toward the campsite.

"What are we going to do about that?" Lark whispered, following her sisters. Behind them, the doctor and Forsythia talked in low tones under the gathering dusk.

"What?"

"Them."

"I think it's lovely, don't you?" Lilac scooped Sofie up and kissed her cheek, which was now filling out a bit with good food and milk.

"But he's only just lost his wife. It seems too soon."

Del stirred cornmeal and flour for a quick corn pone. "Perhaps. But sometimes these things happen."

"Maybe." *Lord, I just don't want my sister to get hurt.*

The next morning, Lark saddled Starbright to head into Salton.

"Could you use some company?" The doctor looked up at her from under his best hat.

"I—don't think so." She didn't mean to be rude, but the lawyer would be expecting Miss Larkspur Nielsen, and she wasn't ready for that conversation in front of the doctor. Though they'd need to let him in on the secret sometime, the way things were looking. "I'd appreciate it if you'd keep an eye on everyone in the camp."

He stepped back and nodded politely, though perhaps wondering why she suddenly considered her sisters helpless females.

Lark clicked her tongue and nudged Starbright toward the town, the morning sun warm on her shoulders. *Lord, help me find this man. And guide us to the place you have for us.*

Salton wasn't much of a town, but several shops, a mercantile, a bank, and two saloons lined the main dirt road, with a church at the end. Lark tied up Starbright in what seemed to be the general area of the address Anders had sent and strode along the raised wooden sidewalk, its heavy planks foreign beneath her boots after weeks on the trail.

Here—this should be it. Anders's letter in hand, she scanned the unassuming shop front. A small lettered sign in the window read *Henry P. Caldwell, Attorney-at-Law.*

Here we go, Lord. She pushed open the door, jingling a friendly bell.

"Good morning." A man with dark sideburns and spectacles looked up from behind a large wooden desk. "Can I help you?"

"I hope so, sir." Lark stepped forward, her palms suddenly sweaty. "I believe you know my brother, Anders Nielsen. He suggested I come see you about some land a homesteader had for sale."

"Anders Nielsen, yes." Mr. Caldwell removed his spectacles and studied her. "But who would you be?"

"Clark—that is, Larkspur." Lark swallowed and removed her hat. "Miss Larkspur Nielsen, sir." *How do I explain this whole morass?*

The attorney's brows rose, and he pushed to his feet. "Well, that explains my surprise. Anders told me his sister would be coming to see me. He failed to mention she would bear more resemblance to a brother." He limped forward and extended his hand. "Please have a seat, Miss Nielsen."

"Thank you, sir." With that revelation out of the way, Lark breathed a bit easier. She sank into the upholstered chair Caldwell indicated. "I hope you aren't too shocked."

"It takes a good deal to shock an old soldier like me." The attorney eased back into his own chair with a faint groan. "Forgive me. Minié ball took off my leg at the Battle of Franklin. A true blessing, these prosthetic limbs, but never quite the same as God's original. But you don't need to hear all that." He leaned back and smiled. "So, if I may ask, why the"—he waved a hand toward her—"disguise?"

"Safety, sir. We thought it best to appear as a man traveling with his sisters, rather than as four women alone. I did the same when I went to get Anders out of that prison camp."

"Of course. Now I remember Anders mentioning that part of the story." Caldwell steepled his fingers and pressed them to his chin. "He was one of the men in my company, you know, taken prisoner just after I was wounded. I blamed myself, that I wasn't there to protect my men as an officer should be. Thank God you got him out of that place."

"We do. Every day."

"So." He slapped his hand on the desk. "You're here about land, not my war stories. Let me pull out the documents I have on this homesteader who is selling his claim. He's already signed off on the deal. Here we are." Caldwell set a stack of papers on the desk.

"You mean, the deal is already made?"

"In a manner of speaking. You still need to sign yourself, of course. But from Anders I had the impression you wanted the land. Since the seller was in a hurry to head back east—he lost his family, wife and infant, recently and thusly his heart for homesteading—I took the liberty of securing it for you."

"Well, we do want land. But I thought we'd look into all our options." Lark's head spun. This seemed to be happening too fast. "What about homesteading ourselves? Wouldn't that be less expensive?"

"Well, yes. Homestead land is yours with a fee simple title after improving the claim and five years of residence. But only heads of households of majority age are eligible to file."

"And I'm a woman." Lark's voice was flat.

Mr. Caldwell held up a finger. "Actually, that's not necessarily a barrier. Single women are allowed to file a claim if they are of age. However, since the law defines a husband as the head of household, women seeking to homestead must not marry until the five years are up and they hold their title free and clear."

Lark didn't have any entanglements of the heart, though only God knew what the future held. But what about Delphinium? The two of them were the only sisters who had reached twenty-one, and they'd talked about each finding a plot of land. She chewed the inside of her cheek. "So this man, he had completed his five years?"

"No—the Homestead Act has only been in effect for three. But he owns his land now thanks to the commutation clause, which allows a homesteader to acquire final title by purchase after living on the land for six months. That's the only reason he can sell. If anyone tries to sell or abandons their homestead before the title is legally theirs, the land reverts back to the public domain."

"I see." The details whirred through Lark's mind. "I'm grateful you know all this. Could we go take a look at the land?"

"Certainly." Mr. Caldwell pushed back his chair and reached for his hat. "Would you like the rest of your family to come along?"

"Yes, please. We're camped just outside of town, along with a doctor and his nephew who are accompanying us." She thought of something. "If, ah, you wouldn't mind not saying anything about my being a woman just yet, I'd be grateful."

"I see." Mr. Caldwell quirked a brow and reached for a nearby cane to assist his walk. "Of course, Miss Nielsen. But you may want to consider dropping your masquerade. Once you start a new life here, I imagine you will want it to be as yourself."

"I'll think on it."

On Starbright, Lark led the attorney in his buggy to the campsite and gathered up her sisters. The doctor agreed to keep the children, though Del brought the baby along in his sling. The land was about two miles northeast of the town. Del, Lilac, and Forsythia rode in the carriage with Mr. Caldwell, while Lark rode alongside and filled them in on the details.

"Here we are." At last the attorney pulled up the reins and nodded to where a sod house rose from the prairie some way to the east, a few spindly trees forming a windbreak alongside it. "That's the half section you would be buying over that way. And this, from here to that line of trees and west to Salt Creek, is the land you'd homestead."

Their land. A shiver ran down Lark's arms as she swung off Starbright's back. Her sisters climbed down, and together they walked, the prairie grass parting around their ankles.

"How many acres?" Lilac asked.

"One hundred sixty for each half section." Mr. Caldwell kept up with their pace, his cane and prosthetic leg notwithstanding. "So the full claim is three hundred twenty."

Was it worth it? "Pretty close to the creek. How is the soil?" Lark asked.

"Nebraska is known for good soil, and as you can see, no rocks or stumps to contend with. Good corn and cattle country. Mr. Skinner already dug a well, for Salt Creek is as it sounds—salty."

By the time they'd walked to one corner of the land, Forsythia was out of breath. Lark's heart smote her for pushing her sister too far. Yet Forsythia had wanted to come.

"Let me bring the buggy over," Caldwell said. "She can rest there till you're finished."

"I'll get it," Lilac offered.

"True, you can move faster than I, young lady." He smiled. "Thank you."

"I'm sorry to cause trouble." Forsythia leaned on Lark's arm as Lilac flew across the prairie toward the buggy. "It seems like a good piece of land, though, Lark."

"It does, doesn't it?" Lark pushed back her hat and let the wind waving the grasses caress her hair. "I just wish I were sure this was best."

"What is the price?"

"Two hundred and twenty-five dollars. Mr. Caldwell says that's reasonable, only a little over what homestead land is valued at, and this has been improved a bit with the sod house and the trees. We have the funds, thanks to my encounter with Ringwald. But would it be a wiser use of our money to just homestead?"

Del looked at her. "We could, as women?"

"You and I could." Lark hesitated. "If we didn't marry for five years. You have to be twenty-one to file and then stay single for five years."

"I see. We talked about all wanting to get adjoining plots of land, but Forsythia and Lilac can't file yet on account of their age," Del said. "Purchasing this could give them something, along with a start for all of us while we look for more land and decide what to do. I hear claims are going fast now that the war is over, so who knows whether land would even still be available once the younger ones come of age."

Forsythia nibbled her lip. "That makes sense."

"Here you are, Sythia." Lilac drove up in the buggy, set the brake, and jumped down. "Your chariot awaits."

"Why, thank you." Forsythia smiled and accepted Mr. Caldwell's hand to climb in. She turned back to Lark as she settled. "Go on, walk the rest of the land. But I think this might be the Lord's provision for us."

Lark wasn't entirely sure. Yet as the rest of them walked the remaining section, she began to see a home growing here. A house there—not just the soddy, but a real one with wood planks and glass windows. A barn with animals, a garden, productive fields. A windmill to draw water from the well. More trees. *Father, is this the place you've prepared for us?*

"What do you think?" Mr. Caldwell asked the four sisters once they arrived back at the campsite.

"I like it." Del jiggled Mikael, who was fussing for his milk. "But you're the eldest, Clark." With the doctor nearby, she'd switched back to their ruse.

Sometimes Lark didn't like being eldest. Too much responsibility. "What do you think, Lilac?"

"It seems to have what we're looking for." Lilac bent to hug Robbie and Sofie, who threw themselves at her skirts, squealing as if she'd been gone a week. "Not far from town, good land, water."

Silence fell, all eyes on Lark. She rubbed her hands together, thinking.

"I did bring the papers, if you decide to sign." Mr. Caldwell opened his leather satchel.

"Well." Lark drew a breath. "All right. I suppose we'll take it."

Smiles and exclamations bubbled all around. Soon Lark leaned against the attorney's buggy, signing the documents.

The doctor walked up. "Sounds like congratulations are in order." He extended a hand to Mr. Caldwell. "Dr. Adam Brownsville. I don't suppose you know of any other good pieces of land for sale in these parts?"

"Henry P. Caldwell, a pleasure. And I can let you know if I do, though you might look into homesteading as well. Or merely setting up a practice—a doctor, you say?"

"I am, yes."

"He's truly been a godsend to us," Forsythia put in. "And everyone on our wagon train, till they left us behind."

"Medical men are needed everywhere, that's certain. Assuredly here in Salton."

"You have no doctor?" Dr. Brownsville slid his hands in his pockets and cocked his head.

"We had one, a supposed physician at least, but he seemed to rely more on patent medicines than anything else. I never trusted him, nor did many others. He left a couple of months ago in the middle of the night, after a woman he was treating died. He left an office, which is still empty, far as I know."

"You don't say." The doctor ran a hand over his beard. "We should talk further."

"Glad to. Your presence could be a real uplift to this town. But tonight"—the attorney glanced at the sky—"I need to get home, or my wife will have my head for being late to supper. Especially on a night she's fixed fried chicken." He winked. "Pleasure meeting you folks. Young Nielsen, come to my office tomorrow, and we'll finalize the sale." He packed the papers, gave one to Lark, and drove off.

The doctor watched him go. "He seems like a good man."

"Anders trusted him with his life. And with us."

"A good recommendation." Dr. Brownsville nodded. "So you took the land?"

"We did." Lark folded the paper in her hands, still heady with the reality. "Two hundred twenty-five dollars for one hundred sixty acres that includes a one-room sod house and some trees and about five acres worked up, plus a well. We'll homestead the adjoining section too. We still need to finalize everything with the banker in town."

The doctor frowned. "One dollar and forty cents per acre. I thought homestead land was only valued at a dollar twenty-five per acre."

"Mr. Caldwell said it was a fair price due to the improvements." Of course she'd run the calculations in her head, multiple times. But doubt sank heavy in Lark's stomach. Had she moved too quickly? *Lord, is this what you truly want us to have?*

21

Had he made the right choice?

Adam walked alongside Henry Caldwell over the raised wooden sidewalks of Salton. It had seemed obvious at the time, leaving the wagon train. But settling in Nebraska—when he and Jesse had planned for California—was a big change.

But then, it hadn't been him and Jesse planning for California, not really. It had been him and Elizabeth. And Elizabeth was gone.

"The empty office is across the street beside the general store. The folks who own the store, Mr. and Mrs. Jorgensen, own that building too." Caldwell waited for a horse and wagon to pass, then led the way across the street, keeping a brisk pace despite his cane and prosthetic leg. Amazing, the mechanical marvels in medicine since the war.

"Do you think they'd be open to selling or renting the space?" Adam paused on the street to examine the simple board front of the building. "Are there rooms behind the office?"

"Above. Let's see if they can let us in." Caldwell pushed open the door of the general store with a friendly jangle.

A slender man with a gray mustache looked up from behind the counter. "Mr. Caldwell, good afternoon."

"How are you, Mr. Jorgensen?"

"Fine, fine, can't complain. What can I do for you?"

"I've got a friend here I think you'll be glad to meet." Caldwell turned and extended a hand toward Adam. "Dr. Adam Brownsville. He's just arrived in the area."

The warmth in Caldwell's brown eyes eased Adam's wondering about this new step. *Friend*—he liked the sound of that.

"Welcome to you, Doctor." Mr. Jorgensen shook his hand, his grip welcoming if not strong. "Planning to stay in these parts?"

"He's interested in your rooms next door, the office Dr. Edson used. Would you let him take a look?"

"Sure, sure." Mr. Jorgensen nodded and took off his apron. "Certainly would be fine to have a decent doctor in these parts after that last humbug."

"He was a real charlatan, eh?" Adam followed.

"Worse." The shopkeeper's hands trembled a bit as he fit a key into a door in the wall separating the store and the office beside it. "He . . . but you'll learn all that soon enough. Here we are."

The door stuck a bit, then swung open. Adam stepped into the musty warmth of a closed-up building. Sunlight beamed through dusty windows, illuminating a desk, several chairs, and an examining table. A cabinet stood in the corner with a few bottles and boxes inside.

Adam opened the cupboard and took out a small brown glass flask. He examined the faded label, then opened the bottle and sniffed. He shook his head. "Calomel."

"Oh yes. He dosed that stuff out like candy, said it was a regular cure-all. He gave it to me when I had a bellyache, but it made me so sick that I threw it out."

"You were wise to. It's mercurous chloride, a form of inorganic mercury. It's still in use by many physicians, fraud or no, but I and others believe it to be highly toxic and dangerous." Adam examined the rest of the bottles. Some patent medicines—mostly whiskey but otherwise fairly harmless, if ineffective. A handful of homeopathic remedies. And in the back, a small bottle each of quinine and digitalis.

"Well, those could actually be useful." He organized the bottles by habit. "But I'd need to order in most of my own supplies. You could do that through the store?"

"Certainly. You're interested, then?"

Adam glanced around the space. "I'd like to see the rooms upstairs, but yes, I'm interested, if you'll have me." He met Mr. Jorgensen's gaze. "I understand it may take a while to gain the town's trust after your last experience."

If he wasn't mistaken, tears glistened in the corners of the older man's eyes. "Any man Mr. Caldwell thinks well of has my confidence. You'd be an answer to many folks' prayers."

Is this the answer to mine, Lord? Adam climbed the dusty steps after Mr. Jorgensen, Caldwell remaining below in deference to his leg. Two rooms, small but serviceable. A bedroom with a window toward the back and a sitting room with a wood stove and space for a cot for Jesse. Not much, but it would do till he could buy or build a house.

Back down in the store, he and Mr. Jorgensen discussed the rent, and Adam promised to bring the deposit by that evening. With a lightened heart, he placed his first order for medical supplies, then looked around for something to bring back to the wagons, something that would make the children smile. And Forsythia.

"Do you have any sweets for sale, Mr. Jorgensen? It's been a while since we've had a treat on this journey."

"My wife is finishing up a batch of her cherry fritters in the kitchen. Our cherry tree is bearing a heap this year, but as soon as I set out her fritters in the store, they're gone before you can say Jack Robinson." His eyes twinkled. "Good thing you caught them early. Lucretia!" he hollered into a hallway that seemingly connected the store with the Jorgensens' living space. "Got those fritters ready?"

"I was just bringin' them out. Needn't holler my ear off." A woman as comfortably round as her husband was slim emerged from the doorway, bearing a tray of hot fritters dusted with sugar.

Adam's mouth watered at the aroma. "Those smell delicious. I'll take a dozen, if I may."

"Twenty-five cents." Mrs. Jorgensen dropped the pastries into a paper bag and handed it over.

"Thank you." The price seemed a bit steep, but he didn't care just now. Adam handed over the coins with a smile, hoping to garner one in return. "We'll look forward to them."

"Lu." Her husband laid a hand on her arm. "This is Dr. Brownsville. He's going to take up practice in the office next door. Isn't that a piece of news?"

Mrs. Jorgensen stopped arranging fritters and for the first time looked Adam straight in the eyes. Her expression caught him in the chest. Grief and—hatred?

"Well, let's hope he doesn't kill anyone fool enough to enter those doors. I told you we shoulda sold that building when we had a chance." She snatched her tray and hurried back down the hallway.

Mr. Jorgensen watched her go, his shoulders slumped. With a sigh, he turned back to Adam and Mr. Caldwell. "You'll have to forgive Lucretia, Dr. Brownsville." He retied his apron, face drawn in regret. "You see, she blames Dr. Edson for the death of our daughter—and she's likely right." The older man seemed about to say more, then shook his head. "I'd best go see to her. Excuse me, gentlemen."

Adam watched the little man hurry after his wife. What on earth had this so-called physician done to this town?

"As you can see, you are needed here," the attorney said after they showed themselves out. "Though the road may not be smooth."

"Few roads are." Adam extended his hand. "Thank you, Mr. Caldwell. For everything."

"Call me Henry." Caldwell shook his hand firmly. "I feel you may be a gift from the Lord to this town, Doctor."

"Then please call me Adam." He returned the grip.

He bid Caldwell good day and wove his way back through the town on his own, headed out to the campsite. When he reached the open space of the prairie once more, a breath he didn't know he'd been holding released from his chest. It was strange to be in civilization again, even as rustic as this. So much was happening so fast. *And yet, Lord, your hand seems to be in this. At least I hope so.* And now, what to do about Forsythia?

He cared for her, that was certain. It seemed so soon after losing Elizabeth—the woman he'd thought the one love of his life. And yet he'd heard of such things happening, especially out on the frontier, where life was precious and love still more so. Love. Could God truly have that for him again? Tears pricked the back of his throat at the thought. He'd thought his heart buried that day back in Independence. But God's mercies truly were new every morning.

And now that he had a stable place to live and practice, perhaps he might speak to her about all this.

Clark met Adam before he reached his wagon. "How did your business go?"

"Well, I think." He paused and nodded. "And yours? Did you meet with the banker yet?"

"We'll be leaving shortly, hoping to finalize the purchase of the homesteader's land and file for the adjoining claim all at once. First, though, I wondered if I could speak with you."

The young man's solemn tone set Adam's heart to pattering, making him feel like a schoolboy gaining courage to face his sweetheart's father.

"Certainly." He swallowed. "Is it about Forsythia?"

"Forsythia?" Understanding dawned on Clark's face. "Ah. Well, that's not a bad idea. But—"

"I understand—you are her older brother, and in lieu of a father, responsible." His words tumbled out too quickly. "Let me assure you, my intentions are entirely honorable—and as soon as I have the chance to—"

"Doctor." Clark held up a hand, consternation in his face. "I would like to discuss Forsythia sometime soon. But I don't have the time right now. And when I do, it—it will be as an older sister, not a brother." His face flushed.

"As a what?" Adam frowned. The words didn't make sense.

"We didn't intend to deceive you for this long. But we haven't been entirely honest with you." The young man took off his hat, unshading a face the doctor had always thought boyishly fine-featured. But now . . . dear Lord.

"My name isn't actually Clark. It's Larkspur. Miss Larkspur Nielsen."

As the words sank in, heat rose in Adam's chest. He should have known.

It hadn't gone well.

Forsythia could tell as soon as Lark stomped back to their wagons, yanking the bandana from around her neck.

"Get the girls and children together. We're going to be late. I've got to get back into those fool women's clothes." Lark hauled herself up into the Durhams' wagon, where they kept the clothing trunks, and jerked the canvas flap closed for privacy.

Forsythia stepped close to talk through the wagon cover. "How did he take it?"

"He's not happy." Rustling inside, then muttered frustration.

"Do you need help?"

"I just have to remember how to do up all these buttons. Britches and men's shirts sure are easier."

Lord, please help Adam to understand. Forsythia called to Del and Lilac to load the children into their wagon, then hurried off for the doctor's. It would take Lark a few more minutes to be ready.

"Jesse, where's your uncle?"

The young man looked up from mending a yoke. "B-behind the wagon."

Forsythia rounded the corner to find Adam splashing water on his face from a basin he'd set against the side of the wagon.

He straightened, toweling his face, then spotted her. His mouth tightened under his beard. He glanced away, folding the towel.

"Doctor." She stepped closer. "I know what you must be thinking."

"And what's that?" He laid the towel neatly on the edge of the basin.

"That we haven't been honest with you. And how could we do that, with all we've been through together?"

He met her gaze. "Well?"

"I don't fully know what to say." Forsythia released a short breath. "Lark—that's what we call her—had gone as a man before in order to rescue Anders from prison camp. And we thought it safer for her to do so again, to become Clark, than to have four women traveling alone. Surely you can see that, conditions as they are." The man who'd attacked Del flashed through her mind, along with the memory of her own knife striking home. She shivered, rubbing her arms. Would she never be free of that image?

"I can." The doctor nodded, but his tone remained steely. "What I cannot see is why you would continue to deceive a friend."

"We didn't intend to." Forsythia raised her arms at her sides, then dropped them again. "It just—we were all so used to it by that time. And we hadn't made it safely to our new land yet, so keeping up the ruse seemed the most natural thing. There never seemed to be a good time. . . . I'm sorry, Adam." Her voice broke on the last word. "I mean, Dr. Brownsville. Forgive me."

Adam sighed, and a little of the stiffness eased from his shoulders. "Forsythia . . . Miss Nielsen. I care for your family very much. I care for . . . you, more than I can say. I had intended to speak of this to you soon, perhaps even tonight. But I need some time to think. To see if I can trust you again."

The words cut deeply. But Forsythia nodded, her throat aching. "I understand."

"Sythia, come on." Lark waved from across the campsite, almost unrecognizable in a calico dress and shawl, a straw bonnet tied over her shorn hair. "We're leaving."

"Excuse me." Without another glance at the doctor, Forsythia hurried away.

She fought an urge to cry all the way into Salton, but by the time they sat down with the banker, Mr. Young, she'd composed herself. Only a sick tightening remained in her stomach, and not from vestiges of dysentery.

"So you are all four purchasing the half section of land from a Mr. Skinner, one hundred sixty acres of improved land with sod house and well, at one dollar forty cents per acre." The banker's voice droned. He glanced around the circle of sisters, all but Lark balancing a small child in their arms. "Is that correct, Misses Nielsen?"

They all nodded.

"And you have the payment for this in full?"

Larkspur reached into her reticule and pulled out a small bag. She set it on the table with a clink.

The payment from her gambling winnings. Forsythia held her breath. *We've waited a long time for this moment, Lord.*

Mr. Young grunted and pulled the purse close. Opening it, he counted the bills and coins. "Very well. All seems to be in order. Sign here, ladies." He pushed the paper first to Lark, who signed and next passed it to Del, then on to Forsythia and Lilac.

"Very well." The banker made a note, then tucked the money bag away. "And in addition, you, Miss Larkspur Nielsen, wish to file a claim to homestead the adjoining section of land, also one hundred sixty acres, is that correct?"

"Yes, sir." Lark sat tall.

"And you are aware of the terms required in order to homestead as a single woman, namely, that you must be the head of your household, that you must reside on the land five years without more than a six-month absence, that you must improve the land faithfully, and that you must refrain from marriage until your five-year residency is complete, unless you choose to acquire final title by purchase after living on the land at least six months?"

"I am."

"Fine." He pushed another paper toward Lark with a nod. "Sign here."

Lark signed, then laid down the pen. "Anything else, sir?"

"Guess that'll do it." Mr. Young gathered and stacked the papers, then palmed the money bag and stood with a grunt. "Quite a venture you young women are undertaking, homesteading and farming without a man to your names. Keep in mind that if you fail in your first attempt to homestead, the government considers you no longer eligible for another claim."

"We don't intend to fail." Lark stood, her slender frame taller than the banker's. "Can we go out to our land? Is it ours?"

"It appears to be." The portly man touched his hat and tipped his head toward the door. "Good day to you, ladies."

"Thank you." Lark's calico skirts swept as regally as a queen's as they filed out of the office.

Once out in the sunshine of the street, Lark turned to her sisters. A smile skipped from her face to each of theirs.

Forsythia even felt the knot in her stomach loosen. She reached for Lark's hand and squeezed it. "Let's thank the Lord. And then go home."

Their new home.

An hour later, Forsythia turned a full circle within the four walls of the sod house on their property, scanning the darkened space. A bit tight for four women and three children, but they'd make do. At least until they could add on or build a real wooden house.

"I never thought I'd be so excited about a house with roots hanging from the ceiling." Beside her, Lilac threw her arms wide. "But it's so nice to have a roof and walls again, even if it's only sod."

"I agree. But it certainly is—well, dirty." Forsythia wrinkled her nose. Even the air was redolent of earth. There might only be so much they could do to keep a sod house clean, but she aimed to try. "Let's start wiping off the furniture, at least."

The homesteader had left a rope-strung bed, a table and chairs, and a cabinet, along with a small woodstove. All covered with a layer of dirt that had sifted down from the ceiling.

Rag in hand, Forsythia wiped the table, then the stove. "We've got to find out how to harden the floor so we're not kicking up dirt all the time. I know there are ways. Where is Del?"

"Planting the rosebushes and apple tree starts. She couldn't wait to get them in the ground," Lilac said.

Of course. Forsythia smiled and stepped to the open doorway to shake out her rag.

Del crouched near the door, patting soil around a rosebush with the help of Robbie and Sofie. They were a bit scraggly, but the bushes had survived, as had two of the three apple tree seedlings.

"I thought I'd plant the trees over there." Del nodded. "Close enough to the house to give some shade, but not so close that we're stepping on fallen apples."

"I like apples." Robbie looked up with a grin, his face dirt-smudged.

"I yike app-uhs too." Sofie nodded and gave the dirt an extra pat.

Forsythia smiled and picked her up. "We all like apples, little one." She hugged the little girl, who was growing a bit sturdier these days, then blew softly under her dimpled chin. Sofie giggled and squirmed to get down. Forsythia lowered her and crouched to touch one of the rosebush's withered leaves. "Makes it feel like we're really coming home, doesn't it? Planting Ma's roses."

"That's what I thought." Del dashed a grimy hand against her cheek. "Our first start on Leah's Garden, you know?"

"Someday we'll have a sign up with that name." Forsythia shaded her eyes and gazed across the land—their land. "We'll have flowers growing everywhere you can see."

"We'll sell seeds and starts, all kinds of things." Larkspur walked up, a spade in her hand. "But to begin with, we need to see what we can still get planted in the garden. The soil's already been dug up for a garden plot. It just needs a little going over to loosen it again after the rains."

Lilac stepped out of the house. "It's late for planting, but we could still put in beans, potatoes, carrots, beets, lettuce, and maybe collard greens. We brought some seeds. Do you think the store will have more?"

"If not, maybe we can order them."

"That sounds good." Forsythia tapped her rag on her palm. "Any idea how to harden the sod floor?"

"I think you wet it down and tamp with a wooden post or something," Lark said. "We'll ask around. Plenty of folks around here must have experience."

Del stood and dusted the dirt from her hands. "There. Help me get the apple trees in the ground?"

Together the sisters dug holes deep in the willing soil and settled the spindly seedlings, covering their root balls with earth.

"Lord, bless these trees and let them bear much fruit for us and to bless others." Del sat back on her heels.

"Amen. Well done, big sister." Forsythia hugged her.

"Since the house is close to the boundary line, we can build a barn on the homestead section. That will be a good start to improving it." Larkspur scanned their land as Forsythia had done. Would they ever grow tired of it?

"And perhaps plant more trees. These apples are a good start, but we could plant more on the homestead side, create a whole little orchard." Right now only a slender cottonwood seedling waved its leaves over the sod house, and a thin windbreak stood off to the north. Stepping to the side, Forsythia pointed to the gentle rise behind the soddy. "Are those graves up there?"

Lilac nodded. "I saw them when Robbie and I were exploring. No headstones, just simple crosses stuck in the ground made from sticks. But it's one large grave and two small ones. Mr. Caldwell said Mr. Skinner lost a wife and a baby. I don't know about the third."

"So sad." Forsythia rubbed her arms. "Is that why he left?"

"Sounds like." Lark lifted her spade. "Let's finish cleaning the house, at least enough to unload some things from the wagons. Maybe at least some of us can sleep indoors tonight."

Forsythia hung back a moment, watching the lowering sun cast shadows and coolness across the prairie. She wondered what the doctor was doing back at the campsite and pictured him moving about the fire and making coffee.

Her heart ached. Could they invite him and Jesse to join them for supper, as they had so many times before? Or would he refuse now?

22

Still no patients.

Adam rearranged the shining instruments in his case once more, then closed the cover. He glanced around his new office. The windows now let the sun shine clearly through the space, the examining table sat clean and ready for use, and he had even managed to restock the cabinet with medicines, bandages, and other supplies, thanks to Mr. Jorgensen.

Yet no one had come for treatment. And it had been over a week. Either this was an exceptionally healthy town, or he had more mistrust to overcome than he had realized. Even his door-to-door visits had done no good.

"U-uncle Adam?"

He looked up to see his nephew descending the stairs from their rooms above. "Yes, Jesse?"

"I g-got that window fixed." Jesse tucked away his hammer and nails in the toolbox and slid it into the bottom of the cabinet. "Anything else you n-need?"

"I think we're pretty shipshape." Adam laid a hand on his nephew's shoulder. "Now if only the townspeople would real-ize we're here."

"M-maybe they're afraid because of what that lady said."

Adam frowned. "What lady?"

Jesse looked a bit shamefaced. "Mrs. Jor-Jorgensen. I h-heard her when I was in the store. She d-didn't see me."

"What did she say?"

"She was talking to some other ladies." Jesse hesitated. "I didn't hear everything, but she said s-something about how the children who traveled with us had all lost their parents. And that it was b-because you couldn't save them, that you were n-no kind of doctor, just like the doctor they had before."

A rock settled in Adam's gut. "When was this?"

"A couple of days ago." Jesse met his eyes, worry in his gaze. "I'm s-sorry if I shoulda told you."

Adam squeezed his shoulder. "None of this is your fault. But thanks for telling me." He stepped to the window and stared out at the men and women hurrying back and forth on the bustling street. Most rushed right past his door. One mother glanced at his sign, then herded her children by with a shake of her head.

So there was even more going on here than he knew. *What do I do, Lord? Have a talk with Mrs. Jorgensen? If she'll even listen to me. Or do I just wait for the truth to make itself known?*

"Th-that man looks hurt." At his shoulder, Jesse pointed out the windowpane.

"Where?" Adam peered closer. A man climbed down from a wagon across the dusty street and started across, cradling his hand, which was wrapped in a bloody rag. A sandy-haired boy of about ten stayed on the wagon seat, holding the reins.

"You're right." Adam stepped to the door and flung it open. "Sir, do you need help?"

"You must be the new doc." The man stepped inside without hesitation and held up his hand with a wry grin. "Appears I'm in need of your services. Guess you saw me comin'."

"My nephew did. Please, have a seat." Adam indicated the

examining table and hurried to wash his hands. "What happened?"

"Bit of a scythe accident while haying." The man grimaced. "You'd think after being out in the hayfields since I was knee-high to a grasshopper, I'd know better."

Adam dried his hands. "May I take a look, Mister . . . ?"

"Oh, sure, sorry. Anthony Armstead." Mr. Armstead unwrapped the red-stained rag.

"And I'm Dr. Brownsville." Adam examined the gash from the thumb webbing across the palm of the hand. Deep and still bleeding freely, but it didn't appear to have severed any tendons, the best he could tell. "This'll need stitching once I clean it. Jesse, fetch me a bowl of clean water and some bandages, would you?"

Anthony Armstead sat back with apparent ease as Adam cleansed the wound and threaded his needle.

"This will sting a bit, I'm afraid."

"I've had worse." Sure enough, Armstead barely flinched as Adam began to stitch the torn edges of his flesh closed. "I must say, I'm glad you were here today. We've needed a good doctor in this town."

"I'm afraid not many share your opinion. You're my first patient."

"You don't say." Armstead drummed his other fingers on his thigh.

"Unfortunately, it seems my landlady may be part of the problem." He snipped off the thread, frustration rising in his chest again. "Apparently, she's been saying some—well, let's just say some twisted versions of the truth."

Armstead's fingers stilled. "Mrs. Jorgensen?"

"You know her?"

"She's my mother-in-law."

Adam looked up, remorse smiting him. He knew better than

to speak of anyone like that, let alone to a patient. "Forgive me. I spoke out of turn. I understand Mrs. Jorgensen recently lost a daughter under the previous physician's care, which no doubt accounts for her mistrust."

"Sure does. But believe me, Doctor, you have my sympathies. Anyone unlucky enough to get on Lucretia's wrong side—well, they won't get out of it for a month of Sundays. I can tell already"—he held up his neatly bandaged hand—"that you're the good kind of doc, the kind we sorely need around here. But if you knew what happened to poor Matilda, you'd understand a bit more why her ma's carrying such a grudge."

"What did happen, exactly?"

Armstead shook his head. "'Twas a terrible thing. Matilda and Elias, they lost a baby stillborn over a year ago and had high hopes for their second. Well, one night last March, Elias came knockin' on our door, asked me to go for the doctor. Matilda was in labor and carryin' on something awful. I went for Doc Edson—truth be told, I still regret it." He met Adam's gaze frankly. "But I didn't know what else to do. My Rachel and I, we heard late the next morning that Edson tried to cut the baby out of her."

"My God." Adam's gut tightened. That procedure was dangerous in the best hands, and in incompetent ones—he could only imagine the result.

Peter grimaced. "Well, both Matilda and her baby died. The doc left not long after. I guess he knew he risked being run out of town if he stayed much longer. Elias just couldn't seem to take life out here anymore without his wife. He up and sold his homestead, then headed back east only a few weeks ago."

Adam stared. "Really? What did you say his name was?"

"Skinner, Elias Skinner."

Skinner. Had that been the name Clark—Lark—mentioned as the former owner of the Nielsens' new land? "His homestead wouldn't be a couple of miles or so northeast of town, would it? With a soddy and a well on it?"

"Sounds like it." Anthony frowned. "Why?"

"I believe I may know the people who bought it, that's all." Adam reined in his curiosity and wiped his hands. "Thank you for telling me this, Mr. Armstead. I am truly sorry for this tragedy in your family."

"Well, thanks for fixin' me up today." Armstead flexed his bandaged hand. "Feels better already. What do I owe you?"

"Please, nothing for today. But if you get a chance to give a good testimony to anyone, I would appreciate it. Take care to keep the wound clean, especially if you change the dressing. I'd like to see you again in a week. Is there anyone who might take over your chores for a few days?"

"Well, I've got three boys, including young Carl out there." Anthony tipped his head toward the window, where they could see the youngster still sitting on the wagon seat, slapping flies and holding the horses calm. "But haying season is a hard time of year for a farmer to take his ease."

"Just do the best you can." Adam saw his patient out the door, giving a friendly wave to the boy before he shut it. He blew out a breath before turning back to Jesse. "Well, between you and Mr. Armstead, it's been an educational morning."

"What are you g-going to do?" His nephew shifted his feet.

"I don't quite know. Pray, for starters, I suppose." Adam lifted the bowl of bloodstained water.

"Uncle Adam? C-can I ask you something?"

"Of course." He'd clean up, then see about their supper, as the sun was lowering. And maybe somewhere along the way, he'd get some insight as to what to do about this mess.

"Miss Lark asked if I'd c-come to work for them. They need help haying the prairie grass and s-some other things. She said they'd p-pay me too."

"I see." Adam stepped out the back door and tossed the water on the struggling daisies by the stoop, then stepped back in. "Do you want to?"

His nephew hesitated, then nodded. "I don't have m-much to do. S-sometimes I don't know what to do with myself." A vulnerability sheened his eyes.

Adam set down the empty bowl, guilt pinching his chest. How long had it been since he'd really talked with his nephew, much less asked after his heart? The boy had been passed from relative to relative most of his life, his wishes seldom consulted. Adam and Elizabeth had vowed to do better than that. And here he was, caught up in his own problems, whether business or matters of the heart.

He leaned back against the examining table. "If you want to do it, of course you should."

"But I thought . . . you m-might not want me to."

"Why not?"

Jesse shrugged. "You aren't too happy with the Nielsens lately."

Perceptive young man. Adam's neck heated. "That needn't enter into this. I'm sure they'll be fair to you." Even if they hadn't been honest with him.

"Maybe you should t-talk to her."

"Who?"

"Miss Forsythia."

"I'd rather not speak of her." The words came out harsher than he'd meant. "Now, go see what you can find in the store for supper. I've got to finish cleaning up this mess." Minor though it was.

The weight of guilt intensified after Jesse left, shoulders slumped. And that was Adam's fault. *Lord, what's the matter with me?* He pressed a fist to his forehead.

His stomach suddenly rumbled for one of the Nielsens' open-fire suppers they'd shared so often on the trail, the laughter and woodsmoke and sweet fellowship over bacon-flavored beans and corn bread. Without a kitchen in their rooms, he and Jesse had subsisted off ham and cheese and salt-rising bread from the store, albeit bought under Mrs. Jorgensen's disapproving nose.

He missed their friends. But he didn't know how to fix this.

Yes, you do, whispered a Voice he knew well.

But did he have the courage?

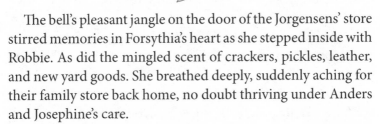

The bell's pleasant jangle on the door of the Jorgensens' store stirred memories in Forsythia's heart as she stepped inside with Robbie. As did the mingled scent of crackers, pickles, leather, and new yard goods. She breathed deeply, suddenly aching for their family store back home, no doubt thriving under Anders and Josephine's care.

"Can I help you, Miss Nielsen?" Somber as usual, Mrs. Jorgensen looked up from behind the counter.

"Good day. I was actually wondering if I could help you." Forsythia stepped up to the counter and nodded at Robbie's silent plea to examine the wooden tops and whistles in a barrel nearby. "Be careful." She smiled at Mrs. Jorgensen. "I've been wondering whether you could use any help in the store. My sisters and I all have experience working in our father's mercantile, and I'm looking for a way to earn a bit of extra income for us."

"Your father had a store, you say?"

"Yes. It's been a part of the family for as long as I can remember."

"Well, Mr. Jorgensen has mentioned wanting an extra hand behind the counter now and again. Sometimes he's busy in the back and I'm busy in the kitchen, and there's no one to mind the front. But I'll have to speak to him."

"Of course. Thank you." Forsythia offered another smile,

never mind that they never seemed to gain a response. What an unhappy woman. "Also, I want to order some garden seeds. Do you have a catalog?"

"Bit late in the season for that." With a grunt, Mrs. Jorgensen slapped a catalog on the counter in front of her. "But we can order whatever you want to take a chance on."

"Thank you." Forsythia perused the pages. Not corn or tomatoes or melons—there wasn't time for those. But quick-growing beans would be good, and greens. Root vegetables, too, which they could harvest in the fall and store for winter. And pray for a late frost, not that root crops froze easily like corn or lettuce.

"That one of the orphaned young'uns I heard about?"

Forsythia looked up in surprise at Mrs. Jorgensen's initiating conversation. Miracles did happen. "Yes. This is Robbie." She reached for the little boy's hand.

"Sure a shame about his ma. That doc didn't do her much good, did he?"

"Dr. Brownsville did everything he could." Forsythia swallowed and pulled Robbie closer. "As did I. Sadly, it wasn't enough."

"Seems it never is." Mrs. Jorgensen sniffed and turned away.

So much bitterness. Forsythia smoothed her hand over Robbie's hair. "I'm almost finished, dear one. Why don't you pick out a stick of candy to take and share with Sofie?" There, that brought the light back to his brown eyes.

When a throat cleared behind them, Forsythia turned. "Why, hello, Jesse."

"Hey, Miss F-Forsythia. Hey, Robbie."

"How are you? We miss seeing you, now that you live in town."

"We're doing fine." He shifted his feet. "You can tell Miss Larkspur that I'll t-take the job like she said. Come out and h-help you all with the haying and whatever else you need."

"That's wonderful. We'll look forward to seeing you. Can you come tomorrow morning?"

"Okay." Jesse turned away, then looked back. "I think my uncle m-misses you."

Her mind stuttered to a stop. "What?"

"He doesn't t-talk about it, but I know." With a little wave, Jesse sidled away toward the grocery section.

Her head abuzz, Forsythia placed an order for seeds, hoping she'd picked the right ones, and guided Robbie out of the store after a promise from Mrs. Jorgensen that they'd be in touch about the job.

Back out on the wooden sidewalk, Forsythia drew a steadying breath. Shadows of the buildings stretched long across the street, heralding suppertime, though the summer sun wouldn't set for some hours.

"Can we go home? I wanna give Sofie her candy." Robbie held up his small paper sack.

"Straightaway." Forcing herself not to look at the building next to the store, lest she see Adam at the window, she led Robbie to Starbright, boosted him up, then climbed up behind him.

As she clucked to the mare, Forsythia couldn't resist one glance back at the doctor's window. And there he was—only a silhouette of his broad shoulders and bearded face, but enough to set her heart pounding. A figure somehow imprinted deep on her heart before she knew how it had happened.

And now what, Lord? She fought tears as she turned Starbright toward home. *If we can't even talk to each other, what's to become of us?*

The next day, Jesse arrived at sunup. He joined them for breakfast, eating as if he hadn't had a home-cooked meal in a week, which was most likely true. Once the sun had dried the dew, Lark, Jesse, Forsythia, and Del headed into the field of waving prairie grass armed with hats, gloves, and scythes.

Lilac stayed near the soddy with the children, Mikael asleep on a blanket under the young cottonwood tree.

"We'll start here and make our way east," Lark said, tipping back her hat. "We don't have a mowing machine, but try to cut it in rows as much as you can. Sythia, don't work too long. You're not strong yet. You can trade with Lilac as soon as you get tired."

Forsythia nodded, but she wanted to help, at least a little. The July breeze, already warm for early in the morning, flapped her sunbonnet against her face.

"All right, spread out and get cutting." Lark sent them out like a general ordering her troops.

Haying was new work to all of them, but soon Forsythia fell into a rhythm with her scythe, enjoying the pull of the muscles in her arms and the satisfying sweep of the blade against the grass. The repetitive motion gave her time to think about Adam.

When had he gone from being "the doctor" to Adam in her mind? Was it when they had tried to save Alice? No, but that had been the first thing to draw them together. Taking in the children, then? Or perhaps it wasn't until she had fallen ill herself. She shook a grasshopper off her sleeve and paused to wipe the sweat from her forehead. Whenever, however, it happened, it had happened. Feelings had bloomed in her heart that she'd maybe no right to, not toward a so recently widowed man. And yet . . . from what Jesse had said, Adam cared for her too.

The thought rushed heat to her cheeks and pattered her heart. To have found a good man to love again, to love her again . . . It was something she'd dreamed of since her sweetheart Aaron died in the war's dreadfulness, yet hardly believed would happen. After all, there weren't nearly enough young men left for all the women these days, and she'd already known love. Yet it had happened again . . . and almost as quickly as it began, it seemed this new love was gone. Snuffed out by hurt and a quarrel. She blinked back tears or sweat from her eyes—she wasn't sure which.

She didn't realize how long she had worked until Del came up behind her.

"Sythia." Her sister touched her sleeve. "Lark says stop, you'd better go rest. Lilac has switchel for us, and then she'll come take your place."

"All right." Forsythia straightened, only now noticing her arms were shaking. She relinquished her scythe to Del and followed her sister back toward the house. Already the field showed their progress in the long swaths of grass lying in rows, though much still remained to cut.

"How long will it need to dry?" Joining the group gathered in front of the soddy, Forsythia sank into a chair Lilac had pulled out from the house and accepted a tin cup of switchel. The cool mixture of water from the well, sugar, vinegar, and ginger poured sweet and spicy over her tongue, easing her stomach and cooling her head. "Mmm, good. Thank you."

"It should dry in two or three days, praying we get no rain." Lark scanned the fields with a farmer's eye. "Then we'll need to stack it to shed rain and save it for the animals this winter. Once we have the barn up, we can store some in there."

"When do you want to start the barn?" Del picked up Mikael, who was opening his eyes and kicking on the blanket.

"Soon as we get the hay cut. We'll cut sod near the property line so we can plow the dirt underneath it for planting, then use the cut blocks to build the barn."

"I can h-help with that too," Jesse said.

"Indeed you can. Sod houses, sod barns." Forsythia shook her head. "I never realized the ground could yield so much building material."

"With how the grass roots hold it together, it's much like

Pharaoh's mud bricks mixed with straw." Lark handed her cup back to Lilac and adjusted her hat. "Well, back we go."

Forsythia took Mikael from Del, and the other four shouldered their scythes and headed back into the field.

"How are you, then, little one?" She bounced the baby in her arms and leaned him back so she could see his face. "You're getting to be such a big boy, aren't you?" He was nearly a month old. Mikael blinked at her, then dimpled in a sudden smile. Forsythia smiled back, her heart easing. She pressed a kiss to the baby's silken cheek, then sat to cuddle him and watch Robbie and Sofie play with their carved animals on the shady blanket. *Thank you, Lord, for children. What a comfort from you they are.*

Jesse stayed for supper that night, all of them weary but glad at the work accomplished. After supper had revived them some, Forsythia brought out her guitar, and with her sisters on the fiddle and harmonica, music sounded around the campfire not far from the sod walls of their new home.

"Savior, Like a Shepherd Lead Us." "How Firm a Foundation." "Come, Thou Fount of Every Blessing." The familiar tunes rose with the lamplight, knitting hearts and voices close once more. They closed with Ma's favorite, "Abide with Me."

Jesse said good night and strode back toward town in the summer moonlight. The children settled on pallets, the sisters slid under their covers—two of them with the baby on the rope bed and the other two spreading their bedrolls under the wagon.

Forsythia laid her head on her pillow with a heart lightened by the music, but still feeling the underlying ache. *Lord, I hate this silent rift between Adam and me. I don't know what to do, or what your will is, but please, let us be able to talk soon.*

23

So much to do.

Larkspur lay awake long after her sisters and the children slumbered, staring up into the darkness of the wagon bed overhead. Tomorrow they'd continue cutting grass for hay, and then they needed to get started on an addition to the house—all seven of them crammed into the twelve-by-twelve-foot space wouldn't work much longer. So much for her plans for the barn. Or rather, some type of shelter for the animals. She was beginning to realize they couldn't manage a full barn yet, not on their own, or even with Jesse's help. They needed to sell or trade the ox that had belonged to the Durhams so they wouldn't have to feed it through the winter. Four oxen, one horse, and a milk cow would need a lot of hay.

Her mind jumped to the building situation. To cut the sod and plow the earth beneath, they'd need a breaking plow. She'd heard some of the men on the wagon train discussing their use of the new land. On the prairies, sod buildings were the least expensive way to go. Lark rolled over. She'd head to the store tomorrow, see what the Jorgensens had or could order. The plow might be expensive, but maybe they could trade an ox or two for it. They had more than they needed now.

Then there was the garden. They had to get seeds in the ground before it was too late, or they wouldn't have any vegetables for winter. First, they needed to spade the plot that had been the garden before. The Skinners had planted a good-sized garden not far from the house last year, at least. The wife had died too early to have planted this year, though, or even prepared the plot.

Stop worrying. Sleep. She squeezed her eyes tight. *Lord, I know you've gotten us this far. But I feel so responsible. Show us how to get it all done.*

The next morning, they all hauled their bedding out of the house, and Lilac and Forsythia set to swabbing the floor with a manure wash again, as Lark had learned in town. The Skinners had started the process, but it took time and repeated applications to get the floor to a hard sheen.

"Laundry time again," Del said, shaking out a coverlet. "I'll get a fire going and heat some water." A wail from Mikael made her pause. "As soon as I feed the baby."

"All right." Lark rolled her lips. So it would be just her and Jesse for haying today. It was too much for two people, really. But the other tasks were important too. *Lord, help us.*

Jesse walked up. "S-sorry to be late."

Lark pulled on her gloves. "I know it's a bit of a walk from town. Has your uncle given any thought to getting a horse?"

"He's t-talking about it."

"Need some breakfast? There's leftovers on the table outside the soddy."

Jesse dipped his head in thanks and stepped over to scarf down some ham and biscuits. By the time Lark had tied on her straw hat—she refused to wear a sunbonnet because it hampered her vision—and sharpened her scythe, he stood ready to work.

They cut the waist-high prairie grass all morning, until the sun beat hot on their backs and sweat mingled with the dust sifting into Lark's bodice and sleeves. She paused to wipe her forehead when Lilac brought them water.

"How's it going with the soddy floor?" Lark drank, grateful. "Thank you."

"Almost finished for this round. I'll be out here to help soon."

They paused for a dinner of ham sandwiches, and then Lilac joined in the haying for the afternoon. By the time the sun lowered toward suppertime, they'd finished nearly half of the field. The drying hay lay in wide stripes across the land, the unevenness of the first rows showing their inexperience.

Lark rolled her sore shoulders. They were getting there. But it had taken days to get this far—would they manage to cut all the hay before another rain ruined it? Should they stop to rake and stack what had been cut already so the livestock would have at least some for the winter? Or just press on with the cutting? So many questions and not enough answers.

Every muscle aching, she trudged back to the house. Jesse and Lilac trailed behind.

"How is it going?" Forsythia met them with Mikael in her arms and a pitcher of switchel.

Lark downed her cup in one swig. "Going. But awfully slow."

"You need more help. Del and I can trade off with the children and the haying tomorrow. Maybe it's just as well I haven't heard from the Jorgensens yet about working at the store."

"I c-could ask my uncle to help."

They both turned to look at Jesse.

He shrugged. "I could ask."

"Sure, thanks." Lark smiled at him. But would Dr. Brownsville come? He'd let Jesse, true, but he had his own practice to get running. And they'd barely seen him or heard a word since the tiff over her masquerading as a man. Lark rubbed her tired forehead. Should she try to talk to the doctor herself? It wasn't fair for Forsythia's hopes to be dashed over something Larkspur had done. But then, it wasn't fair for Dr. Brownsville to blame Forsythia either. They'd all just done what they had to do.

At least she thought so. Lark dragged herself to the washbasin set outside the soddy and splashed cool water on her sweat-grimed face. Having to come west in the first place had been because of her rash actions, and now she'd caused more trouble. If she couldn't get this homestead up and running sustainably, that would be on her shoulders too.

No wonder she carried a yoke heavier than the oxen's lately.

The next day, they cut grass all morning, making progress with Forsythia helping as well as Lilac and Jesse. After the mid-day meal, Lark left the others still working, Del spelling Forsythia now, and headed to town.

She took the wagon and hitched two of the oxen to it—Sam and Soda. Walking alongside with the whip brought back memories of the trail. Had that life really been only weeks ago? It felt strange to drive the oxen wearing a skirt instead of pants.

Lark stopped the oxen outside the store and climbed the wooden steps. The bell jangled a welcome on the door, and she blinked in the dim interior after the sunshine outside.

"Afternoon, Miss Nielsen." Mr. Jorgensen looked up with a cheery smile. "What can I do for you?"

Good, he was easier to work with than his taciturn wife. Lark stepped up to the counter.

"I'm looking to get a breaking plow. Do you carry those, or would I need to order one?"

"Sure, we carry them, though mostly in planting season. I might have one in the back, if you've a mind to wait a moment."

"Of course." Lark scanned the shelves behind the counter while he was gone. Bolts of colorful calico and flannel, bottles of liniment, cans of kerosene. Horse harnesses hung from the rafters overhead.

"Yes, we have one, if you'll bring your wagon around."

She led the oxen behind the building, and Mr. Jorgensen lugged the heavy piece of equipment from the back storage room. The steel blade glinted, ready to bite into the tough prairie sod.

"How much is it? I was wondering if I could trade in a couple of our oxen."

The storekeeper chuckled and shook his head. "Fifteen dollars, but a span of working oxen is worth nearly ten times that. You'd do better to sell them to some homesteader."

"Ah." Clearly she was out of touch with prices around here. Or farming in general. "I'll have to come back, then. I didn't bring enough cash. Would you hold it for me?"

"To be sure. Not much call for new plows this time of year, as I said. If you don't have the cash right now, we can start a tab."

"Thank you," she answered with a nod. They'd had plenty of tabs run at their store at home, too, especially in the winter. "Do you know of anyone who might be interested in the oxen?"

"Not offhand." The shopkeeper shrugged. "You might ask Henry Caldwell, though. He tends to have his finger on the pulse of what's what. Knows who's coming and going, who needs this or that."

It made sense, with how the attorney had arranged the purchase of their land.

"Thank you." Lark reached to tip her hat out of habit, then flinched when her fingers touched her sunbonnet, which she'd conceded to for visiting town. So much to get used to.

Leaving the loaded wagon in the shade of the store, she crossed the street to the attorney's office and rapped on the door. It would be good to see him again.

"Ah, Miss Nielsen." Mr. Caldwell opened the door with a

smile. "What a pleasure to see you." He stepped back and gestured for her to enter. "I was just chatting with a friend of yours."

Lark stepped inside. Dr. Brownsville rose from the chair in front of Mr. Caldwell's desk.

She stopped short, stiffening. "Forgive me." This wasn't a good place for their first encounter after the last conversation. "I didn't mean to interrupt."

"Not at all." Mr. Caldwell waved a hand. "We were just visiting. Dr. Brownsville is looking for a horse, and I know someone who might be willing to swap a horse and buggy for his oxen and wagon. You know him, actually—Mr. Young, the banker who handled your homestead purchase."

Really? She wouldn't have pegged him as a farmer. But then, most of the folks in town probably held dual lives if they'd come out to settle the territory in the first place.

The doctor stood silently, polite but unsmiling. Mr. Caldwell glanced between them, his brow creased.

"I have a similar question, as it happens." Lark focused her attention on the attorney. "I'm looking to sell a span of our oxen as well—or at least the one that belonged to the family of the little boy we took in. Mr. Jorgensen said you might know of someone who'd be interested."

Mr. Caldwell rubbed his chin. "I'll ask around. I believe I heard of a settler looking to try oxen instead of mules on his homestead. May I let you know?"

"Of course. Thank you."

"By the way, my wife has been wanting to have your family to supper one of these days." Mr. Caldwell leaned on his cane. "Would Sunday evening be convenient? She's eager to chat with more womenfolk. She says this territory is overrun with men."

Lark smiled and nodded. "I see no problem with that." Her sisters would be delighted with a social invitation, that was certain. "Please give her our thanks."

"We'll look forward to it."

Silence hung.

"I won't keep you gentlemen any longer. Good day to you, Mr. Caldwell. Dr. Brownsville." Lark turned to go, the doctor's chill in the room outdoing the heat through the sunny window.

"Miss Nielsen." His voice halted her steps.

"Yes, Doctor?"

"My nephew informed me you could use some assistance with the haying. Tell your sisters I'll be out first thing tomorrow."

Shock nearly dropped her jaw. "Th-thank you." By sisters, did he mean Forsythia? Lark searched his somber brown gaze but found no indication. She nodded to both gentlemen again and headed into the welcome sunshine once more.

Well, Lord, at least he's speaking to us again. But by the look of things, he's not ready to forgive, much less forget.

"What was that about?" Henry Caldwell's steady gaze bored into Adam.

"What do you mean?" Adam sat back down, though he couldn't quite meet his friend's eyes.

"With Miss Nielsen, man. You turned into a veritable icicle. Don't tell me you have feelings for her."

"For her? Certainly not." Adam's neck heated.

"Aha. For someone else, then." Henry eased back into his chair and poised his cane like a schoolmaster's rule.

"This has nothing to do with—no." Adam shifted his weight, the anger rising in his chest again, however he tried to rid himself of it. "I simply—I found that I had been deceived by the Nielsen family after we traveled together for some weeks. Or rather, that they had been deceiving me all along."

"Ah." The attorney nodded. "Miss Larkspur and her guise as a man."

"Yes."

"I see." Henry steepled his fingers. "But you do understand why she did it?"

"I do. But not why they kept up the deception so long to a friend."

"And to one of the sisters, you wish to be more than a friend, is that it?" The attorney tipped his head. "Might that be why the seeming betrayal runs deeper?"

Adam couldn't think what to say. He could see how his friend might nonplus defendants in the courtroom.

"Forgive me," Henry said. "I won't press you on this. But let me just say that bitterness, whether in a friendship or something more, is not something to let take root. I speak from experience."

They sat a moment in silence. Adam, feeling somehow a chastened son even if the other man barely had ten years on him, nodded, gazing at the attorney's Bible sitting on his desk. *Have I even talked to you about this, Lord?*

"Well." Henry tapped his cane on the floor and stood. "Enough sermonizing from me. Let's go take a look at that horse."

Half an hour later, Adam stood stroking the nose of a dark bay gelding, the animal's form and teeth showing he had many good years left in him. The horse nuzzled Adam's palm with soft whiskers.

"Sorry, boy. I don't have any sugar for you." Something warmed in his chest, and he laid his palm on the horse's broad cheek and looked into its eyes. It had been some time since he'd had a special bond with a mount of his own.

"I'll take him." He nodded to Hiram Young, the banker. "And the buggy too."

"Fine by me. My son-in-law'll be mighty happy with the oxen and wagon for a wedding present." Mr. Young hooked his thumbs in his vest. "They're sharing our homestead now that our Becky got married, doing the farming for us."

Well, that explained it. Adam couldn't quite picture the portly older man driving oxen.

They finalized the exchange, and Adam hitched the gelding to the buggy and climbed in, testing the feel of the reins in his hands.

"Now you look like a proper doctor." Mr. Young grinned around his cigar.

"If only I could get some proper patients."

"Eh, folks'll come around." The banker shrugged. "That last feller left a bad taste in people's mouths. Just give 'em time. When they need you bad enough, they'll come."

Adam was trying. But how much time was enough before he took further measures, whatever those might be?

Adam drove his new horse and rig back to the office and let the gelding out in the fenced field with the Jorgensens' horses, his mind turning. He didn't want people to go sick or injured without treatment because of fear. Should he consider calling a town meeting, perhaps with Caldwell and Young's endorsement? Surely having the backing of two of the few professional men in town could make a difference.

What to do, Lord? He rubbed the gelding's nose. He needed a name for this fellow.

And what to do about Forsythia? He'd be out at the Nielsens' tomorrow. This issue was going to hit him head on, ready or not.

24

What could Forsythia possibly say to Adam?

She attacked the clumped soil in the garden plot with her spade. Since garden work was easier than haying, she'd been assigned here after a morning in the fields fairly wore her out yesterday. The plot had been plowed and planted the year before, and Lark and Lilac had cleared the worst of the weeds, but the soil needed to be broken up again.

It was good thinking work. And good for releasing frustration over how soon the doctor and Jesse might arrive for the haying.

"Miss Sythia, look!"

At Robbie's call, Forsythia leaned on her spade and smiled at the children following her in the soft dirt. Robbie held up a wriggling earthworm, his grin creasing his face in half.

"I see! Very nice. Put it back, though, Robbie boy. Earthworms are good for the garden."

"Can I show Sofie first?"

"Very well, then back it goes."

"Look, Sofie." Cradling the worm in his hands, Robbie bent to show the little girl, who squatted on her haunches, poking a stick in the dirt in imitation of Forsythia's spading. Her rosebud mouth opened in an *O* as she stared at the moist pink worm.

"All right, put it back now." Forsythia made her voice firm. "We don't want it to dry out."

"Because if it dries out, it'll die, right, Miss Sythia?" Robbie carefully slid the worm back into the furrow.

"That's right."

She still needed to decide what to have Robbie and the other children call her long-term. Auntie Sythia? Mama? What was right? She glanced toward the house, where they'd pulled Mikael's cradle outside. He was quiet, so he was still napping. The cradle had come from the Durhams' wagon, no doubt used for Robbie and allowed to take up valuable space in hopes of the new baby to come. That little one had never used it, but baby Mikael did. She hoped that brought a smile to Alice's face in heaven.

Forsythia turned back to spading, having finished one length of the plot already. Not a bad start this early in the morning, though heat already rose from the sun-soaked earth.

"Sythia! Come look what we've got."

At Lilac's call, Forsythia looked up again. She'd make little progress with this many interruptions.

Lilac hurried toward her, her dark curls flying free of her sunbonnet and face beaming. She clutched her apron around . . . a bundle of wiggling feathers?

"Chickens. Jesse brought us chickens." Out of breath, Lilac hurried to the edge of the garden plot and opened her apron for Forsythia to see. "A batch of chickens someone was giving away. Mr. Jorgensen had them at the store. He was only too glad to get rid of them, Jesse said. Isn't it wonderful? They should be laying by fall. There are more, if we want to go to town to get them."

"Wonderful." Forsythia smoothed her finger over the coppery feathers of one bird. Three half-grown, leggy young chickens stirred in Lilac's apron. "We definitely need a barn of some sort now."

"Jesse and the doctor are going to help us put together a temporary coop before they leave. Lark says she'll go into town for chicken wire." Lilac hesitated. "They're already in the field, but the doctor asked about you."

"He did?" Forsythia's heart flipped.

"Well, he asked where you were, at least." Lilac cocked her head, compassion in her eyes. "You'll speak to him, won't you?"

"If he'll speak to me." Forsythia turned back to her spade.

She didn't see Adam until she took water to the fieldworkers midmorning, carrying Mikael snug in the sling against her.

She was grateful for the baby's distraction for both of them. The doctor kept his eyes on Mikael's face as he took the water dipper from her.

"He's grown." He drank, then took his hat off to wipe his forehead with his sleeve.

Seeing him so close, shirtsleeves rolled up and dark hair curling with sweat, sent Forsythia's heart into her throat. She searched his face, hoping for some sign of forgiveness, but he wouldn't quite meet her eyes.

"Doctor." She gripped the water bucket handle and adjusted Mikael's weight in the sling with her other hand.

"Yes?" He did glance at her then.

"How—how have you been?" Her courage failing, the words stuttered out.

His gaze softened. "I'm well. We have the office and our rooms pretty well set up, and I was able to obtain a horse and buggy yesterday."

"Lark mentioned that." Something released in Forsythia's chest. At least they were talking.

"And you?"

The look in his brown eyes caught her in the throat. He did

still care—surely he did. "Well also. Still not full strength, but I'm fine to work in the garden." She jiggled Mikael with a hand under his bottom. "And tend to these little ones."

"Which you do nicely." He touched Mikael's tiny fist.

"Doctor . . ." she started.

"I'd best get back to work." He handed back the dipper, brushing her hand ever so briefly, then settled his hat and picked up his scythe.

"Of course." Throat stinging in disappointment, she nodded, watching his broad back and arms begin the swinging rhythm of cutting once again.

Well, Lord, thank you. She headed back to the house with Mikael. *It's a start.*

By Saturday, the hay lay cut and drying, and the garden plot was ready for planting. Lark gave Jesse—and his uncle—the day off, and the sisters walked the rows of their garden, seeds in hand. Laughter and chatter rose like steam from the earth in the summer sunshine, the children playing about them. They planted the seeds they'd brought from home, carrots, beets, turnips, and cabbage, and also those ordered from the store, lettuce and beans and seed potatoes. It felt so good to get the vegetables in the ground.

"Tomorrow let's go to the church service," Lark said as they washed their soil-dusted hands once the planting was done. "It's been too long since we gathered for worship."

"Oh, that would be such a gift." Forsythia drew a deep breath at the thought. "I wonder if they have anyone to play music yet."

"I'm not sure. The town is pretty small still, with how many families left after the Indian scare last year."

"Did anything actually happen?" Lilac dried her hands.

"No, but people were terrified by the rumors."

"So much happens because of fear and misunderstanding." Forsythia thought of Little Bear and the friend he had been to them on the trail. How was he faring, and his family on the reservation? And now the distance between her and the doctor . . .

"Then to the Caldwells' for supper, right?" Del scooped a wakening Mikael from his cradle and kissed his cheek, earning one of his increasingly frequent smiles. "There's much to look forward to this Sunday."

Only a few families had gathered in the simple church building at the end of the main street on Sunday morning, but Forsythia already recognized a number of faces. The Jorgensens, and Adam and Jesse, of course. The banker, Mr. Young, and his family. Mr. Caldwell and a kind-faced woman who must be his wife. And a few other people she'd met briefly in the store or passed on the street.

Someday, hopefully, this would be home and all these people their friends. Surely gathering to worship the Savior together was a good step in that direction.

Rev. Pritchard, a slender, earnest young man with slightly disheveled hair, rose to begin the service. Del had told them he was an itinerant preacher, going back and forth between Salton and another town about ten miles away.

"This is the day the Lord hath made," he said, smiling broadly over the little congregation. "Let us rejoice and be glad in it."

Yes, Lord. Forsythia closed her eyes and quieted her heart. *Help me be glad in you, though I don't know what the future holds. But all will be well, as Ma always said. Maybe not in our way, but in yours.*

After the simple service, they gathered out in the sunshine to visit. Del held Mikael while Robbie ran to play with the other children scampering about. Sofie clung to Forsythia's skirts, sober-faced.

"You haven't seen this many people in a long while, have you, little one?" Forsythia picked up the toddler and kissed her hair, braided tightly and tied with a blue ribbon in honor of the day.

Sofie sniffled and leaned her head on Forsythia's shoulder.

"You aren't coming down with something, are you?" She laid her hand on Sofie's forehead. She wasn't feverish, but she seemed a bit under the weather.

"Sythia." Lark waved her over to where her sisters stood talking with the reverend.

With a glance to see Robbie engrossed in a game of tag with some other little boys, Forsythia crossed the churchyard with Sofie in her arms.

Lark introduced her to Rev. Pritchard. "I was asking the reverend if he'd like any help with the music on Sundays. He says yes."

"Accompaniment would be a tremendous boon to our services." Rev. Pritchard rocked on his toes, beaming. "Someday I hope we can have a piano, as we do in my other parish. I fear our a cappella tunes lack the luster and life instruments bring. But with juggling two congregations—you can imagine there's much I haven't managed to accomplish yet."

"It was still lovely to join the congregation in song, a cappella or not." Forsythia shifted Sofie on her hip. "But we'd be delighted to bring our instruments next Sunday, if a guitar, fiddle, and harmonica aren't too rustic for you."

"By no means. Surely any instrument is fit to make a joyful noise unto the Lord. And after all"—he flung his arms wide toward the dusty road and unpainted buildings—"we are plenty rustic here to begin with."

Forsythia laughed. He seemed like a pleasant, good-hearted young pastor, if a bit enthusiastic. She glanced back to check on Robbie and noticed the doctor watching her. What was he thinking, seeing her laugh and chat with a friendly young man?

She turned back and focused on what Rev. Pritchard was

saying. If Adam wanted to talk with her, he was free to do so. In the meantime, let him wonder. The thought gave her a wicked little frisson of pleasure. *Forsythia Peace Nielsen, shame on you. And on the Lord's day too*, Ma's voice niggled in her mind.

"You must be the Nielsen sisters." A gentle hand touched Forsythia's shoulder. "I couldn't leave without greeting you all briefly, though I know we'll see you tonight."

They turned to see Mrs. Caldwell smiling at them, her dark hair laced with silver. Her husband stood back but gave them all a friendly nod.

"Thank you for inviting us." Lark shook the woman's hand. "I meant to ask, is it all right if we bring the children?"

"Oh, goodness, yes. I'd be disappointed if you didn't." Mrs. Caldwell beamed at Sofie, earning a shy smile in return. "I won't keep you now, but we'll see you about six? I look forward to becoming better acquainted."

They said their good-byes and gathered the children to head home. Sofie had started to fall asleep on Forsythia's shoulder and fussed when transferred to the wagon. Robbie, meanwhile, was not pleased at being removed from his new friends. Between the older two and a hungry baby, it made for a rather fractious ride home.

They had a simple cold dinner, since their main meal would be supper today, and then the children napped. By the time they piled back into the wagon to head for the Caldwells', everyone seemed more chipper again.

The evening summer sun still shone when they pulled up at the Caldwells' homestead a short ways out of town.

"A real frame house," Lilac marveled, climbing out of the wagon. "Lark, think we'll have one like this someday?"

"I hope so."

Del and Forsythia collected the children, smoothing Sofie's dress and straightening Robbie's collar, then together they climbed the steps—real wooden steps. Forsythia admired the simple porch with a rocking chair and porch swing. How lovely it must be to sit out here on summer nights to catch a breeze or watch the stars.

Mrs. Caldwell opened the door before they even knocked, beckoning them in. "Welcome, welcome."

Forsythia stepped inside, leading Robbie by the hand, and gazed with hungry eyes about her. Braided rugs, kerosene lamps, framed pictures on the walls, comfortable furniture. Scents savory and sweet wafting from the kitchen, and Mrs. Caldwell's motherly voice. A home—that was what this was. An unexpected lump tightened Forsythia's throat. It felt so long, compared to the actual time since they left home.

Robbie stared speechless at the spread when they all sat down at the supper table. Forsythia felt almost the same. Crisp fried chicken, new potatoes, tiny pole beans from the Caldwells' garden. Even lettuce in a salad with sugar, vinegar, and cream dressing. They must have gotten their garden in early.

Mr. Caldwell prayed. "Father, we thank thee for this food from thy hand, and for new friends and a new life in this land. Bless this evening and our fellowship together. In the name of Jesus, amen."

Forsythia blinked back tears before lifting her head. They hadn't known a homey welcome like this since the Herrons. *Heavenly Father, you knew how much we needed this.*

"I hope our beans will produce before frost. We got them planted yesterday." Lark speared a forkful reverently. "This looks heavenly."

"Make sure you soak the ground and seeds really well," Mrs. Caldwell counseled. "They'll sprout faster that way."

"I hadn't thought of that," Lark answered. "Thanks for the good advice. I'll water it well tomorrow and keep it damp."

Conversation flowed easily, as if they'd known the Caldwells for years. After supper, Forsythia sat in the sitting room—on an upholstered sofa, luxury of luxuries—to cradle a sleeping Mikael and watch Sofie and Robbie play.

"Rests the soul, doesn't it?" Mrs. Caldwell entered and sat beside her. "Watching a sleeping baby."

"Would you like to hold him?"

"You don't mind?" Her eyes held an unexpected vulnerability.

Forsythia transferred Mikael's sleepy weight to the other woman's arms.

"I've always loved little ones." Mrs. Caldwell brushed a gentle hand over Mikael's growing hair. "We couldn't have any of our own, you know."

"I didn't know." One never knew the heartaches behind others' smiling faces.

"I gave that dream to the Lord long ago. But now and then He gives me the gift of loving other people's children." Mrs. Caldwell looked up at Forsythia with eyes whose kindness reminded her more of Ma than anyone she'd met in years. "As it seems He has given you."

"I sometimes feel very inadequate for it." Forsythia folded her hands in her skirt.

"Well, that's a good sign you're not depending on your own strength, then." Mrs. Caldwell rocked Mikael gently. "But perhaps you won't always carry this burden alone? My Henry said something to me of his friend the doctor . . ."

"Oh." Forsythia's face warmed. "I don't—that is, there is no understanding."

"Would you like there to be?"

Their hostess could be direct as well as kind. "I—I might. But I don't think he does, not anymore."

Mrs. Caldwell sat silently a moment. "I'm sorry, dear one.

But be sure of what he thinks before you assume. Sometimes things just need to be talked through a bit."

Perhaps she was right. But it took two to be willing to talk.

A sudden eruption from the children claimed Forsythia's attention as Robbie tugged a wooden train Jesse had carved away from Sofie. Sofie slapped him, then burst into tears.

Forsythia hurried to separate them, lifting the sobbing little girl to her hip. "What's the matter with you today?"

Sofie coughed and rubbed her nose, eyes streaming.

"I'm afraid she might be coming down with a cold. We'd better get her home. I'm so sorry."

"Nothing to be sorry for." Mrs. Caldwell rose. "Let me tell the rest of your family for you."

"Thank you. Robbie, pick up your train. It's time to go."

Sofie fell asleep on Forsythia's lap on the drive home, but the heaviness of her breathing was worrying. The little girl barely woke when they got back to the homestead, undressed her, and tucked her under the covers.

"I don't like the sound of her lungs," Forsythia whispered to Lark, covering the little girl with a blanket. "And she feels feverish. This came on so suddenly. Or else I just haven't been paying close enough attention." Had she been so preoccupied with her own problems that she'd neglected this little one entrusted to her? Guilt smote hard.

"Things do come on suddenly in children. It's not your fault, Sythia." Lark squeezed her shoulder. "Get some sleep yourself. She'll probably be better in the morning."

Lark headed out to the wagon, where she still slept until they could add on to the soddy. Forsythia lay down next to Sofie so she would hear her in the night. She laid a hand on the small back, feeling the gentle rise and fall. Only a slight wheezing now. Hopefully Lark was right, and Sofie would just sleep off whatever this was. *Please, Lord.*

A barking cough woke Forsythia sometime later. She sat up to find Sofie caught in a paroxysm beside her, her little body spasming with coughs so sharp she could barely breathe.

Dear God. Forsythia snatched the little girl up and held her upright against her own body to help her breathe. "There, little one. Sythia's here. Try to breathe, Sofie."

The coughing eased slightly, and Sofie drew several shuddering breaths, then started to cry.

Del sat up on the other side of the bed. "Is she all right?"

"I'm not sure. She was coughing dreadfully." Forsythia rocked the little girl in her arms. Almost immediately, Sofie started to cough again, hacking barks that made Forsythia wince at the sound. "Del, can you get her some water?"

Del scrambled to her feet and lit a lamp, then dipped a tin cup into the water bucket they kept near the stove. "Here, little one." She brought the cup near.

Sofie tried to drink, but she just kept coughing. Water spilled over onto her nightie and Forsythia's.

"Can you get Lark?" Forsythia wrapped a blanket around the little girl and rubbed her back, trying to calm her. Crying certainly didn't help the coughing.

A moment later, Lark knelt beside them. "Sounds like croup. I remember Jonah had it when he was little, and the coughing comes on sudden in the night. Ma used steam to calm Jonah's down."

"Let's boil some water, then. Put some lavender and rosemary in the water from my kit. Those are supposed to help with breathing. Add a few drops of eucalyptus oil."

Lilac was up now and put a kettle on the stove. Thankfully, Robbie and Mikael still slept.

When the water boiled, Forsythia held Sofie so the fragrant steam could rise into her face. Lark settled a towel over their heads to hold in the steam. Though the coughing eased a bit, fits persisted, only giving the little girl a minute or so break between paroxysms. Her breath started to come in high-pitched wheezes.

"Try some warm water." Lark added some hot water to the cold in the cup and offered it to Sofie.

The little girl choked, water dribbling out of her mouth. Grimacing, she twisted against Forsythia, fighting for breath.

"She's not getting better." Panic rose in Forsythia's chest. "What else can we do?" She ran through her list of medicinal herbs in her head, but nothing else came to mind. Plus, if Sofie couldn't drink, what good would they do?

"I don't know." Lark sat back on her heels. "I don't remember Ma doing anything else, but I was still young at the time."

Another coughing fit shook Sofie. Forsythia set her mouth and stood, hugging the little girl to her shoulder. "I'm taking her to Dr. Brownsville."

Lark pushed to her feet. "Wouldn't it be better if I fetch him here?"

"I'm afraid there might not be time." Speaking the words gave shape to her fear, but her gut said she needed to go. Now. "It'll be quicker just to take her there. Will you harness Starbright for me?"

"Of course. And I'll drive."

Del held Sofie while Lark and Forsythia yanked on dresses and boots, then they bundled Sofie into a blanket on Forsythia's lap on the wagon seat.

"We will pray." Lilac squeezed her hand, then let go. "Go with God."

Lark clucked to Starbright. "Come on, girl. Show us your speed."

Holding Sofie upright to help her breathe, Forsythia prayed with every step of the horse and jolt of the wagon. How could two miles seem so long?

At last the darkened shapes of buildings rose in the moonlight. Sofie's coughing fits had grown weaker, the space between them longer. Forsythia kept feeling for the little girl's breathing, her own breath fast with fear. Was she growing worse?

Please, Lord. Please, Lord.

25

A pounding downstairs jolted Adam awake.

His heart pumping hard, he yanked trousers over his nightshirt and clattered down the stairs. Midnight hammering on a doctor's door was never good.

The knocking came again. Adam fumbled to light a lamp in his office, hurried to the door, and flung it open.

Larkspur Nielsen stood on the doorstep, a shadowy horse and wagon behind her. Was that Forsythia on the wagon seat, a bundle in her arms?

"Sofie's got croup," Lark said. "She's not responding to anything we tried."

"Let's get her inside." Adam strode to the wagon and reached up for Sofie. Cradling the child, he carried her into his office, followed by the sisters.

"Can you light another lamp, please?" He set Sofie on the examining table and loosened the blanket. "Let's take a look at you, little one."

Lark brought another kerosene lamp close.

"The paroxysms seemed to ease on the drive, but I don't know if that means she's better or worse." Forsythia stayed close at Adam's side. "She was having such a terrible time getting air before that we couldn't even get warm water down her."

Adam grabbed his stethoscope to listen to the tiny chest. Sofie lay quietly, her breathing hoarse, but it seemed to come without too much effort. She scanned the shadowy, lamplit office with wide eyes.

"She has some lung congestion, but I think you're right, her breathing has eased." Adam removed the listening pieces from his ears. "Cool night air can often calm an attack of croup. Taking her for a ride outside was probably the best thing you could do for her."

"Really?" Forsythia pressed a hand to her mouth. "So we didn't need to disturb you after all. I was so frightened."

"No, I'm glad you did. Acute croup is nothing to be careless with, and children do die of it."

Sofie coughed but not into a fit.

"That's so much looser than it was." Tears in her voice, Forsythia stroked Sofie's hair. "Oh, thank you, Lord."

"Let's try some warm water or tea for her now." Adam turned to Lark. "Would you stir up the fire in the stove? The kettle on top should still be full and perhaps warm." He'd made tea himself in the evening, staying up late to plan for the town meeting he and Caldwell were putting together. He'd only been in bed an hour or so.

"Of course." Lark opened the door of the potbellied stove, poked the still-glowing coals, and added another chunk of wood. She pulled the kettle to the center of the stove.

"The steam will be good for her, too, though I'm sure you already tried that." Adam held one of the lamps close to examine Sophie's face and chest. No bluish tint to her lips or nail beds, and while her nostrils flared slightly with each breath, he didn't see chest retractions, nor was she consistently wheezing, only sporadically.

"I'd like you to stay here overnight so I can monitor Sofie. But the worst seems to be over—of this attack, at least."

"I should go home and let the others know. You stay, Sythia." Lark headed for the door, then turned back. "Thank you, Doctor."

"Of course. I haven't done much." But he heard the stiffness creep back into his voice.

Larkspur left without another word. Forsythia stood with her face averted from him, rubbing Sofie's back.

Finally yielding to the holy prompting within him, Adam stepped away from the examining table. "I'll be right back." He hurried to the door and opened it. "Larkspur—Miss Nielsen?"

She looked down from the wagon seat. "Yes?"

He closed the door behind him and stepped up to the wagon. "I'm afraid I haven't been very kind in my behavior lately."

"I understand why you're upset. I just wish you wouldn't blame Forsythia for it."

"I don't—not really." He ran a hand through his hair. How to explain the mix of emotions tumbling through him lately? "I understand why you did what you did also. I just wish you had told me about it sooner."

"I'm sorry." Lark met his gaze.

He extended a hand up to her. "How about I'll forgive you, if you'll forgive me?"

She shook it, her grip strong. "Agreed."

Adam watched the wagon rumble away in the moonlight, the weight in his chest finally lightening. Except he still needed to speak with Forsythia. *Lord, give me the words.*

She looked up when he stepped back into the office. She'd drawn a chair near the stove so Sofie could breathe the steam puffing from the kettle. She sat bent over the little girl in her arms, and the lamplight flickered on her hair like sparks in the night.

Adam swallowed. He cared for her. He might even love her. But . . . he wasn't ready. Not yet. He'd realized that, in times of prayer these recent days. He didn't want to hurt her any more than he'd already done. But he needed time.

"How is she doing?" He crouched down to Sofie's level and touched the little girl's forehead. Cool to his touch but not clammy. A good sign.

"She's getting sleepy, but I'd like to get some liquid in her. Do you have chamomile? I should have brought my herbs with me."

"I don't know many herbal remedies, but I do have that one." Adam rose and fetched it from his cabinet. He put a pinch of the herb in a small cup, then added water from the kettle and set it aside to steep. He drew a chair close to Forsythia's while they waited.

"Miss Nielsen . . . Forsythia. May I call you that?"

She nodded, some emotion flitting across her face.

"I want to tell you that I spoke with your sister. And we have mended the breach, as it were."

Forsythia closed her eyes. "I'm so glad."

"I want to ask your forgiveness, if I've hurt you by my behavior in recent days." He paused. "No, please erase that *if*. I know I have hurt you. I've seen it in your eyes."

"I've wanted to speak to you . . . Adam." She seemed to taste his name, her eyes asking permission, which he gave with a nod. "I just wasn't sure how to make this right."

"That wasn't your responsibility, not really. I understand what you did, though I may not agree with it. But I think we must put this behind us, perhaps having all learned something from it."

She nodded, and a tear fell on Sofie's nightgowned arm.

"And I've learned something else." He hesitated, then reached for her hand and folded it in his.

Only her faint intake of breath told him what he already suspected. *Lord, this is hard.*

"I care for you, Forsythia." His heart thudded as if he were a schoolboy again. "I care deeply. And I would consider it . . . a privilege and an honor if someday you would give consent for me to court you." Her fingers tensed, slender and warm within his. "But not yet."

She looked up, and the question in her eyes smote him in the chest.

"I've realized I'm not ready. I still . . ." He cleared his throat from a sudden clogging. "I still miss Elizabeth. We've been going so hard since I joined the wagon train that I haven't had time to properly grieve. It hasn't even been three months since I buried her."

"Of course." She pressed his hand, compassion melting the hurt in her eyes.

"And I'll understand if—if you don't want to wait for me." These words came hard, but he pressed them forth. "I know there are plenty of eligible men in these parts who might be eager to win your hand. And I can't say for certain when I'll be ready."

Forsythia shook her head, and another tear slipped down her cheek. "I don't mind waiting."

"Well." He rubbed the back of his neck, feeling it warm. "If you're sure."

Forsythia nodded and sniffed, then withdrew her hand with a small smile. "Perhaps we should see if Sofie's tea is ready."

"Perhaps." Or the nearness and sweetness of this woman might just make him throw all caution and wisdom to the wind. "At least I have some honey here." He dipped out a spoonful and stirred it into the steaming tea.

"You know, there are things you don't know about me," Forsythia said some moments later, after getting several small sips into Sofie.

"What do you mean?" Adam sat back down, leaning his elbow on the examining table.

"I haven't told you this, but . . . I killed a man on our journey here. Shortly after we left home." The hand holding Sofie's cup trembled a bit, and she set down the tea.

"Killed?" That didn't sound like Forsythia. "What happened?"

"He snuck into our camp at night and grabbed Del." As Sofie's eyelids drooped, Forsythia snuggled her close. "He had her by the neck and was threatening awful things. I . . . threw my knife. Pa had taught us all well, but I was the best at knife throwing." Her voice caught, dropping to a whisper. "I didn't mean to kill him."

Adam stroked his beard. "You saved your sister's life."

"That's what Lark says." Forsythia shrugged slightly. "But I had awful dreams afterward. Lark prayed me through it, and it's better now. But sometimes . . . I still see my knife sticking from that horrid man's back." She shuddered. "Anyway, I just thought you should know." She glanced at him, then away.

"Forsythia." Adam leaned forward. "If you are wondering if this changes my opinion of you or my feelings toward you, it does not. Except to strengthen my admiration for your courage. I have no doubt throwing that knife was the hardest thing you ever did. But think if you had not. Does Del wish you had held back?"

"I suppose not." She met his eyes, vulnerability in her blue ones. "But sometimes I can't help wondering, how does the Lord see it? Am I stained forever in His sight?"

"No more than the rest of us are. That's why He's given us the blood of Jesus, after all."

Forsythia blinked hard, then let out a long, trembling sigh. "You're right. Thank you." She glanced down at Sofie, and her mouth tipped up in a smile. "Somebody has fallen asleep."

The next morning, after Forsythia and Sofie had slept on a comfortable pallet he made for them on the office floor and Adam managed to catch a few hours of sleep upstairs, Lark came back to collect her family in the wagon. Sofie had coughed some in the night, but she was vastly improved, and he felt it safe to send them home.

"Feel free to send for me again. But remember, warm steam and then cool night air. The combination often does the trick."

"We'll remember. Thank you." While her gaze was nothing but proper, there was something tender and new in Forsythia's smile as she bid him good-bye.

Adam headed back inside as the Nielsens drove away, Jesse accompanying them. *Lord, why is my heart tugging toward her harder now that I've set the brakes on this thing?*

The town meeting. He'd focus on that. It was set for this evening, after all. Caldwell and Young had agreed to help lead it, and Rev. Pritchard sounded eager to attend as well. Hopefully other families would show up. He wanted to introduce himself to the town, build bridges and connections with the people, as well as suggest they start holding these meetings regularly. After all, the only way to grow a town was to develop community.

He sat at his desk to go over his notes from last night. Sofie's forgotten cup caught his attention, sitting there with the dregs of chamomile tea still inside. He turned it, thinking of Forsythia patiently coaxing the little girl to drink. Tending to Sofie beside her last night, he'd felt the most whole he had since Elizabeth died. Actually, that was how he felt every time he worked with Forsythia.

Pay attention, man. You said you needed time, and you do.

He grabbed a cup of coffee, then forced himself to read over and edit his notes, then buried himself in a medical journal on frontier doctoring. If he was to win the trust of this town, he'd better be sure he was capable of keeping it.

A knock on his door roused him from the pages. Opening it, he found Hiram Young standing outside.

"Welcome, Mr. Young. Can I do something for you?"

"I hope so." Hiram removed his hat and stepped inside, twirling it between his fingers.

Adam closed the door. "Are you ill, Mr. Young?"

"No—no. But I've got a—" The banker grimaced. "A boil that could use tending to."

"I see. Where is it?"

"It's, ah . . ." Hiram's florid face reddened further. "In a place that makes sitting down a bit unpleasant, if you get my meaning."

"Aha." Keeping a straight face, Adam drew the curtains and motioned to his examining table. "I assure you, my practice is one of complete discretion. Please, let's take a look, Mr. Young."

Half an hour later, the boil lanced and dressed, he sent a relieved banker on his way.

Well. Adam washed his hands and instruments. He'd officially seen his third patient in town, if you counted Sofie. And two just this morning. Perhaps things were looking up.

Late that afternoon, as he was starting to think about getting ready for the meeting, Rev. Pritchard stopped by to have Adam treat an ingrown toenail. When Henry Caldwell followed shortly after, asking him to take a look at a spot that sometimes rubbed on his prosthetic leg, Adam folded his arms.

"You rascals are in cahoots, aren't you? Trying to build up my practice before the meeting tonight."

The attorney looked up innocently, folding his trouser leg back down over the prosthetic. "They're all perfectly legitimate complaints, Doctor."

"Indeed. Quite urgent, all of them." Adam shook his head, but he couldn't help but be warmed. So he did have some friends in this town.

"Well, we figured, if anyone questioned your character, we could all truthfully say we'd been patients of yours." Henry pushed to his feet. "Simple as that."

"Thank you." Adam clapped his friend on the shoulder. "But I don't need you as my defense lawyer tonight. Let me speak to the people myself."

That night, he wondered if he'd spoken too quickly when he saw the scattered attendance in the church building and the skeptical looks on the faces of many of the families who were there. The Nielsen sisters slipped into the back, bolstering his spirits more than he'd thought probable.

"Welcome, citizens of Salton." Mr. Caldwell opened the meeting, using the pulpit as a podium. "As resident attorney, I've been asked to officially open our first town meeting. Rev. Pritchard, would you offer a word of prayer?"

The young preacher bounced up and gave an enthusiastic invocation.

"Thank you." Henry adjusted his spectacles and smiled out over the attendees. "As you know, we are gathered for several reasons. But first, we want to welcome an important—and very needed—new member to our community. Dr. Adam Brownsville would like to say a few words to us."

Henry stepped aside, and Adam took his place, grateful for the notes in his hand. He hadn't felt this nervous since his first day of medical school.

"Good evening, citizens of Salton." He gave what he hoped was a friendly smile, though the faces blurred before him. "I didn't plan to settle in your town, but each day I am more convinced this is where the Lord led me. When I first met Mr. Caldwell here, he told me you had need of a doctor." He glanced at his notes, then back up. "He also told me your prior experience with a physician—or with a man claiming to be a physician—had been distressing. Indeed, that this man was a charlatan through and through, and, as I have since learned, was the cause of not only injury but even death to some you held most dear."

He could sense Mr. Jorgensen's gaze from the front row. His wife was not present.

"I make no excuses for such a man. He is not worthy to be called a doctor, a title of which the very essence should be to first do no harm. But I stand before you to tell you my desire is to serve this town in a manner completely opposite to that of my predecessor. I am a graduate of Jefferson Medical College in Philadelphia. Following the completion of my studies, I opened my own practice in Illinois and ran it successfully for six years. I am not a perfect doctor, nor can I save every patient. You may have heard that I failed to save the mothers of the children the Nielsen sisters have taken in."

Murmurs scuttled around the room.

"In fact, I was unable to save even my own wife. She died of pneumonia shortly before I joined the wagon train that led me here." He glanced down again a moment, pushing down the ache in his chest.

The roomful of people quieted.

"But I can promise you this." He tried to meet the gaze of every person he could. "I will not lie to you. I will not carelessly experiment on your loved ones. I will do my best always to help, to ease suffering, and, when God allows it, to save lives. For He is the only One who truly has that power." Adam drew a breath. "I hope to get to know many of you not merely as patients, but as friends. I ask only that you would give me that chance." He paused a moment, but there seemed to be nothing left to say. "Thank you."

He sat down, spent. Henry Caldwell returned to the pulpit,

and discussion ensued regarding getting the school ready to open in September, advertising for a sheriff, and planning some sort of community harvest celebration for the fall. But Adam couldn't focus on any of it.

Had his words made any difference? *Lord, I've done all I can.*

26

A growing race had begun in the garden.

Forsythia breathed in the fresh morning air and bent to brush her fingers over the feathery carrot tops waving above the earth. They'd had gentle rain and plenty of sun, just right for these new seedlings. The beets and turnips were sending tender new leaves up, too, and the potatoes had sprouted like weeds. As for the beans, they seemed to be striving to win the race.

"Ready?" Lark spoke from behind her.

Forsythia turned with a smile and tightened her sunbonnet strings. "Ready."

Lark handed her a spade. "I'll drive the plow, and you and Lilac can come behind and cut the sod strips."

Today was the day to cut sod for their addition to the house. Which would mean more room soon, praise be. Even with Lark still sleeping in the wagon, they always seemed to be stepping on each other.

Larkspur hitched three of the oxen to the breaking plow and started on a section of mown prairie grass near where the barn would eventually be built. Following, Forsythia marveled at how the plow's steel blade cut through the tough sod, slicing off a long strip about four inches deep and—when Lark turned and plowed the other direction—twelve inches wide. She and Lilac came behind with their spades and sliced the sod into bricks about two feet long.

By the time they'd worked for an hour, sweat was pouring down Forsythia's neck inside her bonnet. She huffed a breath to blow the stray hairs off her face. She fully understood why Lark preferred a straw hat.

"Dr. Brownsville's here," Robbie called, running toward them from the house. "Him and Jesse. To help!"

"Wonderful." Lark turned the oxen for another row. "Sythia, ask them to start carrying the sod bricks over to the house. They're heavy, so it will help to have the men for that."

If only she weren't so sweaty and disheveled. Forsythia wiped grimy hands on her apron and headed for the soddy. Del, with Mikael in her arms, stood chatting with the doctor and Jesse.

"Thank you so much for coming, Doctor." Forsythia approached them. "When you're ready, Lark said we could use help lugging the sod bricks we've been cutting over to the house. No hurry."

"We'll be right over." Adam turned to her with the smile that always weakened her knees. "I was just telling Del that the town is in need of a schoolteacher. The woman Rev. Pritchard thought he'd found can't come after all, and the townsfolk want the children to get some schooling in before harvest season pulls them back to the fields."

"I'd have to take the teacher's examination to get a certificate, but I'd like to try." Del's eyes were lit up. "I've always wanted a chance to teach."

"And you'd be good at it." Forsythia wanted to hug her sister, but her hands were too dirty.

"Well, let's get to sod laying, then." The doctor rolled up his sleeves and winked at Jesse. "Before we get roped in to building a schoolhouse next."

"The town already has one, silly." But Forsythia smiled. Something seemed lighter about Adam in recent days. Was it the talk they'd had? Or was God healing his heart?

As for her, she'd known a greater depth of peace since their conversation. Not just over Adam, but over the thief she'd killed. How easy it was sometimes to forget the simple truth of having a Savior. But she was trying hard to remember.

They labored until noon, Lark plowing, Forsythia and Lilac cutting sod bricks, and the doctor and Jesse loading them on the wagon to take over to the house, laying them along the lines Lark had marked on the east side. After stopping for the dinner Del prepared, they all joined in continuing to build the sod walls of the addition.

They laid the bricks end to end lengthwise, then started the next row with half a piece of sod so they could overlap the lay of the bricks, always setting the heavy lengths grass-side down. The walls rose slowly but surely, firm and two feet thick.

"But how do we get in?" Robbie popped out of the main soddy, eager to help. "There's no door in this wall."

"It will be a separate room." Lark paused to wipe her forehead with her wrist, leaving a streak of dirt. She pointed to the soddy wall with no door or window. "We can't cut a door in that wall without compromising the main house, so we'll just have another door, right there." She pointed to the gap with her boot. "But it will provide good storage and a place for a couple of us to sleep. A lot of families build wooden additions instead, since it's hard to join sod walls. But we don't have that much lumber yet, and sod is free."

"It's free 'cause it's dirt." Robbie flung his arms wide. "And we don't have to pay God for it."

Laughter rose above the climbing sod.

Robbie studied the growing room. "Our chickens could live in there too."

Forsythia choked trying to stem her laughter, then gave up. "Oh, Robbie, such a mind you have. But you're right, we need a house for our chickens too."

"They can live with Buttercup." He nodded sagely, a finger against his chin.

The grown-ups all nodded, mostly with faces creased in delighted laughter.

Two days later, Adam and Jesse pounded the wooden planks Lark had bought for the doorframe snug against the sod bricks bordering the door space, and they continued laying sod blocks against them. They nailed another board over the top to complete the frame, then continued laying sod atop it for a couple more rows. Adam climbed onto a ladder to reach the highest part of the wall.

By the time the sun lowered toward supper the next night, the walls of the addition were finished. Weary and thankful, they sat on the grass to survey their handiwork.

"New house!" From Forsythia's lap, Sofie clapped her tiny hands and beamed.

"A new part of our house anyway." Forsythia squeezed her close, so thankful for the ease of her little girl's breathing. *Her little girl.* When had she started to think of Sofie that way? And not just her, but Robbie and Mikael too.

"I'd call that a good day's work." Beside her, Adam stretched his arms, then leaned back on his elbows. "But I think I'll opt for shipping in timber to get my own house in town built."

"We couldn't have done it without you." Forsythia fought the urge to brush a wayward dark curl off his forehead.

He tipped his head back and smiled at her. "That's what friends are for. Besides, it's not like I have patients banging down the door or even at the door." He rolled his eyes, making the others chuckle.

"The meeting didn't make a difference?"

"Not yet. But we'll see."

He and Jesse declined supper, choosing to drive home to get some rest before they came back to help lay the roof in the morning. Forsythia fought disappointment, focusing on Mikael's gurgles and coos as she warmed his milk and fed him from the cup Jesse had carved.

Lord, why is my heart tugging toward Adam so much now, just when he has pulled back?

Adam's back muscles ached as he placed another sod brick atop the closely spaced wooden rafters they had laid across the Nielsens' soddy addition.

He didn't mind helping the Nielsens—certainly they had helped him plenty. It was what neighbors did out here on the frontier, and they'd no men of their own, hardy though these women were. And he hoped someday they might be more than friends, even family, despite his telling Forsythia he needed time.

But even with all the manual labor he'd done in recent months, lifting and laying heavy bricks of sod taxed his muscles in entirely new ways. His shoulders felt like they were on fire, and not from the baking sun.

At a distant noise, he glanced down from his perch on the ladder. A wagon came rattling across the prairie, kicking up dust from the trail leading from the north. The horses pulling it were near galloping.

"Jesse," he called to his nephew, who was helping cut more sod, "can you see who that is?"

Jesse straightened and shaded his eyes. "N-not sure. But they're in a hurry."

Adam clambered down the ladder. No one pushed a team like that on a hot day, not without good reason.

The wagon clattered up, and a man jumped down. Anthony Armstead. Adam's first patient in this town.

"Please, it's my boy. Carl." Anthony was gasping for breath as he gestured to the wagon bed. "A rattler got him."

Adam charged for his buggy, where he always kept his bag ready. "Get me cold wet cloths."

Lilac and Lark ran for the well. Forsythia hurried at his side. "Do you need a knife?"

"Have one." He snatched up his bag and rushed to the Armsteads' wagon.

A boy of about ten lay in the back on a quilt, his mother cradling his head and shoulders. The same youngster Adam had seen driving the wagon the day Anthony came into town with a gashed hand. His trouser leg was rolled up over a bare right foot, the ankle an angry red and swollen to twice its normal size.

"We were raking hay, stacking it." Armstead's words tumbled over each other, and he shoved his hands through his hair. "The snake was hidden in the hay. It darted out and struck him before we even knew it was there."

Made sense—warm, dry hay, the perfect place for a cold-blooded creature to curl up. Adam yanked a strong bandage from his bag and tied it tight around the boy's leg below the knee in a quick jerk. For a tourniquet, it would have to do.

"Hello there, Carl. I'm going to see what I can do for your leg, all right?"

The boy nodded, his eyes glassy. That wasn't a good sign. His mother smoothed his hair back from his damp forehead, her hands trembling.

"Please take my scalpel from my bag and go hold it over the flame in the stove," Adam told Forsythia. "Then you and Anthony hold Carl's leg."

She was already on her way to the soddy with the scalpel as if she'd been reading his mind.

Moments later, Adam pressed his now cooled scalpel to the swollen flesh and made two quick incisions across the bite. Carl moaned, quivering, but Forsythia held his leg firmly. Adam bent his mouth to the cuts and sucked and spat several times into the dry grass. This should have been done immediately after the bite, but he could only hope it might still have some effect.

Lilac appeared at his elbow with a cup of water and the wet compresses. With a nod of thanks, he swished away any remaining poison from his mouth.

Forsythia helped him pack the leg in wet cloths. "This slows the circulation?"

"Yes. We hope." Adam pressed his fingers to the bridge of his nose. *Think, think.* His knowledge of treating snakebites had been purely theoretical until now.

"Ma always said to use indigo for a snakebite." Forsythia's voice cut into his tumbled thoughts, steady and calm. "Or a poultice of gunpowder and egg."

"You have those?" Adam lifted his head.

"Yes." Forsythia scooted out of the wagon. "I'll be right back."

"Bring the wagon closer, into the shade of the sod house." Adam beckoned to Anthony. "We don't want to move Carl directly unless we have to."

Once in the shade, Adam climbed up into the wagon and checked the boy's pulse. Still fast, and his breathing was rapid. But the leg seemed no more swollen or red than before. *Please, Lord. Show us what to do. Save this boy's life.*

"Here." Forsythia emerged from the soddy, Lark behind her. Each held a dish. "Ma never mentioned using both together, but I don't know which is best." She sprinkled the powdered indigo on the incision, then reached for Lark's dish and smeared on the grayish-yellow paste of egg and gunpowder.

"My pa always said egg was good for absorbing all sorts of poison." Mrs. Armstead spoke for the first time, her voice unsteady. "He cured our dog one time when she'd eaten rat poison by forcing raw eggs down her throat."

"Well, we'll see what this does." Forsythia gently repacked the sides of Carl's leg in the wet cloths, then stepped back, her shaky release of breath the first sign of nerves she had shown.

"Let's pray." Lark held out her hands, and her sisters grasped them. Forsythia hesitated, then reached for Adam's. He took hers without letting himself think about it, then placed his other hand on Carl's swollen bare foot.

"Father." Lark's voice held steady. "We lift up Carl to you. We've done all we can, Lord, but nothing is too difficult for you. We ask for your mercy and your healing upon this boy. Amen."

"Amen," came murmurs around the circle.

Carl's eyes had drifted closed. Adam checked his pulse and breathing. "Still rapid, but steady."

"What now?" Anthony raked his hands through his hair again.

"We wait. And keep praying."

Hours slipped away, the sun passing the noon mark in the sky. Adam and Forsythia stayed with the Armsteads, Lilac caring for the children around them and giving the little ones their dinner. None of the adults had any desire for food. They kept the cloths around Carl's leg wet and spooned sips of water down his throat. Lark and Del returned to cutting sod with Jesse's help.

"I should change the poultice again." Forsythia pushed strands of damp hair off her face. The July heat baked around them, even in the scanty shade. She hurried into the soddy, then emerged with a fresh concoction. She climbed back into the wagon and gently peeled the drying poultice away, pausing to examine the bite below.

"What do you think, Doctor?"

It was hard to see with the substances coating it, and yet . . . "It's not any more swollen. I want to say the swelling and redness have gone down a bit."

"Really?" Mrs. Armstead clasped the back of her hand to her mouth, hugging Carl's shoulders with her other arm. Half-asleep, the boy stirred and moaned.

Adam held up his hand. "He's not out of the woods yet. But go ahead with another poultice, Miss Nielsen."

Forsythia smeared the egg and gunpower paste on again.

By the time shadows stretched across the prairie, Carl's pulse had slowed to a more normal level, and that glassy look was gone from his eyes. His leg, though still swollen, had lost some of the awful lividness.

"I think you might take him home now." Adam changed the wet cloths on Carl's leg once more. "Just keep him resting and the leg downward from his heart, and change the poultice once more tonight. I'll come see him in the morning. But I think . . ." Relief exhaled from his chest with the breath. "I think he's going to be all right."

"Thank you, Doctor." Armstead pumped his hand. "Thank you."

"Thank God." *And thank Forsythia.*

After a quick cold supper with the Nielsens, he and Jesse headed home, completely spent. The rest of the addition's roof would have to wait. On the sidewalk outside his office, as his tired fingers fumbled to undo the door latch, Mrs. Jorgensen stepped outside, closing up the store for the night.

Did she know about her grandson's accident? Likely not, since the Armsteads wouldn't have come by here on their way to the Nielsens'. Anthony had told him that a friend who was haying with them had heard that Adam was out helping at the sisters' homestead, so they'd gone directly there. But just in case . . .

"Mrs. Jorgensen." He cleared his throat. "Your grandson was bitten by a rattlesnake this morning."

Her head snapped up.

"He will recover, I assure you. I just wanted to let you know, should you hear anything about it in town. He had a rough go of it, but I believe he will be fine."

"Do you, really?" Her voice dripped with doubt. "Didn't try any newfangled treatments on him, did you?"

"No." His defenses rose. How could this woman do that? "I incised and applied suction to the wound and packed it in cold cloths. Miss Forsythia Nielsen assisted me, and she knew of some herbal remedies from her mother that seemed to prove helpful."

"Hmph. Sounds like she was more use than you were." Mrs. Jorgensen locked the store door with a snap, then turned and stomped around the corner toward their house behind.

Adam swallowed back any words he might retort. *Lord, why do I let that woman irritate me like this? I shouldn't have said anything to begin with. She'd have heard the news from her family tomorrow.*

He opened the door, letting him and Jesse into the welcoming shadows of their rooms.

If even saving—or helping to save—her grandson's life wasn't going to change Mrs. Jorgensen's mind, he might as well give up and leave it in God's hands, as he should have done to begin with. It would save him a lot of grief.

27

"Mail for you, Miss Nielsen."

Larkspur took the envelopes Mr. Jorgensen handed her across the store counter. A letter from Anders! It had been a while, though they'd all written to him and Josephine several times since they got settled on their homestead. What a treat to share with her sisters as soon as she got home. Another letter from the Herrons too.

"Will that be all, then?" The storekeeper wrapped the silk ribbons Lark had chosen in brown paper.

"Yes, thank you." A small thing to come to town for today, but Forsythia, Del, and Lilac had taken the notion to trim up their best dresses a bit more before the harvest celebration tonight. Lark didn't care much for frills and furbelows, so she'd offered to come get the ribbon while the girls added ruffles and tucks.

"How goes the school teaching for your sister?" Mr. Jorgensen was chatty today. Must be the excitement about tonight, which seemed to have spread through the town like locusts. It must have been a while since most folks had a real social occasion.

"Del is enjoying it. They closed the school for the last two weeks, though, since most of her students were busy with harvest." Lark paid the storekeeper and made her escape. She needed to get back to the farm in time for the evening milking before they dressed for the celebration.

Humid air hit her face as she stepped out the door, unseasonably warm for early October. A gust of wind scattered leaves and dry grasses down the dirt street. Was it getting warmer? Lark glanced up at the sky while she untied Starbright from the hitching post. Some dark clouds were building. Was a fall thunderstorm on its way? For her sisters' sake, she hoped it wouldn't dampen the gathering tonight.

Lark swung up on Starbright and rode toward home.

Around her spread the prairie was severe and brown. A triangle of geese honked overhead, heading south. Everywhere, everyone was getting ready for winter. They'd begun their own small harvest, storing the cabbages and root vegetables in the cellar Jesse had helped dig in a rise behind the house. They'd learned from Mr. Caldwell that the Skinners had planned to do just that but not gotten around to it. So much love had gone into this place and then been destroyed.

Dr. Adam, as he'd asked them to call him, hadn't been able to help at the homestead as much lately, as his practice had finally picked up these past couple of months.

Larkspur reached home, stabled Starbright in the three-sided shelter they'd put up for the animals for now, and entered the soddy waving the letters.

"Guess what I picked up along with your ribbons." She tossed the brown-paper package onto Del's lap. Her sisters looked up from where they sat gathered by the one window and open door for light, stitching on dresses piled in their laps. Sofie squealed and pounced on the package.

"Sorry, little one, it's not a treat for you this time."

"Is it from Anders? Read it to us while we sew." Lilac tossed back her dark curls.

Leaning in the doorframe, Lark opened the envelope. Far off, thunder rumbled. She glanced out at the lowering sky. "Looks like we might get a storm."

Lilac shook her head. "I refuse to believe it. Nothing is going to spoil tonight."

"It may blow on past long before. Don't borrow trouble." Del was ever practical. "Go on, Lark, read."

Lark chuckled and began.

My dear family,

We are well and hope you all are too. It seems so long since we have seen your faces, though it has only been months. We do have some news of our own. We are expecting a little one to be born in this house come March. Josephine is tired but well and sends her love to all of you.

Lark paused for the exclamations of delight that flitted around the room. Gladness swelled her own heart. A new little Nielsen. If only they could visit to welcome him or her. Instead of dreaming, she continued.

Another bit of news, not so good. As you know, Climie Wiesel has been helping us in the store, but she recently got a letter from her husband. He did not disclose his location, but the letter was postmarked in Topeka, Kansas. I had hoped he had not made his way so far west, but I thought I should let you know. He threatened to come back for Climie, though of course we do not plan to allow that to happen. He also said that first he still intended to find that 'Miss Lark-uppity Nielsen' and see she got her comeuppance for turning his wife and church against him. I'm afraid in his twisted mind he blames you for his life falling apart, little sense as that may make.

Lark paused, wishing she'd stopped sooner. Silence fell heavy over the room, squeezing joy out the door.

"Deacon Wiesel is a hypocrite and a coward." She glanced from one sister's face to another. "We don't need to fear him."

"Then why did we leave home?" Lilac's voice sounded unusually small.

What could Lark say to that? She returned to the letter. Surely it couldn't get any worse.

Jonah continues to work for Mr. Holt, though not as hard as he could, and I am not convinced he has left his erring ways behind. At least I have not caught him in the saloon of late—not when I've been watching, anyway. Your prayers for our wayward little brother are still appreciated—and needed.

Do let us know how you are and how you are set for the winter. Give my greetings to Captain Caldwell. We miss you.

> *Love from your brother,*
> *Anders Nielsen*

Lark folded the letter. Her sisters sat still, hands idle on their sewing.

"What do we do?" Del asked, ever practical.

"I don't think there's anything we can do." Forsythia's voice came gently. "Not more than we're already doing. Pray, and don't worry. Just keep building the life the Lord has led us to here in our new home and trust Him with the rest."

Something eased in Lark's chest. "I suppose you're right." *But, Lord, please let me not have led my family into any danger here. I thought we'd gotten far enough away.*

As if on cue, a clap of thunder crashed overhead, making

them all jump, and Sofie let out a wail. Lark set the letters aside and picked her up.

"Shh, little one. It's just a thunderstorm, see?" She turned the girl toward the window as the clouds opened in a sudden downpour.

"As fast as this came on, it may indeed blow past quickly." Del reached around Lark to shut the door. Forsythia and Lilac bundled the dresses away from the rain blowing in.

"Can I go outside and catch rain on my tongue?" Robbie danced an impatient jig.

Lightning forked through the gray sky, followed by another crash. Mikael wailed from where he'd been napping in his cradle, and Del hurried to rock him back to sleep.

"Afraid not, Robbie." Forsythia smoothed her hand over his hair. "It's not safe with so much lightning." She glanced at Lark. "It sure is late for a thunderstorm."

Soon the heavy patter of the rain, though muted on the roof of the soddy, lessened, and the rolling booms of thunder grew further in between.

"Sounds like it's moving on." Del straightened from beside the baby's cradle, Mikael slumbering again.

"Do you think we might still be able to go to the celebration?" Forsythia's voice was hopeful.

"Everything will be soaked." Lark shook her head. "Might be wiser to just stay—" She caught sight of Forsythia's face and stopped. Had her sister been looking forward to this that much? She could have kicked herself. Of course. The doctor would be there. "Well, let's do the chores and then see."

She and Lilac pulled on their boots to go feed the animals and milk Buttercup. Lilac opened the door and sniffed. "The air feels strange. Not just the usual after-rain smell."

"Maybe because it's fall." Lark pulled on her hat and grabbed the milk pail, then followed her little sister outside. The air did have a strange smell and a sort of tension to it. Lark shifted her jaw to ease the pressure in her ears.

"Lark." Lilac grabbed her arm, an urgency in her voice. "The sky."

Lark looked up and caught her breath.

In the southwest, snaking from a canopy of dark clouds, a huge funnel stretched near to the earth. Wind gusted into her face.

A tornado. And it looked to be heading this way, with Salton in its path.

"Get the children." Ducking back inside, Lark hurried to the box where they kept their title to the Skinner's property and other important papers, grabbed the most recent letters to tuck among them, then stuffed the box under her arm. "There's a tornado coming. We need to get in the root cellar."

"Will we all fit?" Forsythia caught up Mikael from his cradle.

"We'll have to. Come on."

Lark herded her family outside, Del carrying Sofie and Lilac holding Robbie's hand. Wind whipped their skirts and hair, sending Robbie's hat flying. He wailed, reaching after it, but Lilac scooped him up and pressed on.

"Here." Lark flung open the slanted wooden door of the cellar against the hillside. "Get in and shut the door. I'm going to check on the animals."

Forsythia climbed in first, holding the baby, then looked back up. "Lark, hurry."

"I will." She stared at the twisting funnel, drawing closer by the second.

With her sisters crouching safe in the cellar, Lark circled into the three-sided sod barn built against the house to grab a bucket of grain, then leaned into the wind and headed toward their newly fenced pasture. Buttercup was still out there, along with the oxen.

She called above the approaching storm, rattling the bucket against the gate. *Come on.* Their eyes rolling in fear, the animals skittered about but slowly made their way to her.

Grasping Buttercup's rope, Lark led her toward the barn, the oxen thankfully following. Starbright stamped and whinnied as she led them in. With the livestock under shelter, she shut the chickens in their coop. If only this barn had a full four sides. But how sturdy was a sod building—any building—against a tornado?

A thud outside, then heavy splatting all around. Lark stared out at the prairie. Hail—huge white hailstones falling everywhere, as big as peaches, flattening the grass.

It was now or never. Shielding her head with her arms, she ran for the root cellar. Lilac held the door open for her, and Lark dove inside.

She slammed the cellar cover shut, plunging them into darkness.

Forsythia huddled in the root cellar, crammed between Lilac and Del amid the sacks of potatoes and turnips, and tried to pray. Mikael fussed in her arms, rubbing his face against her shoulder. Poor baby, he needed a change and a feeding—his nap had been disrupted twice. But there was nothing she could do about that now.

And here she'd been nervous about the possibility of seeing the doctor at the celebration tonight, where there was to be dancing. How quickly life could change.

Where was Adam right now? Lark had said the twister looked to be heading straight for town. Where would he and Jesse go? They had no root cellar, she was certain of that. Panic rose in her throat, and she closed her eyes against it. *Please, Lord, watch over them. There's nothing we can do until the storm passes. I will trust and not be afraid.* She repeated the words, running them through her head to keep the crushing horror at bay.

Overhead, the storm roared like the freight train that had passed right by them when they visited Columbus. She'd never heard wind like this. The pressure in the air made her jaw ache. Lark clutched the door handle to keep the door from being lifted open by the wind.

"I'm scared," Robbie whimpered on the other side of Lilac. "My ears hurt. I want to get out."

Mikael screamed and kept on screaming.

"Me too." Sofie started to cry.

Forsythia clutched the baby's head against her shoulder with her other hand over his outside ear, then reached to touch the little boy's knee in the darkness. "We can't get out yet, Robbie boy. We need to stay in here where it's safe."

"But it doesn't feel safe, Mama Sythia."

Despite the circumstances, her heart warmed as it always did at hearing the name for her he had come up with one day. "I know, dear one. I don't like the awful sound either." *Lord, show me what to say.* "Did you know that in the dark and shadows can actually be a very safe place to be?" She spoke directly into his ear so he could hear her.

Robbie sniffled. "They can?"

"There's a psalm that talks about it." Forsythia shifted, rubbing Mikael's back as he settled against her shoulder. "'He that dwelleth in the secret place of the most High . . .'" Her throat tightened too much for her to speak above the roar of the storm.

"'. . . shall abide under the shadow of the Almighty,'" Lark supplied. "'I will say of the Lord, he is my refuge and my fortress: my God; in him will I trust.'"

The clamping in Forsythia's chest eased. There in the darkness, her sisters picked up the familiar psalm.

"'He shall cover thee with his feathers, and under his wings shalt thou trust: his truth shall be thy shield and buckler. Thou shalt not be afraid for the terror by night; nor for the arrow that flieth by day; nor for the pestilence that walketh in darkness; nor for the destruction that wasteth at noonday.'"

Forsythia joined in again. "'For he shall give his angels charge over thee, to keep thee in all thy ways. They shall bear thee up in their hands, lest thou dash thy foot against a stone.'" *Thank you, Ma, for making us learn these words by heart.*

They finished the psalm in unison.

"So you see, Robbie? God's shadow is a very safe place to be."

"Is this God's shadow?" His voice was small.

Del chuckled. "I suppose every place can be in God's shadow, if we stay close to Him."

They stayed in the cellar for what seemed like an hour, though it was probably half that. At last Lark shifted in the darkness.

"It sounds like it has passed. I'll check." She pushed open the door, and they all blinked in the sudden light. Lark climbed out, stretched, and surveyed the landscape.

"It's gone. You all can come out."

Forsythia handed Mikael up to Lark and stumbled out, her legs stiff and numb.

Behind her, Del and Lilac emerged with Sofie and Robbie. Mikael blinked on Lark's shoulder, round-eyed and seeming to have forgotten his stomach and diaper.

"Looks like it completely missed us, other than the hail." Lark blew out a long breath. "Thank you, Lord."

Still, chunks of sod from the barn and new addition had fallen in from the hail. And part of the fence around the pasture lay scattered like sticks in a children's game. Glistening hailstones littered the grass. Robbie and Sofie ran about picking them up, fascinated, then dropping the stones when their hands grew too cold.

"I'll do the milking now, while we can." Lark shivered. The

wind was turning cold. "Lilac and Del, would you feed the animals? Sythia, get the children inside."

Forsythia shepherded Sofie and Robbie into the soddy. The warm darkness inside wrapped around them like a mother's embrace. She laid Mikael in his cradle so she could light a lamp and set it on the table, its glow lighting the checkered tablecloth and showing the neat bedstead covered with a cheery quilt, the filled cupboards and shelves lining the walls. How quickly this had become home. How quickly they could have lost it. *Thank you, Father.*

Mikael kicked and wailed in his cradle, not at all pleased at being deposited there without anything in his tummy.

"Shh, little one." Forsythia scooped him up. Poor baby, he was soaked. "Let's get you changed. Lark will have warm milk for you soon."

While she changed him into a fresh diaper and gown, urgency pricked the back of her mind. What had gone on in town? Had Salton taken a direct hit? Shouldn't they go check? People might need help. Adam might need help.

Lilac came to the door with a foaming pail of milk. "Here you go."

"Thanks." Forsythia strained and bottled the milk, filled one of the newfangled baby bottles they had ordered from the store for Mikael, and sent the rest of the milk out with Lilac to cool in the water tank in the pump house. She sat down to feed the baby, his hungry cries quickly subsiding into eager swallows.

Her sisters came back inside, chilled and windblown. Del started supper.

Mikael having finished his bottle, Forsythia rose and burped him, then crossed the room to Lark, who was pulling on her coat. With darkness falling, the temperature had dropped too. "Where are you going?"

"I think I'd better head into town. See what damage there

might be and if anyone needs help. There sure won't be any celebration now."

"I'm going with you." Her words were firm.

Lark looked at her without surprise. "All right."

Forsythia handed the baby to Del and gathered her herbs and supplies, then tied a scarf over her head and bundled into her coat. Though her heart pounded as to what they might find, a certain knowledge pulsed through her.

Adam needed her.

28

Adam had never seen anything like this.

Standing outside his office doorway, he surveyed the street, the devastation rendering him light-headed. Several buildings on the other side had been flattened, including the saloon and a salt business. The tornado had ripped part of the roof off Henry Caldwell's office as if it were paper. Beams and broken glass littered the remaining fragments of sidewalk amid the hailstones. The schoolhouse had been lifted off as if it had never been, leaving naked ground.

He stepped farther out to look up the street. Several houses on the outskirts of town looked to have taken damage too. Yet his side of the street stood mostly untouched, aside from some missing shingles and other roof damage from the hail. The tornado must have gone straight down the other side. He turned to examine the mercantile next door and drew a quick breath. The big hickory tree that had shaded the store—only a gaping hole remained in the earth. Roots and all, the giant tree was gone.

Mr. Jorgensen burst out of the store, breathing fast. "Doctor Brownsville, help me, please. It's Lucretia. She's hurt."

"Let me get my bag." Adam ducked back into his office to

grab it, calling up to Jesse where he was going, then entered the store through the adjoining door. There was no sign of the Jorgensens, so he hurried through to their house out back.

He found Mr. Jorgensen in the sitting room, cradling his wife's head as she lay on a lounge, her eyes closed.

"One of them hailstones hit her on the head." The older man's voice was unsteady. "I told her to stay inside, but she was bound and determined to get those fool chickens under cover. Next thing I knew, she'd dropped like a stone. I dragged her into the house, but she hasn't woken up since."

"She may have a concussion." Adam examined the gash matting her hair with blood, then lifted her eyelids and examined her pupils. He pulled out his stethoscope to listen to her heart and breathing. "Why don't you crush up some of those hailstones outside with a hammer and wrap them in a cloth. The ice will help lower the swelling and minimize any bruising to her brain."

"Of course." Mr. Jorgensen eased his wife's head down on a pillow and hurried out the door.

Adam wet a cloth in the water jug he found in the kitchen and set to cleaning Mrs. Jorgensen's head wound, wiping the blood from her graying hair.

She moaned and turned her head from side to side, then fluttered her eyelids open. Focusing unsteadily on Adam's face, she frowned. "What are you . . . doing here? Where . . . am I?"

"You're in your home, Mrs. Jorgensen." Adam lowered the cloth. "Your husband called for me. I'm afraid you took a blow to the head during the storm."

"Storm?" She tried to lift her head, then laid it back down with a grimace. "Where's . . . Edgar?"

"Right here, Lucretia." Mr. Jorgensen hurried in, bundle in hand. "I'm here." He handed the rag wrapped around crushed ice to Adam and fell to his knees beside his wife, stroking her hand.

Adam settled the compress on Mrs. Jorgensen's head. "Keep this on until it melts or as long as she will tolerate it. She must have absolute rest for the next twenty-four hours, and watch her carefully for signs of confusion or increased pain." He hesitated, but he should let them know. "Or seizures. If any of these occur, summon me at once."

"Is there nothing else to do?" Mr. Jorgensen laid a hand on the ice compress.

"Not at the moment. But it's a good sign she has come to already. Most concussions heal with rest and time." Adam stood and closed his bag. Likely the storm had left other casualties in town that needed tending. And the storekeeper's wife wouldn't want him around any longer than necessary. "Let me know if there is any change."

"Doctor." Mrs. Jorgensen's weak voice halted him at the door. He turned back.

Her unfocused gaze rested on him, regret in her face. "Thank you."

Adam nodded. "You're welcome."

Jesse met him in the yard, coming from the back door of their place. "Uncle Adam, there's lots of p-people here to see you."

No surprise. He quickened his pace.

Inside, townsfolk filled his office—mothers, fathers, children. Gashed foreheads and a couple of broken limbs, by the look of it. One woman cradled a girl bleeding heavily from her leg.

Adam scanned the gathering, trying to think. How to organize who needed help most? Where to put them all? His office held nowhere near enough room.

Henry Caldwell appeared at his side, his arm wrapped in a bandage. "How can I help?"

Adam grabbed his friend's wrist. "You're hurt."

"Just a scratch." Henry shook him off. "There's many far worse. Where do you want them?"

Adam thought quickly. "Let's open up the store. Mr. Jorgensen won't mind. Jesse?"

His nephew nodded and opened the door adjoining the office to the mercantile, holding it wide.

"Ladies and gentlemen, please." Adam raised his voice above the clamor. "Wait in the store, and I will see you one at a time, the most urgent cases first. You may enter through this door or go around outside. You, ma'am," he said to the woman with the bleeding girl, "stay here, and anyone else who is bleeding heavily or suspects internal damage." He wasn't sure how they would know, but he had to start somewhere.

With Henry and Jesse's help, they got the murmuring crowd moving, slow as a herd of reluctant cattle.

Adam lifted the young girl with the injured leg to his examining table. She was probably about eight years old, and she shrieked as he moved her. He pushed her calico skirt aside and started to unwind the clumsy, blood-soaked bandage.

"She got caught under a falling beam." The mother twisted her hands, her voice choked. "The bone is broken. It's awful."

Adam removed the bandage and swallowed. Indeed, cracked white bone poked through the gash in the girl's shin. A compound fracture, and bleeding heavily.

"We've got to stop the bleeding first. Jesse, bandages." He grabbed the cloths from his nephew and pressed them to the wound. The little girl screamed again, then sobbed, her hands grasping for her mother.

"I'm sorry, child." The pain would be horrific. He needed to give her some laudanum before trying to set the bone. "Jesse, do you know where the laudanum is?"

"I d-don't know." Jesse crossed to the cupboard and opened it, staring inside.

"Which shelf is it on?" Henry limped over to help him.

"The top, I think." Adam squinted, trying to picture his cupboard. "A small brown bottle."

"This?" Henry held out a brown glass vial.

"No, that's quinine." He couldn't let up the pressure on the girl's leg. She'd bleed to death before they could set her leg.

"Let me look." A quiet feminine voice entered the conversation. Forsythia Nielsen hurried past him, unwinding a scarf from her head as she went. "It's laudanum you need?"

"Yes." Relief expanded in his chest. *Oh, Forsythia, you knew I needed you.*

Gently she pushed past Henry and Jesse to the cabinet, then moved to Adam's side with the correct bottle in hand. "How many drops?"

"Try ten to start."

"Here you are, dear one." Forsythia laid a hand on the little girl's shaking shoulder. "Open your mouth. That's it. This will help." She dispensed the dosage, and the child lay back, still trembling but quieted by Forsythia's touch.

Forsythia set the bottle aside and took off her coat. "An open break, then?"

"Yes." Adam checked beneath the cloth he'd been pressing. "The bleeding's slowing a little. As soon as the laudanum takes effect, we need to set her leg." He glanced around. "Henry, can you go into the store and get a tally of who is here and what their injuries are? I need to know who needs care most urgently."

Caldwell nodded and disappeared through the door, relief on his face.

Good. His friend excelled at organization and managing people, but clearly not so much with medicine.

The little girl's eyelids fluttered, the pain relaxing from her face.

"Jesse, I'll need you to help hold her leg."

His nephew stepped near. "S-sorry I c-couldn't find the laudanum." His face twisted in regret.

"That's all right." Adam smiled and shifted the child's leg into position. "Perhaps I should just make Miss Nielsen my official nurse. Forsythia, you hold her shoulders. Jesse, I need all your weight across her ankles." He glanced at the child's mother. "Ma'am, you may not want to watch this."

With a shudder, the woman turned away.

"Ready?" At his assistants' nods, Adam clenched his jaw and pulled. A horrible grating sound, then a click. Despite the laudanum, the little girl tensed and cried out.

"There." He released a breath. This was never a doctor's favorite chore, but the bone had been set back into place. "Now we just need to close the wound."

Forsythia was already gathering his suturing supplies. How did she even know where they were? Adam sent Jesse to monitor the front door, where more patients were already assembled, then started cleaning and stitching the little girl's leg back together.

Henry Caldwell stepped back in from the store. "We've got an older man who got caught under the saloon when it collapsed. He doesn't say much, but his chest—" The attorney shook his head. "It doesn't look good. Otherwise, some possible broken arms and head injuries. The rest seem mostly minor."

"Thank you." Adam tied off the stitching. "Jesse, help bring in that older man."

Jesse and another young man hauled in a wizened little man who must have been out in these parts long before most settlers arrived. He wore a bulky coat and an uncomplaining expression, which was probably why Adam hadn't noticed him earlier. But when he got the coat off and opened up the old man's shirt, Adam drew a sharp breath. Deep bruises and lacerations covered his chest.

"It's bad, ain't it?" The older man gave a resigned sigh and winced at the effort. "Well, I had a good life."

Forsythia met Adam's gaze over the man's head, her eyes anxious.

Adam set his stethoscope in his ears and listened to the man's lungs, then gently palpitated his ribs.

"Yow," the man yelped. "If a man's gotta go, let him go easy."

"I wouldn't set your affairs in order just yet." Adam removed his earpieces and smiled. "You've got some cracked ribs, which will make breathing painful for some time, I'm afraid. But as best I can tell, your lungs are intact."

The old man blinked up at him. "You mean I ain't gonna die?"

"Only the Lord knows our time, my friend. But I don't think yours is just yet. Forsythia, get me the bandages, please. We'll wrap his ribs tightly to help stabilize them and ease the pain."

Darkness fell, and still they worked together, cleaning and stitching and bandaging wounds, and setting more broken limbs. Lark, who had been helping Mrs. Caldwell clean up some of the mess inside Henry's office, came by and assisted for a few hours as well.

It was nearly midnight when the last patient hobbled out of the office. Many families who had lost homes or endured damage were bedding down with others for the night. Adam made up cots in his office for the little girl with the compound fracture and the man with broken ribs, wanting to keep them close overnight for observation.

"Where is your sister?" he asked Forsythia, concerned by the exhaustion lining her face.

"Lark went home to update the others and get some extra blankets for you here. She'll be back for me." She leaned on the back of a wooden chair.

"Come upstairs and have a cup of tea." Adam extended a hand to her. "Our patients are sleeping, and thanks to the gift of laudanum, I don't think they'll need us anytime soon. We'll hear Lark when she drives up."

Forsythia hesitated, then accepted his assistance up the stairs. In the little sitting room, she sank into the rocking chair he kept pulled close to the stove. Nearby, Jesse snoozed on the sofa.

"This is cozy." She held out her hands, warming them. "Thank you."

Adam set the teakettle to boil. "No, thank you. I don't know what I would have done without you tonight." Weary to the bone himself, he sank into another chair beside her and met her eyes, hoping she could see how much he meant it. "I can't think of anyone else who would have worked beside me like you did."

"What, not Henry or Jesse?" She quirked a smile.

"Definitely not Henry or Jesse." He chuckled.

"What about Elizabeth?"

Adam stilled.

"Forgive me." Forsythia twisted her hands together. "I shouldn't have said that."

"No." Adam reached across and laid his hand over hers, stilling her nervous fingers. "It's all right. And no, not even Elizabeth. She was my first love, the light of my life. And she unfailingly supported me in my work. But sharing it . . . that has been something new with you, Forsythia."

Her fingers trembled under his, and he gripped them tightly. He hadn't meant to speak just yet, but suddenly he knew it was time.

Forsythia sat still, barely daring to breathe. Every ounce of her pulsed with the awareness of Adam's hand over hers, the warmth of his fingers. What was he saying?

"I know I told you I needed time."

"And I understood. I understand."

"And that has meant more than I can say. But what I'm trying to tell you, dearest Forsythia, is that . . . I think I have had enough. Time, that is." He shifted and slipped from his chair to kneel beside hers.

"You have?" She dared to meet his eyes. Those wonderful, warm brown eyes.

He twined his strong fingers through hers. "When the tornado hit, and Jesse and I were hunkered down in the barn out back, all I could think was that I wanted to be at your side, wherever you were, whatever you were doing. And to have you at mine. Then when I needed help in the clinic . . . you were there."

Forsythia lifted her hand and brushed a wayward dark curl from his forehead, as she had so often longed to do. "And all I could think was that you needed me."

He lowered his head, brushing his lips across her knuckles, then looked up again. "You know I am not perfect. I'm as flawed as any man, and I can't even promise I'm finished grieving Elizabeth. But if you still want me, with all my imperfections . . . then I would ask you, Forsythia Nielsen—would you do me the honor of becoming my wife?"

A tear slipped down her cheek. "I don't come unencumbered either. Are you sure you want three ready-made children?"

He caught her tear on his finger. "Elizabeth and I couldn't have children—at least, she couldn't. And your care for those little ones is one of the things I loved first about you."

Love. Lord, he loves me. Forsythia closed her eyes.

"I'd say those three are less encumbrances than extra blessings, wouldn't you?"

She nodded, teary laughter bubbling up. "Then, Dr. Adam Brownsville, yes. I would be honored to become your wife." And then, to the surprise of both of them, she leaned forward and kissed her doctor squarely on the mouth.

"Hello?" A step sounded on the stairs. "Anyone home?"

Lark. Forsythia pulled back with a gasp. "You said we'd hear her."

"Well, I didn't know we would be quite so distracted." A grin lighting his face, Adam kissed her quickly once more and then jumped up. "Yes, Miss Nielsen. We're here."

Forsythia pressed her fingers to her lips, her heart pounding. *Lord, I love him, but are we truly ready for this? And what is Larkspur going to say?*

29

So much to be thankful for.

Standing within the plain wooden walls of the Salton church, Lark stood in charge of the pot of hot cider at the community Thanksgiving meal, breathing in the sweet, spicy scent rising beneath her nose. Children scampered around, their laughter and squeals mingling with the chatter of women spreading food on the tables. The wooden pews had been cleared to the sides to make way for the tables and benches now lining the sanctuary, laden with the fruits of the farming families' harvest.

"Isn't it wonderful?" Del appeared before her, beaming, and Lark dipped her a cupful of cider. "I was just talking with some of the parents of my students, and we think we've already raised nearly enough for the new schoolhouse."

"Just with the plate charge for the meal?" Lark served cider for a little boy and his mother.

"A few people made generous extra donations too—Mr. Young, even Dr. Brownsville. Plus, we've still got the pie auction after dinner."

"I guess you won't be holding class in the church too much longer, then."

"Well, we won't be able to raise the school building until the snow is off the ground. But hopefully in the spring."

Lark loved seeing the shine in Del's eyes and the happy flush in her cheeks when she talked about teaching. Truly her sensible sister had found her passion.

"Miss Nielsen." A small girl ran up and tugged at Del's hand. "Come see the new piano."

"Piano?" Lark raised a brow and turned to see where the child pointed. At the back of the church, Rev. Pritchard and some other men were wrestling a bulky item through the door.

"Oh, I heard about this." Del set down her cup. "Rev. Pritchard's home church back east donated a piano to us. I can't wait to see Sythia's face. Excuse me . . ." She followed the little girl's tugging hand to go see the instrument the men were hauling to the front of the sanctuary.

A piano. What a gift. Lark couldn't hold back her smile. Now the Nielsens' musical offerings during services would sound complete once more. She closed her eyes. *Thank you, Lord.*

"You look mighty happy about somethin', ma'am."

At the soft drawl, Lark opened her eyes with a start.

The man standing before her had trimmed his scruffy beard and exchanged his ragged army uniform for simple farmer's clothes, but she'd recognize that voice anywhere.

"Isaac McTavish?" she blurted.

He frowned. "Do I know you?"

"Oh." Lark's ears heated. How to explain this? And what was he doing here? "Forgive me. I'm Larkspur Nielsen. You met my family when we were on the trail and also at the Herrons'. When I was . . . Clark Nielsen." That likely made little to no sense. "We played music?"

Isaac's face cleared. "I remember now. Mrs. Herron mentioned something in her letter about your, shall I say, necessary subterfuge?" His eyes twinkled.

Lark relaxed. At last, someone who didn't take her masquerade too seriously. "You might say that. I'm glad you aren't too shocked."

"I've seen a heap too much these past few years to shock easy. Besides"—he tipped his head to the side, studying her— "can't say but that it's rather a nice surprise."

Lark didn't know what to say to that. Her cheeks warmed.

"Be that as may be, might a weary traveler get a cup of cider?"

"Oh, of course." Grateful for the distraction, Lark dipped him a cup of the hot, spiced brew. "So what brings you out here, Mr. McTavish?"

"Well, I've been lookin' for what might be the next stop on my journey. I've been traveling hither and yon between here and Ohio, helpin' with harvestin' and such. Then I heard about the cyclone damage y'all suffered up here, and havin' word from Mrs. Herron that my friends the Nielsens had settled up here— well, I thought I'd see if I could be of any help."

"So you knew we were here." He'd come all this way to find them?

"Better to settle where one finds friends, I believe. They're a precious possession in this world."

Lark met the frank gaze of his gray eyes. "Indeed."

At the soft chime of piano keys, they both looked toward the front of the church. Lark's throat tightened with sudden tears.

Forsythia was playing.

It had been so long.

Forsythia caressed the keys, the worn ivory of the hand-me-down piano a familiar friend beneath her fingertips. She segued from one hymn into another, her hands knowing the notes without her even having to think about them. Their beloved "Abide with Me" moved into "My Jesus, I Love Thee," followed by "Now Thank We All Our God." It was Thanksgiving, after all.

Someone slid onto the bench next to her, and she glanced up to see Adam's bearded, smiling face. She smiled back, her heart too full for words.

He sat quietly a moment, watching her, and then, to her surprise, lifted his own hands to the keys and added harmonizing chords to the last round of the hymn of thanksgiving. Their four hands blended beautifully on the final notes of the *amen*.

She turned to him. "I didn't know you played."

"Nothing like you, my love. But a little."

"Do you know 'Come, Ye Thankful People, Come'?" She ran her fingers over the keys again, shifting through arpeggios. It was like her hands couldn't stop playing, so much had they missed it.

"I think so. You start, and I'll see if I can follow."

Forsythia eased into a melodic introduction, then began. After a few measures, Adam pressed the keys again, softly adding chords. His touch was slower than hers, yet sure, with a depth and richness to it, like her doctor himself.

Her doctor. Her heart warmed again with the wonder of it.

She hadn't realized her sisters were gathering around them until Lark's contralto picked up the first verse, then Lilac joined in, followed by Del. Soon other families gathered round, and they were all singing, Forsythia lifting her soprano alongside Adam's hearty baritone.

> "Come, ye thankful people, come,
> Raise the song of harvest home;
> All is safely gathered in,
> Ere the winter storms begin.
> God our Maker doth provide
> For our wants to be supplied;

Come to God's own temple, come,
Raise the song of harvest home."

They finished all four verses, and Forsythia concluded with a triumphant chord. Applause rose enthusiastically from around the church.

"And on that lovely note, let us gather and give thanks." Rev. Pritchard raised his voice above the swelling chatter. "And then eat!"

Still on the piano bench, Forsythia bowed her head and closed her eyes. Adam's hand covered hers, his fingers warm against her skin. Much to be thankful for, indeed.

They all feasted on turkey and duck, mashed potatoes and turnips, canned corn and beans, preserves, pickles, breads, and pastries. Then the pie auction began, the women of Salton—and even an occasional man—having given the best of their baking skills toward the schoolhouse cause. Pumpkin and mince, apple and custard, lemon, raisin, and even vinegar pies were lavishly praised by Mr. Caldwell, the appointed auctioneer, and generously bid on by the townsfolk.

At last, with bellies unable to hold another bite and children falling asleep, the Nielsens piled into their wagon to head home. A November sunset painted the sky toward swiftly falling night as they rode.

Adam and Jesse joined them for Thanksgiving evening, though no one except the children had room for any supper save coffee and a few bites of leftover pie.

Once Robbie, Sofie, and Mikael had tumbled sleepily into their beds, the grown-ups lingered around the table, sipping coffee and visiting.

"This reminds me of home—I mean, home back in Ohio." Lark cupped her hands around her drink. "Ma always said family conversation around the table was the best kind, remember?"

"I do." Del tipped her head. "We must keep up that tradition in our new home. Never stop gathering around the table together—even if it's a bit crowded yet."

They all chuckled, for here in the cramped main room of the soddy, they barely had room for a table large enough for all of them to squeeze around, especially when the doctor and Jesse joined them. They'd had to move another bed into the addition to make it possible.

"Someday we'll have a bigger house. Not too far off, I hope." Lark nodded. "How are your plans coming for your house, Doctor?"

Forsythia glanced at Adam, loving the way his eyes lit at the question.

He leaned forward. "Well, I've bought the land, just a short ways out of town, and have already spoken with an architect and a builder. We've finalized the plans and should be able to start building as soon as the snow clears in spring." He took Forsythia's hand. "I wish it could be ready for our wedding. But my sweet bride has graciously assured me she doesn't mind spending the winter in my rooms above the office. Jesse will move in with the Jorgensens for the time being."

Del raised a brow. "You aren't waiting till spring to get married?"

Adam's grip tightened on Forsythia's fingers. He shot her a glance.

She cleared her throat. "We're thinking of getting married at Christmas." That was Adam's desire, and she hadn't contradicted it. Though whenever she thought of being married in just a few short weeks, she found it a little hard to breathe. Was it only from excitement?

"I see." Del said nothing more, but her lips thinned.

Forsythia noticed Lark studying her before steering the conversation toward the church plans to celebrate the upcoming

Christmas season. But a strain hung over the rest of the evening, spoiling the festive spirit they'd all shared.

Adam and Jesse soon said good night, and Forsythia walked her doctor out to their buggy. The air hung clear and bitter cold, the black sky frosted with stars above. She shivered even in her coat, her breath puffing in the night air.

"You must hurry back inside." With Jesse already in the buggy, Adam laid his mittened hands on her shoulders. "Are you all right?"

She hesitated, then nodded. "I think so."

He pressed a kiss to her woolen hood. "I love you, you know."

"I love you too." She watched the buggy drive off over the frozen ground, wondering if the chill in the air heralded snow. They'd only had dustings so far.

She hurried back into the lamplit warmth of the soddy. Lark and Lilac were looking at some of Lilac's latest drawings by the fire while Del washed the coffee cups.

Forsythia joined her, taking a dish towel to dry. "So what was that about?"

"What was what about?"

"You know. Adam's and my wedding, at the table." Irritation prickled. "You were unhappy about something. Spit it out."

Del sighed. "I just . . . I hope you aren't moving too fast."

"We've known each other nearly six months. These things can move swiftly out here on the prairie." Hearing herself repeat the arguments she had run so often through her own head, Forsythia paused, letting her defenses lower. "You think we are?"

"I can't say for certain. Only . . ." Del laid her dishcloth down and looked at her sister. "You say nearly six months . . . Sythia, it's *only* been six months, just half a year since his wife died. You love each other, and are no doubt God's gift to one another. I don't question that. But I do question not giving it a bit more time."

Forsythia stared at the coffee cup in her hand, rubbing the rim with her drying cloth over and over. Though she hadn't wanted to admit any barrier to moving forward, the wisdom in her sister's words sank into her head and heart. A sigh rose up from the soles of her feet, or so it felt. "I'll talk to him."

Del squeezed Forsythia's hand with her damp one. "Forgive me if I've overstepped, little sister. I just don't want you to make a mistake."

Nor did she wish to, certainly. *But oh, Lord, how am I going to tell Adam?*

30

What do you mean, you don't want to get married yet?" Adam's brows drew together in a darker frown than Forsythia had ever seen except for when he first found out about Clark being Lark.

"It's not that I don't want to." She twisted her hands together, sitting on one of the chairs in Adam's office, where she'd found him organizing medical supplies. "It's just that I've begun to wonder if we're moving too fast."

"Because of what your sister said." Adam slammed a drawer harder than necessary.

"But she's right, Adam." Forsythia bored her gaze into his bent head, willing him to understand. It had taken her a few days since her talk with Del to work up the courage to talk to him about it, but she knew it was the right thing to do. "It's only been six months since you lost Elizabeth. We've been acquainted even less time. Does that not seem fast to you?"

"And God can work quickly, when He's of a mind. Or do you—or your sisters—doubt that too? I've heard of far faster courtships on the frontier than ours."

"And does that mean we shouldn't even consider the timing just because others have moved more quickly?"

He huffed out a breath and dug through his medical bag. "Where in tarnation did I put my stethoscope?"

Forsythia rose and quietly crossed to him. She gently reached behind his shoulders and lifted the instrument from his neck.

"Oh." He took it, a bit shamefaced, and hung it on its hook, then sank into his chair, rubbing his forehead. He sat there for a moment, head in his hand, then looked up at her. "I dearly want to marry you, Forsythia Nielsen."

"And I you." She drew near and laid her hands on his shoulders. The vulnerability in his brown eyes set her heart to thudding. "So very much, Adam. But at the right time. Not sooner than we should, simply because we don't want to wait." She glanced at the narrow staircase leading up from the office. "Besides, wouldn't it, in some ways, be better to wait till the house is ready anyway?"

Adam sat still for a moment, then leaned his head back and groaned a sigh. "I suppose. I've been fighting that thought, but yes, in a strictly practical sense, it would be the wiser move. And no doubt in the other ways you mention as well. As much as I didn't want to hear it, I value the strength in you to say it." He gave her a wry smile. "Very well. We'll postpone the wedding till spring. But once a livable frame for the house exists, I warn you, I will brook no more excuses to carrying you over its threshold just as soon as Rev. Pritchard can pronounce us man and wife."

Forsythia kissed him right on those penitent lips. "It's a pact."

The decision was right. She knew it by the holy peace in her heart. *But oh, Lord, these will be another six very long months.*

It was snowing.

Balanced on a ladder leaned against the sod wall of the newly enclosed barn, Lark tipped her head back to see the fluffy flakes falling fast from above.

"Think it means to stick this time?" Isaac McTavish, who had been helping them finish the barn before winter, asked from where he crouched near the roof's peak, helping lay the final sod bricks across the closely spaced rafters. Snow already dusted white over the patched shoulders of his coat.

"Looking likely." Lark brushed snowflakes from her eyelashes. Though they were only a week from Christmas, the snow until now had been meager. "How's the roof seem?"

"Tight as we can make it. Your stock'll be snug as bugs this winter, I'm thinkin'."

"Praise be." Lark climbed down the ladder, then held it steady for Isaac to descend.

"Is the roof f-finished?" Jesse came up, leading Buttercup. "I thought I should get the animals in from the s-snow."

"Good thinking." Lark patted his shoulder. What would they have done without this faithful young man? "And yes, the barn is finished." A weight lifted from her chest with the words. At last, their homestead was ready for winter. And just in time too.

"Stay for supper?" she asked Isaac, blinking through the snowfall, which was thicker and faster now.

"I'd best get back to the Youngs' before I get myself stranded." Since Thanksgiving, Isaac had taken up lodging in the banker's barn, helping his son-in-law run the farm—not that it abounded with work just now, hence his helping the Nielsens and whatever other families had need. He touched his hat with a gloved hand. "But thank you kindly. Perhaps another time."

Of course he wouldn't want to stay with the snowstorm. "Would you join us for Christmas dinner, then? Weather permitting, that is."

"I just might do that. Evenin', Miss Larkspur." Turning up his coat collar against the snow, Isaac touched his hat again and headed off, disappearing into a blur of white.

The snow did indeed stick, falling steadily overnight and building to six inches by morning. Robbie and Sofie stared with wide-eyed wonder, then spent the morning playing in the new white world, all aglitter in the winter sunshine. Del and Forsythia watched by the window while sewing linens for Forsythia's trousseau, baby Mikael playing on his quilt by their feet, but Lark and Lilac donned hats and mittens for an old-fashioned snowball fight with the children.

When a cold, wet missile splatted directly in her face, Lark shrieked and fell backward into the snow, arms flailing.

"Children, this is how you make snow angels." She spread her legs and arms. "See?" Her laughter bubbled with Robbie's as he threw himself down to imitate her. *Lord, it feels so good to laugh.* She squinted up into the deep blue sky. *Can I dare to think we are truly home—that this journey I started us on last spring has come to such a good end? That we seem to be safe here and settled at last?*

A verse floated through her mind. *"Yea, the Lord shall give that which is good; and our land shall yield her increase." Truly, you have been faithful to that promise, Father. Thank you.*

And before they knew it, it was Christmas.

Robbie and Sofie woke early and squealed over the little gifts filling their stockings. After a simple breakfast, the sisters set to work preparing their first Christmas dinner in Nebraska. They had no turkey this year, but a plump goose Lilac had shot had been roasting since before dawn in the oven of their new, larger cookstove, bought with some of Lark's remaining winnings. Del mashed potatoes and baked squash, while Forsythia whipped fresh butter for the hot rolls, a treat now that Buttercup was with calf and her milk was starting to dry up. They mostly had to save it for Mikael.

The doctor and Jesse arrived, coats and scarves frosted with fresh snow. Lark set the table, listening to the children chatter as Robbie played with his new wooden train, carved by Jesse, and Sofie crooned to her rag doll, fashioned in secret by Del to tuck in the little girl's stocking that morning.

Lark glanced out the window. It was snowing harder now, and there was no sign of Isaac. Likely he wouldn't come at this point. She fought a nagging disappointment and straightened the forks on Ma's lace tablecloth.

"Dinner is ready." Del squeezed her shoulder. "Shall we go ahead?"

Lark looked out the window once more. She could barely see the barn through the snow. "I think so."

Around the table they gathered, dressed in their best, the table set with the nicest dishes they had managed to bring on the journey. Lilac had gathered winterberry and sumac branches and entwined them between Ma's pewter candlesticks as a centerpiece, and the candlelight glowed on the crimson berries.

At the head of the table, Lark reached for Del's and Robbie's hands on either side to say the blessing. At the other end, she saw Forsythia clasp hands with her doctor, and the hands continued to join around the table until they formed an unbroken circle.

Lark closed her eyes. "Father, we thank thee." A sudden lump filled her throat. So much to be thankful for . . . so very, very much. Yet suddenly, awareness of those missing from this table pressed on her heart, those they wouldn't feast with again until heaven. Ma and Pa. Dr. Adam's Elizabeth, and Jesse's parents. Thomas and Alice Durham, and Sofie and Mikael's mother and father. So many broken pieces, and yet the Lord had woven them all together into a family, as only He could do.

"We thank thee," she began again. "For bringing us all to

this place to gather around this table. For the food thou hast provided for us, and for the love of family and friends. And most of all, for the gift of thy Son, whose coming as Immanuel we celebrate this day. Bless this food and our fellowship around it."

The "amen" echoed heartily around the table.

They dug in, laughter and chatter rising with the fragrance of roast goose and apple pie. After dinner and the washing up, they gathered back around the table. Forsythia brought over her guitar and tuned the instrument. Lilac fetched the fiddle and passed the mouth organ to Lark.

"What shall we start with?" Forsythia's fingers picked over the strings.

"'Joy to the World'?" suggested the doctor.

She smiled and swung into those joyous chords, Lilac and Lark adding fiddle and harmonica to the singing. Sofie and Robbie clapped along, and then Robbie requested "Jingle Bells."

"Maybe something quieter now?" Del cuddled a sleepy Mikael, who lay against her, chewing on the leather teething ring he had found in his stocking. They expected a tooth to poke through any day now.

"How about that new one we learned last Christmas, 'Silent Night'?" Lilac played the intro on the fiddle.

"Good idea." Forsythia finger-picked the guitar and softly began to sing. "'Silent night, holy night . . .'"

Was that a knock at the door? Lark cocked her head, halting her own singing for a moment. Perhaps it was only the wind—no, there it came again. She pushed to her feet and hurried to the door.

Isaac McTavish stood outside the soddy, his shoulders and boots crusted with snow. He removed his hat, sending a shower of white to the ground. "Did I miss dinner?"

"We've plenty left." Lark held the door wide, feeling her smile stretch her cheeks. "Come in. You must be half-frozen."

"Not once I heard that music." Isaac stepped inside, nodding to everyone. "Near to lost my way in the storm at one point, and then I heard this glorious sound. I said to myself, either I'm freezing to death and that's a heavenly choir, or I've near made it to the Nielsens." He smiled, lighting those gray eyes of his. "As much as I look forward to glory one day, I must say, I'm glad it was the latter."

They set a chair for Isaac by the stove and provided him with a cup of coffee and as much food as a plate could hold, then settled back into their places once more.

"Do you have a favorite Christmas carol, Mr. McTavish?" Lark asked.

"Always been partial to 'O Come, All Ye Faithful.' And please, it's time you call me Isaac. You folks are the closest I have around here to a real home."

With a strum and a nod, Forsythia led off.

> "O come, all ye faithful, joyful and triumphant!
> O come ye, o come ye to Bethlehem;
> Come and behold Him
> Born the King of angels;
> O come, let us adore Him,
> O come, let us adore Him . . ."

Home, Lark thought, her heart echoing Isaac's words as she sang. The Nielsen sisters had come home at last.

Epilogue

L ilac popped her head through the church doorway. "Sythia? They're ready for you."

Standing on the steps outside, Forsythia drew a quick breath as Del put the final touch on the sprigs of Queen Anne's lace tucked in her hair. This was really happening.

Lark handed her the nosegay of Ma's roses, brought from Ohio and now blooming again. "You look beautiful."

"Thank you." Forsythia gazed at her sisters for a moment, imprinting their smiling faces on this day deep in her heart. They all wore new springtime dresses, their hair wreathed with flowers from their garden—Ma's garden.

Mr. Caldwell stepped near and held out his arm with a fatherly quirk of his brow.

Forsythia tucked her hand through the crook of his arm. "I'm ready."

Her sisters slipped through the door ahead of her. In a moment, soft chords sounded from the piano—not from her fingers today. It turned out Mrs. Caldwell had a fair musical background as well.

Grateful for the attorney's steady arm, Forsythia stepped inside the church, her knees unexpectedly wobbly. *Lord, I know this is what you have for me. But it will be such a change for all of us. Be thou with us in this new season.*

Then she looked up and saw Adam standing in his dark coattails near the simple wooden altar.

And she forgot everything else.

A few moments later, she stood before a beaming Rev. Pritchard, her hands clasped in her doctor's, his grip so loving and sure that all the tumbling in her heart settled back into its rightful place. She gazed into his brown eyes, saying those words that echoed across centuries with sacred weight.

". . . to have and to hold, from this day forward . . . for better, for worse, for richer, for poorer, in sickness and in health, to love and to cherish, till death do us part . . . according to God's holy ordinance . . . and thereto I plight thee my troth."

"By the power vested in me, I now pronounce you man and wife." Rev. Pritchard's grin seemed about to split his face. He'd confided this would be his first wedding conducted in Salton, since he'd only started his circuit the year before.

Adam enveloped Forsythia in his arms with a kiss that swept her boots off the plank floor.

A flurry of embracing and congratulating, then everyone proceeded to their wagons and made their way to the doctor's new house just outside of town. Forsythia and Adam drove ahead in his buggy.

"I can hardly believe we are really—that I am really Mrs. Doctor Adam Brownsville." Forsythia smoothed the skirt of her blue-sprigged lawn dress, sewed specially for the wedding. "Can you?"

"I've waited long enough." Adam covered her hand with his and smiled into her eyes, letting the horse find its own way on the familiar path.

They pulled up at the house, and Adam lifted her from the buggy. She slipped her hand through his elbow as they walked up to the broad front porch of the two-story white frame house that still smelled of paint and freshly sawed beams.

"Oh, Adam, it's lovely." Tears stung her eyes. "A real home-place."

"For us and for the children." He put his arm around her and hugged her close. "And any more God chooses to add to our family."

"And Jesse." She looked up at him.

"Always Jesse."

The rattle of wagons announced their reception guests' arrival.

"I nearly forgot." Adam quirked a teasing grin, then scooped Forsythia up in his arms.

She squealed. "What are you—?"

He hurried up the porch steps and flung open the front door. "Carrying you over the threshold, of course. I did promise."

Soon beloved family and friends filled their new home, bearing food and gifts of dishes, pots and pans, and linens. Jesse presented a beautiful rocking chair for the sitting room with his characteristic shy grin, and her sisters laid a large bundle wrapped in a sheet in Forsythia's arms.

"What is it?" She stared at it, feeling the soft weight.

"Open it."

She unwrapped a large quilt, patterns of flowers stitched all over it in loving hands, each block bearing a different flower in an appropriate color.

"It's Ma's garden, see?" Lilac touched a square of primroses. "We embroidered the names of each flower and herb next to it."

"So you did." Forsythia caressed the block for rosemary. "It's beautiful. How did you ever manage to keep it a surprise?"

Lark rolled her eyes. "Let's just say we were glad for every

hour you spent working at the store. Or that we could get Adam
to spirit you away."

They all laughed.

Soon the guests drifted away with well wishes and tired children. But with Adam's blessing, Forsythia had one more journey
to make before bidding her sisters good-bye and truly beginning her new life.

Adam drove her in the buggy, following the Nielsen wagon
back to the sisters' homestead, only a little over a mile from the
Brownsville residence. The fields waved green, and the shoots in
the cornfield near the house were just beginning to sprout above
the dark earth. Ma's rosebushes bloomed against the soddy, soon
to be replaced by a frame house also, hopefully. But sweetest
of all was the flower garden on the other side of the house,
still small, but already blooming lavender, pink, and yellow. A
foretaste of what would someday be, Lord willing.

"You don't need to drive all the way up, Adam." She touched
his arm. "I'll only be a minute."

Lark stopped at the end of the lane, and Adam halted their
horse too. Her sisters piled out of the wagon with the children,
who would be staying here for a few days, until Adam and
Forsythia got settled.

Holding her husband's hand, Forsythia climbed down from
the buggy and joined her sisters at the turning from the road
to the Nielsen lane.

Lark lifted the engraved wooden sign from the back of the
wagon bed, and Lilac pounded the iron signpost into the dirt.

"I hereby christen our homestead"—Lark held up the plaque
for them all to see— "Leah's Garden." She hung the sign on the
iron hooks.

It swayed gently in the late spring breeze, the curling letters
and carved flowers around the words seeming to evoke Ma's
gentle presence.

"I love it." Lilac threw her arms around Del. "It feels like we've truly come home at last."

Adam stepped up beside Forsythia, and she leaned her head on his shoulder with a full heart. Truly this had been such a season of change. Yet here in this new land, surrounded by those she loved, in many ways she knew her journey was just beginning.

Lauraine Snelling is the award-winning author of more than ninety books, fiction and nonfiction, for adults and young adults. Her books have sold more than five million copies. Besides writing books and articles, she teaches at writers' conferences across the country. She and her husband make their home in Tehachapi, California. Learn more at www.laurainesnelling .com.

Kiersti Giron grew up loving Lauraine's books and had the blessing of being mentored by her as a young writer. Now it is her joy and honor to collaborate with Lauraine on this new series. Kiersti holds a lifelong passion for history and storytelling, seen in her award-winning novel manuscripts, and loves writing about reconciliation, healing, and God's story weaving into ours. She lives in California with her husband, their lively young son, and two cats.

Sign Up for Lauraine's Newsletter

Keep up to date with Lauraine's news on book releases and events by signing up for her email list at laurainesnelling.com.

More from Lauraine Snelling

After several years of widowhood and hardship, Ingeborg focuses on the good she's been given while she watches her widowed stepson fall in love once again. But not everything is comfortable for Ingeborg; one of her dearest friendships is changing—and she will have to decide if her settled life is worth more to her than a future she hardly dares to imagine.

A Blessing to Cherish

You May Also Like . . .

In 1910, Signe, her husband, and their boys emigrate from Norway to Minnesota, dreaming of one day owning a farm of their own. But the relatives they've come to stay with are harsh and demanding. As Signe's family is worked to the bone to repay the cost of their voyage, can she learn to trust God through this trial and hold on to hope for a better future?

The Promise of Dawn by Lauraine Snelling
UNDER NORTHERN SKIES #1
laurainesnelling.com

When a stranger appears in India with news that Ottilie Russell's brother must travel to England to take his place as a nobleman, she is shattered by the secrets that come to light. But betrayal and loss lurk in England too, and soon Ottilie must fight to ensure her brother doesn't forget who he is, as well as stitch a place for herself in this foreign land.

A Tapestry of Light by Kimberly Duffy
kimberlyduffy.com

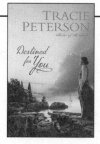

After smallpox kills her mother and siblings, Gloriana Womack is dedicated to holding together what's left of her fractured family. Luke Carson arrives in Duluth to shepherd the arrival of the railroad and reunite with his brother. When tragedy strikes, Gloriana and Luke must help each other through their grief and soon find their lives inextricably linked.

Destined for You by Tracie Peterson
LADIES OF THE LAKE #1
traciepeterson.com

◊ BETHANY HOUSE

More from Bethany House

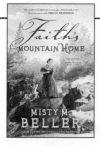

Nate Long has always watched over his twin, even if it's led him to be an outlaw. When his brother is wounded in a shootout, it's their former prisoner, Laura, who ends up nursing his wounds at Settler's Fort. She knows Nate wants a fresh start, but struggles with how his devotion blinds him. Do the futures they seek include love, or is too much in the way?

Faith's Mountain Home by Misty M. Beller
HEARTS OF MONTANA #3
mistymbeller.com

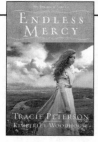

When Madysen Powell's supposedly dead father shows up, her gift for forgiveness is tested and she's left searching for answers. Daniel Beaufort arrives in Nome, longing to start fresh after the gold rush leaves him with only empty pockets, and finds employment at the Powell dairy. Will deceptions from the past tear apart their hopes for a better future?

Endless Mercy by Tracie Peterson and Kimberley Woodhouse
THE TREASURES OF NOME #2
traciepeterson.com; kimberleywoodhouse.com

After receiving word that her sweetheart has been lost during a raid on a Yankee vessel, Cordelia Owens clings to hope. But Phineas Dunn finds nothing redemptive in the horrors of war, and when he returns, sure that he is not the hero Cordelia sees, they both must decide where the dreams of a new America will take them, and if they will go there together.

Dreams of Savannah by Roseanna M. White
roseannamwhite.com

BETHANYHOUSE